Clara E. C. Waters, Katherine E. Conway

A Handbook of Christian Symbols and Stories of the Saints

as illustrated in art

Clara E. C. Waters, Katherine E. Conway

A Handbook of Christian Symbols and Stories of the Saints
as illustrated in art

ISBN/EAN: 9783337339722

Printed in Europe, USA, Canada, Australia, Japan

Cover: Foto ©Andreas Hilbeck / pixelio.de

More available books at **www.hansebooks.com**

A HANDBOOK

OF

CHRISTIAN SYMBOLS

AND

STORIES OF THE SAINTS

As Illustrated in Art

BY

CLARA ERSKINE CLEMENT

EDITED BY

KATHERINE E. CONWAY

FIFTH EDITION

BOSTON AND NEW YORK
HOUGHTON, MIFFLIN AND COMPANY
The Riverside Press, Cambridge
1895

PREFACE.

THE title of the present work sufficiently indicates its general scope and purpose. It has been undertaken to satisfy a want often felt personally by the writer and often expressed to her by others. Those who go abroad and travel in Christian lands meet at every step, through town and country, in the broad light of day and in the mysterious gloom of sacred places, symbolic forms which are known in a general way to represent the mysteries and facts of the Christian faith, but which fail to recall them to the uninitiated beholder in anything like a distinct and accurate manner. Churches are dedicated to saints hitherto unheard of; and streets, sometimes large cities, bear their names. Pictures, even of saints best known, are seen, in churches and art galleries, coupled with incidents and surroundings that fairly bewilder the mind.

Nor need one go abroad to feel thus puzzled and perplexed. The very pictures and prints, copied from the Great Masters, which adorn our own homes, affect us similarly. In the books which lie on our tables, in the contributions of the art critics to our newspapers and magazines, we are constantly lighting on references to names and facts of which we want ampler knowledge. They come to us invested with a halo of sanctity and mystery, and we long to have at hand some book, simple and

accessible, which will tell us all about them; and this is just
our aim in the following pages.

Though containing much that belongs to history proper, our
book does not profess to be in all respects a true history of
persons and facts.   Its purpose is rather to show forth the
conception of them which is embodied and illustrated in art.
History and legend unite in this conception.   The artist's individual fancy must also be allowed for.   It would be extremely
difficult to isolate what is purely historical.   It is thus in all
records of the past.   The difficulty is still greater in all religious
narratives, save only the Inspired Writings, on account of the
marvellous, which forms a part of them, and which can be
neither wholly accepted nor wholly rejected.   Wonders related
in the lives of the saints, which have undoubtedly a basis in
historical fact, have often come down the years exaggerated,
distorted, or invested in "showy human colors," — as Cardinal
Newman warns us in his consideration of " The Internal Character of Ecclesiastical Miracles," — either through the infirmity
of credulous or over-zealous chroniclers or through the malice of
the enemies of the Church.

That some of the miracles attributed to the saints should
have been merely fabled, need not startle nor scandalize even
the Catholic reader, nor excite prejudice against the great mass
which rest on evidence at least as firm as that on which we accept the records of profane history ; for, to quote again from
the above-named eminent authority, " it as little derogates from
the supernatural gift residing in the Church that miracles should
have been fabricated or exaggerated, as it prejudices her holiness
that within her pale good men are mixed with bad."

An additional difficulty arises from the fact that the origina-
tors of many strange stories — such, for example, as those which

are related of St. Christopher, St. Hilarion, St. Nicholas of Myra,
St. George the Soldier-Saint, etc., and some of the wonder-tales
which have gathered about the records of St. Gregory the Great
— chose, like the Greeks of old, that mythical form of narration
simply to indicate more strongly some moral lesson.   Hence
they never appealed to the faith of their hearers; nor did any
of these, save only the most ignorant, take the stories in their
literal sense.   For this method of popular instruction we have
even a divine precedent, — Christ himself instructing the
multitude by parables.

The difficulties of the historian, however, are no concern of
ours.   We tell in words the story told in art, adding only as
much of real fact as the mind naturally desires to know in connection with the subject.   In heroes of the supernatural as well
as of the natural order, —

"Our elder brothers, and of one blood," —

we feel, so to speak, a family pride, not alone for their actual
achievements, but even for the fond exaggerations of their
disciples and admirers.

As to what must be set down as unmistakably legendary, independent of its helping to elucidate the great works of art, it
has often an intrinsic beauty of its own, and is deeply interesting
as illustrative of the religious mind of past ages, — ages of faith
more ardent than our own, which merited and often won open
and extraordinary recompenses.

TABLE OF CONTENTS.

PAGE

SYMBOLISM IN ART 1

LEGENDS AND STORIES ILLUSTRATED IN ART 37

GENERAL INDEX 325

SYMBOLISM IN ART.

St. Augustine calls the representations of art *libri idiotarum* (" the books of the simple "), and there is no doubt that the first object of Christian art was to teach; and the aim of the artist was to render the truth he desired to present without regard to the beauty of the representation : he adhered to the actual, and gave no play to imagination or æsthetics. But later in its history, this art has been influenced by legends and doctrines in the choice of subjects, and these have been variously rendered, in accordance with the character, the æsthetic cultivation, and the refinement of the artist. But from its infancy to the present time, there have been certain characteristic figures, attributes or symbols, which have made a part of the language of what may be called Christian Art. These are meaningless — or worse, perhaps a deformity — to the eye of one who understands them not; but they add much to the power of a representation, to the depth of sentiment and expression when rightly apprehended. These symbols are used in two ways, — to express a general fact or sentiment, or as the especial attribute or characteristic of the person represented. My present limits allow but an imperfect and superficial consideration of this subject.

1

I. GENERAL SYMBOLS.

The Glory, Aureole, and Nimbus, all represent light or bright-ness, and are the symbols of sanctity. The nimbus surrounds the head; the aureole encircles the whole body, and the glory is the union of the nimbus and aureole. The nimbus belongs to all holy persons and saints as well as to the representations of divinity. The aureole, strictly speaking, belongs only to the persons of the Godhead; but the Virgin Mary is invested with it, (1) when she holds the Saviour in her arms, (2) in pictures of the Assumption, (3) when she is represented as the intercessor for humanity at the last judg-ment, (4) when represented as the Woman of the Apocalypse. The aureole has also been used as a symbol of the apotheosis of holy persons; but this is a degeneration from its original design and the use assigned it in ancient traditions. The glory also belongs espe-cially to God and the Virgin. The oblong aureole is called, in Latin, *vesica piscis;* in Italian, the *mandorla* (almond). The cruciform or triangular nimbus, or the figure of a cross in the nimbus, belongs properly to the persons of the Trinity; the nimbus of saints and lesser beings should be circular. A square nimbus is used for persons still living when the representation was made; the hex-agonal nimbus for allegorical personages. These symbols did not appear in Christian art until the fifth century, and during the fif-teenth and sixteenth centuries they disappeared. They are, however, employed in the present day, although not with the careful distinc-tion in the employment of the various forms which characterized their earliest use. The color of these symbols in painting is golden, or that which represents light; in some instances, in miniatures or on glass, they are of various colors. Didron believes these to be symbolical, but is not sure of the signification of the colors.

The Fish. A fish, most frequently a dolphin, was the earliest and most universal of the Christian symbols. It has several signi-fications. The Greek word for fish, ΙΧΘΥΣ, is composed of the initial letters of the Greek Ἰησοῦς Χριστός, Θεοῦ Υἱός, Σωτήρ, the Latin translation of which is "Jesus Christus, Dei filius, Salvator," —thus forming the initial anagram of this title of Jesus; and these characters are found in many ancient inscriptions and upon works of art. The fish is an emblem of water and the sacrament of baptism;

of the vocation of the Christian apostle, or "fisher of men," especially in the hands of St. Peter and others who were eminently successful in making converts; it is emblematic of Christians generally, they being likened to fish in the call of the Apostles (Matt. iv. 19), and also typified by the miraculous draught of fishes (John xxi.). But it is not true that the fish is always a Christian emblem; according to Didron it is never met as such in Greek art, and he believes that this emblem on the tombs in the catacombs at Rome signified the occupation of the person buried in them.

THE CROSS has a deeper meaning than that of other symbols; it is in a certain sense not merely the instrument of the sufferings of Christ, but himself suffering, — *ubi crux est martyr ibi.* In Christian iconography the cross holds a most important place. According to the tradition or legend of the True Cross, it was co-existent with the world, and will appear at the last judgment. Chosroes believed that in possessing the cross of Christ he possessed the Saviour, and so it was enthroned at his right hand. Thus in early representations of the three persons of the Godhead the cross without the figure was considered not only to recall Christ to the mind, but actually to show him. There are four differently formed crosses: The Latin, or Roman, Cross (1) is believed to be like that on which Christ suffered, and is the one placed in the hand of a saint. This cross is in the form of a man with the arms extended; the distance from the head to the shoulders being less than from the shoulders to the feet, and the length of the arms less than that of the whole figure. The Greek Cross (2) has four equal branches. The Cross of

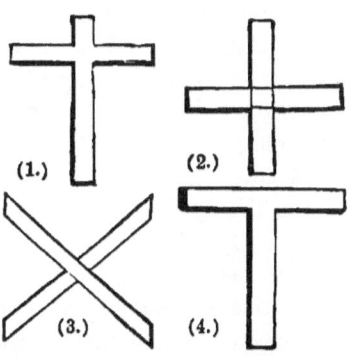

St. Andrew (3) is a cross saltier, or an X; and the Egyptian, or "Tau," Cross (4) has but three branches, like the letter T. This last is also called St. Anthony's Cross, because this saint is represented with a crutch in the shape of the "Tau," and it is embroidered on his vestments. It is also assigned as the cross of the Old Testament, and the brazen serpent is represented on a pole with this form. The Patriarchal Cross is of the same shape as the Latin Cross, but has two horizontal bars. There are numerous varieties of the Greek and Latin crosses, such as the Maltese Cross, the Cross of Dorat, and various others which pertain in some cases to certain localities. The cross is often interlaced or combined with the first two letters of the name of Christ in Greek. This monogram itself is called the Labarum, or the Cross of Constantine, this being the form of the legendary cross which he saw in the sky, and which was inscribed, according to Eusebius, EN TOYTΩ NIKA ("Conquer by this"). Frequently, when the cross was made of gold or silver, the five wounds of Christ were represented by inserting in it as many carbuncles or rubies, there being one in the centre and one at each extremity.

The Lamb has been an emblem of the Saviour from the earliest period of Christian art. It was the type of him in the Old Testament, and the name given him by St. John the Baptist (John. i. 28). When standing, bearing the cross or a banner, with a nimbus about the head, it is the Lamb of God, and is frequently inscribed *Ecce Agnus Dei.* The Twelve Apostles are represented by as many lambs; while the thirteenth, the symbol of Christ, bears the cross or has a nimbus about the head, and is frequently larger than the others. The lamb, called the Apocalyptic Lamb, has seven horns and seven eyes (Rev. v. 6). The lamb is also a general symbol of modesty, purity, and innocence, as when made the attribute of St. Agnes.

The Lion is another symbol of Christ, the "Lion of Judah," and is sometimes represented with a cruciform nimbus. According to an Eastern tradition, the cub of the lion is born dead, and is licked by its sire until it comes to life on the third day. Hence it is symbolical of the resurrection. It is given. to St. Jerome and other hermits as the emblem of solitude; to those who perished in the amphitheatre as the symbol of their death; and is placed at the feet of some to denote their courage and fortitude under the sufferings of martyrdom.

The Pelican, who tears open her breast to feed her young with her blood, is the emblem of our redemption through the sufferings of Christ; it is also a symbol of the Eucharist.

The Dragon is the symbol of Satan and sin. It is represented as conquered by Christianity, as in the legends of St. Margaret, St. Michael, St. George, and St. Sylvester. In the legend of St. Martha it represents a flood and pestilence. The "jaws of hell" are represented by the open mouth of a dragon emitting flames.

THE SERPENT, another emblem of sin, is sometimes placed beneath the feet of the Virgin; sometimes twined around a globe, to indicate the power of sin over the entire world. In some symbolic pictures of the Crucifixion the serpent lies dead at the foot of the cross, "or, if alive, looking impotently up at the second Adam upon the tree of our salvation, as before, according to art, he looked triumphantly down upon our first parents, from the tree of our fall."

THE HIND OR HART is the especial attribute of St. Eustace, St. Procopius, St. Giles, and St. Hubert. It was made the symbol of religious aspiration by the "sweet singer of Israel" (Psalm xlii.), and is also an emblem of solitude and hermit life.

THE UNICORN. This fabulous creature was said to be able to evade all pursuers except a virgin of perfect purity in heart, mind, and life. It is given as an attribute only to the Virgin and St. Justina, and is the emblem of female chastity.

THE PEACOCK is seen on tombs, sarcophagi, and among funereal emblems. It symbolizes the change from life to immortality. It was borrowed from pagan art, where it represented the apotheosis of an empress. It was the bird of Juno, but was not the symbol of pride until modern times.

THE DOVE is the emblem of the soul when represented as issuing from the mouth of the dying; an emblem of purity when given to the Virgin and certain female saints; also the symbol of the Holy Ghost and of spiritual inspiration. It symbolizes the divine Spirit when it hovers over holy men, as the emblem of their heaven-sent inspiration; and is seen in pictures of the Baptism of Christ, the Pentecost, and the Annunciation.

THE OLIVE, as the emblem of peace, is given to the Archangel Gabriel and to some saints. It is seen upon the tombs of martyrs, and is sometimes borne by the angels who announce the nativity.

THE PALM. The use of the palm as the symbol of martyrdom is authorized by Scripture (Rev. vii. 9).

It belongs to all the "noble army of martyrs." It is placed in their hands and carved on their tombs. It is sometimes brought to them by angels as if from heaven itself. It is very much varied in form and size.

THE LILY, wherever seen, has but one signification, which is chastity and purity. It belongs especially to pictures of the Annunciation and to St. Joseph, whose rod was said to have put forth lilies.

FRUIT OR FLOWERS, although frequently employed merely as ornaments, have, under certain circumstances, different significations. As the apple is an emblem of the fall in Paradise, in many pictures, so when presented to the infant Saviour, or in his hand, it signifies redemption. Roses are illustrative of the legends of St. Elizabeth of Hungary, St. Cecilia, and St. Dorothea, and a type of the Virgin as the "Rose of Sharon." A bursting pomegranate is the symbol of a hopeful future. Any fruit in the hand of St. Catherine is a symbol of "the fruit of the Spirit."

THE LAMP, LANTERN, OR TAPER is most frequently the symbol of piety. But the lamp, as the attribute of St. Lucia, signifies heavenly wisdom, or spiritual light.

FIRE AND FLAMES are emblems of zeal and fervor of soul, or of the sufferings of martydom.

THE FLAMING HEART is symbolical of fervent piety and spiritual love.

THE CROWN, when on the head of the Madonna, makes her the Queen of Heaven and Regina Angelorum. When the attribute of a martyr, it signifies the victory over sin and death, or denotes that the saint was of royal blood; in the latter case it is usually placed at the feet. Among the Jews the crown was the ornament of a bride, and to the present time it is placed on the head of a nun when consecrated as the Bride of Christ. For this reason it is more frequently seen on the heads of female saints, while those

of the other sex hold it in the hand. It is sometimes a mere circlet, often a chaplet of flowers; and again it is magnificent with gold and precious jewels.

THE SWORD, AXE, LANCE, AND CLUB are all symbols of martyrdom, and are the attributes of certain saints, and signify the manner of death they suffered. The sword is also an attribute of the warrior saints, and sometimes is an emblem of a violent death, without being the instrument employed.

THE SKULL AND SCOURGE symbolize penance.

THE SHELL, pilgrimage.

THE BELL signifies the exorcism of evil spirits.

THE ANVIL is the attribute of St. Adrian, and is the symbol of his death.

THE ARROW is the attribute of St. Sebastian, St. Ursula, and St. Christina.

THE PONIARD, of St. Lucia.

THE CALDRON, of St. Cecilia and St. John the Evangelist.

THE SHEARS AND PINCERS, of St. Agatha and St. Apollonia.

THE WHEELS, of St. Catherine.

THE STANDARD, OR BANNER, is the symbol of victory. It belongs to the military saints, and to those who carried the gospel to heathen lands. It is borne by Christ after the resurrection. St. Reparata and St. Ursula are the only female saints to whom it is given.

THE CHALICE is the emblem of faith, and is an attribute of St. Barbara. With a serpent, it is that of St. John the Evangelist.

THE BOOK, in the hand of St. Stephen, is the Old Testament; in the hands of the Evangelists it represents their own writings. In other cases it is the Scriptures, or the symbol of the learning and writings of the saint who bears it.

THE CHURCH, in the hand of St. Jerome, is the symbol of his love and care for the whole Christian Church. In other cases it is generally the model of some particular church, and the saint who bears it was its founder or first bishop.

THE SHIP. In early times the ark was the symbol of the Christian Church, but later any ship has had this significance. The boat of St. Peter, tempest-tossed and guided by Christ, is symbolical of his watchful care of his Church.

THE ANCHOR is one of the earliest Christian symbols. It is seen in the catacombs and on very ancient gems. It is the emblem of immovable hope and untiring patience. It is an attribute of some saints in illustration of their legends, as in the case of St. Clement.

THE SYMBOLS OF THE PASSION AND CRUCIFIXION are numerous; and although rarely seen in the catacombs and in early sculpture, they are constantly found in churches. They are, the two swords of the Apostles, the ear of Malchus, St. Peter's sword, the pillar and cord, the scourge, the crown of thorns, the three dice, the spear, the sponge, the nails, the cross, the thirty pieces of silver, the hammer and pincers, the ladder, the lantern, the boxes of spice for embalming, the seamless garment, the purse, and the cock. The five wounds are represented by the hands and feet with a heart in the centre, each pierced with one wound; or by a heart alone, with five wounds.

EARS OF CORN AND BUNCHES OF GRAPES were symbols of the bread and wine of the Holy Eucharist; while the representations of the labors of the vintage were typical of those of Christians in the vineyard of the Lord. The vine or vine leaf was an emblem of the Saviour, the true vine.

THE CANDELABRUM was an emblem of Christ and his Church, the light of the world. With seven branches it refers to the seven gifts of the Spirit, or to the seven churches (Rev. i. 20).

LITTLE NAKED BODIES are the symbols of the souls of men, and are seen in pictures of St. Michael when he is represented as the Introductor of souls. They are also placed in the hand which symbolizes God the Father.

II. SYMBOLISM OF COLORS.

In ancient art each color had a mystic sense or symbolism; and its proper use was an important consideration, and carefully studied.

WHITE is worn by the Saviour after his resurrection, by the Virgin in representations of the Assumption, by women as the emblem of chastity, by rich men to indicate humility, and by the judge as the symbol of integrity. It is represented sometimes by silver or the diamond; and its sentiment is purity, virginity, innocence, faith, joy, and light.

RED, the color of the ruby, speaks of royalty, fire, divine love, the Holy Spirit, creative power, and heat. In an opposite sense it symbolized blood, war, and hatred. Red and black combined were the colors of Satan, purgatory, and evil spirits. Red and white roses are emblems of love and innocence, or love and wisdom, as in the garland of St. Cecilia.

BLUE, that of the sapphire, signified heaven, heavenly love and truth, constancy and fidelity. Christ and the Virgin Mary wear the blue mantle; St. John, a blue tunic.

GREEN, the emerald, the color of spring, expressed hope and victory.

YELLOW OR GOLD was the emblem of the sun, the goodness of God, marriage, and fruitfulness. St. Joseph and St. Peter wear yellow. Yellow has also a bad signification when it has a dirty, dingy hue, such as the usual dress of Judas, and then signifies jealousy, inconstancy, and deceit.

VIOLET OR AMETHYST signified passion and suffering, or love and truth. Penitents, as the Magdalene, wear it. The Madonna wears it after the crucifixion, and Christ after the resurrection.

GRAY is the color of penance, mourning, humility, or accused innocence.

BLACK with white signified humility, mourning, and purity of life. Alone, it spoke of darkness, wickedness, and death, and belonged to Satan. In pictures of the Temptation, Jesus sometimes wears black.

III. SYMBOLS OF GOD THE FATHER.

Before the twelfth century there were no portraits of God the Father, and the symbol used to indicate his presence was a hand issuing from the clouds. This hand when entirely open is in the act of bestowing, and has rays from each finger. It was generally represented in the act of benediction; and the position showed whether it belonged to Eastern or Western, or to Greek or Latin art, — for the benedictory gesture differs in the two churches. "In the Greek Church it is performed with the forefinger entirely open, the middle finger slightly bent, the thumb crossed upon the third finger, and the little finger bent. This movement and position of the five fingers form more or less perfectly the monogram of the Son of God." The Latin benediction is given with the third and little fingers closed, the thumb and the other two fingers remaining open and straight. This

is said to symbolize the three persons of the Trinity by the open
fingers, and the two natures of Christ by the closed. The hand is
frequently surrounded by the cruciform nimbus, which in the early
centuries was given to God alone. The hand is most frequently seen
in pictures of the Baptism of Christ; the Agony in the Garden; in
the Crucifixion, where it is placed on the summit of the cross in the
act of benediction; and when Jesus is represented as reascending to
heaven after his death, bearing the cross in his hand, the right hand
of the Father is extended to him as if "in a manner to assist him to
rise." In another representation of the hand of God it is filled with
little naked figures whose hands are joined as if in prayer. These
are the souls of the righteous who have returned to God.

The next symbol of the Father was a face in the clouds, then a
bust; and gradually by the end of the fourteenth century a figure
and distinct characteristics represented the first person of the Godhead. In the beginning there was little or no distinction between
the representations of the Father and Son; but gradually the Father
was made older, while the place of honor, the royal crown on his head,
and the globe in his hand indicated a superior dignity and consideration.[1] From this time to that of the Renaissance, however, the
representations of God were but little more than those of a pope or
king; the triple tiara was indeed increased by the addition of two
more crowns, and when in the garments of a king a nimbus encircled
the crown. With the æsthetic genius and progress of the Renaissance, with Michael Angelo, Perugino, and Raphael, came representations of God that more satisfactorily embody that mental conception
which can never be embodied, — the conception of God, of Jehovah,
the Creator and Ancient of days. But at length it came to be remembered that no personal representation of the Father should ever be
made. No mortal man hath seen or can see him; and Jesus, being
the Word, was the speech of God, and was the fitting representation
of the Father whenever he had spoken. Since the sixteenth century
the Father has been symbolized by the triangle, which is his linear
emblem, or some other geometrical figure inscribed with his name,
and surrounded with rays of light. This radiating circle is itself an
emblem of eternity. Sometimes a flood or blaze of light alone is
the symbol of the "appearance of brightness" which the prophet

---

[1] Christ as God, equal to the Father; as man, inferior to the Father.

describes (Ezek. viii. 2); but the triangle became extremely popular on account of the ideas or teaching which it embodied. Here the Father, represented by his name, in Hebrew, occupied the centre of the triangle which symbolized the Trinity, and all was contained in the circle of Eternity.

This abstruse symbol is often seen in the decorations of the churches of the present day and upon the vestments of bishops.

IV. SYMBOLS OF GOD THE SON.

The usual symbols of Christ have been mentioned under the head of general symbols; for they are capable of various significations, and are employed as attributes of saints or to denote their characteristics. They are the glory, aureole, or nimbus, the fish, cross, lamb, and lion. The traditions of the earliest portraits of Christ will be found by referring to the legends of King Abgarus and St. Veronica. From the beginning of Christian art, Christ has been represented by portraits rather than symbols, and in such a manner as to render them quite unmistakable. In the earliest representations of the Crucifixion, it was surrounded with various symbols; and the aim of the artists who painted them was to portray the mysterious death which convulsed Nature, raised the dead, and wrought mighty miracles, rather than the mere physical sufferings and human death which later art presents.

Among the symbols thus used were the sun and moon, represented by the classic figures of Sol and Luna, with the rays and crescent, or seated in their orbs surrounded with clouds, with their right hands raised to the cheek, an ancient sign of sorrow. Again, they bore torches reversed. Figures are seen rising from tombs and from the water, showing that the dead shall rise from sea and land. Earth and Ocean are also symbolized. In one ancient ivory, Earth is half nude and sits beside a tree; in one hand she holds a cornucopia, the symbol of abundance, while a serpent nurses at her breast, the emblem of life nourished by the earth. The ocean is as a river-god, riding on a dolphin, or holding a subverted urn, from which the water pours forth. The church and the synagogue are typified by females; the one on the right or place of honor, the church, holds a banner and gazes up at the Saviour, while on the left the synagogue turns her back as if rebellious. The Virgin and St. John are ever present at the crucifixion, from earliest to latest time. Their hands are often raised to the cheek in token of affliction, and the disciple bears the Gospel in his hand. Angels sometimes hold a crown above the head of Christ, or hang from the cross in attitudes of anguish. The presence of the Father is shown by the hand before described, which holds the crown or is in the act of blessing. Other symbols are the serpent twined about the foot of the cross; the pelican tearing her breast to feed her young, an emblem of redemption, also of the sacrament of the Eucharist; a female figure crowned with towers supposed to represent Jerusalem; a skull symbolizes Adam; the sacrifice of a heifer typifies the Jewish rites; and sometimes the Evangelists are represented writing their Gospels, while their winged symbols whisper in their ears. These are the most important accessories of the symbolical representations of the Crucifixion; the historical easily explain themselves. In many ancient crucifixions the figure of Christ is clothed in a robe. Some had a drapery from the hips to the knees. The draped figures are mostly, if not all, of Byzantine origin; and there is a legend which is given as a reason for this mode of representation : "A priest who had exhibited to the people a figure of Christ only cinctured with a cloth was visited by an apparition which said, 'All ye go covered with various raiment, and me ye show naked. Go forthwith and cover me with clothing.' The priest, not understanding what was meant, took no notice; and on the third day the vision appeared again, and having scourged him severely with rods, said, 'Have I not told you to cover me with garments? Go now and cover with clothing the picture in which I appear crucified.'"

V. SYMBOLS OF THE HOLY GHOST.

From the sixth century to the present time, the dove has been the constant and universal symbol of the Holy Ghost. It appears in illustrations of the Scripture scenes, in which the Holy Spirit is mentioned from the "moving upon the face of the waters" to the Day of Pentecost. There are also many representations of his appearance in historical scenes, and in others which are partly or wholly legendary. The dove is often present at the Nativity and the Annunciation: it issues from the rod of Joseph, thus designating him to be the spouse of the Virgin; it hovers above the heads of holy men and saints, showing that their inspiration is heaven-sent, — among these are David, St. John the Evangelist, St. Jerome, St. Teresa, and others. Another representation, intensely symbolical, is that of the Saviour surrounded by seven doves; they are of snowy whiteness, and have the cruciform nimbus; they are emblems of the seven gifts of the Spirit with which Christ was endowed, — wisdom, understanding, counsel, strength, knowledge, piety, and fear (Isa. xi.). These doves are frequently placed with three on each side and one at the top, thus forming a kind of aureole. It may not be out of place to observe that during the Middle Ages seven was esteemed a mystic number. There were seven gifts of the Holy Ghost; seven sacraments; seven planets; seven days in the week; seven branches on the candlestick of Moses; seven liberal arts; seven churches of Asia; seven mysterious seals; seven stars and seven symbolic trumpets; seven heads of the Dragon; seven joys and seven sorrows of the Virgin; seven penitential psalms; seven deadly sins; seven canonical hours. Even Mohammed says, in the Koran, that "God visited the skies, and formed there seven heavens" (Koran ii. 27). Some cathedrals have seven chapels, as those at Rheims and Chartres. During the tenth century the Holy Ghost was sometimes represented as a man; but this representation was never received with as much favor as the other. He was made of every age, from the earliest to the latest years of life. As a little child, he floated on the waters; as a young child, he was in the arms of the Father; his age is according to the fancy of the artist, or the supposed requirements of the representation. Among the legendary pictures in which he was thus represented, is that of the reception of Christ in heaven, after his earthly mission was ended; the Holy Ghost is seated by the Father, and has a book, symbolizing wisdom. He blesses Jesus, as does the Father; he also assists at the coronation of the Virgin. In some instances the two representations of the Holy Ghost were combined by the figure of a man with a dove on his head or hand. Still another symbol is that of a dove from which emanate rays of light, spreading out in every direction, forming a radiating aureole about it. The dove is also one of the general symbols of art, and as such is emblematical of purity and innocence, which signification was made most emphatic by its use as the sacrifice for purification, under the Jewish law. As before mentioned, it is the attribute of certain female saints, denoting chastity and purity.

VI. SYMBOLS OF THE TRINITY.

Representations of the Divine Three in One were employed in art from its earliest ages. It was symbolized by the combination of three triangles, three circles, three fishes, and many other representations more obscure in their meanings. In later art the three persons of the Trinity have been represented by three human figures, each with its special attribute, that of the Holy Ghost being the dove. Another mode represents the Father and Son with the dove between them; in the thirteenth and fourteenth centuries the dove was often seen hovering between the first and second persons of the Trinity, with the tips of the wings touching the lips of each. This representation is called the double procession of the Spirit; illustrative of the words of the Nicene Creed, "proceeding from the Father and the Son." This representation belongs to the Latin Church. In these representations, when the locality is heaven, the figures are always seated. There is a device called the Italian Trinity, which was popular from the twelfth to the seventeenth century. In this the Father holds a crucifix by the ends of the transverse beam, the figure of Christ hanging between his knees; the dove proceeds downwards from the lips of the Father, and touches the head of the Son, or is merely sitting on the cross. Some attempts have been made to embody this mystery, by the representation of a body with three heads, or a head with three faces; but they are only frightful and monstrous.

VII. SYMBOLS OF ANGELS.

According to Dionysius the Areopagite, there are three divisions of angels, and these each divided into three classes or choirs, making nine in all :—

I. COUNCILLORS OF GOD, consisting of —

1. THE SERAPHIM, represented as covered with eyes.

2. THE CHERUBIM, represented with six wings, and usually standing on wheels, according to the description of Ezekiel. Sometimes

they have an open book. These two orders stand always before God, praising and adoring him.

3. THRONES are represented carrying a throne or tower, and their duty is to support the throne of God.

II. GOVERNORS. — These rule the stars and regulate the universe.

4. DOMINATIONS, represented with a sword, a triple crown and sceptre, or an orb and cross.

5. VIRTUES. — These carry a battle-axe and pennon or a crown and censer, and are in complete armor.

6. POWERS. — These hold a baton, or are in the act of scourging or chaining evil spirits.

III. MESSENGERS OF GOD.

7. PRINCEDOMS OR PRINCIPALITIES. — These are in armor, with pennons, or holding a lily.

8. ARCHANGELS. — Of these, three are universally known by name, especially venerated, and depicted in Christian Art : —

a. MICHAEL ("like unto God"), captain-general of the host of heaven, protector of the Hebrew nation, conqueror of the hosts of hell; lord and guardian of souls, patron saint and prince of the Church Militant.

b. GABRIEL ("God is my strength"), guardian of the Blessed Virgin, the bearer of important messages, the angel of the Annunciation, the preceptor of the patriarch Joseph.

c. RAPHAEL ("the medicine of God"), the chief of guardian angels, the conductor of the young Tobias.

Tradition names four other archangels : —

d. URIEL ("the light of God"), the strong companion, the regent of the sun, the teacher of Esdras.[1]

e. CHAMUEL ("one who sees God") is believed by some to be

---

[1] Uriel is represented in Christian Art as holding in his right hand a drawn sword across his breast, with flames on his left. Another tradition names the three last-mentioned archangels as follows : Sealtiel, the Praying Spirit, said to be the angel who appeared to Agar in the wilderness, whom Art depicts with face and eyes cast down, and his hands clasped upon his breast, as if he were a penitent; Jehudiel, the Remunerator, supposed to be the angel whom God sent before the children of Israel, and who in pictures holds a golden crown in his right hand, and a scourge of three black cords in his left; Barachiel, the Helper, said to be the angel who spoke to Abraham, and who rebuked Sara when she laughed, and who is painted with the lap of his cloak filled with white roses.

the one who wrestled with Jacob, and appeared to Christ during his agony in the garden; but others believe that this was Gabriel.

f. JOPHIEL ("the beauty of God") the guardian of the tree of knowledge, and the one who drove Adam and Eve from the Garden of Eden, the protector of those who seek truth, the preceptor of the sons of Noah, the enemy of all who pursue vain knowledge.

g. ZADKIEL ("the righteousness of God"). According to some authorities he stayed the hand of Abraham from sacrificing Isaac; but others believe that this was done by Michael.

The attributes of Michael are the sword and scales; of Gabriel, the lily; of Raphael, the staff and gourd of the pilgrim; of Uriel, a roll and book; of Chamuel, a cup and staff; of Jophiel, a flaming sword; and of Zadkiel, the sacrificial knife. When represented merely as archangels and not in their distinctive characters, they are in complete armor, holding their swords with points upwards, and sometimes with trumpets.

9. ANGELS. — Variously represented according to the purpose for which they are sent forth.

The Greek word for angel signifies literally "a bringer of tidings;" therefore this term, though applied to all heavenly beings below the Godhead, belongs most properly to archangels and angels who are brought into communication with mankind. When Christ is represented with wings in Greek art, it is as "the great angel of the will of God." John the Baptist and the Evangelists are angels, also, inasmuch as they were God's messengers, and they are sometimes represented with wings.[1] A glory of angels is a representation in which the Trinity, Christ, or the Virgin is surrounded by circles of angels, representing the different choirs. The interior circles, the Seraphim and Cherubim, are symbolized by heads with two, four, or six wings, and are usually of a bright red or blue color. Properly the Seraph, whose name signifies "to love," should be red; and the Cherub, whose name signifies "to know," should be blue. Angels should always be young, beautiful, perfect, but so represented as to seem immortal rather than eternal, since they are created beings. In early art they were always draped; and although all colors are employed in the drapery, white should be the prevailing one. Wings

---

[1] See the Angels, or Bishops, of the Seven Churches, in the Apocalypse, or Revelations, of St. John.

are seldom wanting, and the representation of them as the attribute of celestial beings did not originate in Christian art. This symbol of might, majesty, and divine beauty is found in the remains of Egypt, Babylon, and Nineveh, as well as in Etruscan art.

VIII. SYMBOLS OF THE VIRGIN.

Among the symbols of the Blessed Virgin, the titles by which she is known, and from which certain pictures and effigies are named, are by no means the least interesting, showing as they do the estimation in which she is held, and the tenderness, as well as sacredness, of the love she engenders in the hearts of her faithful clients. As the protector of the afflicted she is represented with her robe so spread out as to cover the votaries who pray for her gracious aid. In this character she has several titles, such as —

Santa Maria di Misericordia, Our Lady of Mercy; and by this title, Nuestra Señora de la Merced, she is known as the patroness of the Spanish Order of Mercy. When painted for their institutions, she frequently holds a badge of the order on a tablet.

Santa Maria del buon Consilio, Our Lady of Good Counsel.

S. M. della Grazia, Our Lady of Grace.

S. M. Auxilium Afflictorum, Help of the Afflicted.

S. M. del Pianto, del Dolore, Our Lady of Lamentation, or Sorrow.

S. M. del Soccorro, Our Lady of Succor, or of the Forsaken.

S. M. de buon Cuore, Our Lady of Good Heart.

S. M. Consolatrice, della Consolazione, or del Conforto, Our Lady of Consolation.

S. M. Refugium Peccatorum, Refuge of Sinners.

S. M. della Speranza, Our Lady of Hope.

She is invoked by women in travail as —

S. M. del Parto, Our Lady of Good Delivery.

Again, by the people, as —

S. M. della Pace, Our Lady of Peace.

S. M. del Popolo, Our Lady of the People.

S. M. della Vittoria, Our Lady of Victory.

By students she is invoked as —

S. M. della Sapienza, Our Lady of Wisdom.

S. M. della Perseveranza, Our Lady of Perseverance.

When painted for colleges and institutions of learning, she frequently holds a book.

By prisoners she is called, —

S. M. della Liberta, or Liberatrice, Our Lady of Liberty.

S. M. della Catena, Our Lady of Fetters.

There are also many titles derived from the circumstances of her life, or from certain accessories of the representation, as —

S. M. della Cintola, Our Lady of the Girdle, when she gives her girdle to St. Thomas.

S. M. del Libro, when she holds the book of Wisdom.

S. M. del Presepio, Our Lady of the Cradle, when in a Nativity.

S. M. della Lettera, the Madonna of the Letter, which illustrates the legend that she wrote a letter, A. D. 42, from Jerusalem to the people of Messina. This is her title as protectress of that city.

S. M. della Scodella, when with a cup she dips water from a fountain.

S. M. della Rosa, Our Lady of the Rose, when she holds a rose.

S. M. della Spina. This is her title as protectress of Pisa, when she holds the crown of thorns.

S. M. de Belem, Our Lady of Bethlehem. With this title she is the patroness of the Jeronymites.

S. M. di Loretto, Our Lady of Loretto. See legend of the Santa Casa.

S. M. del Pillar. This is her title as protectress of Saragossa. According to the tradition, she descended from heaven, standing on a marble pillar, and appeared to St. James when he was preaching in Spain. This legend is often seen in Spanish pictures, and the pillar is preserved in the cathedral of Saragossa.

S. M. del Carmine, Our Lady of Mount Carmel, under which title she is the protectress of the Carmelites.

S. M. della Neve, Our Lady of the Snow. See legend of Santa Maria Maggiore.

S. M. del Rosario, Our Lady of the Rosary. See the Rosary.

S. M. della Stella, Our Lady of the Star, when the star is embroidered on her mantle as an attribute.

S. M. del Fiore, Our Lady of the Flower. This is her title as protectress of Florence.

Certain prophets are sometimes represented as attending on Mary

and the infant Jesus. They are those who have referred especially to
the Incarnation. They are : —

Moses, because he beheld the burning bush.

Aaron, whose rod blossomed miraculously.

Gideon, whose fleece was wet with dew when it was dry all around.

Daniel (Dan. ii. 45).

David, both prophet and ancestor.

Isaiah, who prophesied that a virgin should conceive and bear a son.

Ezekiel (Ezek. xliv. 2).

Frequently the figures of these prophets are omitted, and symbols
of them introduced, as the burning bush for Moses, the dewy fleece
for Gideon, the rod for Aaron, etc.

Certain women, too, are regarded as types of Mary, and are often
seated at her feet, or otherwise represented near her, as —

Judith and Esther, who were emblems of the Virgin, in having
brought deliverance to Israel.

Ruth, because she was the ancestress of David.

Bathsheba, because she sat on the right hand of her son.

Abishag, who was "the virgin who was brought to the king."

There are certain general symbols which are also given to Mary,
with peculiar significations.

THE APPLE, when in the hand of the infant Saviour, signifies the
sin in Paradise, which made his coming necessary ; but in the hand
of the Virgin, it designates her as the second Eve.

THE SERPENT, the general emblem of Satan and sin, has a peculiar meaning when placed beneath the feet of the Virgin, and is illustrative of the prophecy, *Ipsa conteret caput tuum* ("She shall bruise
thy head ").

THE GLOBE, beneath the Virgin and entwined by a serpent, is the
symbol of her triumph over a world fallen through sin.

THE POMEGRANATE, the emblem of hope, is frequently given to
the Virgin by the child Jesus.

BIRDS, in ancient pictures, figured the soul, or the spiritual,
as the opposite of the material. Thus the dove is the Holy Spirit
hovering above her; while the seven doves, which typify the gifts
of the Spirit, when surrounding the Virgin, make her the Mater Sapientiæ, or the Mother of Wisdom. When doves are near her while
she reads or works, they express her gentleness and tenderness.

THE BOOK in the hand of Mary, if open, represents the book of Wisdom ; if closed or sealed, it is a mystical symbol of the Virgin, which will be further explained.

FLOWERS were consecrated to the Virgin ; and FRUITS signify "the fruits of the Spirit, — joy, peace, and love."

Lastly, there are many symbols of the Virgin, derived from the Canticles and the Litanies of the Virgin, and which belong especially to her :

THE LILY.   "I am the rose of Sharon, and the lily of the valley " (Cant. ii. 12).

THE ROSE is one emblem of love and beauty, and especially dedicated to Mary.   A plantation or garden of roses is often represented.

THE ENCLOSED GARDEN (Cant. iv. 12).

THE STAR is often embroidered on her veil or mantle.   When she has a crown of twelve stars it is illustrative of the description in

Tetramorph.

the Revelation.   She is also called Stella Maris, the Star of the Sea ; Stella Jacobi, the Star of Jacob ; Stella non Erratica, the Fixed Star ; and Stella Matutina, the Morning Star.

THE SUN AND MOON refer to her as the woman of the Apocalypse : " A woman clothed with the sun, having the moon under her feet, and on her head a crown of twelve stars."

THE STEM OF JESSE is represented as a green branch twined with flowers (Isa. xi. 1).

THE PORTA CLAUSA, or Closed Gate (Ezek. xliv. 4).

THE WELL, FOUNTAIN, CITY OF DAVID, TEMPLE OF SOLOMON, AND TOWER OF DAVID are all symbols borrowed from the Canticles.

THE OLIVE, THE CYPRESS, AND THE PALM are all emblems of the Virgin.   The first signifies peace, hope, and abundance ; the second points to heaven, and the third speaks of victory.

THE CEDAR OF LEBANON, by its height, its perfume, its healing qualities, and its incorruptible substance, symbolizes the greatness, goodness, and beauty of the Virgin.

THE SEALED BOOK, in the hands of the Virgin, alludes to the text, "In that book were all my members written," and also to the sealed book described by Isaiah (xxix. 11, 12).

THE MIRROR is borrowed as an emblem from the book of Wisdom (vii. 25): *Specula sine maculâ.*

The explanation of the seven joys and the seven sorrows of the Virgin, as well as that of the mysteries of the Rosary, will be found, by reference to them in their alphabetical order, in the next division of this book.

IX. SYMBOLS OF THE EVANGELISTS.

When the Evangelists are represented together, it is in their character of witnesses, upon whose testimony the truth of Christianity rests; when they are single, they are usually presented as teachers or patrons. The earliest symbol of the Evangelists was a Greek cross, with a scroll or book in each angle, — emblems of the writers of the four Gospels. The second symbol was that of the four rivers which rise in Paradise. Sometimes the

(Mosaic.) St. Mark.

Saviour with a lamb, or the symbolic Agnus Dei, was represented on an eminence, with the four streams, symbolizing the Evangelists,

St. Mark.

flowing from beneath him. Their next symbol was the four fiery creatures of Ezekiel's vision (Ezek. i. 5). These were interpreted by the Jews, as representing the archangels; also the prophets Isaiah, Jeremiah, Ezekiel, and Daniel; but the early Christians explained them as emblems of the Evangelists.

The four "beasts" of the Apocalypse received the same explanation, and in the seventh century they had become the distinctive symbols of these inspired witnesses.

(Mosaic, 5th Century.) St. Luke.

St. Jerome explains the individual application of these symbols thus : —

1. The Cherub, which most resembles a human being, was given to St. Matthew, because he speaks more of the human than of the divine nature of our Saviour.

2. The Lion symbolizes St. Mark, for three reasons : —

a. He commences his epistle with the mission of St. John the Baptist, "The voice of one crying in the wilderness."

b. The king of beasts is a type of the royal dignity of Christ, which St. Mark makes so apparent.

c. According to an Oriental tradition, the young lions are born dead, and after three days are made alive by the breath or the roar of the sire ;

(Mosaic, 11th Century.) St. John.

thus they are an emblem of the Resurrection, of which St. Mark is called the historian.

3. The Ox was given to St. Luke because he especially sets forth the priesthood of Christ, and the ox is symbolical of sacrifice.

4. The Eagle was given to St. John as an emblem of the lofty flights of his inspiration.

Others regarded these "beasts" as shadowing forth the Incarnation, Passion, Resurrection, and Ascension of Jesus ; and they are also believed to represent the fourfold character of Christ as man, king, high-priest, and God.

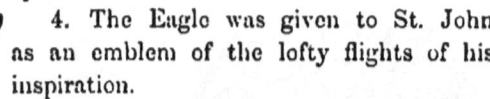

(Mosaic, A. D. 700.) St. Luke.

These symbolic creatures were always represented as winged. The union of all four "beasts" forms that mysterious emblem called the Tetramorph. In another symbol a woman represents the new Law, or the Church. She is crowned and seated on a creature who has the four heads of these symbolic beasts, the body of a horse, and four feet, embracing one of each of the four creatures. Again the Church is in a triumphal chariot, driven by a cherub or angel, and drawn by the lion, ox, and eagle. The next advance was the combination of the human form with the heads of these mystic beasts. Figures formed in this way were sometimes represented alternately with the figures of the prophets, all forming a circle. These ideas seem to have been borrowed from the winged bulls, with human heads, found at Nineveh.

At length the only symbol retained in the representations of the Evangelists was the wings. These were attached to the human form;

they bear their books, and the symbolic creatures were represented near them or at their feet.

The Evangelists were often represented together, with four prophets, thus symbolizing the old and new law; or with four doctors of the Church, as witnesses to, and interpreters of the truth.

In later art, the Evangelists appear without emblems or attributes; sometimes with their names inscribed above or beneath their representations. In speaking of the different stages of this symbolism, Mrs. Jameson says: "It will be in-

(Fra Angelico.)

(Fra Angelico.)

teresting to pause for a moment and take a rapid, retrospective view of the progress, from first to last, in the expression of an idea through form. First, we have the mere fact, — the four scrolls, or the four books. Next, the idea, — the four rivers of salvation, flowing from on high to fertilize the whole earth. Thirdly, the prophetic symbol, — the winged cherub of fourfold aspect. Next, the Christian symbol, — the four beasts in the Apocalypse, with or without the angel-wings. Then the combination of the emblematical animal with the human form. Then the human personages, each of venerable or inspired aspect, as becomes the teacher and witness; and each attended by the Scriptural emblem, — no longer an emblem, but an attribute marking his individual vocation and character. And lastly, the emblem and attribute both discarded, we have the human being only, holding his gospel, — that is, his version of the doctrine of Christ." [1]

X. SYMBOLS OF THE APOSTLES.

The earliest purely symbolic representation of the Twelve Apostles was that of twelve sheep surrounding Christ, the good Shepherd, while he bore a lamb in his arms; or again, Jesus, as the Lamb of God, is on an eminence, from which flow the four rivers of Paradise, while on one side six sheep leave Jerusalem, and on the other side the same number leave Bethlehem. They were very rarely represented by doves. The next advance was to represent them as men, and all

St. John.

bearing sheep; or in place of sheep, scrolls, and distinguished from each other by the inscription of their names above them.

According to tradition, the Apostles, before separating, composed the Apostles' Creed, of which each one furnished a sentence or article. These

(Hans Beham.)

are inscribed on their scrolls as follows : St. Peter, — Credo in Deum Patrem omnipotentem, creatorem cœli et terræ ; St. Andrew, — Et in Jesum Christum Filium ejus unicum, Dominum nostrum ; St. James

---

[1] Sacred and Legendary Art.

Major, — Qui conceptus est de Spiritu Sancto, natus ex Maria Virgine; St. John, — Passus sub Pontio Pilato, crucifixus, mortuus et sepultus; St. Philip, — Descendit ad inferos, tertia die resurrexit a mortuis; St. James Minor, — Ascendit ad cœlos, sedet ad dexteram Dei Patris omnipotentis; St. Thomas, — Inde venturus est judicare vivos et mortuos; St. Bartholomew, — Credo in Spiritum Sanctum; St. Matthew, — Sanctam Ecclesiam Catholicam, sanctorum communionem; St. Simon, — Remissionem peccatorum; St. Matthias, — Carnis resurrectionem; St. Thaddeus, — Et vitam æternam. From the sixth century every one of the Apostles had his especial attribute, which was taken from some circumstance of his life or death, and which will be found in their respective legends. These attributes are as follow : —

St. Peter, the keys or a fish.

St. Andrew, the transverse cross which bears his name.

St. James Major, the pilgrim's staff.

St. John : the chalice with the serpent is the proper attribute of this Apostle ; but the eagle, which is his attribute as an Evangelist, is sometimes seen when he is with the Apostles.

St. Thomas, generally, a builder's rule ; rarely, a spear.

St. James Minor, a club.

St. Philip, a small cross on a staff or crosier, surmounted by a cross.

St. Bartholomew, a knife.

St. Matthew, a purse.

St. Simon, a saw.

St. Thaddeus, a halberd or lance.

St. Matthias, a lance.

Sometimes St. Paul, St. Mark, and St. Luke are represented with the Apostles, and some others are left out, as the number is always twelve. In such cases, St. Paul bears either one or two swords.

(Fra Angelico.)

The Apostles have also been represented seated on clouds, surrounding the Saviour, as they are supposed to be in heaven. Later art has not only distinguished each of the Apostles by his own attribute, it has also attempted to represent the character of each in the face and bearing ; and the illustration of the legends which develop the characteristics drawn from the Scripture history enables the artist to accomplish this object, sometimes with wonderful effect.

XI. SYMBOLS OF THE MONASTIC ORDERS.

To a student or lover of art there is a world of interest connected with the monastic orders, with their founders, their artists, their pictures. While they instituted schools, built cathedrals, and founded hospitals, they were the most munificent patrons of art the world has ever seen. To them we are indebted for many of the rarest gems of painting. Intended for the seclusion of church and cloister, *they now belong to all the world;* for who that has gazed on the Madonna di San Sisto, on the spirit-moving pictures of Angelico the Blessed, and many, many others, does not feel that he has a possession in them; that they have imparted something to him that was *his,* — something intended for him, and held in trust until he came to claim his own? There are certain peculiarities in what may be called monastic pictures, which were most fitting when these were in their proper places, but which seem incongruous when these pictures appear in the galleries of art or on the walls of palaces. I refer especially to the representation of the personages, and the peculiar habits and symbols of the different orders for which the pictures were painted. For instance, in pictures of the Annunciation, and other scenes from the life of the Virgin or the Saviour, we see the founders of orders and institutions in their distinctive dress; and until we consider that the pictures were painted for these orders, and in honor of these very founders and saints, we wonder at, and are disturbed by the seeming inappropriateness of the representations.

That these things are so, makes it a necessity that some attention should be given to these symbols and habits. A knowledge of them enables one to decide for what order a picture was intended, and explains much of its import and purpose.

There are certain general symbols which have a peculiar significance in monastic pictures : —

THE NIMBUS is given only to a canonized saint, never to a *beato;* sometimes the picture is painted before canonization, and the nimbus added afterwards.

The Infant Christ is often placed in the arms of a saint; or, in some pictures of the Virgin, she bends down and places the child in the arms of holy men and women. These are generally representations of visions which these saints have had, or have arisen from legends like that of St. Anthony of Padua, which relates that the Saviour came in this form, and stood on his book while he preached the Gospel.

The Standard, surmounted by the cross, belongs especially to such as were missionaries and apostles, and carried the Gospel to heathen nations. It is also an attribute of the warrior saints connected with the monastic orders.

The Crown at the feet of saints indicates that they were of royal birth, or resigned their kingdoms for the monastery. If they retained their rank until death, they wear the crown; and female saints of royal blood frequently wear the diadem outside the veil.

A Seraph distinguishes the saints of the Seraphic Order.[1]

The Stigmata, or Similitude of the Wounds of Christ, belong properly to St. Catherine of Siena and St. Francis alone, but are sometimes given to St. Maria Maddalena de' Pazzi.

The Book in the hand has the general signification of the Gospel; but accompanied by the pen or ink-horn, it indicates that the saint was an author, and the book is sometimes lettered with the proper titles of his works. The open book in the hand of a founder is the symbol of the rule of his order, and is often inscribed with the first sentence of the rule.

The Crucifix in the hand signifies a preacher; it is also an emblem of penance and faith.

The Flaming Heart is an emblem of divine love. It is given to St. Augustine. The heart crowned with thorns belongs to St. Francis de Sales. The heart inscribed with I. H. S. is given to Jesuit saints, to St. Teresa, St. Bridget of Sweden, and St. Maria Maddalena de' Pazzi.

The Crown of Thorns on the head or in the hands is the symbol of suffering for Christ's sake.

The Palm is not a general symbol for the monastic saints, but is given to St. Placidus, St. Boniface, and St. Thomas à Becket, of the

---

[1] The Order of St. Francis.

Benedictines; to St. Angelus and St. Albert, of the Carmelites, and to St. Peter Martyr, of the Dominicans, and but few others.

THE SCOURGE is the symbol of self-inflicted penance.

WALKING ON THE SEA represents a miracle attributed to the saint who is so painted.

THE CARDINAL'S HAT is given to St. Bonaventure. He is distinguished from St. Jerome by the Franciscan girdle.

THE MITRE AND PASTORAL STAFF belong to abbots and bishops. The staff without the mitre is proper only to abbesses.

SLAVES WITH BROKEN CHAINS, as well as beggars, children, and lepers at the feet of a saint, signify beneficence.

ROSES are significant of the name of the saint, or are connected with some circumstance in their lives, as with St. Elizabeth of Hungary, and St. Dorothea.

THE LILY is an emblem of purity and chastity, and of very general use; but it belongs especially to St. Clara, St. Anthony of Padua, St. Catherine of Siena, as well as to those who made vows of celibacy, like St. Casimir and others. The crucifix twined with lilies belongs to St. Nicholas of Tolentino. The lily also belongs to such as devoted themselves especially to the Blessed Virgin.

THE STAR over the head or breast expresses the divine attestation to the sanctity of the saint.

THE SUN on the breast is the symbol of the light of wisdom.

THE DOVE is the emblem of the direct inspiration of the Holy Ghost.

THE FISH, as the emblem of baptism, belongs to some early missionaries and to such as converted the heathen.

THE LAMB is proper to St. Francis as the symbol of meekness.

WILD BEASTS at the feet of a saint signify that he cleared a wilderness or founded a convent in a solitude.

THE HIND OR STAG is the emblem of solitude.

THE DRAGON at the feet is sin conquered; but chained to a rock or led by a chain, it is heresy vanquished.

The habits and special symbols of different orders are important. First, the *Benedictines*, with St. Benedict as their general patriarch, embrace, —

THE CAMALDOLESI, founded by St. Romualdo;

THE VALLOMBROSIANS, founded by St. John Gualberto;

The Carthusians, founded by St. Bruno ;

The Cistercians, founded by St. Bernard of Clairvaux ;

The Olivetani, founded by St. Bernardo Ptolomei ;

The Cluniacs, founded by St. Peter of Clugny ;

and some other less important branches which are governed by the Rule of St. Benedict.

The color of the habit is not especially determined in the Benedictine Rule. In the early pictures of St. Benedict he wears black ; but in some pictures painted for the reformed Benedictines, he is in a white habit. The black habit is given to St. Scholastica and the pupils of St. Benedict, St. Maurus, and St. Placidus, and to St. Flavia ; also to St. Boniface, the Apostle of Germany ; St. Bennett, Bishop of Durham ; St. Benedict of Anian ; St. Dunstan of Canterbury ; St. Walpurgis of Eichstadt ; St. Giles of Languedoc ; St. Ildefonso of Toledo ; St. Bavon of Ghent ; and to nearly all Benedictines who lived before the year 1020.

The Camaldolesi and their founder wear white.

The Vallombrosians, gray or ash color.

The Cluniacs, black.

The Cistercians, white. Their habit is long and loose, with very wide sleeves.

The Carthusians, white.

The Olivetani, white.

These orders furnished the earliest artists and architects of Europe. The monastery of Monte Cassino was founded by St. Benedict. Its church and cloisters contain many works of art, and among them the statues in marble of the most noted members and benefactors of the community. The cave at Subiaco, the Sacro Speco, is of great interest, and painted with very ancient frescos. They were done in 1219, and are important in the history of art. Among the finest edifices of the Benedictines may be mentioned the Basilica of San Paolo (fuori-le-mura) at Rome, San Severino at Naples, San Giustina at Padua, the monastery of Bamberg in Germany, St. Maur, Marmontier, and Fontevrauld in France. For their convent at Piacenza, the Madonna di San Sisto was painted ; for that at Grotta Ferrata, the life of St. Nilus by Domenichino ; at San Severino, the life of St. Benedict by Antonio lo Zingaro. For the Vallombrosians, Perugino painted the Assumption. Taddeo Gaddi painted many pictures for the Camaldolesi; and for different Benedictine orders, Ghirlandajo and Andrea del Sarto painted some of their finest pictures. The Certosa di Pavia is unequalled in many points, and has works of Luini, Borgognone, and many other famous masters. This is a Carthusian monastery, as is also the Certosa at Rome, built by Michael Angelo. Zurbaran and Carducho painted for the Spanish Carthusians, and Le Sueur the life of St. Bruno for those at Paris.

The Cistercians have many pictures of the Blessed Virgin, as they especially honor her and dedicate their churches under her patronage.

The beautiful church of San Lorenzo in Cremona, and that of Santa Maria in Organo at Verona, belong to the Olivetani, whose artists excelled in Tarsia or Intarsiatura, a beautiful style of inlaid work. In England many of the finest cathedrals were Benedictine foundations, and the word "abbey" belongs especially to this order.

THE AUGUSTINES.

These orders reverence St. Augustine of Hippo as their general patriarch and founder. They embrace, —

THE SERVI, founded by St. Philip Benizi;

THE ORDER OF MERCY, founded by St. Peter Nolasco;

THE BRIGITTINES, founded by St. Bridget of Sweden.[1]

The Augustinians reverence St. Joseph, the husband of the Virgin Mary, as their patriarch and patron saint. The habit of the Augustinians is black. St. Augustine and his mother, St. Monica, are the principal personages in the pictures of the order. St. Joseph and all the events of his life are also favorite subjects; and the earliest martyrs and bishops, though common to all orders, are especially honored by the Augustinians. The primitive hermits, St. Anthony and St. Paul, also receive much veneration; but their chief saint is Nicholas of Tolentino. The most important churches of the Agostini in Italy are the Sant' Agostino at Pavia, which contains the magnificent shrine of their founder, which has in all two hundred and ninety figures worked in marble. The principal events of the life of St. Augustine

---

[1] Some other orders of men and women follow the Rule, or a modification of the Rule, of St. Augustine.

are represented, and there are also statues of the Evangelists, Apostles, and many saints. The Sant' Agostino at Rome is the church for which the Isaiah of Raphael was painted. The Eremitani at Padua and the San Lorenzo of Florence are rich in works of art. The cathedrals at Cologne, Strasbourg, and Mayence belong to the Augustinians; and there are many churches, dedicated to St. Lawrence, St. Sebastian, St. Mary Magdalene, and St. Antonio Abbate, ministered to by priests of this order.

THE FRANCISCANS.

With St. Francis at their head, this order embraces —
THE CAPUCHINS ;
THE OBSERVANTS ;
THE CONVENTUALS, and
THE MINIMES.

These monks, as well as the Dominicans, are called *frati*, or "brothers," instead of *padri*, or "fathers ;" and the humility of St. Francis caused him to add the word *minori*, or "lesser," to his community. The habit of the Franciscans was first gray, and remained so for two centuries, when it was changed to dark brown. It is a plain tunic with long full sleeves, but not as ample as those of the Benedictines. This tunic is bound about the waist with a knotted cord, which is the emblem of a beast subdued ; and this was the light in which St. Francis considered the body when subjected to the spirit. A scanty cape hangs about the shoulders, to which is attached a hood to be drawn over the head in cold weather. The nuns wear the same dress, with a veil in place of the hood. The third order of St. Francis is distinguished by the cord worn as a girdle. The Franciscans are barefooted or with a sandal known in Italy as the *zoccolo ;* hence the name Zoccolanti, by which these friars are sometimes called. The Minimes are distinguished by a scapulary which hangs a little below the girdle in front and is rounded at the ends ; to this is attached a small round hood, while that of the Capuchins is pointed. The Franciscans aspired to extreme sanctity, and were greatly beloved by the people. They have several royal saints ; but first are their eight principal saints, called *I Cardini dell' Ordine Serafico* ("the chiefs of the Seraphic Order").

1. St. Francis, Padre Serafico, patriarch and founder.

2. St. Clara, Madre Serafica, first Franciscan nun and foundress of the Povere Donne, or Poor Clares.

3. St. Bonaventura, il Dottore Serafico, the great prelate of the order.

4. St. Antony of Padua, who is, next to St. Francis, the saint most renowned in the order for miracles.

5. St. Bernardino of Siena, their great preacher and reformer.

6. St. Louis, King of France.

7. St. Louis, Bishop of Toulouse.

8. St. Elizabeth of Hungary.

Then follow St. Margaret of Cortona, St. Rosa di Viterbo, St. Felix de Cantalicio, and a host of others.

The churches of the Franciscans have been magnificently adorned. The parent convent and church at Assisi was three hundred years in the hands of the greatest artists of Italy. Raphael, Pinturicchio, Giotto, Taddeo and Angelo Gaddi, Giottino, Luca della Robbia, and Benedetto da Maiano, all contributed to the decoration of Franciscan edifices. The St. Antonio-di-Padova is filled with art treasures. It has bronzes of Donatello and Andrea Riccio; pictures by many of the great painters of Upper Italy, and marbles of Lombardi, Sansovino, and Sammichele. Murillo painted many of his wonderful pictures for this order in Spain.

THE DOMINICANS.

These are called the Preaching Friars, and have St. Dominick at their head. They wear a white woollen habit, fastened with a white girdle; over this a white scapular, which hangs to the feet from the neck, both before and behind, like a long apron; over all a black cloak with a hood. The scapular of the lay brothers is black.

The Dominicans always wear shoes. Their traditions teach that this habit was adopted in accordance with the directions of the Blessed Virgin. The white symbolizes purity; the black, mortification and penance. Their four principal saints are St. Dominick, St. Peter Martyr; St. Thomas Aquinas, the Angelic Doctor; and St. Catherine of Siena. The Dominicans have embraced some of the most splendid artists and patrons of art. The shrine of St. Dominick is in the church of his order at Bologna. It is called, in Italy, the Arca di San Domenico. Niccolo Pisano built the church and executed the shrine, but the church has been rebuilt in modern style. At Rome the Santa Maria-Sopra-Minerva is their most important church; and here sleeps Angelico da Fiesole, "Il Beato," and Leo X., with Cardinal Howard, Cardinal Bembo, and Durandus. This church is filled with beautiful pictures, and here is Michael Angelo's statue of Christ. At Florence the Dominicans have the Santa Maria Novella; in this church is the Chapel Dei Spagnuoli, painted by Taddeo Gaddi and Simone Memmi; — the Strozzi Chapel, by Andrea Orcagna; and here is the Madonna and Child, by Cimabue.

In Florence is the convent of St. Mark, in which lived and painted Fra Angelico and Fra Bartolomeo. The first of these entered this convent when twenty years old, and passed the remainder of his long life in painting the spiritual conceptions of his devout and gentle mind. He believed that God granted him his benediction on his labors; and so impressed was he with the religious importance of them, that he is said to have painted much upon his bended knees, as if performing an act of devotion. His principal works are in his own convent, in the church of Santa Maria Novella, and in the Chapel of Nicholas V., in the Vatican. Fra Bartolomeo is also called Baccio della Porta and Il Frate.

At Siena the Dominicans have the Madonna by Guido da Siena, and the frescos of Razzi. For this order Leonardo da Vinci painted his Last Supper, and Titian his San Pietro Martire.

Their churches were built without aisles, having a nave only, in order that the preaching, which was their especial duty, might be heard in every part; this form of edifice was very advantageous also for the setting forth of their pictures.

THE CARMELITES.

This order claims the prophet Elijah as its founder, and also that Mt. Carmel has been inhabited by a direct succession of hermits ever since the time of that prophet. The members wear a brown tunic with a white mantle, and are also called White Friars. Their most interesting church is the Carmini at Florence, in which is the Brancacci Chapel, which was painted by Masaccio, Filippino Lippi, and Masolino. As an order, the Carmelites are not important in art.

THE JERONYMITES.

These monks claim St. Jerome as their founder, and adorn their edifices largely with pictures of that saint, and scenes from his life. The Escurial and the monastery of St. Just, in Spain ; the monastery of Belem, in Portugal ; and that of St. Sigismond, near Cremona, in Italy, — all belong to this order, which is remarkable for the magnificence of its edifices.

THE JESUITS.

The members of this order are not easily distinguished in art. They wear the black frock buttoned to the chin, which is so unfavorable for a picture that they are often represented in the priestly vestments, as in the case of St. Ignatius Loyola and St. Francis Xavier ; or in cassock and surplice, as in the case of St. Aloysius and St. Stanislaus Kostka. If the head is covered, it is by a square black cap. The Jesuits did not appear to value art as highly as many of the older orders. They lavished large sums of money on their churches ; but it was spent in brilliant decorations of gold and silver, rare marbles, and even jewels, rather than in pictures and statues ; and yet they were (after some royal personages) the chief patrons of Rubens and Van Dyck, who decorated the splendid church of their order at Antwerp.

XII. VOTIVE PICTURES, ANACHRONISMS, Etc.

There are large numbers of what are known as votive pictures, which are painted in fulfilment of a vow, in gratitude for some signal blessing, or to avert some anticipated danger. Many commemorate a recovery, or escape from sickness or accident. The donor, and sometimes his entire family, are seen in the picture, and are frequently represented as grouped about the Madonna and Child. In early art the donor or votary was represented as very diminutive, to express humility ; but in later times they appear of a natural size. The figure of a bishop kneeling, while all others stand, signifies that he is the person who presents the picture ; when he stands it is difficult to determine who he may be, for there are hundreds of bishop-martyrs and patrons who are thus represented.

In many works of art there is an apparent anachronism in the choice of the persons represented ; as, for instance, when the Virgin is surrounded by those who lived either centuries before or after herself. It must be borne in mind that such pictures were not intended to represent physical facts, but are devotional in their character and meaning. And if the persons represented are not living, they know no more of time; for them it no longer exists, and that which at a careless glance appears to be the result of ignorance or bad taste is, in fact, a spiritual conception of the "communion of saints," who belong no more to earth. When thus considered, there appears no incongruity in these representations, of which the Correggio at Parma is a good illustration. In it St. Jerome presents his translation of the Scriptures to the infant Christ, while an angel turns the leaves, and Mary Magdalene kisses the feet of Jesus. Neither is the grouping in many pictures strictly in accordance with what might be termed propriety. The Sibyls dancing around the cradle of Jesus, and the representations of Greek poets and philosophers in ecclesiastical art, are explained by the fact that everything was regarded in but a single aspect, — that is, in its relation to Christ and his Church. All those who preceded him foreshadowed him, and prophesied of his coming. Therefore these Greeks sometimes bear scrolls inscribed with sentences from their writings which are interpreted as relating to the Saviour. In the examination of large numbers of religious pictures, chronology should be entirely forgotten, for time was not thought of in their arrangement, and many other considerations determined the artist in his association of persons. Certain saints are brought together, because they are joint patrons of the place for which they were painted, as in the Venetian pictures of St. Mark, St. George, and St. Catherine. Again, they are connected by the same attributes, or similar events, in their lives, as is the case with St. Roch and St. Sebastian, — the first having tended the sick who suffered from the plague, and the last being a protector against it. Or they were friends on earth, as St. Cyprian and St. Cornelius; or they rest together in death, as St. Stephen and St. Laurence. Some of these, or other like reasons, which were good and sufficient to the minds of artists and their patrons, always explained the apparent inconsistencies of these pictures, and were perfectly understood in the age to which they belonged. Again, some saints are so much more frequently represented than others as to occasion surprise and remark. This may be explained in part by the fact that some saints were universal patrons honored throughout Christendom, while the veneration for others was confined to special localities or to certain orders. St. Joseph, St. George, St. Sebastian, St. Christopher, St. Cosmo, St. Damian, St. Roch, St. Nicholas, St. Catherine, St. Cecilia, St. Barbara, St. Margaret, and St. Ursula are of the former class.

In particular schools of art this frequent representation of certain personages is governed by the locality in which they were painted, or that for which they were intended. A Florentine artist would introduce St. Donato and St. Romulo; a Neapolitan, St. Januarius; a Frenchman, St. Denis, etc.; or as in an existing picture, St. Peter, St. Leonard, St. Martha, and St. Mary Magdalene are united to indicate that the society for which it was painted redeemed prisoners, ransomed slaves, labored for the poor, and converted the fallen and sinful.

Thus it is apparent that it is for the advantage of the careful observer to consider that however bizarre a picture may appear, there is some reason for its arrangement, which, if understood and appreciated, adds meaning to it, helps to discern its intention and sentiment, and shows that what seems at first to be the result of chance, or an ignorance of the fitness of things, is in truth that of deep and earnest thought, of delicate and poetic conceptions, and a lofty desire to teach grand and holy truths as well as to give pleasure and delight the eye.

Badge of the Order of Mercy.

LEGENDS AND STORIES

WHICH HAVE BEEN ILLUSTRATED IN ART.

St. Abbondio was born at Thessalonica. He was the fourth Bishop of Como, in the time of Leo I. He is represented in the cathedral of Como, and is the apostle and patron saint of that portion of Italy.

Abgarus, King. The apocryphal gospel spoken of by Eusebius, and called "Christ and Abgarus," begins with "A Copy of a Letter written by King Abgarus to Jesus, and sent to Him by Ananias, his Footman, to Jerusalem, inviting Him to Edessa." This letter opens with greetings to the Saviour, and goes on to urge him to go to Edessa, to cure the king of a serious disease. It adds: "My city is indeed small, but neat, and large enough for us both." Jesus returned an answer that he could not go, as he must fulfil his mission at Jerusalem, but promised that after his ascension he would send a disciple, who would cure the king and give life to him and to all who were with him. This account ends here; but up to the tenth century there were a variety of additions made to it, until then it had assumed the following form: "Abgarus, King of Edessa, suffering from the twofold infliction of gout and leprosy, withdrew from the sight of men. Ananias, one of his servants, returning from a journey to Egypt, tells him of the wonderful cures by Christ, of which he has heard in Palestine. In the hope of obtaining relief, Abgarus writes to Christ, and charges Ananias, who was not only a good traveller but a skilful painter, that if Christ should not be able to come, he should at all events send him his portrait. Ananias

finds Christ as he is in the act of performing miracles, and teaching
the multitude in the open air. As he is not able to approach him
for the crowd, he mounts a rock not far off. Thence he fixes his
eyes upon Christ, and begins to take his likeness. Jesus, who sees
him, and also knows in spirit the contents of the letter, sends
Thomas to bring him to him, writes his answer to Abgarus, and gives
it to him. But seeing that Ananias still lingers, Jesus calls for
water, and having washed his face, he wipes it on a cloth, on which,
by his divine power, there remains a perfect portrait of his features;
this he gives to Ananias, charging him to take it to Abgarus, so that
his longing may be satisfied, and his disease cured. On the way
Ananias passes by the city of Hierapolis, but remains outside the
gates, and hides the holy cloth in a heap of freshly made bricks.
At midnight the inhabitants of Hierapolis perceive that this heap
of bricks is surrounded with fire. They discover Ananias, and he
owns the supernatural character of the object hidden among the
bricks. They find not only the miraculous cloth, but more still;
for, by a mysterious virtue, a brick that lay near the cloth has
received a second impress of the divine image. And as no fire is
discoverable, except the light that proceeds from the picture, the
inhabitants keep the brick as a sacred treasure, and let Ananias go
on his way. He gives King Abgarus the letter and the cloth, who
is immediately healed." This last legend was edited by the Emperor Constantine Porphyrogenitus, and in his time the original napkin was at Constantinople; two others at Rome and Genoa, while a
false copy had been sent to the King of Persia. The brick, too, had
remained in its first city, but had furnished images to other cities. In
fact, the Roman one still exists in the church of San Silvestro. But
Constantine has given a third version, which is that Christ, on the
way to Calvary, wiped his face on a piece of linen on which the impress
of his countenance was left, and gave it to Thomas, commanding that
after his ascension Thaddeus should take it to Abgarus in order to fulfil the promise which Jesus had made. This was done; but Thaddeus
first goes to the house of a Jew in Edessa, determined to do some
miracles which shall attract the attention of the King. And he heals
the sick, until Abgarus hears of him and sends for him, hoping that
he is the disciple whom Christ had promised him should come. As
Thaddeus enters the room, he lifts up the picture; and so great a

light proceeds from it, that Abgarus springs from his bed, forgetting all his lameness, and goes to receive the picture. He touches with it his head and limbs, and receives strength. The leprosy disappears except from his forehead. He is converted; and when he is baptized, even the last marks of the leprosy disappear. This legend has been often represented in painting.

St. Achilleus and St. Nereus. These are Roman saints, and the church dedicated to them is near the Baths of Caracalla. They were chamberlains of Flavia Domitilla. They persuaded her not to marry Aurelian, the son of the consul, to whom she was betrothed, because he was an idolater. For this they were beheaded. Flavia Domitilla was the grand-niece of the Emperor Domitian. Her parents had been martyred because they were Christians. She also suffered death for the same cause, at Terracina. Nereus and Achilleus are represented in secular habits, standing on each side of Domitilla. She is dressed as a princess. They all bear palms. May 12.

St. Adelaide, or Alice, of Germany was the daughter of Ralph II. of Burgundy. Her father died when she was six years old, and at sixteen she married Lothaire, King of Italy. Her husband did not live long; and after his death Adelaide was imprisoned at Pavia, by Berengarius III. She at length escaped, and fled towards Germany. She was met by the Emperor Otho I., who was marching with his army to release her. Otho made a treaty with Berengarius, and married Alice. But the treaty was soon broken, when Otho sent Berengarius a prisoner to Germany, and he himself was crowned emperor at Rome. Adelaide made use of her rank and power to do good, and educated her son Otho II. with carefulness. The emperor died after a reign of thirty-six years; and his son suffered himself to be influenced by evil advisers, and especially by his second wife, Theophania, so that he banished his good mother from the court. But being overtaken by misfortune, he recalled her and attempted to atone for his wicked cruelty. He died after a reign of nine years, and his wife, so long as she lived, insulted St. Adelaide by the most disrespectful treatment; but she soon died also, and Adelaide became regent. From this time she devoted herself to good works, and built many religious edifices. The people, who loved her, were guided by her into virtue and piety. She died at Salcis, when on a journey.

A part of her relics are preserved in a shrine in Hanover. December 16, A. D. 999.

St. Adelaide was the wife of St. Lupo, and the mother of St. Grata, who together with St. Alexander the martyr, are saints belonging especially to Bergamo, the last two being the patron saints of that city. St. Grata, after the death of her husband, became a Christian, and converted her father, who was Duke of Bergamo, and her mother, St. Adelaide, to the same faith. Through the influence of St. Grata, St. Lupo founded the cathedral at Bergamo. After the death of her parents Grata governed Bergamo, and founded three churches and a hospital, where she herself ministered to the sick. St. Alexander was a soldier of the Thebau Legion, and was beheaded outside Bergamo. Grata wrapped the head in a napkin, and gave honorable burial to the remains. St Adelaide is represented with a crown and a long veil, St. Lupo with a royal crown, St. Alexander as a Roman warrior with a palm, and St. Grata as carrying the head of Alexander.

St. Adrian (*Gr.* Ἅγ. Ἀδριανός; *Lat.* S. Adrianus; *Fr.* St. Adrien; *Ital.* Sant' Adriano) was a military saint, and for ages was considered next to St. George in Northern Europe. In the North of France, Flanders, and Germany, he was the patron saint of soldiers, and protector against the plague. He is also the patron of Flemish brewers. He was a noble Roman, son of Probus. At the time of the tenth persecution of the Christians at Nicomedia, a city of Bithynia (A. D. 290), he served in the guards of the Emperor Galerius Maximian. He was less than thirty years old, and was married to Natalia, who was a Christian secretly. She was exceedingly virtuous and beautiful. The imperial edict was torn down by St. George, which so infuriated the emperor that thirty-four Christians were sentenced to the torture at one time. It fell by lot to Adrian to superintend the execution of the sentence. When he saw the manner in which the Christians suffered for their faith, he was suddenly converted, and seating himself in their midst, exclaimed, " Consider me also as one of ye ; for I too will be a Christian." He was immediately imprisoned. Natalia, hearing this, was full of joy, and going to him encouraged him to suffer for Christ. Adrian was soon condemned to die; and the night before his execution, he bribed his jailer to permit him to visit Natalia. She, hearing that her

husband had left his prison, was in great sorrow, and tearing her garments threw herself down, saying, "Alas! miserable that I am! I
have not deserved to be the wife of a martyr! Now will men point
at me and say, Behold the wife of the coward and apostate, who for
fear of death hath denied his God." But Adrian, who had now come,
hearing these words, said, "O thou noble and strong-hearted woman!
Oh, bless God that I am not unworthy of thee! Open the door that
I may bid thee farewell before I die." Joyfully she opened the door
and embraced him, and returned to prison with him. The next day
Adrian was scourged and tortured, and sent back to prison. The
tyrants, hearing of the devotion of Natalia, ordered that no woman
should be admitted to the prison. She then cut off her beautiful
hair, and dressed as a man, and so gained admission to Adrian. She
found him torn and bleeding. She took him in her arms, and said,
"O light of mine eyes and husband of mine heart! Blessed art
thou, who art called to suffer for Christ's sake!" Thus she so
strengthened his heart that he was able to endure to the end. The
next day his limbs were struck off on an anvil, and he was beheaded.
Natalia supported him in his sufferings, and he expired in her arms
before the last blow. Kissing him, she took one of his hands, which
she wrapped in linen with spices and perfumes, and placed it at the
head of her bed. His body was taken by Christians to Byzantium,
since Constantinople. There is a tradition that in the ninth century
it was removed to the convent which bears his name, at Grammont,
in Flanders. After this the emperor threatened to marry Natalia to
a tribune of the army. She fled to Argyropolis, near Byzantium, and
passed her life near the tomb of Adrian. He often appeared to her
in visions, and asked her to follow him, which she soon did; and
when she died, Adrian with rejoicing angels met her, and together
they entered the presence of God. An anvil is the attribute of
Adrian, and is represented at his feet or in his hand. His sword
was long kept as a relic, at Walbeck, in Saxony; but the Emperor
Henry II. (St. Henry) girded it on himself when preparing to go
against the Turks and Hungarians. A. D. 290.

St. Afra was the daughter of St. Hilaria, and is the patroness
of Augsburg. She was for a long time a courtesan in that city, and
had three maidens as dissolute as herself, — Digna, Eunomia, and
Eutropia. At length Narcissus, a holy man fleeing from persecution,

came to her house, not knowing her character. When she found he was a priest, she was overcome with fear, and for the first time was ashamed of her life of sin. He told her of Christ, and at length she besought him to allow her to be baptized. He, knowing that Christ did not reject even the greatest sinners, baptized her and assured her of forgiveness. By her aid Narcissus escaped to his native Spain. Through her influence her mother and the three maidens were also converted. Afra was seized, and accused of having assisted Narcissus to escape and of being herself a Christian. The judge, Gaius, who had known of her former life, was amazed at her modesty, and the firmness with which she acknowledged her new faith, and asked her how one so vile could expect to be received by Jesus. To which she replied, " It is true I am unworthy to bear the name of Christian ; nevertheless, He who did not reject Mary Magdalene when she washed his feet with her tears, will not reject me." She was burned alive ; and as she prayed in the midst of the fire, angels bore her spirit to heaven. Shortly after, her mother and the three maidens were executed for their faith, and suffered with constancy. August 5, A. D. 304.

St. Afra, patroness of Brescia, is supposed to have been of noble family. She was converted by the works of San Faustino and San Giovita (Faustinus and Jovita), and suffered martyrdom with Calocerus. The church dedicated to her is one of the finest ornaments of Brescia.

St. Agatha (*Lat.* Sancta Agatha ; *Fr.* Ste. Agathe ; *Ital.* Santa Agata ; *Ger.* Die Heilige Agatha), virgin and martyr ; patroness of Malta and Catania, also protectress against fire and all diseases of the breast. The Emperor Decius strangled his predecessor, Philip ; and desiring to make it appear that he did this because Philip was a Christian, and not for his own advancement, he instituted great persecutions of the Christians throughout his empire. He made Quintianus king of Sicily. Here, at Catania, dwelt Agatha, a maiden of great beauty, whom Quintianus tempted with presents, flattery, and promises, without success. He then gave her to Frondisia, who was a courtesan with nine daughters, all as wicked as possible, and promised her great riches if she would subdue Agatha to his wishes. Frondisia attempted to influence Agatha by every means in her power for thirty-three days ; but she remained fixed

in her purity, and her faith in Jesus. At the end of that time
Frondisia said to Quintianus, "Sooner shall that sword at thy side
become like liquid lead, and the rocks dissolve and flow like water,
than the heart of this damsel be subdued to thy will." Then Quintianus in fury commanded her to be brought, and attempted to
move her by threats; but she said, "If thou shouldst throw me
to the wild beasts, the power of Christ would render them weak
as lambs; if thou shouldst kindle a fire to consume me, the angels
would quench it with their dews from heaven; if thou shouldst
tear me with scourges, the Holy Spirit within me would render
thy tortures harmless." Then the tyrant ordered her to be beaten,
and her bosom to be torn with shears. After that she was thrown
into a dark dungeon. At midnight there came an aged man bearing
a vase of ointment, and a youth with a torch. It was St. Peter
and an angel, but Agatha did not know them; and the light which
filled the dungeon so frightened the guards that they fled, leaving
the door open. Then one said to the maiden, "Arise and fly."
But she replied, "God forbid that I should fly from my crown of
martyrdom, and be the occasion that my keepers should suffer,
for my flight, tortures, and death; I will not fly." Then St.
Peter healed all her wounds with celestial ointment, and vanished
from her sight. The rage of Quintianus not being satisfied, he sent
for her again, and was astonished at the wonderful cure of her
wounds. "Who hath healed thee?" asked he; she replied, "He,
whom I confess and adore with my heart and with my lips, hath
sent his apostle, and healed me, and delivered me." Then Quintianus ordered her to be burned; and as she was thrown in the
fire, a great earthquake shook the city, and the people ran to the
palace, crying, "This has fallen upon us because of the sufferings
of this Christian damsel;" and they threatened to burn Quintianus
if he did not desist. So he ordered her to be taken from the flames,
and she was borne again to prison, scorched, and in great agony.
Here she entreated God to release her and take her to heaven;
which prayer was heard, for immediately she died. The Christians
embalmed her body, and placed it in a tomb of porphyry. Near
to Catania is a volcano which the people call Mongibello (Mt. Ætna),
and about a year after the death of Agatha this mountain opened
and sent forth streams of fire. When the fire had almost reached

the city, the people took the veil of Agatha from her tomb, and placing it on a lance bore it in procession towards the fire, and when they came to it the fire was stayed and the city saved. When the heathen saw this miracle, they were all converted and baptized. There is in Malta a subterranean chapel dedicated to St. Agatha. It is cut out of the rock, and the walls are frescoed. Tradition asserts that the ground once belonged to the family of the saint. St. Agatha is usually represented with a palm in one hand and a salver in the other, on which is the female breast. Sometimes the shears are beside her. She wears a long veil. February 5, A. D. 251.

St. Aglae (*Gr.* 'Αγ. 'Αγλαις) was a Greek by birth, and lived with her lover, Boniface, in sin and luxury for many years. In the time of the last persecution of the Christians, they were both converted from their sins, and became followers of Christ. Aglaë sent Boniface with great treasures to assist the martyrs and to bury their remains. In his zeal, he exposed himself and suffered martyrdom. His body was brought to Aglaë. She built, on the western side of the Aventine, an oratory, wherein she placed the remains of Boniface, and she spent the remainder of her life in prayers and penitence. May 14. Boniface died, about 307; Aglaë, fifteen years later.

St. Agnes (*Lat.* Sancta Agnus; *Ital.* Sant' Agnese; *Sp.* Santa Inez; *Fr.* Ste. Agnès). St. Agnes was a Roman maiden of great beauty, and a Christian from her infancy. She was not more than thirteen years old when the son of the prefect Sempronius saw her, and so loved her that he sought her for his wife. But she refused his request, saying that she was already affianced to a husband whom she loved, meaning Jesus. The young man knew not to whom she referred; and his jealousy and disappointed love made him sick, almost unto death. Then the physicians said, "This youth is sick of unrequited love, and our art can avail nothing." When the prefect questioned his son, he told his father of his love for Agnes, and that unless she would be his wife he must die. Then Sempronius begged of Agnes and her parents that she should marry his son; but she replied, as before, that she preferred her betrothed to the son of the prefect. When he had inquired her meaning, and found that she was a Christian, he was glad; for there was an edict against the Christians, and he felt she was in his power. He then told her that since she would have no earthly husband, she must become a Vestal Virgin.

But she refused with scorn the worship of vain images, and declared that she would serve none but Jesus. Sempronius then threatened her with the most horrid death, and put her in chains, and dragged her to the altars of the gods. But she remained firm. Then he ordered her to be taken to a house of infamy, to suffer the most fearful outrages. The soldiers stripped off her garments; but when she prayed, her hair was lengthened till it was as a cloak about her, covering her whole person, and those who saw her were seized with fear. So they shut her in a room; and when she prayed to Christ that she might not be dishonored, she saw before her a shining white garment, which she put on with joy, and the room was filled with great light. The son of the prefect, thinking she must be subdued, now came to her. But he was struck blind, and fell in convulsions. Agnes, moved by his sufferings and the tears of his friends, prayed for his recovery, and he was healed. When Sempronius saw this, he wished to save her; but the people said, "She is a sorceress; let her die." So she was condemned to be burned; but the flames harmed her not, while her executioners were consumed by them. Then they cried out the more, "She is a sorceress: she must die." Then an executioner was commanded to ascend the pile, and kill her with the sword. This he did; and gazing steadfastly towards heaven, she fell dead upon the pile. She was buried on the Via Nomentana, and the Christians were accustomed to visit her tomb to weep. But she appeared to them, and forbade that they should sorrow for one who was happy in heaven. St. Agnes is a favorite saint of the Roman, and, in general, of young Catholic women. There is one church dedicated to her, on the Piazza Navona, on the spot where stood the house of infamy to which she was carried; and another of great interest beyond the Porta Pia, said to have been built by Constantine, at the request of his daughter, Constantina, to commemorate the burial-place of St. Agnes. Next to the Evangelists and Apostles, there is no saint whose images are older than those of St. Agnes. She is most frequently represented with a lamb. January 21, A. D. 304. She is one of the four great virgin martyrs of the Latin Church.

St. Agnes of Monte Pulciano. This saint was remarkable for her piety from her very infancy. At nine years of age she was placed in a nunnery, and at fifteen was made prioress of a new convent at Procino, of the Dominican Order. She slept on the ground with a stone pillow, and lived on bread and water for fifteen years, until she was obliged to diminish her austerities on account of her health. At length the people of Monte Pulciano, being desirous that she should return to her native town, built a convent on a spot where they had destroyed a lewd house; of which convent St. Agnes became the superior. She had the gifts of miracles and prophecy, and was greatly beloved. St. Catherine of Siena made a pilgrimage to the tomb of St. Agnes with two of her nieces, who took the veil on that occasion. She is greatly venerated in Tuscany. April 20, A. D. 1317.

St. Alban was the first saint and martyr in England, on which account the Abbot of St. Alban's had precedence over all others. This saint was a native of Verulam. He lived in the time of Aurelian, and went to Rome. While still an idolater, he was noted for his hospitality, charity, and many virtues, as well as for his great learning. When the persecution of Diocletian invaded Britain, St. Alban gave shelter to a priest, who was the means of his conversion, and baptized him. When the priest was pursued to his house, St. Alban put on his long robe and gave himself to the soldiers to save his guest. He was condemned to death, as he would neither worship idols nor surrender the priest. He was first tortured, and then led out for execution. It was necessary to cross the river Coln to reach the place where he was to suffer. The crowd was great, and the bridge so narrow that they could not pass; but when the saint said a short prayer, the waters were divided, and all went over dry-shod. When on the hill of execution, he prayed for water to quench his thirst and a spring gushed out at his feet. He was beheaded. His burial-place was forgotten, but disclosed in 793 by a miracle. An angel commanded King Offa in a vision that he should find the remains of this saint, and secure to them the veneration of the people. He found them at Verulam, and built a church for them, near which arose a great Benedictine monastery and the town of St. Alban's in Hertfordshire. His attributes are the sword and a fountain springing at his feet. June 22, A. D. 305.

St. Albert (*Lat.* S. Albertus; *Ital.* Sant' Alberto) was Bishop of Vercelli and Patriarch of Jerusalem. He is reverenced as the founder of the Order of the Carmelites. He was murdered at Acre, when embarking to attend a council at Rome. At the cathedral at Cremona is a vessel in which, tradition says, St. Albert kneaded bread for the poor. He is represented in his episcopal robes, and carries the palm.

Albertus Magnus, sometimes called Sant' Alberto Magno, was a teacher of St. Thomas Aquinas, and is represented in art in company with that saint.

St. Alexander (*Ital.* Sant' Alessandro; *Fr.* St. Alexandre). March 18, A. D. 251. See St. Adelaide.

St. Alexis (*Lat.* S. Aletius; *Ital.* Sant' Alessio; *Fr.* St. Alexis; *Ger.* Der Heilige Alexius). In the time of Pope Innocent I. and the Emperor Honorius, there lived on the Cœlian Hill a man of great rank and wealth, named Euphemian. His wife was called Aglæ. For many years they had no child, and on this account prayed earnestly to God, until at length they had a son, whom they called Alexis. From his childhood he devoted himself to the service of God, and wore beneath his rich clothing a shirt of hair, and when in his own chamber bewailed his sins and those of the whole world, and made a vow to serve God alone. At length Euphemian selected a beautiful maiden of noble rank to be the wife of Alexis. When he saw the loveliness of his bride and remembered his vow, he trembled. He did not dare to disobey his father, and the wedding was celebrated with great pomp. Then Alexis went to the chamber of his bride, and gave her a gold ring, a girdle of precious stones, and a purple veil, and bade her farewell, and was seen no more. His mother and his wife passed their time in the deepest grief, while his father sent through all the world to find him. Alexis, disguised as a pilgrim, reached the mouth of the Tiber in a small boat, and sailed from Ostia for Laodicea. Thence he went to Edessa, in Mesopotamia, where he dwelt, ministering to the poor and sick, until the people called him a saint. Fearing popular favor, he sailed for Tarsus to pay his devotions to St. Paul. But the vessel in a storm was driven to Ostia. So, then, Alexis went to his father's house, and begged that he might live upon his charity. Euphemian, not recognizing him, thought upon his son, that he too might be poor and in need, and gave orders that he should be provided for. But the servants ill-treated him, and gave him no lodging but a hole under the marble steps of the house. But the hardest thing he had to endure was to hear his wife and mother constantly lamenting for him and complaining of his absence. By this was he sorely tempted, but he yielded not. Thus passed many years, till at length he knew that he must die. Then he asked for pen and ink, and wrote an account of all his life, and put it in his bosom. Now, on a feast day, as Pope Innocent was singing high mass, the Emperor Honorius present, and Euphemian was standing by the latter, a voice cried out, "Seek the servant of God, who is about to depart from this life, and who shall pray for Rome." And the people fell on their faces, and another voice said, "Where shall we seek him?" And the answer was, "In the house of Euphemian the patrician." So they all went instantly, and Euphemian led the way; and as he came near home, they told him that the beggar had died, and they had laid him on the steps before the door. When he uncovered the face, it was as the face of an angel, and a great glory of light shone from it. Then he said, "This is the servant of God, of whom the voice spoke just now." And the pope took the letter from the dead hand of Alexis, and read it aloud. The father was overwhelmed with grief. The wife and the mother rushed out and threw themselves on the dead body. Seven days they watched beside it, and many sick and infirm were healed by touching the holy remains of Alexis. He is the patron of pilgrims and beggars, and on the spot where stood his father's house is now the church of St. Alexis. The marble steps beneath which he lived and died are preserved in the church; and a statue of the saint, in the dress of a pilgrim with a staff beside him, and a letter in his hand, is extended beneath them. Cardinal Wiseman wrote a charming drama on the story of St. Alexis, entitled "The Hidden Gem." July 24, A. D. 400.

St. Alphege was an English nobleman. He was a most holy man, and was made Archbishop of Canterbury in 1006. Six years later the Danes took the city and cathedral of Canterbury. They put the people to death and burned the city. St. Alphege was kept seven months in prison, and then stoned to death because he refused to pay a large ransom for his life. The place where he met his death was at Greenwich, and the same as that on which the parish church now stands. It is said that ten years after death his body was found entire and incorrupt. It was removed from St. Paul's to the Canterbury Cathedral, and enshrined near the high altar. He is represented with his chasuble full of stones. April 19, A. D. 1012.

St. Ambrose (*Lat.* S. Ambrosius; *Ital.* Sant' Ambrogio; *Fr.* St. Ambrose; *Ger.* Der Heilige Ambrosius). St. Ambrose is one of the Fathers of the Church. He was born at Treves, A. D. 340, and was a son of a prefect of Gaul of the same name. He studied at Rome, and being at length appointed prefect of Æmilia and Liguria (Piedmont and Genoa), he resided at Milan. He was very eloquent; and the same story that is told of Plato and Archilochus is told of him, — namely, that when an infant in his cradle a swarm of bees alighted on his mouth without injuring him. This was thought to indicate his future eloquence. Shortly after his going to Milan the bishop died; and a great dispute arose between the Catholics and Arians concerning the succession, when Ambrose by his eloquence quieted them. In the midst of it a voice like that of a child cried out, "Ambrose shall be bishop." To this he greatly objected, especially as he was only a catechumen. But the people would not listen to this refusal; and being baptized, in due time he was consecrated Bishop of Milan. He first gave all his property to the poor, and then devoted himself to such studies as would fit him for his office. St. Ambrose was an eloquent advocate of the advantages of celibacy for both sexes, and of the supremacy of the Church above all other powers. He had no fear of man, forbidding even the Emperor Theodosius to enter the Church until he had atoned for his sin in permitting the massacre of seven thousand men at Thessalonica, by public penance. He founded the Basilica of Sant' Ambrogio Maggiore at Milan in 387, and dedicated it to all the saints. He is the patron saint of Milan. There are many wonderful and miraculous circumstances related in his life; and at his death it was said that Christ visited him, and that he ascended to heaven in the arms of angels. He is represented as a mitred bishop with the crosier; sometimes with a beehive at his feet; but his usual attribute is a knotted scourge with three thongs. April 4, A. D. 397.

St. Anastasia (*Fr.* Ste. Anastasie; *Gr.* Ἁγ. Ἀναστασίη). Just under the Palatine Hill is the church dedicated to this saint, who, while she has great fame among Greek Christians, was a Roman lady. She was condemned to the flames in the persecution of Diocletian. She suffered greatly at the hands of her husband and family because she openly professed Christianity. St. Chrysogonus (Grisogono) is chiefly celebrated for his influence over Anastasia and for the courage with which he inspired her. He was slain by the sword and thrown into the sea. They are said to have suffered at Illyria; but Anastasia was buried by Apollina in her garden, near the Circus Maximus, where

her church now stands. It is said that St. Jerome once celebrated
mass in this church. There is also a beautiful church at Verona
dedicated to St. Anastasia. The church of Chrysogonus in the Trastevere, built in 599, was rebuilt in 1623 by Scipio Borghese, Cardinal
of San Grisogono. December 25, A. D. 304.

St. Andrea of Corsini was born in 1302. He was of the Corsini family of Florence. He was extremely wild until he was sixteen
years old, when his mother, in despair, told him of a dream which
she had before his birth, in which she dreamed of giving birth to
a wolf; but this wolf on entering a church was changed to a lamb.
This greatly affected Andrea, and he went to a Carmelite church to
pray, where such a change was begun in him that at seventeen he
became a friar. He was Bishop of Fiesole. The Florentines attributed to the protection of this saint their victory of the battle of
Anghiari. February 4, A. D. 1373.

St. Andrew (*Lat.* S. Andreas; *Ital.* Sant' Andrea; *Fr.* St. André;
Gr. Ἅγ. Ἀνδρέας). St. Andrew was the first called to be an Apostle.
He was the brother of Simon Peter. Very little is said of him
in Scripture. Legends tell that he travelled into Scythia, Cappadocia, and Bithynia, and converted multitudes by his preaching.
The Russians believe that he preached to the Muscovites in Sarmatia.
He returned to Jerusalem, and after visiting Greece came to Patras,
a city of Achaia. Here, among many others, he converted Maximilla,
wife of Ægeus, the proconsul. He also persuaded her to make a
public confession, which so enraged her husband that he condemned
St. Andrew to be scourged and crucified. There is a variety of opinions as to the form of the cross on which he suffered; but the one
called by his name is generally believed to be like that on which he
died. It is said that he was fastened with cords rather than nails.
When he approached his cross, he venerated it as having been sanctified by Jesus. He was gloriously triumphant in his death. In the
fourth century a part of the relics of St. Andrew were taken to Scotland, since which time he has been the patron saint of that country
and of its first order of knighthood. He is the patron of the Order
of the Golden Fleece of Burgundy, as well as of Russia, and of its
great order of the Cross of St. Andrew. He is represented leaning
on his cross, the Gospel in his hand; his hair and beard are silvery
white, and his beard divided. November 30, A. D. 70.

St. Angelus, the Carmelite, came from the East, and preached in Palermo and Messina. There was a certain Count Berenger, who led an openly shameful life with his own sister. Being rebuked by Angelo, he commanded him to be hung upon a tree and shot with arrows. The legend, and in fact the very existence of this saint, have been disputed; but pictures said to represent him are seen at Bologna. May 5, A. D. 1225.

St. Anianus, or **Annianus.** In the Acts of St. Mark we are told that this saint was a shoemaker whom St. Mark healed when he first entered the city of Alexandria. He became so zealous a convert, and learned so rapidly, that St. Mark made him bishop during his absence. He governed the church at Alexandria four years with St. Mark, and eighteen years after his death. There was a church in that city dedicated to him. April 25, A. D. 86.

St. Anna, the mother of the Blessed Virgin, whose name signifies "gracious," is much honored in the Church, and numerous miracles have been attributed to her intercession. About 550 Justinian I. built a church at Constantinople, and dedicated it to St. Anna. Her body was removed from Palestine to Constantinople in 710. July 26. See St. Joachim.

St. Ansano of Siena. This saint was a Roman, Ansanus Tranquillinus. His nurse, a Christian woman, named Maxima, had him secretly baptized. His faith was not disclosed until he was nineteen years old, when he began to preach with great success. He suffered much during the persecution of Diocletian, and was at last beheaded on the banks of the river Arbia. St. Ansano was, until the end of the thirteenth century, the great patron of Siena; and there is, in the Duomo of that city, a fine statue representing him as baptizing the Sienese converts.

St. Anthony (*Ital.* Sant' Antonio Abbate, or l'Eremita; *Fr.* St. Antoine l'Abbé; *Ger.* Der Heilige Anton, or Antonius). St. Anthony, an Egyptian, was born at Alexandria. At eighteen years of age he was left an orphan, with one sister. He had great rank and wealth. Thoughtful from childhood, he feared the temptations of the world. Entering a church one day, he heard these words: "Every one that hath forsaken houses, or brethren, or sisters, or father, or mother, or wife, or children, or lands, for my name's sake, shall receive a hundred-fold, and shall inherit everlasting life;" and at another time, "If thou wilt be perfect, go, sell all thou hast, and give it to the poor, and thou shalt have treasure in heaven." He was so impressed by these things that he took them as a warning from God. He divided his wealth with his sister, gave all his share to the poor, and joined a company of hermits in the desert. Here he lived so pure a life as to arouse the hatred of Satan, who sent demons to tempt and torment him. They whispered to him of all he had left behind, and pictured before his mind the attractions of the world. But he prayed until great drops stood on his brow, and the demons despaired. They then placed delicious food before him, and, assuming the forms of lovely women, tempted him to sin. Again he resisted all their arts with prayer; but he suffered so much that he determined to go yet farther into the desert, and he found a cave where he thought Satan could not discover him. But here the demons came, and tortured him with all kinds of horrible pains, and tore him with their claws, till a hermit who carried him food found him lying as if dead. He bore him to his cell; but as soon as Anthony revived, he insisted upon returning to his cave, and when there he cried out, "Ha! thou arch tempter! didst thou think I had fled? Lo, here I am again; I, Anthony! I have strength to combat still!" Then was Satan furious, and he set his demons to try all their powers to overcome him. They surrounded him with lions, tigers, serpents, scorpions, and all the horrible shapes they could conceive, and they were roaring and hissing all around him. But in the midst of all this came a great light from heaven, and the beasts vanished; while Anthony, looking up, cried out, "O Lord Jesus Christ! where wert thou in those moments of anguish?" And Christ said gently, "Anthony, I was here beside thee, and rejoiced to see thee contend and overcome. Be of good heart; for I will make thy name famous through all the world." Then he resolved to go even farther into the desert. As he travelled he saw heaps of gold and silver, but he knew they were the temptations of Satan; and when he looked away, they disappeared in the air. He was now thirty-five years old, when he shut himself in a cavern for twenty years, and saw no one, neither was he seen of any; but when he came forth, all could see that he had been miraculously sustained, for he was not wasted or changed, except that his hair was white and his beard long. And now he preached the love of God to all men; comforted the sick and afflicted, and expelled demons, over whom he had gained great power. Multitudes were converted and came to the desert, until there were five thousand hermits in the caves and ancient tombs, and St. Anthony did many miracles. At length, when he had lived in the desert seventy-five years, he began to be proud of his life of self-denial, and a voice said to him in a vision, "There is one holier than thou art, for Paul the hermit has served God in solitude and penance for ninety years." So he resolved to seek Paul; and as he journeyed he met a centaur, who pointed the way to him; and again a satyr, who besought him to pray for him and his people. The third day he came to the cave of Paul. At first Paul would not receive him; but at length, moved by his prayers and tears, he admitted him. Then they held communion together; and as they sat, a raven brought them a loaf of bread, when Paul blessed God and said, "For sixty years, every day, hath this raven brought me half a loaf; but because thou art come, my brother, lo! the portion is doubled, and we are fed as Elijah was fed in the wilderness." And they ate and returned thanks. Then Paul said, "My brother! God hath sent thee here that thou mightest receive my last breath and bury me. Go, return to thy dwelling; bring here the cloak which was given to thee by that holy Bishop Athanasius, wrap me in it, and lay me in the earth." Then Anthony wondered, for the gift of the cloak was unknown to all. But he kissed Paul, and hastened to bring the cloak; for he feared he should not reach him again before his death. Returning, when he was about three hours from his cave he heard heavenly music, and looking up saw the spirit of Paul, as a star, borne by prophets, apostles, and angels to heaven. Then Anthony lamented, and went with haste to the cave where Paul was dead, in the attitude of prayer. Then he wept over him and recited the office for the dead, and he thought how he could bury him, for he had not strength to dig a grave. Then came two lions across the desert, roaring as if in sympathy, and with their paws they dug a grave, in which Anthony laid Paul, wrapped in the cloak of Athanasius. When he had returned to the convent, he told all these things, which were believed by the whole Church, and Paul was canonized. Fourteen years after, Anthony, being one hundred and four years old, felt that he must soon die; and after going to a lonely place with a few brethren, he charged them that they should keep secret the place of his burial. Gently his spirit passed away, and angels conveyed it to heaven. St. Anthony is represented with various attributes. He wears a monk's habit, as the founder of Monachism. In Greek pictures the letter Θ is on the cope on the left shoulder, and always in blue. It is the first letter of Θεός, God. The crutch is a symbol of his age and feebleness. The bell signifies his power to exorcise evil spirits, as a bell which has been blessed is used in exorcisms. The asperges, or rod for sprinkling holy water, is a symbol of the same idea. The hog represents the sensuality and appetites which he conquered. Flames of fire under his feet, or a city or house burning, signify that he is a protector against fire in this world and the next also. Paul is represented as old, meagre, half clothed in palm-leaves, his hair long and white, seated on a rock in meditation, and a palm-tree near him. St. Anthony, January 17, A. D. 357.

St. Antonio, Archbishop of Florence, was a native of Florence. He was born about 1384. His thoughtfulness and studiousness caused his friends to regard him as fitted for a religious life. He went to Fiesole, and asked admission to the Dominican Convent at fifteen. The prior, after talking with him, told him that when he had learned perfectly the Book of Decrees, he would receive him. This he did in one year, and then was sent to Cortona to pass his novitiate in study. He took his vows at Fiesole, and there formed a tender attachment to the wonderful painter-monk, Fra Giovanni, called Il Beato and Angelico. It is believed that the great learning of Antonio was of advantage to the heavenly mind of Angelico, and that their communion was not without its effects upon the latter's pictures. The Archbishop of Florence dying, the pope wished to give the office to Angelico; but he begged that Antonio should have it instead, which the pope granted. This greatly pleased the Florentines, as he was not only much beloved, but a native of their city. He died at the age of seventy, thirteen years after he was made archbishop, during which time he was distinguished for his wisdom and holiness. He is always represented as an archbishop, and wears the pallium over the habit of the Dominicans. May 10, A. D. 1461.

St. Antony of Padua (*Lat.* S. Antonius Thaumaturgus; *Ital.* Sant' Antonio di Padova, Il Santo; *Sp.* San Antonio de Padua, Sol brillante de la Iglesia, Gloria de Portugal, etc.). This saint was a Portuguese by birth. He became a Franciscan, and stands in that order next to its founder. After the martyrdom of the first missionaries in Morocco, Antony determined to be himself a missionary and martyr, and went to convert the Moors. But he was seized with an illness that compelled him to return to Europe. He was driven by the winds to Italy, and came to Assisi, where St. Francis was holding the first chapter of his order. St. Francis found him a valuable assistant, and he preached at the universities of Padua, Bologna, Paris, and Toulouse, but at length he preached to the people. He did much good in Italy as a preacher. His imagination was vivid, and his language effective. His similes were very beautiful. He died at thirty-six, after a ministry of ten years. Great honors have been paid his memory, and the church of Sant' Antonio at Padua is wonderfully rich in adornments of both ancient and modern art. He performed many miracles, which are represented in pictures in various churches and convents, especially in Italy and Spain. One of these is thus related. When preaching at the funeral of a very rich man, he denounced his love of money, and exclaimed, "His heart is buried in his treasure-chest; go seek it there, and you will find it." The friends of the man broke open the chest, and to their surprise found the heart; they then examined his body, and found that his heart was indeed wanting. His attributes are the lily and crucifix. He is young, and wears the habit and cord of St. Francis. June 13, A. D. 1231.

St. Apollinaris of Ravenna (*Ital.* Sant' Apollinare; *Fr.* St. Apollinaire). This saint came with the Apostle Peter from Antioch to Rome; and Peter, having laid hands on him, sent him to preach in the east of Italy. He became the first Bishop of Ravenna, and performed such miracles, and so preached, as to convert multitudes. At length he was seized and imprisoned. His jailer allowed him to escape; but his enemies pursued him, beat him, and wounded him so that he died. The Basilica of Apollinaris-in-Classe is on the spot where he was martyred. July 23, A. D. 79.

St. Apollonia of Alexandria (*Fr.* Ste. Apolline). The parents of Apollonia were heathens, and had no children, though they constantly prayed the gods to grant them a child. Her father was a magistrate. At length there came three pilgrims to Alexandria, begging in the name of Jesus and the Blessed Virgin. The wife of the magistrate, hearing them, asked if the Virgin could grant her prayer for a child. Being told of her great power, she gave the pilgrims food and money, and, full of faith, invoked Mary's intercession, who answered the prayer by the birth of Apollonia. She was very beautiful; and as her mother constantly told her the story of her birth, she grew up a Christian, and sought St. Leontine that he might baptize her. As soon as he did so, an angel appeared with a garment dazzlingly white, which he threw over her, saying, "This is Apollonia, the servant of God! Go now to Alexandria and announce the faith of Christ." She obeyed, and converted many; but others accused her to her father, who gave her to the heathen governor. He commanded her to worship the idol of the city. But she made the sign of the cross before the idol, and commanded its demon to depart. The demon broke the statue and fled, crying, "The holy virgin Apollonia drives me forth." Then they bound her to a column, and drew her teeth out one by one with pincers, and then, kindling a fire, they burned her. She is the protector against toothache, and all diseases of the teeth. Her attributes are a pair of pincers with a tooth, and the palm; sometimes a golden tooth suspended on her neck-chain. February 9, A. D. 250.

St. Athanasius (*Gr.* Ἅγ. Ἀθανάσιος; *Lat.* S. Athanasius, Pater Orthodoxiæ; *Ital.* Sant' Atanasio; *Fr.* St. Athanase). This saint, best known by the creed which bears his name, was an Alexandrian, and a pupil of St. Anthony. He first studied science and literature; and, being converted, he was ordained deacon. His opposition to Arius at the Council of Nice gained for him the title of the "Father of Orthodoxy." He became Bishop of Alexandria, and during the great heresy of his age materially aided by his perseverance in the victory of the Catholic Church. He was bishop forty-six years, but he was in exile during twenty years of that time. May 2, A. D. 373.

St. Augustine, or St. Austin (*Lat.* S. Augustinus; *Ital.* Sant' Agostino; *Fr.* St. Augustin). The father of St. Augustine was a heathen; his mother, Monica, was a Christian. He was born in Tagaste, Numidia. In his youth he was so devoted to pleasure that his mother feared the destruction of his character, and in her sorrow sought advice of the Bishop of Carthage. He comforted her with the assurance that her prayers would be answered at last. At length Augustine went to Rome, and became famous as a lawyer. But he was restless and unhappy. He went to Milan, and was there converted by the preaching of St. Ambrose, who baptized him in the presence of his mother. The "Te Deum," it is thought, was composed for this occasion. St. Augustine and St. Ambrose recited it as they approached the altar. He was Bishop of Hippo; and after thirty-five years Hippo was besieged by the Vandals, and St. Augustine perished at the age of seventy-five. It is said that his remains were removed to Pavia. He was the third doctor of the Church, and his writings are celebrated. One of the scenes in his life most frequently illustrated in art is that of a vision, related by himself, and which he saw while writing his Discourse on the Trinity. He was walking on the sea-shore, lost in meditation on his great theme, when he saw a little child bringing water and endeavoring to fill a hole which he had dug in the sand. Augustine asked him the motive of his labors. The child said he intended to empty all the water of the sea into this cavity. "Impossible," exclaimed St. Augustine. "Not more impossible," answered the child, "than for thee, O Augustine, to explain the mystery on which thou art now meditating." He is the patron of theologians and learned men. August 28, A. D. 430.

St. Augustine of Canterbury is believed to have introduced the Benedictine Order into England. He was sent from Rome as missionary to Britain, by St. Gregory. Fearing the dangers represented to exist in England at that time, he and his companions were seized with dread, and Augustine went to beg the pope to recall his command. This Gregory refused to do. He made Augustine bishop over those who should be converted. They landed in Kent, where there was great hatred of Christianity; but Queen Bertha was a Christian, and for her sake King Ethelbert permitted them to enter Canterbury, which they did, singing praises, and carrying the image of Christ. Ethelbert and his people became Christians, and were baptized in a little chapel which Bertha had built near Canterbury, and, being a French princess, had dedicated to Martin of Tours. St. Augustine desired greatly to see the ancient Britons, Christians whom the English had driven into the mountain regions of Wales, reclaimed from certain abuses which had crept in among them. He also wanted their

assistance in his missionary work among the English.   But the Britons' hatred of their oppressors sadly obstructed St. Augustine's pious
and pacific wishes.   In virtue of his authority as Papal Legate, he
visited all the British bishops ; and these willingly responded to his
invitation to a conference at Ausric, on the edge of Worcestershire,
near Herefordshire, a place later called Augustine's Oak.   Augustine required of them aid in converting the pagan English ; con-
formity to the custom of the Universal Church as to the time of
celebrating Easter, and as to the manner of administering baptism.
These things they refused, because of their hatred of their national
enemies.   Whereupon St. Augustine prophesied that "if they would
not preach to the English the way of life, they would fall by their
hands under the judgment of death."   This prediction was fulfilled after the death of St. Augustine, when Ethilfrid, king of the
pagan Northern English, mightily overthrew the Britons at Chester,
and slew twenty-two hundred of the British monks of Bangor, who
prayed in sight of the battle-field for the victory of their countrymen.
Those who account St. Augustine instigator of this massacre, which
took place years after his death, know not his tender charity, whose
only weapons against sinners were prayers for their conversion.   He
should be represented in the Benedictine habit, with the staff and the
Gospel, or as bishop with pallium, cope, and mitre.   A. D. 604.

St. Balbina was the daughter of the prefect Quirinus, and discovered the lost chains of St. Peter.   The church dedicated to her
at Rome is very ancient.   She is represented veiled, with chains in
her hand or near her.

St. Barbara (*Ital.* Santa Barbara ; *Fr.* Ste. Barbe).   This
saint was of the East, and daughter of Dioscorus, who dwelt in Heliopolis.   He was rich and noble, and loved his only daughter so fondly
that he shut her up in a high tower lest she should attract suitors
by her beauty.   Here she passed her time in study, and while watching the wonders and beauties of the heavens, felt that the idols could
not be gods, or the creators of the world.   But she had heard of no
other God.   At length the fame of Origen reached her from Alexandria, and she sent him a letter by a trusty servant, asking that he
should teach her.   He sent a disciple disguised as a physician, who
instructed her, and, after her conversion, baptized her.   Her father
had set workmen to make a bathroom in her tower ; and when they

had made two windows, she desired them to add another. They were afraid to do this, but she insisted; and when her father asked the cause, she said, "Know, my father, that through three windows doth the soul receive light, — the Father, the Son, and the Holy Ghost; and the three are one." Then her father would have killed her with his sword; but she fled to the top of the tower, and angels concealed her and bore her away to a place of safety. A shepherd betrayed where she was hidden, and her father dragged her by the hair and put her in a dungeon. He then delivered her to the proconsul Marcian, who scourged and tortured her, but she did not yield; and at last her father carried her to a mountain near the city, and himself beheaded her. Immediately a great tempest arose, and the lightning entirely consumed the father. St. Barbara is the patroness of Ferrara, Mantua, and Guastala; also of fortifications and fire-arms, as well as of armorers and gunsmiths. She is also invoked as a protector against lightning and the explosions of gunpowder. A tower with three windows is her peculiar attribute. She also has the book, palm, and sword. She is further invoked by all who desire the sacraments of the Church in their dying hours. December 4, A. D. 303.

St. Barnabas (*Ital.* San Barnabà; *Fr.* St. Barnabé). The name of Apostle is also given this saint; and if not fully entitled to it, he is at least next in holiness to the Apostles with whom he labored. He was a native of Cyprus, — a Levite, and a cousin of St. Mark. He labored with Paul at Antioch and Lystra; and the legends tell us that he was of so noble a presence that he was called Jupiter, while Paul was styled Mercurius. At length, on account of a difference concerning Mark, they separated; and Barnabas preached in Italy as well as in Asia Minor and Greece, and it is said he was the first Bishop of Milan. Tradition says he preached from the Gospel of St. Matthew, written by the Evangelist himself, which he carried always with him, and that it had power to heal the sick when laid upon their bosoms. He was at last seized by the Jews and cruelly martyred, while preaching in Judæa. Mark and other Christians buried him, and in the time of the Emperor Zeno his resting-place was revealed in a vision to Antemius. He was found with the Gospel in his bosom. This was taken to Constantinople, and a church was built under the invocation of the saint. June 11.

St. Bartholomew (*Lat.* S. Bartholomeus; *Ital.* San Bartolomeo; *Fr.* St. Barthelemi). The origin of this saint is doubtful, it being disputed whether he were the son of a prince, Ptolomeus, or of a husbandman. After the ascension of our Lord, he travelled through India, carrying the Gospel of St. Matthew. He preached in Armenia and Cilicia. He suffered a horrible death at Albanopolis, being first flayed, and then crucified. His attribute is a large knife. Sometimes he has his own skin hanging over his arm. August 24.

St. Basil the Great (*Gr.* Ἅγ. βασίλειος; *Lat.* S. Basilius Magnus; *Ital.* San Basilio Magno; *Fr.* St. Basile). This saint is the second in honor in the Greek Church, as well as the founder of the Basilians, almost the only monastic order known in that church; for the Order of St. Anthony has but a few houses at Sinai and Lebanon, and by the shores of the Red Sea. He was born at Cæsarea, in Cappadocia, in 328, and was of a family of great sanctity, — his grandmother, father, mother, two brothers, and a sister all being saints. He wrote many theological works. He attributes his early education to his grandmother, St. Macrina. He studied at Constantinople and at Athens, where he was associated with both St. Gregory of Nazianzen and with Julian, afterwards the Apostate. His great talents at one time so aroused his pride that but for the influence of St. Macrina, his sister, he would have perilled his salvation. He was then about twenty-eight, and after this gave himself entirely to religion, — passing some years in the desert as a hermit, where he lost his health, from the austerity of his living. He was made a priest in 362, and eight years after Bishop of Cæsarea. The 14th of June, the day of his ordination, is a great feast in the Greek Church. He lived with the same abstinence on the throne as in the desert. He vigorously opposed the Arian heresy; and when the Emperor Valens required him to communicate religiously with the Arians, he refused. The emperor threatened him, even with death, without effect. At length he thought to awe Basil by coming to church in great state, with all his court and soldiers. It was on the day of the Epiphany. Instead of overawing the saint, he was himself overawed by the piety of the congregation and the angelic devotion of the great bishop. The emperor afterwards conferred with Basil; and though he remained unconverted, he made some concessions to the Catholics. It is related of Basil, as of two other saints, that while he preached, the Holy

Ghost, in the form of a white dove, rested on his shoulder, to inspire his words. June 14, A. D. 380.

St. Bavon (*Flem.* St. Bavo, or St. Baf; *Ital.* San Bavone). He was born a nobleman; some authorities claim, Duke of Brabant. He was converted from idolatry by St. Amand of Belgium, first Bishop of Maestricht. Bavon was then nearly fifty years old, a widower, and had led a dissipated life. He gave all his riches in charity, and was placed by St. Amand in a monastery in Ghent; but he left that, and lived a hermit in the forest of Malmedun. His shelter was a hollow tree, and he subsisted on herbs. It is related of him, that after becoming a Christian he met one who had been his slave and cruelly treated. Bavon besought him to bind and beat him, and cast him in prison, as he had formerly done to him. This was of course refused; but the saint so insisted that finally it was done, and while in prison he passed his time in doing penance for his former sins. He is the patron of Ghent and Haerlem. His attribute is a falcon; he is sometimes represented as a hermit, and sometimes in his ducal robes. October 1, A. D. 657.

St. Bede the Venerable was born at Jarrow, in Northumberland, in 673. He was eminent for his learning and piety, and some even thought him superior in eloquence to St. Gregory. He died dictating the last words of a translation of the Gospel of St. John. He was called "the Venerable," and was known by this name at a Council at Aix-la-Chapelle. There is a legendary account of the way in which he received this title. It says that, his scholars wishing to put an inscription on his tombstone, one of them wrote : —

> "Hac sunt in fossa
> Bedæ   ossa,"

leaving the blank as above, because no suitable word occurred to him. He fell asleep thinking of it; and when he awoke, "venerabilis" had been inserted by an angel's hand. There are other ways of accounting for the title, but this is the favorite one. Bede's works are extant, and his "Ecclesiastial History" is the only authentic record we have of the early English Church. May 27, A. D. 735.

Bel and the Dragon. When Cyrus was King of Babylon, and Daniel was his friend, and greatly honored by him, the Babylonians had an idol called Bel, to whom were given every day "twelve great measures of fine flour, and forty sheep, and six vessels of wine." And the number of the priests who attended him were threescore and ten, and they had wives and children. Now Cyrus worshipped Bel, but Daniel worshipped his own God; and when Cyrus demanded the reason of this, Daniel replied that he could not " worship idols made with hands, but the living God," who had created all men and the world in which they lived. Then Cyrus asked Daniel if Bel were not living, and reminded him of how much he ate and drank every day. Then said Daniel, "O king, be not deceived; for this is but clay within and brass without, and did never eat nor drink anything." So the king was wroth, and said to the priests, "If ye tell me not who this is that devoureth these expenses, ye shall die. But if ye can certify me that Bel devoureth them, then Daniel shall die: for he hath spoken blasphemy against Bel." And Daniel replied, "Let it be according to thy word." Then the priests said to the king, "Lo we go out, but thou, O king, set on the meat, and make ready the wine, and shut the door fast, and seal it with thine own signet; and to-morrow when thou comest in, if thou findest not that Bel hath eaten up all, we will suffer death; or else Daniel, that speaketh falsely against us." Now they did this because they had an entrance which was hidden under the table, and by that they could go out and in as they liked. Then the king set the food before Bel, as the priests had said; and Daniel commanded the servants to bring ashes, and he strewed them upon the floor; and when all was ready they closed the temple, and the king sealed it with his own seal. Then in the night the priests came with their wives and children, as they were accustomed to do, and consumed all that had been provided. Now in the morning the king came with Daniel, and they found the seals whole, and they broke them and went in. And when the king saw that the food was gone, he cried out, "Great art thou, O Bel, and with thee is no deceit at all!" Then Daniel laughed, and said to the king, "Behold now the pavement, and mark well whose footsteps are these." So when the king saw the footsteps of men, women, and children, he was angry, and took the priests with their wives and children, and these showed him the door where they had gone in and out. Then the king slew them, and gave the idol Bel to Daniel, and he destroyed both the god and his temple. Now in the same place was a great dragon, which was also worshipped by the Babylonians; and the king said to Daniel, "Wilt thou also say that this is of brass?

Lo, he liveth, he eateth and drinketh : thou canst not say that he is no living God ; therefore, worship him." But Daniel declared that he would not worship him, and that he could slay him without sword or stave. And the king gave him leave. Then Daniel took pitch and fat and hair, and made lumps of it, and put them in the dragon's mouth, until he burst asunder. Then the people were filled with indignation, and they came to the king, and demanded that he should deliver Daniel to them, or they would destroy him and his house. Then the king, being sore pressed, gave up Daniel, and they threw him into the lions' den, where he remained six days. Now there were seven lions in the den, and each day they had given them two carcasses and two sheep, but now they gave them nothing, so that they might devour Daniel. There was in Judæa a prophet whose name was Habakkuk ; and he had made him a mess of pottage, and had put bread in a bowl, and was about to give it to the reapers in the field ; but the angel of the Lord came to him, and commanded that he should carry it to Babylon, and give it to Daniel, who was in the lions' den. Then Habakkuk said, "Lord, I never saw Babylon ; neither do I know where the den is." Then the angel of the Lord took Habakkuk by the hair of his head, and set him in Babylon over the lions' den ; and Habakkuk cried, saying, "O Daniel, Daniel, take the dinner which God hath sent thee." Then Daniel thanked God that he had not left him to perish, and arose, and ate the food which the prophet had brought, and the angel set Habakkuk again in his own place. Now, upon the seventh day, the king came to the den to bewail Daniel, and he found him alive. Then cried the king, "Great art thou, O Lord God of Daniel, and there is none other beside thee." Then he took Daniel out of the den, and cast in those who had accused him, and they were devoured in a moment, before his face.

St. Benedict (*Ital.* San Benedetto ; *Fr.* St. Benoit ; *Sp.* San Benito). This saint was the founder, the patriarch, and the first abbot of the great order of the Benedictines. He was of noble birth, and a native of Norcia, in the duchy of Spoleto. He studied at Rome, but soon wearied of the profligacy of those about him ; and imbibing the ideas of St. Jerome and St. Augustine in favor of solitude, at fifteen he became a hermit. His nurse, who loved him extremely, followed him into his retirement, and ministered as much as possible to his comfort. But he, regarding this as a drawback to perfect holiness, fled from her to Subiaco, a wilderness forty miles from Rome. Here he lived for three years, entirely unknown, except to Romano, another hermit, who shared with him his bread and water. Here he was greatly tempted by the recollections of the world he had left, and especially, at one time, by the remembrance of a beautiful woman he had seen at Rome, when, to overcome his great desire to return to her, he flung himself into a thicket of briers and thorns, and rolled himself therein until he was torn and bleeding. At the monastery of Subiaco they show roses, said to have been propagated from these briers. The fame of his sanctity at last brought great crowds to him, who begged his prayers, and that he would heal their diseases; and a company of hermits near by requested that he would be their head. But when they saw the severity of his life, they attempted to poison him. When he made the sign of the cross before the poisoned cup, it fell to the ground in fragments. He then returned to his cave and again dwelt alone. But so many hermits came to Subiaco and lived in huts and caves, that at length, for the sake of order, Benedict commanded them to build twelve monasteries, and he placed twelve monks in each. Two senators of Rome brought to him their sons, Maurus and Placidus, to be educated as Christians. They were but twelve and five years of age, and they became the special charge of Benedict. But Satan, much troubled at all this, put it into the heart of a priest, Florentius, to traduce the character of St. Benedict, and to poison him with a loaf of bread. These plans failing, he at last brought seven young women into one of the monasteries to try the chastity of the monks. Then Benedict left Subiaco, and immediately Florentius was crushed to death beneath a falling gallery in his own house. Benedict even wept for his fate, and imposed a penance on Maurus when he rejoiced at it. There still remained at this time, on Monte Cassino, a temple of Apollo. Thither Benedict went, and by his miracles and preaching converted the idolaters, so that they broke the statue and altar, and burnt the grove. The saint then built up two chapels, and dedicated them to St. John the Baptist and St. Martin of Tours. On the summit of this mountain he founded the monastery which has always been regarded as the parent of all others of the Benedictine Order. Hence he promulgated the rules of his order. His sister Scholastica followed him to Monte Cassino, and he visited her once a year during the last years of his life. In 540 Totila, King of the Goths, visited Benedict, and entreated his blessing. The saint reproved him for his past life, and it was thought that after this the Goth was less ferocious. Before his death monasteries of his order were instituted in all parts of Europe. He was at last seized with fever, and on the sixth day he ordered his grave to be dug, and after standing upon the edge of it, supported by his disciples, and in silent contemplation, he was borne to the altar of the church, and receiving the last sacraments there died. March 21, A. D. 543.

St. Benedict of Anian (*Fr.* St. Benoit d'Aniane). This saint was page and cup-bearer at the court of Pepin-le-Bref, and a distinguished commander in the army of Charlemagne. He was born at Maguelonne, in Languedoc, and his original name is unknown. He had an extremely narrow escape from drowning, after which he entered on a religious life. He went first to the abbey of St. Seine; but disapproving of the habits of the monks, he dwelt a hermit on the banks of the Anian. At length, a number of hermits having joined him, he founded a Benedictine monastery, with great severity of rule. He was called to Aix-la-Chapelle by Louis-le-Debonnaire. Here he founded another monastery. He presided at a council for the reformation of the monastic orders. William, Duke of Aquitaine, was a great warrior, and had vanquished the Saracens in the south of France. He was converted by St. Benedict, and built a monastery, in which he lived and died a monk. St. Benedict conferred upon William the monk's habit. February 12, A. D. 821.

Benedict, Bennet Biscop, or St. Bennet of Wearmouth, did much for art as well as for piety in England. He was of a noble Northumbrian family. He founded the monasteries of St. Peter's at Wearmouth and St. Paul's at Jarrow. He had a cultivated taste, and went five times to France and Italy. He brought to England stone-workers and glaziers to introduce a new style of building. He brought, too, many books and pictures, and also a certain John, Abbot of San Martino, who was a teacher of music, and who introduced chanting into English cathedrals. St. Bennet wrote many books of instruction for monks, and died at an advanced age, celebrated for piety and munificence. January 12, A. D. 703.

St. Benno is noted especially for his connection with the Emperor Henry IV. He was a German Benedictine, and Bishop of

Meissen; and when Henry, after being excommunicated, attempted to enter the cathedral, Benno locked the doors and threw the key into the river Elbe. He then went to Rome. On his return to Meissen, he ordered a fisherman to cast his net into the river, and a fish was taken, in which was found the key. His proper attribute is a fish with a key in its mouth.

St. Bernard of Clairvaux (*Lat.* S. Bernardus, Doctor mellifluus; *Ital.* San Bernardo di Chiaravalle, Abbate; *Ger.* Der Heilige Bernhard; *Fr.* St. Bernard) was a man of great power and importance. He was born in 1190, at Fontaine, near Dijon. He was the son of a noble; and his mother, Alice, was a remarkable woman. She had a large number of children, all of whom she nursed at her own breast, as she believed that infants imbibe with the milk the temperament of the nurse. According to all authorities she gave her son his early education. From the age of fifteen he practised great self-denial, and from it his health suffered. He had great personal beauty. After studying at the University of Paris, he entered, at twenty, the Benedictine monastery of Citeaux. He resisted all temptations; and it is related of him that, finding himself gazing on a beautiful woman with a feeling of pleasure, he rushed into a half-frozen pool and remained there until nearly frozen himself. The abbey of Citeaux became so crowded that Bernard was sent at twenty-five to found another monastery. He went with twelve companions to what was then called the "Valley of Wormwood," and there founded the abbey of Clairvaux. In a few years Bernard became famous, and his abbey very much crowded. He was considered an authority in matters of law as well as of religion. He was judge between Anacletus and Innocent II., deciding in favor of the latter, to the satisfaction of the whole Church. He also reconciled the disputes between the clergy of Milan and Rome. He preached a second Crusade, succeeded in rousing the people to great enthusiasm, and was invited to assume the command. He was also the adversary of Abelard and Arnold de Brescia. St. Bernard is one of the Fathers of the Church. In his writings he sets forth with great power the perfections of the Blessed Virgin, especially in the "Missus Est;" and it was believed that she appeared to him twice: once, when ill and unable to write, she restored him by her presence; and again she moistened his lips with the milk of her bosom, so that his eloquence was irresistible. His health suffered greatly from his labors and fasts, and he died at sixty-three. His attributes are the demon fettered behind him; three mitres on his book or at his feet, emblems of three bishoprics which he refused; the beehive, a symbol of eloquence. The mitre and crosier, as Abbot of Clairvaux, are given him but rarely. August 20, A. D. 1153.

St. Bernard of Menthon was by birth a noble Savoyard. In his youth he was serious and studious, showing such traits of character as indicated a religious vocation. His father wished him to marry; but he preferred to study, and put himself under the teaching of Peter, Archdeacon of Aoust. In 966 Bernard was made archdeacon, which was at that time a responsible and laborious office, as its duties comprised the whole government of the diocese. By great devotion and constant preaching for forty-two years, he did much good in the dioceses of Aoust, Sion, Geneva, Tarantaise, Milan, and Novara. He destroyed an idol on a mountain in the Walais, and exposed the deception of the heathen priests. He founded two roads and two monastic hospitals, the Great and Little St. Bernard, the former of which was near the site of the heathen idol before spoken of. At these hospitals the monks, assisted by their dogs, search out and care for travellers who are lost in the passes of the mountains, where the storms are severe and the cold intense. St. Bernard died at Novara, at eighty-five years of age. His body is in the monastery at Novara, and his head is shown in a rich case at the monastery of Monte-Joye, in the diocese of Aoust. May 28, A. D. 1008.

St. Bernardino da Feltri shares the honor of having founded the "Monts-de-Piété." He was a most eloquent man, and preached at the church of Santa Croce in Florence, against Jews and usurers, and on the necessity that the poor should be protected from them. It is certain that the two Bernardinos labored in this matter, but not easy to decide to which belongs the greater honor.

St. Bernard Ptolomei (*Ital.* San Bernardo dei Tolomei). He was of an illustrious family of Siena; born in 1272. He distinguished himself as a lawyer; but at length, seized with the religious passion of the age, he went into a mountain, called the Mount of Olives, about ten miles from Siena. Here he formed the order called "Olivetani." They followed the Rule of St. Benedict, and wore a white habit. August 21, A. D. 1348.

St. Bernardino of Siena. This saint was of the family of Albizeschi. He was born at Massa, a Sienese town, in 1380. His mother dying, he was educated by an aunt, whose influence developed not only his talents, but great purity of character also. At seventeen he joined a brotherhood whose members were devoted to the service of the hospitals. A pestilence soon broke out, which destroyed great numbers, and among them physicians and priests. For four months Bernardino with twelve others cared for the inmates of the plague hospital. His health suffered greatly from his labor. He became a Franciscan at twenty-three. He was a celebrated preacher, and went all over Italy. He endeavored to reconcile the Guelphs and Ghibellines. He was offered three bishoprics, which he refused. The Duke of Milan, offended at his preaching, threatened him in vain; he then sent him money, with which he went to the prisons and liberated poor debtors. He founded the order called in Italy "Osservanti," and in France "Frères de l'Observance," because they observe strictly the Rule of St. Francis, going barefoot and keeping strictly the vow of poverty. When preaching, he held in his hand a tablet on which was the name of Jesus in a circle of golden rays. A man who had lived by making cards and dice complained to the saint that on account of the reforms in religion, his occupation was gone. Bernardino advised him to carve tablets like his, to sell to the people. He did so; and a peculiar blessing being attached to them, he sold large numbers, and made a fortune in this way. St. Bernardino is said to have founded those institutions called still in France "Monts-de-Piété," where money is loaned on pledges. In the commencement they were entirely charitable and for the benefit of the poor. He died at Aquila, in the Abruzzi, where his remains are preserved in a silver shrine in the church of San Francisco. May 20, A. D. 1444.

St. Bibiana was a Roman lady, who, together with her father, mother, and sister, suffered martyrdom in the reign of Julian the Apostate. She was scourged and then pierced with a dagger. The church dedicated to her is between the Santa Croce and the Porta Maggiore. The column to which she was bound is shown within the church. December 2, A. D. 362.

St. Blaise of Sebaste (*Gr.* Ἅγ. Βλαισός; *Ital.* San Biagio; *Fr.* St. Blaise; *Ger.* Der Heilige Blasius: signification, "crooked").

This holy man was bishop over the Christians at Sebaste, in Cappadocia, and in the time when Agricolaus was governor, was obliged to flee to the mountains to escape persecution. There were great numbers of wild beasts there, but instead of harming the saint, they came to him in numbers every morning to receive his blessing ; and when Agricolaus sent to obtain beasts for the amphitheatres, the hunters found St. Blaise surrounded with them. He nursed the sick ones, reproved the ferocious, and gave his benediction to all. The hunters, amazed at this, seized him and took him to the governor. As they went, they met a woman whose child was choking from a bone stuck in its throat. The mother cried out, " O servant of Christ, have mercy on me ! " He laid his hand on the throat of the child and prayed, and it was healed. Again, they met a woman whose pig had been carried off by a wolf ; and as it was all she had of worldly goods, she was in much distress. St. Blaise commanded the wolf to bring back the pig unharmed, which was done. The governor sentenced him to be scourged and imprisoned without food ; but the poor woman had killed her pig, and brought a part, with bread and fruit, to the holy man. A second time the governor tortured him by tearing his flesh with iron combs, such as are used to card wool ; when, as he still remained firm in his faith, he was beheaded. He is the patron of Ragusa, also the patron of wool-combers, of those who suffer from throat diseases, and of wild animals. He is a popular saint in France and England, and especially in Yorkshire, where once in seven years a festival is held in his honor. The iron wool-comb is his proper attribute. February 3, A. D. 316.

St. Bonaventura was the great prelate of the Seraphic Order, and was styled " il Dottore Serafico." His fame is not confined to his order, as he is considered one of the brightest lights of the whole Church. His name was Giovanni Fidanga, and he was born at Bagnarea, in Tuscany, in 1221. In his infancy he was so ill that his life was despaired of, and his mother took him to St. Francis to be healed. When the saint saw him he exclaimed, " O, buona ventura ! " whereupon his mother dedicated him to God by the name of Bonaventura. His progress in study was amazing ; and at twenty-two he became a Franciscan, and went to Paris to study theology. He soon became celebrated ; but his humility was so great that he felt unworthy to receive the Holy Communion, and legends

tell us that the Host was presented to him by angels. Louis IX.
(St. Louis) greatly honored him while at Paris, and he was chosen
General of his order at thirty-five.   He was appointed Archbishop of
York, but declined the honor.   At length he was made Cardinal and
Bishop of Albano.   When the pope's nuncios carried him the cardinal's hat, they found him in the garden of a convent, near Florence,
washing the plate from which he had just eaten; and he requested
them to hang the hat on a tree until he could take it.   In 1274,
when a council was held at Lyons to reconcile the Greek and Latin
churches, he, being one of the most distinguished of preachers, first
addressed the assembly.   The fatigues of his labors here brought on
a fever, of which he died, being fifty-three years old.   He was buried
in the church of the Franciscans at Lyons; but the Calvinists, in
1562, broke open his shrine and threw his ashes into the Saône.
July 14, A. D. 1274.

   St. Boniface, martyr (*Lat.* and *Ger.* S. Bonifacius; *Ital.* San
Bonifaccio).   The history of St. Boniface is one of the most authentic, as well as beautiful, of the legends of his age.   Justice can by
no means be done to his character in the space allotted him here.
His name was Winfred, and he was born of a noble family at Crediton, in Devonshire.   He taught literature and the Holy Scriptures
at the Benedictine abbey of Nutsall, or Nuscella, near Winchester,
until he was thirty-six years old.   For some years he had not been
happy in his quiet vocation, but was constantly haunted by a desire
to preach the Gospel in Germany.   He went first to Friesland, but it
was in the days of Charles Martel, and a time when he could hope
for no results from his labors; so he returned to Nutsall, but soon
left England for the last time, and went to Rome to entreat the
aid of the pope in his German labors.   It is said to have been at
this time that he changed his name.   Receiving a commission from
the pope, he now travelled through Bavaria, Thuringia, Saxony,
and Friesland, preaching with great success.   In 732 he was made
Archbishop and Primate of all Germany; and soon after, King Pepin-
le-Bref, whom Boniface had anointed, named him the first Bishop
of Mayence.   But when seventy-four years old, he gave up all his
honors, and girding on the plain habit of a Benedictine monk, devoted himself again to missionary labors.   At length, while in his
tent, on the banks of a small river in Friesland, where he awaited a

company of proselytes, to whom he was about to administer the sacrament of confirmation, he was attacked by a band of pagans who
had sworn to murder him. He always carried in his bosom a copy
of the "De Bono Mortis" of St. Ambrose. This was stained with
his blood, and was preserved as a sacred relic at Fulda. In 1835
King Louis of Bavaria, in honor of the twenty-fifth anniversary of
his marriage, founded a magnificent basilica, and consecrated it to St.
Boniface. In it are fine frescos, representing the various scenes in
the life of this wonderful man. June 5, A. D. 755.

St. Boniface. See St. Aglaë.

St. Brice (*Lat.* S. Britius) was Bishop of Tours and successor
to St. Martin. He is represented with coals in his hands, which he
carries unhurt, to prove himself innocent of false accusations made
against him; and again he carries a child in his arms. November 13,
A. D. 444.

St. Bridget of Ireland. Although nearly every vestige of this
saint is gone, she still lives as their patroness in the hearts of the
Irish people. Her mother was very lovely, and the captive, taken in
war, of a powerful chieftain. His wife, being jealous of her, turned
her away before the birth of Bridget. But two disciples of St. Patrick took pity on them, and baptized the mother and child. Bridget
grew up with such beauty of mind and person that she became
famous, and her father desired to have her, and to marry her to a
chief. But Bridget devoted herself to God's service, especially to the
instruction of women. She received the veil at the hands of St.
Patrick. She went to Kildare, "the cell or place of the oak," and
not only taught, but performed miracles. Her fame drew about her
many women who lived in huts, and from this arose the first religious
community of women in Ireland. The convent and city of Kildare
were afterwards both flourishing and famous. Here was preserved
unextinguished, for many centuries, the sacred lamp which burned
before her altar, —

> "The bright lamp that shone in Kildare's holy fane,
> And burned through long ages of darkness and storm.

February 1.

St. Bridget of Sweden was the founder of the Order of the
Brigittines, or Brigitta, and is one of the patron saints of Sweden.
She was of royal blood, and married to the Prince of Norica, named

Ulpho. She was very devout, and influenced her husband and their eight children to live religiously. After the death of Ulpho she built monasteries at Wastein for monks and nuns, respectively, and handsomely endowed both. Their rule was principally that of St. Augustine, though modified by directions Bridget received in visions, of which she had many. Her order was approved by the pope, under the title of the "Rule of the Order of our Saviour." She made many pilgrimages to Rome and Compostella.

St. Bruno was the founder and first abbot of the Carthusian Order. He was of a noble family of Cologne, and on account of his great talents was sent to Paris to study theology under Raymond. He afterwards taught in the school at Rheims; but, after long reflection, determined on a monastic life. With six companions he went to Grenoble, when Hugo, the bishop, having been warned in a dream of their coming, gave them some barren land at Chartreux. Here Bruno founded his first monastery, and his order was confirmed by the pope. The robes and hoods of the Carthusians are white, and their whole heads shaven. Urban II. had been a pupil of Bruno at Rheims, and when he became pope, sent for him to aid him in his great cares, and desired to make him Archbishop of Reggio. But this Bruno refused, and not liking the life at court, retired to Calabria, where he founded another monastery. He died in 1200. The order which he established is of great interest. It is among the most severe in its rule of all the monastic orders, and adds almost perpetual silence to the usual vows. Only once a week can these monks talk together. They never taste flesh, and make but one meal a day of pulse, bread, and water, and this is eaten separately. They labor, too, with great diligence, and their discipline has been described as most fearful in its severity. In spite of all this, they have an extreme love of the beautiful, and have done much for art. Their churches and gardens were wondrous in their perfection; and their pictures at the Chartreuse of Paris (now in the Louvre), in the Chartreuse of Santa Maria de las Cuevas near Seville, at Paular, and other places, possess a world of interest. July 18.

Cædmon the Poet lived in the monastery of the Abbess Hilda, as a servant, until past middle life. He knew nothing of literature or poetry; and when it came his turn to sing at table, he went away. Once as he did this, and went to the stable to care for the horses, he fell asleep, and an angel came in a dream and told him to sing. He answered that he could not sing, and for that reason had left the table. But the angel said, "You shall sing, notwithstanding;" and when he asked what he should sing, the reply was, "Sing the beginning of created beings." Then Cœdmon began to sing praises to God; and when he awoke he remembered all he had sung, and was able to add more also. When he told this to Hilda, she believed him to be inspired, and received him into a monastery whose monks were under her jurisdiction. He was instructed in Scripture; and as he read, he converted it into verse. His paraphrase of Scripture is still preserved in the Bodleian Library at Oxford. He died peacefully, while making the sign of the cross.

St. Casimir, patron saint of Poland, was the son of Casimir IV. of Poland and Elizabeth of Austria. From his childhood he participated in none of the pleasures of his father's court; and as he grew up he composed many hymns. He refused the crown of Hungary, and lived more and more secluded, devoting himself to religious pursuits, until his death in 1483. March 4.

St. Cassian (*Ital.* San Casciano) was a schoolmaster of Imola; and being denounced as a Christian, the judge who condemned him to death allowed his scholars to be his executioners. They hated him on account of his severe discipline, and they tortured him most cruelly, by piercing him with the iron styles used in writing. He is the patron saint of Imola. August 13.

St. Catherine of Alexandria, virgin and martyr (*Lat.* Sancta Catharina; *Ital.* Santa Catarina dei Studienti, or Santa Catarina delle Ruote; *Fr.* Madame Ste. Catherine; *Sp.* Santa Catalina; *Ger.* Die Heilige Katharina von Alexandrien). This saint was the daughter of Costis (half-brother to Constantine the Great) and Sabinella, Queen of Egypt. Before the birth of Catherine her mother was prepared by a dream to find her a remarkable child; and at the moment of her birth a halo of light played about her head. Her acquirements and her wisdom were most wonderful, and the philosophy of Plato was her favorite study while a child. She had seven learned masters, and chambers fitted with everything to aid her in her studies. Her father died when she was fourteen, leaving her heiress to the kingdom. She gave herself up to study and retirement, which displeased her subjects and they begged her to marry. They said she was possessed of four notable gifts, — that she was of the most noble blood in the world, and that she surpassed all others in wealth, knowledge, and beauty; and they desired that she should give them an heir. She replied that as she had four gifts, so he whom she would marry must likewise be of such noble blood that all would worship him; and so great as not to be indebted to her for being made a king, richer than any other; so beautiful that angels should desire to see him; and so benign as to forgive all offences. Such an one only could she marry. Then Sabinella and the people were sorrowful, for they knew of no such man. But Catherine would marry no other. Now a hermit who dwelt in a desert not far from Alexandria was sent by the Blessed Virgin, who appeared to him, to tell Catherine that her Son was the husband she desired to have, for he possessed all the requirements, and more; and the hermit gave Catherine a picture of Mary and Jesus. When she gazed on his face she loved him, and could think of nothing else, and her studies became dull to her. That night she had a dream in which she went with the old hermit to a sanctuary on a high mountain; and when she approached it angels came to meet her, and she fell on her face. But an angel said, "Stand up, our dear sister Catherine; for thee hath the King of glory delighted to honor." Then she stood up and followed them, and they led her to a chamber where the queen was, surrounded by angels, saints, and martyrs, and her beauty none could describe. The angels presented Catherine to her, and besought her to receive her as her daughter. The queen bade her welcome, and led her to our Lord. But the Lord turned away, saying, "She is not fair and beautiful enough for me." At these words Catherine awoke, and wept till morning. She called the hermit, and demanded what would make her worthy of her celestial Bridegroom. He, perceiving the darkness of her mind, instructed her in the true faith; and she, and also Sabinella, were baptized. That night, as Catherine slept, the Virgin and her Son, attended by many angels, appeared to her; and Mary again presented her to Jesus, saying, "Lo, she hath been baptized, and I myself have been her godmother." Then Christ smiled on her, and plighted his troth to her, and put a ring on her finger. And when she awoke the ring was still there; and from that time she despised all earthly things, and thought only of the time when she should go to her heavenly Bridegroom. At length the good Sabinella died. At this time Maximin came to Alexandria, and declared a great persecution against those who did not worship idols. Then Catherine came forth to the temple, and held an argument with the tyrant and confounded him. He then ordered fifty learned men to come from all parts of the empire to dispute with her; but she, praying to God, overcame them all, so that they too declared themselves Christians. Then Maximin, enraged, commanded them to be burned; and Catherine comforted them when they could not be baptized, saying that their blood should be their baptism, and the flames glorious crowns for them. Then the emperor, admiring her beauty, tried to overcome her virtue; and when he could not do this, and was about to go to war, he commanded Porphyry, his servant, to cast her into a dungeon and starve her. But angels came to feed her; and when, after twelve days, they opened the dungeon, a bright light and a fragrance filled all the place. Then the empress and Porphyry, with two hundred others, fell at the feet of Catherine, and declared themselves Christians. When Maximin returned, he put the empress and all to death, and admiring Catherine's beauty still more than at first, offered her to be mistress of the world if she would listen to him. When she still rejected his offers, he ordered the most dreadful tortures for her, — wheels revolving in different directions, that should tear her in many pieces. When they had bound her to these, an angel came and consumed the wheels in fire, and the fragments flew around, and killed the executioners and three thousand people. But again Maximin ordered her to be scourged and beheaded. Then angels came and bore her body to the top of Mt. Sinai, and there it rested in a marble sarcophagus. In the eighth century a monastery was built over her burial-place, and her remains are still greatly venerated. It is said by some that Maximin was consumed by an inward fire; by others, that wild beasts devoured him. Catherine is patroness of education, science, and philosophy, of all students, and of colleges. As patroness of eloquence, she was invoked for all diseases of the tongue. She is also patroness of Venice, and a favorite saint of ladies of royal birth. She is represented as richly dressed; and her peculiar attribute is the wheel, either whole or broken. She has also the martyr's palm, the crown of royalty, the book which expresses her learning; and frequently she tramples on the head of

Maximin, thus symbolizing the triumph of her Christian faith over paganism and cruelty. The marriage of St. Catherine to the Saviour is a favorite and extremely beautiful subject of art. November 25, A. D. 307.

St. Catherine of Bologna, or Santa Caterina de' Vigri, has been greatly venerated in her own city for about four centuries. She was of noble family, and for a time a maid of honor at the court of Ferrara. She entered a convent of Poor Clares, and became distinguished as a painter. There are said to be several pictures of hers in Bologna. Her remains, dressed in brocade and jewels, are to be seen in her convent at Bologna. March 9, A. D. 1463.

St. Catherine of Siena (*Lat.* Sancta Catharina Senese, Virgo admirabilis, et gloriosa Sponsa Christi; *Ital.* Santa Caterina di Siena, la Santissima Vergine). She was the daughter of a dyer who dwelt near the Fonte-Branda, at Siena; his dwelling is now the Oratory of St. Catherine. She dedicated herself to a religious life as early as in her eighth year, and prayed Christ to be her Bridegroom, as he was that of Catherine of Alexandria. Her father and mother were angry at her refusal to marry, and greatly persecuted her, putting the most menial labors upon her and treating her with great harshness. But at length her father saw her at prayer with a white dove resting upon her head, of whose presence she seemed unconscious. From this time she was allowed to choose her own course in life. She never entered a convent as a professed nun, but she made a vow of silence for three years, and led a life of the greatest self-denial. She went every day to the convent of St. Dominick to pray, and there she had many wonderful visions. She was greatly tempted of Satan; she inflicted upon herself the most severe penances, and Christ came to her in visible presence to console her. She nursed the sick, even those who had the most loathsome diseases. Her fame spread through all Tuscany and to Milan and Naples. At length the Florentines, having rebelled against the Holy See, were excommunicated by the pope, and they sent Catherine to him as their mediator. The pope, then at Avignon, was so much pleased with Catherine that he left her to decide the terms of peace between himself and the Florentines.[1] Catherine felt it to be a

---

[1] St. Catherine reconciled the Florentines to the Holy See, in 1378, during the Pontificate of Urban VI.

great cause of misrule in the Church, that the popes were absent from Rome, and she used all her powers to persuade Gregory XI. to return to the Lateran, which he did. In the great schism which followed the death of Gregory, Catherine took the part of Urban VI., who appointed her ambassadress, with St. Catherine of Sweden, to the court of Joanna II. of Sicily, who had sided with the anti-pope, Clement. But her failing health prevented her from fulfilling the mission. Catherine died at thirty-three, after great physical suffering, — still full of zeal and faith. She was one of the most noted of female saints, and is known at Siena as "la Santa." The facts of her history render her life interesting in many ways. She is represented in pictures in the habit of the Dominican Order, with the stigmata, which she is said to have received. April 30, A. D. 1380.

St. Cecilia (*Fr.* Ste. Cécile). She is supposed to have lived in the third century, and the honor paid to her can be traced to that time. She was the daughter of a noble Roman, who, with his wife, had secretly become Christians. Cecilia was in childhood remarkably serious and pious. She early made a vow of chastity, and devoted herself to a religious life. She always carried a copy of the Gospels in her robe. She especially excelled in music, and composed and sung hymns so sweet that angels came to listen to her. But the instruments employed in secular music were insufficient to express the music of her soul, and she invented the organ, and consecrated it to God's service. Her parents desired her, when sixteen years old, to marry Valerian, a rich young noble. She did so; but beneath her bridal robes she wore a garment of penance, and remembering her vow prayed God to help her to preserve her chastity. He so answered her prayer that when she told Valerian of her faith, he became converted, and was baptized, and respected her vow. Cecilia had told Valerian that she had a guardian angel; and when he returned from his baptism, he heard sweet music, and saw the angel standing near her with two crowns, made of the immortal roses which bloom in Paradise. Cecilia and Valerian knelt, and the angel crowned them with the flowers, and told Valerian that because he had listened to Cecilia and respected her vow, whatever he most desired should be granted him. Then Valerian said, " I have a brother, named Tiburtius, whom I love as my own soul; grant that his eyes also may be opened to the truth." This request was pleasing to God ; and when Tiburtius entered soon after and perceived the fragrance of the roses, he was surprised, for it was not the time of flowers. Then Cecilia told him of their faith, and he too was converted and baptized. They then gave themselves up to a religious life, and did much good to the poor and persecuted Christians. But the prefect, Almachius, commanded them to worship Jupiter; and when they would not, he cast the brothers into prison, and gave them a keeper, called Maximus, and he also became a Christian. This so enraged the prefect that he commanded the three to be beheaded. Cecilia cared for, and buried their remains in the cemetery of Calixtus. Desiring to have her great wealth, the prefect then commanded Cecilia to worship Jupiter, and threatened her with fearful tortures. She only smiled her scorn. He then commanded her to be thrown into her bath, filled with boiling water. This did not hurt her at all; so he then sent an executioner to slay her with the sword. His hand trembled, so that he inflicted three wounds on her neck and breast, and yet did not kill her. She lingered three days. She gave her money to the poor, and desired that her house should be made a church. She died sweetly singing, and was buried beside her husband. In the ninth century, when Paschal repaired her church, he had a vision of St. Cecilia, in which she told him her burial-place. Her body was found, and also the bodies of Valerian, Tiburtius, and Maximus. They were placed in her church, now called St. Cecilia-in-Trastevere. Her bathroom is a chapel, and the stones and pipes for heating the bath still remain. In the sixteenth century the church was again repaired, and her coffin opened, when the celebrated statue of " St. Cecilia lying dead " was made, which represents her as she appeared in the coffin. She is the patroness of music and musicians. Her proper attribute is the organ and a roll of music. She also has the crown of roses, and an attendant angel. She is richly dressed, and often has jewels. November 22, A. D. 280.

St. Celsus (*Ital.* San Celso). This was a young disciple of St. Nazarius, who was a converted Jew. Together they travelled through Gaul as missionary preachers. At Genoa the people threw them into the sea ; but they were miraculously saved, and came at last to Milan, where Protasius and Gervasius had become Christians, whom they strengthened. Both Celsus and Nazarius were beheaded at Milan, where there is a beautiful church, San Nazaro Maggiore. There is also at Ravenna the remarkable Byzantine church of SS. Nazaro-e-Celso. They are always represented together, and bear the swords and palms of martyrs. Nazarius is old and Celsus quite young. July 28.

St. Cesareo, or Cæsarius. The veneration of this saint seems to be confined to Rome. He perished at Terracina because he opposed the worship of Apollo. He was famous both in the East and West in the sixth century. The church of San Cesareo in Rome is also called "in Palatio," from its situation near the ancient palace and baths of Caracalla on the Via Appia, not far from the Porta St. Sebastiano. He was put into a sack, and cast into the sea, together with a priest named Lucian. November 1, A. D. 300.

St. Chad of Lichfield became, in 659, abbot of the Priory of Lastingham, which had been founded by his eldest brother, Cedd. He was famous for his religious life, and being made bishop of the Mercians and Northumbrians, he preached as a missionary through all the country. He had his episcopal see in Lichfield, "the field of the dead;" and there he built a habitation where he lived with a few brethren, and a church where he baptized his converts. After living in this way more than two years, he had a vision in which he was warned of his death. He saw his brother with a troop of angels. They sang and called him to follow them to God, and still sweetly singing ascended to heaven. He advised the brethren how they should live, and soon died. His church may be considered the origin of the cathedral of Lichfield, where the shrine of St. Chad was deposited in 1148, and is greatly venerated. March 2, A. D. 673.

Chantal, la Mère. Ste. Jeanne-Françoise de Chantal was the grandmother of Madame de Sévigné. She was devoted to the Faith even in childhood, and would not receive a gift from a Calvinist. In obedience to her parents, she married Baron Chantal, but made a vow to dedicate herself to a religious life if she should ever be a widow. Her husband died when she was twenty-nine, and for ten years she devoted herself to her children and to the preparation for the fulfilment of her vow. She assisted St. Francis de Sales to establish the Order of the Visitation, and assumed the direction of it, as "la Mère Chantal." Her children loved her passionately, and sought to keep

her with them ; but she remained firm in her determination. At the
time of her death, in 1641, there were seventy-five houses of her
order in France and Savoy. She was canonized in 1769. August
21, A. D. 1641.

St. Charlemagne [1] — whose history as Charlemagne the Great,
Emperor of France, Italy, and Germany, is so familiar to all — stands at
the head of royal saints in the countries over which he ruled, although
if a strict chronology were observed, St. Clotilda and St. Sigismond
would precede him. He is frequently represented with a book, in
remembrance of his having caused the Scriptures to be correctly
translated and widely promulgated. January 28, A. D. 814.

St. Charles Borromeo (*Ital.* San Carlo). This saint was of one
of the noblest families of Lombardy. Being the second son, he was
early dedicated to the Church. At twelve years of age he received
the revenues of a rich Benedictine monastery, but would only reserve
a mere pittance for himself, devoting the remainder to charity. At
twenty-three he was made cardinal and Archbishop of Milan, by his
uncle Pius IV. His elder brother died when Charles was twenty-six.
He went at once to take possession of his diocese and estate. His
incomes he dedicated to public uses, only spending for himself enough
to buy his bread and water, and straw on which to sleep. He sent
missionaries to preach in every part of his diocese, and went also
himself to see that his people were cared for. In public he lived as
became his rank, and gave feasts of which he never partook. His
charities were most munificent. At the time of the plague at Milan,
he went into the city, when all others fled, and tended the sick and
performed all the duties pertaining to his office. His example inspired
twenty-eight priests to join him, all of whom with St. Charles escaped
unhurt. He lived in a time when the clergy had fallen into great
laxity of discipline, and he may be regarded as a powerful instrument
in restoring them to zeal for the duties of their vocation. He was
hated by those priests who had been in the habit of using the revenues of the Church for their own indulgence; and one, Fra Farina,
attempted to kill him by firing upon him while he was celebrating
the evening service. He finished the prayer, although he believed
himself mortally wounded, and the people considered him to be mirac-

---

[1] He is not mentioned in the Catholic Calendar of Saints, save as Blessed. His
feast, January 28, has been kept by the Germans and French only since 1486.

ulously healed. He died November 4, 1584, and with his last breath exclaimed, "Ecce venio." His remains repose in a rich shrine at Milan. He is represented in cardinal's robes and barefooted, a rope about his neck and one hand raised in benediction, with a book in the other. November 4, A. D. 1584.

St. Cheron was a disciple of St. Denis, and was Bishop of Chartres. He was attacked by robbers, and his head was struck off, when on his way from Chartres to Paris to visit St. Denis. Taking his head in his hand, he continued his journey. One of the windows in the cathedral of Chartres represents the history of St. Cheron.

St. Christina (*Ital.* Santa Cristina ; *Fr.* Ste. Christine). She is supposed to have been born at Tiro, a town on the borders of Lake Bolsena, which has since been swallowed up in the lake. The legend of this saint has been rejected by the Church, but she is celebrated in central and northern Italy. She was the child of a Roman patrician who governed the city. She called herself Christina because she had been converted to the doctrines of Christ. As she stood, one day, watching those who begged alms, and had nothing to give, she thought of the golden idols of her father, and she broke them in pieces and gave them to the poor. Her father was furious, and ordered his servants to beat her and throw her into a dungeon. Here angels came and healed her wounds. Her father then commanded her to be thrown into the lake with a mill-stone tied to her neck. But angels bore her up, and God clothed her with a white robe and led her safely to land. She was then thrown into a fiery furnace, wherein she remained unharmed five days and sung God's praises. Her father then ordered her head to be shaved, and that she should be taken to the temple of Apollo to sacrifice ; but when she came there the idol fell down before her, which so frightened her father that he died. But Julian, hearing that she sang in her prison, sent orders that her tongue should be cut out, when she still continued to sing, to the amazement of all. She was next shut up with poisonous reptiles, but she was not harmed. At last, in despair, he commanded her to be bound to a post and shot with arrows till she died. Thus was she martyred, and angels bore her soul to heaven. On an island in the lake of Bolsena, which few travellers visit, is a church dedicated to St. Christina, the paintings in which are attributed to the Caracci. The cathedral of Bolsena is consecrated to her, — patroness of Bolsena

6

and the Venetian States.   Her proper attribute is the mill-stone; but she sometimes has arrows alone, when she might be mistaken for St. Ursula.   She has also the martyr's palm and crown.   July 24, A. D. 295.

St. Christopher (*Lat.* St. Christophorus; *Ital.* San Cristofero, or Cristofano; *Fr.* St. Christophe, or Cristofle; *Ger.* Der Heilige Christoph).   St. Christopher might well be called the giant saint. He was of the land of Canaan, and before performing the deeds which won him saintly renown, was called Offero, which signifies "the bearer."   He was proud of his vast size and strength; but in spite of this, his poverty compelled him to become a servant.   So he resolved that the most powerful monarch of the earth alone should be his master, and he went to seek him.   At length, after many days of wandering, he came to the court of a king said to excel all others in power and wealth, and to him he offered his services.   The king accepted him gladly, for no other monarch of all the earth could boast of such a servant.   Now Offero knew nothing of the power of Christ or Satan, and supposed his master to be afraid of no one, since he was the greatest monarch of the earth; but one day, as he stood beside him, a minstrel who was singing mentioned frequently the name of Satan, and every time he did so the king trembled and crossed himself.   Offero asked the meaning of this; and when the king did not answer, he said, "If thou dost not answer me this, I leave thee."   Then the king said, "I make this sign that Satan may have no power over me; for he is very mighty, and as wicked as strong, and I fear lest he shall overcome me."   Then Offero felt himself deceived, and said, "Since there is one whom thou fearest, him will I seek and serve; for my master must fear no one."   So he wandered again, seeking Satan; and crossing a great desert, he saw a terrible being with the appearance of great power, marching at the head of an armed legion.   He did not seem to notice the great size of Offero, and with an air of authority said, "Whither goest thou, and for what dost thou seek?"   Then said Offero, "I wish to find Satan; for I have heard he is the most powerful of all the earth, and I would have him for my master."   Satan, well pleased, replied, "I am he, and your service shall be an easy and pleasant one."   Offero then bowed before him, and joined his followers.   After a time, as they journeyed on, they came to a cross, erected by the wayside, where four roads met. When the Devil saw this he turned with great haste and fear, and went a long distance out of his way to avoid the cross. Then said Offero, "Why is this? What is this cross, and wherefore dost thou avoid it?" But Satan spoke not. Then said Offero, "Except thou tellest me I must leave thee." Being compelled, the wicked one replied, "I fear the cross, because upon it Jesus died; and when I behold it I fly, lest he should overcome me." Then said Offero, "Tell me who is this Jesus; for since thou fearest him, he is more powerful than thou, and him will I seek and serve." So he left Satan, and wandered many days in search of Christ. At length he came to a hermit, whom he entreated to tell him where Christ could be found. Then the hermit, seeing that he knew nothing of Jesus, began to teach him, and said, "Thou art right in believing that Christ is the greatest king; for his power extends over both heaven and earth, and will endure throughout eternity. But thou canst not serve him lightly; and if he accepts thee, he will impose great duties upon thee, and will require that thou fast often." Then said Offero, "I will not fast, for it is my strength that makes me a good servant: why should I waste it by fasting?" "And besides, thou must pray," said the hermit. "I know not how to pray, neither will I learn. Such a service is for weak ones, but not for me," said the proud giant. Then said the hermit, "If thou wilt use thy strength, knowest thou a deep, wide river, that is often swollen with rains, and sweeps away in its swift current many of those who would cross it?" Offero said, "I know such a stream." "Then go there," said the hermit, "and aid those who struggle with its waves; and the weak and the little ones bear thou from shore to shore, on thy broad shoulders. This is a good work; and if Christ will have thee for this service, he will assure thee of his acceptance." Then was Offero glad, for this was a task which suited him well. So he went to the river and built upon its bank a hut of the boughs of trees. And he aided all who came; and many he bore upon his shoulders, and was never weary by day or night in assisting those who crossed the river. And after he began his work, not one perished, where before so many had been swept away. For a staff he used a palm-tree which he pulled up in the forest, and it was not too large for his great height and strength. As Jesus beheld this he was well pleased with Offero and his labor; for though he would neither fast nor pray, yet had he found a way to serve him. At length, after Offero had spent a long time and did not weary of his toil, as he rested one night in his hut, he heard a voice like that of a weak child, and it said, "Offero, wilt thou carry me over?" And he went out quickly, but he could find no one. But when he had again lain down, the same voice called as before, and at the third call he arose and sought with a lantern. At last he found a little child who besought him, "Offero, Offero, carry me over to-night." He lifted him up, and carrying his staff, began to cross the stream. Immediately the winds blew, the waves were tossed, and the roar of the waters was as many thunders, and the little child grew heavy and more heavy, until Offero feared he should himself sink, and both be lost. But with the aid of his palm staff, at length he crossed and put his burden safely down upon the other side. Then he cried out, "Whom have I borne? Had it been the whole world, it could not have been more heavy!" Then the child replied, "Me thou hast desired to serve, and I have accepted thee. Thou hast borne not only the whole world, but Him who made it, on thy shoulders. As a sign of my power and of my approbation of thee, fix thou thy staff in the earth, and it shall grow and bear fruit." Offero did so; and the staff was soon covered with leaves, and the dates hung in huge clusters upon it. But the wonderful child was gone. Then Offero knew that it was Christ whom he had borne, and he fell down and worshipped him. After that, Offero went to Samos, where there was a great persecution of Christians, and in spite of his great strength a heathen struck him, when he said, "Were I not a Christian, I would take vengeance on thee." He permitted himself to be bound and taken to Dagnus, the King of Lycia, in which country was Samos. At the sight of the giant the king fainted. When he was himself again, he said, "Who art thou?" and the giant answered, "My first name was Offero, the Bearer, but now I serve Christ, and have borne him on my shoulders; for this I am now called Christ Offero, the bearer of Christ." Dagnus sent him to prison, and tried to seduce him to idolatry by sending beautiful women to him, who urged him to sin. But Christopher was faithful, and by his influence the women became Christians, and suffered death, because they, too, worshipped Jesus. Then Dagnus tortured him greatly, and commanded him to be beheaded. When they led him to execution, he kneeled down and prayed that all who beheld him and believed in Christ should be delivered from earthquake, fire, and tempest. It was believed that his prayer was effectual, and that all who piously invoke St. Christopher are safe for that day from all dangers of earthquake, flood, or fire. The sight of him is thought also to impart strength to the weak and weary, which idea is expressed in many inscriptions more or less similar to the following one, which accompany his pictures : —

> " Christophori Sancti speciem quicumque tuetur,
> Illo namque die nullo languore tenetur."

("Whoever shall behold the image of St. Christopher shall not faint or fail on that day.") July 25, A. D. 364.

St. Chrysanthus (*Ital.* San Grisante). This saint came to Rome from Alexandria, and St. Daria came from Athens. They were betrothed, but Chrysanthus persuaded Daria that a state of virginity was more favorable to a religious life than that of marriage. They were remarkable for their devotion to the Faith. They were at length accused and martyred, — in the reign of Numerian, according to some; but Baillet believes, in the persecution of Valerian. It is said that soon after their burial a large number of Christians who were praying at their tomb were walled up in the cave, and thus buried alive. The part of the catacombs where they were interred was long called the cemetery of SS. Chrysanthus and Daria. The Greek Church honors them on March 19 and October 17; the Latins, October 25. A. D. 237.

St. Chrysogonus (*Ital.* San Grisogono). See St. Anastasia.

St. Clair (*Lat.* S. Clarus) is one of the beheaded saints. He was an Englishman of noble extraction, and lived and labored in the county of Vexin, in France. He preached with great faithfulness, and was murdered at a village which bears his name by ruffians hired by a lewd woman who could not overcome his chastity. This village is between Rouen and Pontoise. His shrine is greatly venerated and visited by pilgrims. He is represented on a window at St. Maclou in Rouen. November 4.

St. Clara (*Lat.* Sancta Clara; *Ital.* Santa Chiara; *Fr.* Ste. Claire). Clara d' Assisi was the daughter of a nobleman, Favorino Sciffo; her mother was named Ortolana. Her beauty and the great wealth of her family caused her to receive many offers of marriage. She had early dedicated herself to a religious life, and went to

St. Francis to ask his advice. He encouraged her to renounce the world, and appointed Palm Sunday as the day for her to make her profession. She went to church with all her family richly attired, as was the custom on that day. When the others approached the altar she remained afar off; and St. Francis, admiring her humility, came down from the altar to give her the palm-branch. At evening she concealed herself in a veil, and escaped to the Porzioncula, where St. Francis dwelt. She was conducted to the altar, where St. Francis cut off her hair with his own hands, and she, putting off her rich garments, was covered with the personal penitential robes of Francis, which he threw over her. Thus she became his disciple, and the " Madre Serafica," or the foundress of the Order of Franciscan Nuns, or, as they are better known, the "Poor Clares." The rules of her order were severe in the extreme. Clara went, by the wish of St. Francis, to the convent of St. Paolo. Her family and friends tried every means to induce her to return to them without effect; and in a short time she was followed by her sister Agnes, only fourteen years old; by many ladies of rank, among whom were three of the house of Ubaldini; and, at length, by her mother. Clara so strictly adhered to the rules of her order as to injure her health, and for a long time she was bedridden. On one occasion when the Saracens, to whom Frederick had given the fortress of Nocera, came to ravage her convent of San Damiano, she arose from her bed, where she had so long been confined, and placing the Pyx which contained the Host upon the threshold, she kneeled down and began to sing, when the infidels threw down their arms and fled. Innocent IV. visited her and confirmed her order; and before her death it had spread throughout Christendom, and many noble ladies had joined it. She died at sixty in a rapturous trance, believing herself called to heaven by angelic voices. Her sister Agnes succeeded her as abbess. When the nuns removed from San Damiano to San Giorgio, they bore her remains with them. The latter is now the church of Santa Chiara d' Assisi, and is the most famous one of her order. St. Clara is a favorite saint all over Europe, but especially so in Spain. Her proper attribute is the Pyx containing the Host. She wears a gray tunic, and the cord of St. Francis, with a black veil. She also bears the lily, the cross, and the palm. August 12, A. D. 1253.

St. Clara of Monte-Falco. This saint was of the Augustinian order. In her own country she is called St. Clara; she was canonized December 8, 1881, by Pope Leo XIII. Her birth took place in 1268, and she lived quietly in her own city, which from its height overlooks the Umbrian valleys. The fame of her miracles and the sweetness of her life were well known through all the country.

St. Clement (*Ital.* San Clemente) is supposed to be spoken of by the Apostle Paul (Phil. iv. 3). He was the third pope and bishop of Rome. During the many years of his episcopate he made numerous converts, among whom was Domitilla, the niece of the Emperor Domitian; and by her influence he was protected during the reign of her uncle. In the persecution under Trajan, the prefect who governed Rome in the absence of the emperor commanded Clement to worship the idols; and when he would not, he banished him to an island where there were large stone quarries worked by convicts. Many Christians had been sent there before him, and others went with him to share his exile. Clement found those on the island suffering for want of water; he knelt and prayed, and looking up saw a lamb on the summit of a hill, which was invisible to all others. He knew it to be the Lamb of God. He went to the spot where he had seen it, and upon digging found a large, clear spring of water. After this miracle, he was condemned to be cast into the sea, bound to an anchor. But when the Christians prayed, the waters were driven back for three miles, and they saw a ruined temple which the sea had covered, and in it was found the body of the saint with the anchor round his neck. For many years, at the anniversary of his death, the sea retreated for seven days, and pilgrimages were made to this submarine tomb. At one time a woman was praying there, and her child had fallen asleep, when the waters arose and she fled, forgetting the child in her fear. The next year the boy was found quietly sleeping as she had left him. The church of San Clemente in Rome is of remarkable interest, and the scenes of his life are represented in paintings of the twelfth century. According to tradition, the relics of the saint are now here, and also those of St. Ignatius of Antioch. His proper attribute is the anchor. November 23, A. D. 100.

St. Clotilda (*Fr.* Ste. Clotilde). St. Clotilda was a Burgundian princess, and the wife of Clovis. She is famed as having Christianized France. Her husband, after long resisting her attempts for his conversion, called upon the God of Clotilda in the midst of an unfortunate battle. Immediately the fortunes of his arms were changed; and by this he was converted, and was baptized by St. Remi. At his baptism it is said that the oil was brought from heaven by a dove; and tradition says that an angel came down bearing three lilies, which he gave to St. Remi, and he in turn gave them to Clotilda, and at this time the arms of France were changed from the three toads (crapauds) of earlier days, to the fleurs-de-lys, the emblems of purity and regeneration. June 3, A. D. 545.

St. Cloud was a grandson of St. Clotilda, who when his brothers were murdered escaped to a convent, and became a monk of the Benedictine Order. September 7, A. D. 560.

Constantine, Emperor. Constantine, while still an idolater and a persecutor of the Christians, was afflicted with a leprosy. The priests of the idols prescribed that he should bathe in children's blood. Three thousand children were collected to be slain; but as the emperor rode to the place where they were, the mothers of the children so entreated him that he stopped his chariot and said, " Far better is it that I should die, than cause the death of these innocents." He then commanded the children to be restored to their mothers, to whom he gave large gifts to compensate for their sufferings. That night in his sleep, St. Peter and St. Paul appeared to him, and told him that Christ had sent them to him because he had spared the innocents. They told him to send for Sylvester, who would show him a pool in which he could wash and be clean, and that from that time he should cease to persecute the Christians, and himself worship their God. Now Sylvester was the Bishop of Rome, who had hid away from the cruelties of Constantine and was in a cave near Monte Calvo. The emperor sent for him; and when the soldiers found him and led him away, he thought it was to his execution. They took him to the emperor, who asked him who the two gods were who had appeared to him the previous night. Sylvester replied that they were not gods, but the apostles of Jesus. Constantine then desired to see the effigies of these apostles. Sylvester

showed him some pictures of Peter and Paul, and Constantine saw
that they were like those whom he had seen in the vision. Sylvester then baptized him, and he came out from his baptism cured of
his disease. The next day, Constantine commanded that Christ
should be worshipped in all Rome as the only God ; the next day,
that those who blasphemed against Him should lose their lives ; the
third day, that any one who insulted a Christian should forfeit half
his goods ; the fourth day, that the Bishop of Rome should be the
first bishop of the world ; the next day, he gave the privilege of
sanctuary to the Christian churches ; the sixth, he ordered that no
churches should be built without the consent of the bishop ; the
seventh, that the tithes of the domains of Rome should belong to
the Church ; and the eighth day, he founded the Lateran, by digging
himself and carrying on his shoulders twelve hodfuls of earth and
laying the first stone. Another account of the manner of his conversion to Christianity, and one frequently illustrated in art, is that
during the campaign of 312, while on his march to Rome, he saw a
luminous cross in the sky, with the inscription, " By this conquer,"
and that on the night before his last battle with Maxentius, he was
commanded in a vision to inscribe the sacred monogram of the name
of Christ upon the shields of his soldiers. Three different localities
claim the honor of having been the place where Constantine beheld
the cross ; these are Autun, Andernach, and Verona. But to these
miraculous directions and the success which followed his obedience
to them is ·attributed his belief in Christianity. The Empress
Helena told him that it would have been better to become a Jew
than a Christian. So he wrote her to bring to dispute with Sylvester the most learned of the Jews. She came to Rome with one
hundred and forty doctors of the law. A day was appointed for
the discussion ; and Zeno and Crato, Greek philosophers, were appointed arbitrators. Then Sylvester, praying for wisdom, utterly
defeated these learned Rabbis. Then one of them, Zambri, who
was a magician, desired that a fierce bull should be brought, and
said that when he should speak in his ear the name of his God, he
should fall dead. The bull was brought ; and as the magician had
said, he fell dead at his feet as soon as he had whispered to him.
Then Sylvester was attacked with fury ; the arbitrators were astonished, and Constantine was shaken in his faith, but Sylvester said

that the name he had spoken was Satan's, for Christ did not destroy but gave life. He desired that Zambri should restore the bull to life. This he could not do; but Sylvester made the sign of the cross, and commanded him to rise, when the bull obeyed and rose up as gentle as before he had been fierce. Then all who saw this believed and were baptized. Awhile after this, it was told the emperor that since his conversion, the dragon which dwelt in the moat had killed three hundred persons daily, by his poisonous breath. Then Sylvester went down to the dragon, and exorcised him in the name of Christ, and bound up his mouth with a thread, and sealed it with the sign of the cross. Sylvester also gave aid in his house to a Christian who was afterward slain for his faith. The governor believed that Sylvester had riches which belonged to the martyr, and threatened him with tortures if he did not give them up. Sylvester told the governor that his soul should be in torments that night; and as he ate his dinner he was choked to death. There is no need to remind one that history and the legends greatly differ regarding Constantine. As for Sylvester, he was at the great Nicene Council, and after governing the Church for nearly twenty-four years, he died and was buried in the cemetery of Priscilla at Rome. The proper attribute of St. Sylvester is the bull; sometimes the portraits of St. Peter and St. Paul. His festival is December 31, and he died in 335.

St. Cosmo and St. Damian (*Lat.* SS. Cosmus et Damianus; *Ital.* SS. Cosimo e Damiano gli santi medici Arabi; *Fr.* SS. Côme et Damien). These brother saints are seldom separated in thought or representation. They were Arabians, but dwelt at Ægæ, in Cilicia. Their father died early; and their mother, Theodora, trained them in Christian virtue. Their charities were extensive; and they studied medicine for the purpose of relieving suffering, and refused all compensation for their labors. They did not refuse to relieve even animals, when in their power. They became most skilful physicians. In the time of Diocletian they were seized by the proconsul Lycias, and thrown into the sea, but were saved by an angel. They were also put in the fire, which would not burn them, and bound to crosses and stoned; but none of the stones reached them, so that at last they were beheaded. They were patrons of medicine, and succeeded to the honors of Æsculapius among the Greeks. They have also the title of Anargyres ("without fees"). They were patrons of the Medici family, as is seen on the coins of Florence. September 27, A. D. 301.

St. Costanzo, Bishop of Perugia. Nothing is known of this saint but that he suffered martyrdom in the reign of Marcus Aurelius. The country between Perugia and Foligno is called the Strada di Costanza, and he is much venerated in that portion of Italy.

St. Crispin and **St. Crispianus** (*Ital.* San Crispino e San Crispiano; *Fr.* SS. Crespin et Crespinian). These saints were brothers, who went with St. Denis from Rome to preach in France. They supported themselves by making shoes, and were supplied with leather by angels to make shoes for the poor. Being denounced as Christians, they were cruelly tortured, and then beheaded at Soissons. The Roman tradition fixes their death in A. D. 300, but other authorities give the date thirteen years earlier. Their proper attributes are the awl and shoemaker's knife. October 25.

St. Cunegunda. March 3, A. D. 1040. (See St. Henry of Bavaria.)

St. Cunibert, to whom one of the most ancient churches of Cologne is dedicated, was bishop of that city. He was the adviser of King Dagobert and some of his successors, and an intimate friend of Pepin d'Heristal. He held his diocese thirty-seven years. According to the legend, St. Cunibert was directed by a dove to the spot where St. Ursula and her companions were buried. He is represented in the episcopal dress, holding in his hand the model of a church. The dove is his attribute. November 12, A. D. 660.

St. Cuthbert of Durham was a shepherd in his youth, in the valley of the Tweed. In his childhood an angel appeared to him and urged him to a pious life. He was instructed at a monastery near his home, where St. Aidan was the prior. One night, as Cuthbert tended his flocks, he saw a dazzling light, and looking up beheld angels bearing St. Aidan to heaven. He then entered the monastery, and soon became a noted preacher. He not only made converts, but he preached much to such Christians as lived unworthy lives. It was said that when he appealed to them an angelic brightness shone in his face, and none could deceive him or conceal the sin of their hearts. He wandered among the mountainous regions, and preached in villages considered almost inaccessible. He later dwelt on an island on the coast of Northumberland, called afterwards Holy Island, in memory of his sanctity. Here he supported himself upon what he raised by his own labor, and it is said that angels brought him bread from Paradise. He was afterwards Bishop of Lindisfarne. Miraculous things are told of him during his life, and of his relics after his death. His shrine became a place of pilgrimage. His relics are now in the cathedral of Durham. His attribute is the head of St. Oswald, buried in the tomb of St. Cuthbert, when the former was slain in battle. He also has the otter, which was said to have licked him into life when he had almost perished from cold and exposure. March 20, A. D. 687.

St. Cyprian, and **St. Justina of Antioch** (*Ital.* San Cipriano il Mago e Santa Giustina; *Fr.* St. Cyprien le Magicien et Ste. Justine). The histories of these saints cannot be separated. Saint Justina was an exceedingly lovely and virtuous Christian maiden of Antioch. Her father was a priest of the idols, but she converted both him and her mother to her own faith. A nobleman named Aglaides sought her love in vain, and at length he applied to the famous magician Cyprian, for his aid in winning her heart. Now Cyprian was very learned in astrology and necromancy, and doubted not his power to overcome all obstacles. But when he saw Justina, he also loved her and determined to win her for himself. He sent demons to her to fill her mind with unchaste and voluptuous images, but she remained unaffected. At length he sent the prince of evil spirits to tempt her, but all without success. Then Cyprian was so astonished at the power of her virtue that he resolved to serve the God of this pure maiden. So he went to her filled with repentance, and confessed himself a Christian. Justina, in her joy at so great a victory for Christ, cut off her beautiful hair, and made of it an offering to the Virgin. Cyprian was soon baptized, and became as famous for his piety as he had before been for his wickedness. When the last persecution of the Christians broke out, the Governor of Antioch commanded these saints to be thrown into boiling pitch, which, by a miracle, had no power to harm them. He then sent them to Diocletian at Nicomedia, who ordered them to be instantly beheaded. September 26, A. D. 304.

St Cyprian of Carthage, and archbishop of that place, perished in the persecution of Valerian. His martyrdom is one of the most authentic in history. He is very rarely represented in works of art; and perhaps the picture by Paul Veronese, in the Brera at Milan, is the only one likely to come within the observation of the traveller. September 16, A. D. 258.

St. Cyril (*Lat.* S. Cyrillus; *Ital.* San Cirillo; *Fr.* St. Cyrille). This saint was Patriarch of Alexandria from the year 412 to 444. He wrote much upon theology, and was earnestly engaged in the contests of the early Church. Some non-Catholic writers have sought to connect him with the terribly cruel murder of Hypatia, the female mathematician and philosopher.[1] He is as highly venerated in the Greek as in the Latin Church, and is the only bishop whom they represent with his head covered. January 28, A. D. 444.

St. Cyril and **St. Methodius.** St. Cyril was a philosopher, and St. Methodius an artist. They were of the Order of St. Basil, and were sent by the Patriarch of Constantinople as missionaries to the people who lived on the borders of the Danube. Bogaris, the King of Bulgaria, desired Methodius to paint a picture in the hall of his palace that should impress his subjects with awe. Methodius painted the "Last Judgment," with Christ enthroned and surrounded with angels; also the happiness of the blessed and the miseries of the lost. When finished, the king desired an explanation of this terrible picture; and Cyril gave it with such power that the monarch, and all who listened, were converted. So they labored among the neighboring nations with success. Methodius painted, and Cyril so explained his pictures as to convince large numbers of the truth of the Christian faith. St. Cyril also learned their languages, made an alphabet for them, and translated a part of the Gospels. He obtained, too, the

---

[1] The Rev. Alban Butler, in his sketch of St. Cyril's life, touching on the deplorable murder of Hypatia, says: "She was much respected and considered by the governor, and often visited him. The mob, which was nowhere more unruly or more fond of riots and tumults than in that populous city, the second in the world for extent, upon a suspicion that she incensed the governor against their bishop, seditiously rose, pulled her out of her chariot, cut and mangled her flesh, and tore her body in pieces in the streets, to the great grief and scandal of all good men, especially of the pious bishop, Cyril." And the same authority adds: "It is very unjust in some moderns to charge him [Cyril] as conscious of so horrible a crime, which shocks human nature. . . . The silence of Orestes and of the historian Socrates, both his declared enemies, suffices to acquit him."

privilege of celebrating mass in the Sclavonic tongue. These saints are generally represented together; St. Cyril with a book and St. Methodius with a tablet on which is a picture. The Greeks honor St. Cyril March 9, and St. Methodius May 11 ; the Latins, both on March 9. They are honored as the apostles of the Sclavos. Their millenary was lately celebrated with great splendor.

Dale Abbey, the legend of. This legend is represented in five pictures. In the first the abbot shoots the deer with a cross-bow, because it had eaten his wheat. In the second the foresters complain of him, and the king commands him to be brought before him. In the third and fourth he is in the presence of the king, who grants him as much land as he can encircle by a furrow from sun to sun ; the plough to be drawn by two wild stags from the forest. In the fifth he ploughs with the stags.

St. Damian. See St. Cosmo.

St. Daria. See St. Chrysanthus.

Dead Nuns, the legend of. There were two noble ladies who joined the sisterhood of St. Scholastica. They were fond of scandal and vain talk. St. Benedict, hearing of this, reproved them, and sent them word that unless they reformed he would punish them. For a while they remembered the admonition, but relapsed again, and so died. They were buried in the church near the altar. One day, as Benedict celebrated mass, when the deacon said, "Let those who are in penance and forbidden to partake, depart and leave us," these nuns arose from their graves, and with sad appearance left the church. This occurred every time the mass was celebrated there, until St. Benedict, pitying them, prayed for their souls, and they rested peacefully.

St. Delphine. See St. Eleazar de Sabran.

St. Denis of France (*Lat.* S. Dionysius ; *Ital.* San Dionisio or Dionigi ; *Fr.* St. Denis). The truth of the legend which makes St. Denis the same with Dionysius the Areopagite will not be confirmed upon a critical examination of facts ; but as they are thus represented in works of art, it must be given to make the representations of them understood. Dionysius was an Athenian philosopher. He was a judge of the Areopagus, and for his wisdom in heavenly things was called Θεόσοφος, Theosophus. He went to Egypt to study astrology, and was at Heliopolis at the time of the crucifixion of our Lord. He was greatly troubled at the darkness which endured for three hours, because he could not understand it. He was converted at Athens by St. Paul, and became first bishop of that city. In his letters he tells of his visit to the Blessed Virgin at Jerusalem ; his astonishment at the dazzling light which surrounded her, and his presence at her death and burial. He went to Rome and attended St. Paul at his martyrdom. He was then sent by Pope Clement to preach in France with two deacons, Rusticus and Eleutherius. After his arrival in France he was called Denis. He found Paris a beautiful city, seeming to him like another Athens. He dwelt here, and by his preaching converted many. He sent missionaries to all parts of France and to Germany. At length he was accused of his faith to the Roman Emperor, who sent Fescennius to Paris to seize him, with his companions. They were all condemned to death. At the place of execution St. Denis knelt down and prayed, and the deacons responded in a loud Amen. Their bodies were left as usual, to be devoured by wild beasts. But St. Denis arose, and taking his head in his hands walked two miles, to the place now called Mont Martre, the angels singing as he went. This miracle converted many, and among them Lactia, wife of Lubrius, who was afterwards beheaded also. The bodies of St. Denis and his deacons were buried, and a church erected over them by St. Geneviève ; but in the reign of Dagobert they were removed to the abbey of St. Denis. He is the patron saint of France, and his name the war-cry of its armies. The oriflamme, the standard of France, was consecrated on his tomb. When Stephen II. became pope, the name of this saint began to be venerated in all Europe. Stephen had been educated at the monastery of St. Denis. There is a beautiful life of the saint in the royal library of Paris, with a large number of exquisite miniatures. His attribute is the severed head. October 9.

St. **Diego d'Alcala** was an humble Capuchin brother in a convent of Alcalà. It is said that the infant Don Carlos was healed through his intercession, when severely wounded. Philip II. promoted his canonization on this account.[1] About 1600 a wealthy Spaniard residing at Rome dedicated a chapel to this saint in the church of San Giacomo degli Spagnuoli, which was painted by Anni-

---

[1] Other wonders were also wrought through St. Diego's intercession ; for, as our readers know, three miracles of the first class are required for the canonization of a saint.

bal Caracci and Albano, who was then his pupil. These frescos were transferred to canvas. There are also pictures of St. Diego by Murillo, the most important being in the Louvre.

St. Digna. See St. Afra of Augsburg, whose handmaiden she was.

St. Dominick (*Lat.* S. Dominicus, Pater Ordinis Prædicatorum ; *Ital.* San Domenico, San Domenico Calaroga ; *Fr.* St. Dominique, Fondateur des Frères Prêcheurs ; *Sp.* San Domingo). This saint was a Castilian of noble descent, of the house of Guzman.[1] His mother dreamed, before his birth, that she had brought forth a dog with a torch in his mouth. At his baptism a star descended from heaven to crown his brow. He studied at Valencia, and became, at the instance of the Bishop of Osma, a regular canon of St. Augustine at the age of twenty-eight years. When thirty years old he went to France, and being shocked at the heresies of the Albigenses, he preached with such effect as to convert many. He went the second time to France with his bishop to conduct to Castile the young princess who was to espouse Prince Ferdinand. Her death, just as he arrived, was a great shock to him ; and thenceforth his zeal and religious devotion were greatened. He obtained permission from the pope in 1207 to preach to the Albigenses in the Vaudois. He wrote out the articles of faith ; and it is said that when this book was thrown in the fire it would not remain, but leaped out uninjured. As the heretical books were burned, this miracle had the effect to convince and convert many. As to the persecution of the Albigenses, it is certain that he was extremely earnest in his prayers and endeavors to secure the triumph of the Church.[2] He united with several priests, who went about to preach barefoot. From this arose his order, which was confirmed in 1216. St. Dominick, by heavenly inspiration, instituted the devotion of the rosary. A rosary should have fifteen large, and one hundred and fifty small beads. The large represent the Paternosters, and the small the Ave-Marias. This use of the rosary was a great assistance to St. Dominick in his labors.

---

[1] The ex-Empress Eugenie of France is a scion of the house of Guzman.

[2] St. Dominick maintained that to labor with success among these heretics, persuasion and good example should be employed, and by no means terror. Himself knew no other arms than those of instruction, patience, penance, fasting, watching, tears, and prayer. He was a zealous advocate of popular education.

In 1218 St. Dominick was commissioned by the pope to reform the nunneries at Rome. From this originated the Order of the Dominican Nuns, for whom he made a rule, which they adopted. He founded many convents in the principal cities of Europe, none of which are more famous than the splendid one of his order in the Rue St. Jacques at Paris. It is from the situation of this convent that the Dominicans were called Jacobins in France. At length he returned to his convent at Bologna, where he died of a fever, brought on by his arduous labors. Two years after his death he was canonized, and his remains placed in the magnificent Arca di San Domenico at Bologna. It is said his true portrait was brought from heaven by St. Catherine and St. Mary Magdalen to a convent of Dominican nuns. His attributes are, the dog by his side; the star, on or above his head; a lily in one hand and a book in the other. There are many interesting legends of his wonderful miracles. At one time, it is said, he restored to life the young Lord Napoleon, nephew of Cardinal Stephano di Fossa-Nova, when he had been killed by a fall from his horse. When, at the convent of St. Sabina, they had not sufficient food, St. Dominick pronounced the blessing upon the little they had, and immediately two angels appeared with bread and wine, which was celestial food, and sweeter than any of earth. St. Dominick had a vision, in which he saw the Saviour with the arrows of divine wrath in his hand. The Virgin asked him what he would do; and when he replied that he would destroy the earth on account of its wickedness, she besought him to wait, and presented to him St. Francis and St. Dominick, saying that they would traverse the whole earth and subdue it to Christ. August 4, A. D. 1221.

St. Donato of Arezzo (*Lat.* S. Donatus; *Fr.* St. Donat). This saint was of noble birth, and in childhood a companion of the Emperor Julian. Julian, after his apostasy, put many Christians to death, and among them the father of Donatus. Donatus then fled from Rome to Arezzo, and had for his companion the holy monk Hilarion. They preached, and performed many miracles. At one time a tax-gatherer of the province went on a journey, and left the money which he had with his wife, Euphrosina. She died suddenly, and told no one where she had hidden the treasure. When her husband returned he was in great distress; and fearing to be punished as a defaulter, he appealed to Donatus, who went to the tomb

7

and called upon Euphrosina to tell him where the money was. She answered him, and this was heard by many. Donatus was made Bishop of Arezzo; and as he celebrated the Holy Mass, the cup which held the wine, and which was of glass, was broken by some idolaters. When Donatus prayed, it was made whole, and not a drop of wine spilled. This miracle was the cause of the conversion of so many that the pagans, in their rage, tortured and beheaded him. Hilarion was scourged to death, and with Donatus is interred beneath the high altar of the cathedral of Arezzo. August 7.

St. Dorothea of Cappadocia, virgin and martyr (*Ital.* Santa Dorotea; *Fr.* Ste. Dorothée). She was a noble virgin, and the most beautiful of the city of Cæsarea. She was a Christian, and devoted to prayer, fasting, and almsgiving. Sapritius or Fabricius, the governor, hearing of her beauty, sent for her, and threatened her with death if she would not worship the idols. She depicted to him the joys of heaven, and declared that she preferred the death which would give her these to a life of idolatry. She was taken to prison; and two sisters, Calista and Christeta, who had renounced Christianity through fear of torture, were sent to induce Dorothea to follow their example. But she so influenced them that they left her, declaring themselves again Christians. Then Fabricius commanded the sisters to be burned, and Dorothea to witness their sufferings. She encouraged them through all, and was then condemned to be tortured and beheaded. She endured the tortures with great courage. As she was led to execution, a young lawyer, called Theophilus, jeered her, and asked her to send him fruits from the gardens to which she was going. She told him that his request should be granted. When at the place of execution, she knelt and prayed; and suddenly there was beside her a beautiful angel with a basket, in which were three roses and three apples. She commanded him to take them to Theophilus, and tell him she had sent them, and should await him in the gardens from which they came. Then she was beheaded. When Theophilus received the fruit and tasted of it, he too became a Christian, and at last suffered martyrdom. Her attributes are roses in the hand or on the head, or a basket with three apples and three roses held by an attendant angel. February 6, A. D. 303.

St. Dunstan was born in 925. He became a monk at Glastonbury. He was a fine scholar, a remarkable musician, a painter, and a worker of metals. He went to court when quite young, and was a great favorite of King Edmund, who admired his musical talents. He had such an influence over the king that he was accused of sorcery and driven from the court. One day, as the king was hunting the stag, his dogs leaped down a fearful precipice. The king feared that he could not rein in his horse and must follow to death. He prayed, and thought of his cruelty to Dunstan. The horse stopped on the bank. The king then begged Dunstan to return to him. It is related that as the saint labored one night at his forge, the Devil came to tempt him in the form of a beautiful woman. Dunstan seized the Devil by the nose with his red-hot tongs. One day his harp hanging on the wall played to him the hymn, "Gaudete animi." Dunstan was made the king's treasurer and Abbot of Glastonbury; but when Edwin came to the throne and lived a shameless life with Elgiva, he drove Dunstan again from court. When Edgar was king, the saint was again honored. He was made Bishop of Worcester, and then Archbishop of Canterbury. In 960 he went to Rome, and received great honors as Primate of the Anglo-Saxon nation. On his return he founded numerous schools and monasteries. He relates in his writings a vision in which he beheld his mother espoused to Christ while angels sang around them. One of the angels asked Dunstan why he did not sing; and when he replied that he was ignorant and could not sing, the angel taught him the hymn, and the next day he could sing the same to his monks. May 19, A. D. 988.

Duns Scotus was a Franciscan, and a rival in theological controversy of St. Thomas Aquinas. Their opinions gave rise to the parties called Thomists and Scotists. He was one of the most zealous defenders of the doctrine of the Immaculate Conception. He was an Englishman, and went to Paris about 1304, where he wrote his commentaries. He was sent to Cologne in 1308, where he was received with great honor; and there he died in the same year. There was a fable of his having been buried alive, which is disputed by good authorities.

St. Ebba of Coldingham. This saint was abbess of the largest monastery which existed in her time, and had monks as well as nuns under her rule. About the year 870 there was an incursion of Danish pirates, and St. Ebba was alarmed for her chastity and that of her nuns. She assembled them in the chapter-house and made an appeal to them; she then took a razor and cut off her nose and upper lip. Her example was followed by the whole community; and when the pirates came, the frightful spectacle the nuns presented protected their virginity. The pirates in their disappointment set fire to the monastery, and the nuns perished in the flames. April 2.

St. Edith of Wilton, daughter of King Edgar. Her mother was a beautiful nun, Wilfrida, whom the king took from her convent by force. As soon as she could escape from him she returned, and Edith was born in the nunnery. She refused to go to court, and was celebrated for her sanctity, learning, and beauty. She spent the fortune her father gave her in founding a nunnery at Wilton, which has since become the seat of the Earls of Pembroke. Edith was remarkable for the costliness and elegance of her attire; and when she was rebuked for it by St. Ethelwold, she insisted that this was of no importance, for God regarded the heart alone, and that he could read beneath any garment. "For," answered she, "pride may exist under the garb of wretchedness; and a mind may be as pure under these vestments as under your tattered furs." [1] She died at the age of twenty-three. She lived to see the consecration of the church she had built in honor of St. Denis, but died forty-three days after. St. Dunstan was warned of her approaching end, while celebrating mass on the occasion of the consecration. September 16, A. D. 984.

Edith of Polesworth. See St. Modwena.

St. Edmund, king and martyr. The ecclesiastical legend of King Edmund is this: Ragnar Lodbrog was a Dane of royal blood. He went out fowling in a small skiff, and, a storm coming on, he was driven upon the English coast in Norfolk. He was taken to King Edmund, who much admired the strength of the Dane and his skill as a huntsman, while Lodbrog was dazzled by the accomplishments of the young king and the splendor of his court. The huntsman of Edmund became jealous of the Dane, and killed him. A dog which Lodbrog had reared watched over his body until it was discovered. The huntsman confessed his crime, and as a punishment was put

---

[1] So far the legend, on which some poems have been made. But, as our readers know, the dress of nuns of every order is regulated by a strict rule; and the legendary answer of the nun Edith to St. Ethelwold, though embodying an unquestioned truth, is not in accordance with the humble submission of Christian virgins to the authorities of the Church.

adrift in the same boat which had brought Lodbrog to England. He was carried to the home of the Dane, where his two sons seeing the boat of their father and supposing him to be murdered, were about to kill the huntsman. But he told them that Edmund had done the deed. Then they swore vengeance, and collecting a great fleet, went to invade England. They landed in Northumbria, and destroyed everything within their reach as they advanced to the territory of Edmund. They demanded of him one half his kingdom. He took counsel with Bishop Humbert, and determined never to submit to a heathen power. He then prepared for battle, and met the Danes near Thetford, where they fought. King Edmund was surrounded by his enemies, and with Humbert took refuge in the church. They were dragged out, and the king was bound to a tree and scourged; his body was then filled with arrows from the Danish bows, and finally he was beheaded. Humbert also was martyred. At length, when the Christians who had hidden came forth, they found a large gray wolf watching the head of the king. This they buried in a spot whereon were afterwards built a church and monastery, and then a town, which was called in memory of the king, Bury St. Edmunds, which name it still retains. November 20, A. D. 870.

St. Edward the Martyr was the son of King Edgar. One day when he was hunting he went to Corfe Castle, where his stepmother, Elfrida, was living with his brother Ethelred. His mother received him kindly, but commanded one of the servants to stab him in the back as he was drinking. He, finding himself wounded, rode away and died in the forest. Elfrida and her son gave him a shameful burial, and instituted rejoicings at his death. But God shed a celestial light on his grave, and those who came to it were healed of all infirmities. Multitudes made pilgrimages to his grave; and when St. Dunstan reproved Elfrida as a murderess, she was struck with remorse, and desired herself to go there. But when she mounted her horse for the journey he would not move, and no power could make him; so Elfrida, perceiving the will of God in this, walked barefooted to the place. His remains were removed with great honors to the nunnery at Shaftesbury, which Alfred the Great had endowed. March 18, A. D. 978.

St. Edward, king and confessor. This saint was son of King Ethelred, who had before his birth two other sons. But when it was near the time for this third one to be born, Ethelred called upon his council to decide who should succeed to the throne. St. Dunstan was present, and he prophesied the early death of those already born; so the council decided in favor of the expected prince, who was afterwards the saint of whom we speak. All the nobles took the oath of fealty to him *dans le sein de sa mère.* The coronation of Edward was on Easter Day, 1043. He freed his subjects from the tax called Danegelt, because when a large sum of this tribute was brought to the palace, and the king was called to look at it, he beheld a rejoicing demon dancing upon the money. This saint had many visions during his life, and also possessed miraculous powers of healing. His history is told in bas-reliefs in his chapel in Westminster Abbey. January 5, A. D. 1066.

St. Eleazar de Sabran was a Franciscan. His mother was a woman of remarkable character and great piety. He was early married to Delphine, heiress of Glendênes. She was as pious as her husband; and they were both enrolled in the Third Order of St. Francis. As Count of Sabran, he administered his affairs with great ability and justice. He died at twenty-eight. St. Delphine then resided for some time with Sancha, Queen of Naples, but at last withdrew to perfect seclusion. St. Eleazar is represented in art holding a package of papers to commemorate a noble act of his life. After the death of his father he found papers which had been written to induce his father to disinherit him, and which attributed to him all manner of evil. Instead of taking revenge on the writer of these calumnies, he sent for him, and burned the letters in his presence. He thus made of his bitter enemy a devoted friend.

St. Elisabeth, mother of John the Baptist (*Lat.* Sancta Elisabetha; *Ital.* Santa Elisabeta; *Sp.* Santa Isabel; *Ger.* Die Heilige Elizabeth). The Hebrew signification of this name is "worshipper of God," or "consecrated to God." The Gospel describes Elisabeth as walking in all the commandments of the Lord blameless; a woman "well stricken in years" when she was "exalted to a miraculous motherhood," and chosen for high honors by God. She should not, however, be represented as decrepit and wrinkled, but as elderly, dignified, and gracious. She appears as an important personage in art, and yet in most cases as the accompaniment to those of still greater importance. She is first seen in pictures of the Visitation or

Salutation, when with prophetic utterance she exclaims, "Whence is this to me, that the mother of my Lord should come to me?" Then in the representations of the birth of John the Baptist, and in various scenes from his life; one of which illustrates the legend that as Elisabeth fled from the massacre at Bethlehem, a huge rock opened and received her and St. John, whom she bore in her arms, into its bosom, where they were concealed until the danger was past. Again St. John is taking leave of his parents to go away into his life in the desert. But the Holy Families in which St. Elisabeth appears are far more numerous than any other representations of her, and are by far the most pleasing. Elisabeth is frequently presenting her child to the Saviour, and teaching him to kneel and fold his hands as if in worship. The matronly age, the dark complexion, and coifed head of Elisabeth are in beautiful contrast with the virgin bloom, the abundant hair, and the youthful grace of the Madonna.

St. Elizabeth of Hungary (*Lat.* Sancta Elizabetha, Mater Pauperum; *Ital.* Santa Elisabeta di Ungheria; *Fr.* Madame Ste. Elisabeth; *Sp.* Santa Isabel; *Ger.* Die Heilige Elizabeth von Ungarn, or von Hessen; Die liebe Frau Elizabeth). This legend is almost entirely historical, with just enough of the marvellous to entitle it to a place in "legendary lore." She was the daughter of the King of Hungary, and was born in 1207. The year of her birth was full of blessings to her country, and from her earliest days she was regarded as an especial favorite of God and one who should bring good to her people. The first words she uttered were those of prayer, and at three years old she showed her charity by giving her toys and garments to those less fortunate than herself. When Herman of Thuringia heard of these things, he desired this princess as a wife for his son, Prince Louis, and sent an embassy to solicit her of her father. His ambassadors were of great rank; and with them went the noble Bertha of Beindeleben, with a train of knights and ladies, and many rich presents. Their request was granted, and the little Elizabeth, only four years old, was given to them. Her father gave her a silver cradle and bath, a rich wardrobe and a train of twelve maidens. He also sent to Herman and his wife Sophia many splendid and precious things which he had obtained from Constantinople. The princess was received at the castle of **Wartburg, at Eisenach,** with great and imposing ceremony. The next day she was betrothed to Louis; and being laid in the same cradle, they smiled and played in such a manner that it was considered an omen of a happy marriage. From this time they were never separated, and grew together in perfect love. Elizabeth was soon seen to be very different from all other children; her mind was devoted to heavenly things, and charity was her chief characteristic. As long as Herman lived, Elizabeth was happy, and he was her true friend and father; but after his death, which happened when she was nine years old, the mother and sister of Prince Louis did all they could to prevent the marriage, because they did not like her devotion and piety. But although she suffered many insults, she never resented them, and Louis remained true to her in spite of all. Sometimes he feared she was too pure and holy to be any other than the bride of Heaven; but at length when he was twenty the marriage took place. They lived a life of most perfect love, but she continued all her religious penances. Louis sometimes remonstrated, but he secretly felt that he and his people should receive in some way great blessings from the sanctity of his wife. Her confessor had told her that the imposts for the support of the royal table were unjust, and from that time, while others feasted, she ate bread and drank only water; but one day Louis took the cup from her hand and tasted, and he thought he drank wine more delicious than he had ever had before. He questioned the cup-bearer, who declared he had given Elizabeth only water. Louis said nothing, for he believed that angels attended her. At another time, when Louis entertained a company of princes, he desired Elizabeth to dress magnificently. When she was attired and about to enter the apartment of Louis, a wretched beggar sought her charity. She told him she could not attend to him then, but he entreated her in the name of John the Baptist. Now this was her patron saint, and she could not refuse what was asked in his name; so she tore off her costly mantle and gave the beggar, and sought her chamber fearing what her husband might say. Just then Louis came to seek her, and as he hesitated whether to blame or praise her, a servant brought the mantle, saying she had found it hanging in its place. Then Louis led her forth to his guests with his heart full of love and wonder; and a bright light was about her, and the jewels on her mantle glowed with celestial brilliancy. Tradition tells us that the beggar was none other than our Blessed Lord. Another time, when visiting the poor of Eisenach, she found a leprous child whom none would care for. She carried him in her arms and laid him in her own bed. This enraged the mother of Louis; and when he returned she told him what sort of person was in his bed in his absence. Almost out of patience, he went to see; and, behold! when he looked he found a sweet infant, and as he gazed it vanished away from his sight. This, too, was believed to have been Jesus. When Louis was absent, Elizabeth spent all her time in visiting the poor; and as she one day descended to Eisenach carrying food in her robe, she met her husband. The path was icy, and she bent with the weight of her burden. When Louis demanded what she did, she did not like to show him, and pressed her robe more firmly together. He insisted, and opened her mantle, when he saw only red and white roses, more lovely than the earthly roses of summer; and this was in winter. Then he was about to embrace her; but such a glory seemed to surround her that he dared not touch her, but he put one of the roses in his bosom and went on, thinking of all these wonders. In 1226 Louis went to Italy with the Emperor Frederick II. A great famine afflicted all Germany, but especially Thuringia. Elizabeth was untiring in her charities and labors. The famine was followed as usual by a plague; and again she labored, with her own hands tending the sick. She founded several hospitals, and went constantly from one to the other. She exhausted the public treasury, and gave away her own robes and jewels. When Louis returned, his counsellors made great complaints of Elizabeth; but he, only thankful that she was still spared to him, said, "Let her do as she will." But she, kissing him many times, said, "See! I have given to the Lord what is his, and he has preserved to us what is thine and mine!" The next year Louis went to the Crusades. The grief of the hearts of this husband and wife at parting was such that Elizabeth was carried home more dead than alive; for she had journeyed two days with him before she could find strength to leave him. It was their final parting; for Louis died in Calabria, in the arms of the Patriarch of Jerusalem. He commanded his retainers to carry his body to his wife, and to defend her and his children, even with their lives, from all wrong. Her grief was so great that God alone could sustain her by miraculous comfort. The brother of Louis, Henry, now drove her forth with her children, and took possession of the Wartburg. It was winter time; she carried her newly born baby in her arms, and was followed by her three other children and her women. It is said that she fell, and that one whom she had cared for in the hospital mocked at her. She found a shelter for her children, and supported herself by spinning wool. But when the knights returned with the body of Louis, they obliged Henry to accept the office of regent until her son Herman could reign; and Elizabeth received as her dower the city of Marbourg. And now she gave herself up to the direction of her rigid confessor, Conrad. She lived a life of penitential humiliation, and even separated herself from her children lest she should love them too well. She drank the very dregs of the cup of penance, and clothed in rags and mocked by the children in the streets as a mad woman, she spun wool until she had no strength remaining. It is said that she was comforted by celestial beings, and that even the Blessed Virgin talked with her. When dying she sang sweet hymns, and at last she said, "Silence," and died. Tradition says that angels bore her spirit to heaven, and as they ascended were heard to chant, "Regnum mundi contempsi." She was twenty-four years old, and Louis had been dead three years and a half. She was canonized four years after her death. Her shrine in the church at Marbourg, which bears her name, was visited by pilgrims, and its stone steps worn away by their knees. In the Reformation so-called, this shrine was desecrated, and her remains scattered, no one knows where. The shrine is still preserved as a curiosity in the sacristy of the church. The castle of Wartburg is in ruins. There are many pictures of this lovely saint; but the most celebrated was painted by Murillo for the church of the Caritad, at Seville. November 19, A. D. 1231.

St. Elizabeth of Portugal (*Sp.* Sant' Isabel de Paz). This Elizabeth was the daughter of the King of Aragon, and the grand-niece of Elizabeth of Hungary. She was married to Dionysius, King of Portugal. He was most faithless and cruel as a husband, but a good king to his subjects. After forty years of great domestic trials she was left a widow. She died at sixty-five, and can be distinguished from the other St. Elizabeth of whom we have spoken, by her age, as the former is always represented as young, while this one is old and venerable. She was so patient, and so often reconciled the troubles of her family, as to acquire in Spain the title "Sant' Isabel de Paz." She is the heroine of Schiller's "Fridolin," though the scene is in Germany, and her name "Die Gräfin von Savern." July 8, A. D. 1336.

St. Eloy of Noyon (*Lat.* S. Eligius ; *Eng.* St. Loo ; *Ital.* Sant' Alò, or Lò ; Sant' Eligio). This saint was born at the village of Chatelas. He was of humble origin. He was at school at Limoges, and there learned the trade of a goldsmith, in which he so excelled that when he went to Paris he attracted the attention of the treasurer of the king, Clotaire II. The king desired to have a throne of gold set with jewels, and it was important to find a skilful and an honest man. Eloy was selected, and of the material furnished him for one throne he made two. The king was so pleased with the beauty of the work and the probity of the workman, that he from that time employed him in State affairs. His successor, Dagobert, made Eloy Master of the Mint. He cut the dies for the money, and there are known to be thirteen pieces bearing his name. He was at length, after the death of Dagobert, made Bishop of Noyon. He was remarkable for his eloquence, and was sent to preach in Belgium ; and by some he is believed to have been the first to carry the Gospel to Sweden and Denmark. Before his Episcopal consecration, while holding a high place at court, he still labored as a goldsmith, and made many beautiful shrines for saints, and holy vessels for churches. The Devil tempted St. Eloy, as he did so many of the saints ; and it is said of him, as of St. Dunstan, that he seized the Devil's nose with his hot tongs. One of the miracles attributed to this saint, and represented on the exterior of Or-San-Michele at Florence, is that a horse being brought to him to be shod, which was possessed by the Devil, he cut off the leg and quietly put on the shoe ; this being done, he made the sign of the cross, and replaced the leg, to the great astonishment of all. He is patron of Bologna and Noyon, of goldsmiths and all other metal-workers, and of farriers and horses. December 1, A. D. 659.

St. Elphege. See St. Alphege.

St. Enurchus, or **Evurtius,** was sent into France by the pope, to attend to the redeeming of captives. The people were electing a Bishop of Orleans. A dove alighted twice upon the head of Enurchus ; **and this was considered as showing so remarkable sanctity in him**

that he was made bishop, which office he held more than twenty years. One of the miracles which he did, was this : when laying the foundations of his Church of the Holy Cross, he directed the men to dig in a certain place, and they there found a pot of gold which was enough to pay for the church. September 7, A. D. 310, or about that time.

St. **Ephesus** and St. **Potitus** are represented on the walls of the Campo Santo at Pisa, and seem to belong especially to that city. St. Ephesus was an officer under Diocletian, and was sent to destroy all the Christians in Sardinia. But he was so warned by a dream that he himself became a Christian, and turned his arms against the pagans. He suffered martyrdom with his friend Potitus.

St. **Ephrem of Edessa,** who on account of his writings is one of the Fathers of the Greek Church, was a hermit of Syria. He is represented in a very curious Greek picture, called the "Obsequies of St. Ephrem," which is one of the best representations of hermit life. Greek festival, January 28 ; Latin, February 1, about 378.

St. **Erasmus of Formia** (*Ital.* Sant' Elmo, or Erasmo ; *Sp.* St. Ermo, or Eramo ; *Fr.* St. Elme). This saint suffered a most horrible martyrdom under Diocletian at Formia, now Mola di Gaeta. He so withstood all common tortures that he was cut open and his entrails wound off like a skein of silk on wheels. He was a bishop, and is represented as such, with the implement of his torture in his hand. There is an altar dedicated to him in St. Peter's, over which a mosaic represents his death. It is a copy of a picture by Poussin. St. Erasmus is invoked, under the name of Elmo, by the mariners on the shores of the Mediterranean, in Spain, Sicily, and Calabria, and is believed to have power over the tempests. At Naples a monastery and fortress bear his name. June 3, A. D. 296.

St. **Ercolano** (Herculanus) was Bishop of Perugia at the time of the invasion of the Goths under Totila. He labored hard and encouraged the people through the siege of Perugia ; and when the city was taken, by order of Totila, he was beheaded on the ramparts. He was thrown into the ditch, and was found lying beside a dead child, who was buried in the same grave with the saint.

St. **Ethelberga.** Of this saint there is little known but the one fact that she was the abbess of the first Benedictine nunnery in England, which was at Barking, in Essex. October 11.

St. Ethelreda. This saint is also called St. Audrey. She was the foundress of the magnificent cathedral of Ely. Her father was Ina, King of the East Angles; and when she married Toubert, or Touberch, Prince of the Gervii, the isle of Ely was her dowry. She had a second husband, Egfrid, King of Northumbria; but after living with him in a state of continency for twelve years, she took the veil at Coldingham, with his consent. King Egfrid later repented his complaisance, and attempted to drag her from the convent. She fled to a rocky point called St. Ebb's Head. Egfrid pursued her; but the tide suddenly rose, and made the rock inaccessible. He married another wife. St. Ethelreda crossed the Humber with two virgins, who watched beside her while she slept, and had a miraculous dream, in which she thought that her staff, being stuck in the ground, had put forth branches and leaves, and become a large tree. A miracle was wrought through her intercession about four hundred years after her death. A wicked man, Britstan, being very sick, repented, and desired to dedicate himself to God in the monastery at Ely; but on his way thither he was arrested and imprisoned. He implored the aid of St. Ethelreda; and at night she, with St. Benedict, came to him, and when she touched his fetters they fell from his feet. After being buried sixteen years in the common cemetery, she was placed in a beautiful sarcophagus of marble, which was probably a relic of the Romans, but the people believed it to have been wrought for the saint by angels. June 23, A. D. 679.

St. Eugenia was the daughter of Philip, Proconsul of Egypt in the reign of Commodus. She was very learned. She was converted to Christianity, put on the attire of a man and became the monk Eugenius. She went to Rome, and was put to death in the time of the Emperor Severus. December 25.

St. Eulalia of Merida. The story of this saint is told by Prudentius. Eulalia was but twelve years old at the time of the publication of the Edict of Diocletian. She went to the prefect who judged the Christians, and reproached him for his cruelty and impiety. The governor immediately seized her, and placed on one side of her the instruments of torture, and on the other the offerings for the idol. She trampled the offerings under her feet, threw down the idol, and spat at the judge. She was then tortured to death; and as she died, a white dove issued from her mouth and flew to heaven. She is much venerated in Spain, and is buried at Merida. Another St. Eulalia is buried at Barcelona. December 10.

St. Eunomia. See St. Afra, of Augsburg.

St. Euphemia of Chalcedonia (*Gr.* 'Αγ. Εὐφημία; signification, "praise;" *Ital.* Sant' Eufemia; *Fr.* Ste. Euphémie). She was a Greek saint, and in the Eastern Church is styled Great; for such was the fame of her beauty and her courageous endurance. There is a homily upon St. Euphemia among the writings of Asterius, who wrote about 400. She suffered death not far from Byzantium, about 307. She was very beautiful in person. After suffering many tortures she was thrown to the lions, who licked her feet, and refused to do violence to her. Priscus, her judge, was so enraged at this that one of the soldiers, who desired to please him, killed the maiden with his sword. Within a century from the time of her death there were many churches dedicated to her, both East and West. In Constantinople alone, there were four. Leo the Iconoclast ordered her relics to be cast into the sea, but they appeared again in the island of Lemnos. Hence different portions of her remains were carried to many places. September 16, A. D. 307.

St. Eustace (*Lat.* S. Eustatius; *Ital.* Sant' Eustachio; *Fr.* St. Eustache). Before his conversion this saint was called Placidus. He was captain of the guards of the Emperor Trajan. He was a lover of hunting; and one day when in the forest, he pursued a white stag, which fled and ascended a high rock. As he looked, he saw between the horns of the stag a radiant cross, and on it an image of Jesus. He fell on his knees; and the figure on the cross spake, announcing itself as the image of the Redeemer, and demanding of Placidus that he should believe. He answered, " Lord, I believe." He was then told that he should suffer much for Christ, but he declared himself ready to do so. He returned to his home, and was baptized, together with his wife and two sons, and was called Eustace. Misfortune soon came. His property was taken by robbers, and his wife carried away by pirates, and he wandered in poverty with his sons. One day he wished to cross a stream, and swam over with one child, whom he left on the bank, while he returned for the other. But when he was in the midst of the river, there came on one side a lion, and on the other a wolf, which beasts carried off the two boys. He went to a village where he labored for his support for fifteen years. Then the Emperor Adrian required the services of Placidus, and searched for and found him. He was put again at the head of his troops, and his honors restored to him with new power and riches. But his heart was lonely, and he mourned for his wife and sons. Now these had been rescued from their dangers, and at last they were all again restored to the husband and father. Then Eustace believed that his troubles were ended; but soon Adrian ordered a great sacrifice to the gods, and when Eustace refused to join in it with his household, he and they were shut up in a brazen bull, and a fire kindled beneath it. September 20, A. D. 118.

St. Eutropia. See St. Afra of Augsburg.

St. Ewald the Black and **St. Ewald the Fair.** These saints were twins, and Saxons. They left England in the days of St. Boniface, and went to Ireland to study. They then went through Friesland to Westphalia, where they were to preach. Here they sought out the prince of the country, and asked permission to preach; but they were murdered by the barbarians and their bodies thrown into the river. A light was seen above the spot where they sank, and their remains were recovered and carried to Cologne, and buried in the church of St. Cuthbert. They are patron saints of Westphalia. October 3, A. D. 695 or 700.

St. Fabian was made Bishop of Rome in A. D. 236. Eusebius says he was chosen because a dove alighted on him while the people and clergy were choosing a pope. At the time he was a stranger to all present. He died a martyr in the persecution of Decius. January 20, A. D. 250.

St. Faith (*Lat.* Sancta Fides) was born at Agen, in Aquitaine. She had great beauty, but from her youth was insensible to the pleasures of the world. Because she refused to sacrifice to Diana, while still very young, Dacian, the Prefect of the Guards, subjected her to the most fearful tortures. She was beaten with rods, then half roasted on a brazen bed, and at length beheaded. The crypt of old St. Paul's in London was dedicated in the name of this saint. October 8, A. D. 290.

St. Faustinus and **St. Jovita** (*Ital.* San Faustino and San Giovita). These were brothers who were converted by the preaching of St. Apollonius, at Brescia. They preached, ministered to the poor, and zealously devoted themselves to a Christian life. By the command of Adrian they were seized and thrown into the amphitheatre.

The beasts did not attack them, and they were afterwards beheaded outside the walls of Brescia, of which city they are the patron saints. February 15, A. D. 121.

St. Felicitas and her seven sons (*Ital.* Santa Felicità, *Fr.* Ste. Félicité). This saint was of an illustrious Roman family. A widow, she devoted herself to the care of her children and to pious works of charity. She had great riches, which made her enemies anxious to accuse her as a Christian, so that they might share the spoils; and her influence having converted many to her religion, gave them a powerful plea against her. It was in the time of the great persecution of the Emperor Marcus Aurelius Antoninus. She was called before Publius, a prefect of Rome, who commanded her to sacrifice to the gods she had rejected. This she refused; and when reminded of the dangers which threatened her children no less than herself, she replied that they knew how to choose everlasting life in preference to eternal death. She witnessed the tortures and death of her sons, never ceasing to exhort them to remain true to their faith. Januarius, the eldest, was scourged with thongs loaded with lead. Felix and Philip were beaten with clubs. Sylvanus was thrown from a rock. Alexander, Vitalis, and Martial were beheaded. After they had all thus suffered martyrdom, Felicitas praised God that she had been the mother of seven sons whom he had deemed worthy of being saints in Paradise. Her only desire was that she might quickly follow them. But she was kept four months in prison, with the hope that this prolonged agony would destroy her faith and strength. But at length she was tortured and killed. Some say she was beheaded, and others that she was thrown into a caldron of boiling oil. In art she is represented as hooded or veiled like a widow, with the martyr's palm, and surrounded by her sons. The representations of this Roman family are sometimes confounded with those of the Seven Maccabees and their heroic mother. The only guide by which to distinguish them is that St. Felicitas was not recognized in the East. In Byzantine art, seven young martyrs with their mother probably represent the Jewish rather than the Roman saints. St. Felicitas is the patroness of male heirs. November 23, A. D. 173. Festival of the sons, July 10.

St. Felix de Valois. November 20, A. D. 1212. See St. John de Matha.

St. Felix de Cantalicio. This saint was a native of Citta Ducale in Umbria. He was born in 1513. His parents were very poor. He entered a Capuchin monastery as a lay brother. Later, he was appointed questor of a community of the Capuccini at Rome. Here for forty-five years he daily begged the bread and wine for his convent; and such an abundance of these articles was never known there as during his time. On this account he is represented in the habit of his order, with a beggar's wallet, which has two ends like a purse thrown over his shoulder, to contain the alms begged for his convent. The extreme devotion of his life won the admiration not only of the brotherhood to which he belonged, but of all who saw him. It is told of him that as he went out on a stormy night to beg, he met an angelic child, who gave him a loaf of bread and a benediction, and then vanished from his sight. He was the first saint of the Order of the Capuchins. May 21, A. D. 1587.

St. Felix, or **Felice.** July 12. See St. Nabor.

St. Ferdinand of Castile (*Sp.* El Santo Rey, Don Fernando, III.). This great king, warrior, and saint was the eldest son of Alphonso, King of Leon, and Berengaria of Castile. His parents were separated by the pope, because being within the prohibited degrees of consanguinity they had married without a dispensation. Their children were, however, declared legitimate. Berengaria returned to her father's court and lived in retirement. The influence she had over Ferdinand was extraordinary, and endured throughout his life. Berengaria, when she came into possession of Castile, gave up her rights to her son; and when at his father's death he succeeded to the throne of Leon, the two kingdoms were united. Ferdinand was married to Joan, Countess of Ponthieu, who was as obedient and loving to Berengaria as was her husband. Ferdinand fought bravely against the Moors, and expelled them from Toledo, Cordova, and Seville. It is related that, at the battle of Xeres, St. Iago appeared at the head of the troops, conducting the fight. Thousands of Moors were slain; but there was only a single Christian killed, and he was one who had gone into battle refusing to forgive an injury. At the time of his death, Ferdinand was planning an expedition to Africa. In the "Annals of the Artists of Spain" we are told that he founded the cathedral of Burgos, "which points to heaven with spires more rich and delicate than any that crown the cities of the Imperial Rhine. He also

8

began to rebuild the cathedral of Toledo, where during four hundred years artists swarmed and labored like bees, and splendid prelates lavished their princely revenues to make fair and glorious the temple of God intrusted to their care." When urged to tax his people, in order to recruit his army and fill his empty coffers, he made a reply which reflects more glory upon his character than his victories or his cathedral foundations can give. "God," he replied, "in whose cause I fight, will supply my need. I fear more the curse of one poor old woman than a whole army of Moors!" He died as a penitent, with a cord about his neck and a crucifix in his hand. His daughter, Eleonora, was married to Edward I. of England. She possessed the piety and courage of her father. It was she who sucked the poison from her husband's wound. When the decree of Ferdinand's canonization reached Seville, the greatest religious festival ever held there took place. He was buried in the cathedral of Seville. There is a portrait of St. Ferdinand, thought to be authentic, in the convent of San Clemente at Seville. May 30, A. D. 1152.

St. Filomena (*Lat.* Sancta Philumena; *Fr.* Ste. Philomène). Within the past half-century this saint has grown in the popular veneration. We know but little of her history. In the beginning of the present century a sepulchre was discovered in the Catacomb of Priscilla at Rome, in which was the skeleton of a young girl. It was adorned with various rudely painted symbols, and a portion of an inscription, the beginning and end of which were gone. It was, —

—lumena pax te cum fi—

These remains, supposed to be those of a martyr, were placed in the treasury of relics in the Lateran. When Pius VII. returned from France, a Neapolitan prelate was sent to congratulate him. One of the priests in his train begged for some relics, and the remains described above were given him. The inscription was translated, "Saint Philomena, rest in peace. Amen." Another priest had a vision, in which St. Filomena appeared with great glory, and revealed that she had suffered death for preferring the Christian faith and her vows of chastity to marriage with the emperor, who wished to make her his wife. Afterwards a young artist was told in a vision that this emperor was Diocletian; but it is also thought to have been Maximian. The priest, Francesco da Lucia, carried the relics to Naples. They were inclosed in a case made in the form of a human body. It was dressed in a crimson tunic and a white satin petticoat. The face was painted, a garland of flowers put upon the head, and a lily and a javelin, with its point reversed, emblematic of her purity and her martyrdom, were put in her hand. She was placed, half sitting, in a sarcophagus with glass sides. After lying in state in the church of Sant' Angiolo, she was carried in procession to Mugnano, amid the acclamations of the people, miracles being wrought through her intercession on the way. Jewels of great value now decorate her shrine. Her image is found in Venetian churches, in Bologna and Lombardy. At Pisa, in the church of San Francisco, and at Paris, in the churches of St. Gervais and St. Merry, there are chapels dedicated to St. Filomena. August 10, A. D. 303.

St. Fina of Gemignano. This saint was not a martyr, but received the honor of canonization on account of her patience and cheerfulness during long and fearful sufferings from disease. She labored as long as was possible for the relief of all the poor and wretched within her reach. She is scarcely known outside of the little town where she dwelt; but there her name is typical of patience, fortitude, and charity. She was warned of her death by a vision of St. Gregory, whom she especially honored, and at the moment of her decease all the bells in San Gemignano were miraculously tolled. As her body was borne to the grave, she raised her hand as if to bless her aged nurse, who from that time was healed of a troublesome disease. The life of this saint is beautifully painted on the chapel dedicated to her in the cathedral of San Gemignano. March 12, A. D. 1253.

St. Flavia was the daughter of a Roman Senator, and sister of St. Placidus, who was taken by his father at the age of five years to Subiaco to be educated by St. Benedict. Flavia followed her brother to Sicily, whither he was sent by his superior; and she, with Placidus and thirty of their companions, was slain by the barbarians outside of their convent near Messina. This narrative is not considered authentic by later Benedictine writers. October 5, A. D. 540.

St. Florian is one of the guardian saints of Austria. He was a Roman soldier, who, on account of his Christian faith, was put to death in the reign of Galerius. A millstone was tied round his neck, and he was thrown into the river Enns. Many miracles were attributed to him, one of which was that with a single pitcher of water he extinguished a large conflagration. Representations of this saint are frequent in Austria and Bohemia, and often adorn pumps and fountains. A magnificent monastery bearing his name commemorates his life and its painful end. A picture of St. Florian by Murillo is in St. Petersburg. May 4.

St. Francesca Romana. The church dedicated to this saint in Rome was the scene of her fasts and vigils, and is now called by her name rather than that of Santa Maria Nuova, which it formerly bore. In the Torre de' Spechi is her convent, which has been the best school in all Rome for the girls of the higher classes. Her father was Paolo di Bassi. She was born in 1384. She was extremely pious from her childhood, and would have preferred the veil of the nun to that of a bride; but her father married her to Lorenzo Penziano, a rich nobleman. She shunned the society and pleasures belonging to her station, and devoted herself as far as possible to a religious life. Every day she recited the entire Office of the Virgin, and went in disguise to her vineyard beyond the gate of San Paolo to gather fagots, which she brought on her head into the city, and distributed to the poor. During the lifetime of her husband she collected the company of women whose superior she became after his death. Their principal labor was teaching the young, but they took no vows. She spent so much time in prayer that she was frequently interrupted by the demands of her family. Once it happened that while reciting the Office of Our Lady she was called away by her husband four times at the same verse; when she returned the fifth time, she found this verse written on the page in golden letters. This was done by her guardian angel, who attended her in visible form. Many wonderful works are attributed to her: the raising of a dead child to life, the staying of an epidemic by her prayers, and the increasing of bread by prayer, when there was not enough for the inmates of her convent, are some of the most important evidences of her favor with Heaven. She died of a fever at the house of her son, whom she had gone to comfort on the occasion of some affliction. Her fame was not by any means confined to Rome, but was great in all Italy. March 9, A. D. 1440.

St. Francis of Assisi (*Lat.* S. Franciscus, Pater Seraphicus; *Ital.* San Francisco di Assisi; *Fr.* St. François d'Assise). St. Francis — called "the Seraphic," from the fervor of his love of God — was the founder of the Franciscans, one of the three Mendicant Orders of Friars. His father, Pietro Bernardone, was a rich merchant. His baptismal name was Giovanni, but he acquired the title of Francisco (the Frenchman) from the fact that his father had him early instructed in French as a preparation for business. In his early years Francis was beloved for his generous and compassionate heart, and remarkable for his prodigality and love of gay pleasures. In a quarrel between the inhabitants of Assisi and those of Perugia, Francis was taken a prisoner, and held for a year in the fortress of Perugia. On reaching home he was very ill for months, and it was during this sickness that his thoughts were turned to the consideration of the wicked uselessness of the life he had lived. Soon after his recovery he met a beggar, in whom he recognized one who had formerly been known to him as rich and noble. Francis exchanged garments with him, putting on the tattered cloak of the mendicant, and giving him the rich clothes in which he was dressed. That same night, in a vision, he thought himself in a splendid apartment, filled with all kinds of arms and many rich jewels and beautiful garments, and all were marked with the sign of the cross. In the midst of them stood Christ, and he said, "These are the riches reserved for my servants, and the weapons wherewith I arm those who fight in my cause." From this Francis thought that he was to be a great soldier, for he knew not as yet of the spiritual weapons Christ gives his disciples. Afterwards, when he went to pray in the half-ruined church of San Damiano, as he knelt he heard a voice say, "Francis, repair my Church, which falleth to ruin." Taking this in its most literal sense, he sold some merchandise, and took the money to the priests of San Damiano for the repairing of their church. His father was so angry at this that Francis hid himself many days in a cave in order to escape from his wrath. When he returned to the city he was so changed, so haggard, and so ragged that he was not recognized, and the boys hooted him in the streets. His father believed him insane, and confined him; but his mother set him at liberty, begging him at the same time to return to his former mode of life, and not to provoke his father and disgrace them all by his strange conduct. At length his father took him to the bishop, to be advised by him. When Francis saw the holy man, he threw himself at his feet; he abjured his former life, and throwing his garments to his father said, "Henceforth I recognize no father but Him who is in heaven." The bishop wept with joy and admiration; and taking a coarse cloak from a beggar who stood by, he gave it to Francis, who gladly received it as the first fruits of the poverty on which he was resolved. He was now twenty-five years old. The first labor he performed was that of caring for the lepers in a hospital; and this was considered the more meritorious from the fact that before this he could not look on a leper without fainting. The next years of his life were passed in prayer and penitence. He wandered among his native mountains, begging alms, every penny of which that could be spared, after supplying the imperative wants of nature, was given for the reparation of churches. He dwelt in a cell near the chapel of Santa Maria degli Angeli; and several disciples, attracted by the fame of his piety, joined him here. Poor as he was, his attention was attracted to the text, "Take nothing for your journey, neither staves, nor scrip, nor bread, nor money, nor two coats;" and he cast about him to see if he had any superfluous comfort. He could find nothing that he could spare, save his leather girdle; and casting that away, he used instead a rope of hemp. This has also been adopted by his followers, from which peculiarity they are called Cordeliers. He preached with marvellous effect, and soon had many followers. Among his female converts none are of greater note than the first, Clara d'Assisi, the beautiful "Gray Sister," the foundress of the order of the "Poor Clares." The vow of poverty, the most complete and absolute, was insisted upon by St. Francis in his order. One of the Franciscan legends is that as he journeyed to Siena, "St. Francis was encountered by three maidens in poor raiment, and exactly resembling each other in age and appearance, who saluted him with the words, 'Welcome, Lady Poverty!' and suddenly disappeared. The brethren not irrationally concluded that this apparition imported some mystery pertaining to St. Francis, and that by the three poor maidens were signified Chastity, Obedience, and Poverty, the beauty and sum of evangelical perfection; all of which shone with equal and consummate lustre in the man of God, though he made his chief glory the privilege of Poverty." This legend has been illustrated by various pictures; and Giotto made Poverty the bride of St. Francis, who did indeed woo the sufferings which she brought with a more devoted ardor than that with which most lovers seek the sweet and sometimes glittering rewards of more attractive mistresses. At length Francis went to Rome to obtain the confirmation of his order. At first the pope, Innocent III., considering him as an enthusiast, repulsed his suit. That night in a vision the pope saw the walls of the Lateran tottering, and only kept from falling by the support of the very man to whom he had refused his aid. He immediately sent for Francis, and granted him the privileges he desired for his order, and full permission to preach. The saint then built cells for his disciples near his own, and gave his brotherhood the name of "Fratre Minori," to signify that humility should be their chief attribute, and that each should strive for the lowest rather than the highest place; while in his own eyes he was himself the basest of men, and he desired to be thus considered by all. His fear that his disciples should seek any other than the deepest poverty led him to forbid the building of any convent, and he commanded that the churches built for them should be the plainest and most inexpensive. Another marked peculiarity of this holy man was what is termed the "gift of tears." He wept and prayed continually, on account of his own sins and those of the whole world; and he resolved to go to preach to the heathen, and indulged the hope that God would grant him the great glory of martyrdom. He attempted at different times to go to Syria and Morocco; but he was driven back by a storm the first time, and the second, was arrested by sickness. But he did many miracles, and founded convents in Spain. Ten years after the establishment of his order he held the first general chapter, at which there assembled five thousand friars. They seemed to be thoroughly inspired with the spirit of their leader, and even he found it necessary to caution them against an excess of austerities and penances. From this assembly he sent forth missionaries to other countries, and again started himself to preach in Egypt and Syria. He succeeded only in reaching Damietta, where he was taken before the sultan, who would neither allow him to preach nor to suffer martyrdom in his territory, but sent him back to Italy, looking upon him with Oriental

regard and kindness as one insane or wanting in mental capacity.
A few years later, having obtained from Pope Honorius the confirmation of his order, he resigned his office as its head, and retired
to a cave on Mt. Alverna.   Here he had many trances and visions of our Saviour and his Blessed Mother ; and it is said that
the saint was sometimes raised into the air in ecstatic raptures of
devotion.   Here it was that he had the wonderful vision, and
received the especial marks of the favor of God, which obtained for
him the title of "the Seraphic."   "After having fasted for fifty days
in his solitary cell on Mt. Alverna, and passed the time in all the
fervor of prayer and ecstatic contemplation, transported almost to
heaven by the ardor of his desires ; then he beheld as it were a
seraph with six shining wings, bearing down upon him from above,
and between his wings was the form of a man crucified.   By this
he understood to be figured a heavenly and immortal intelligence,
subject to death and humiliation.   And it was manifested to him
that he was to be transformed into a resemblance to Christ, not by
the martyrdom of the flesh, but by the might and fire of Divine
love.   When the vision had disappeared and he had recovered a
little from its effect, it was seen that in his hands, his feet, and
side he carried the wounds of our Saviour."   It is piously believed that these wounds were really impressed by a supernatural
power.   Francis in his humility desired to conceal the great favor
and honor he had received ; but notwithstanding his endeavors, they
were seen by many.   His last days were full of suffering.   As death
approached, he commanded those about him to place him on the
earth.   He attempted to repeat the 141st Psalm, and at the last
verse, " Bring my soul out of prison," he breathed his last.   He had
requested that his body should be buried with those of the malefactors, at a place called the Colle d' Inferno, outside the walls of his
native city.   This request was fulfilled ; and as his body was borne
past the church of San Damiano, Clara and her nuns came out to
take a farewell of all that remained of him who had shown her the
way of religious perfection.   Only two years passed before his canonization, and the beginning of the church which covers his remains.
These are still entire and unviolated in their tomb, which is in a
hollow rock.   There are numberless legends connected with St.
Francis, a vast number of which are written in picture history.

Many of them are illustrative of his love for all lower animals and even insects; for he felt that love of Christ in our hearts should fill us with sympathy for everything that can suffer pain or be benefited by kindness. When in Rome, he had always with him a pet lamb. One instance of his tenderness is thus given : " One day he met a young man on his way to Siena to sell some doves which he had caught in a snare ; and Francis said to him, 'O good young man! these are the birds to whom the Scripture compares those who are pure and faithful before God ; do not kill them, I beseech thee, but give them rather to me;' and when they were given to him he put them in his bosom and carried them to his convent at Ravacciano, where he made for them nests, and fed them every day until they became so tame as to eat from his hand. And the young man had also his recompense ; for he became a friar and lived a holy life from that day forth." There is in the church at Assisi a picture of St. Francis, painted soon after his death, under the oversight of those who had known him well. It has almost the value of a portrait. October 4, A. D. 1226.

St. Francis de Paula. This saint, though a native of Paola, a small city of Calabria, is more important in France, and in connection with French history, than in his own country. It was for this saint that Charles VIII. founded the church of the Trinità-di-Monti at Rome. At the age of fifteen he went with his parents to the shrine of St. Francis at Assisi. On his return he became a hermit and lived in a cave near Reggio. His fame drew disciples about him, for whom the people built cells and a little chapel. He called his little band Minimes, or the Hermits of St. Francis, for they followed the Franciscan Rule, adding to it even greater austerities than it already prescribed. They kept Lent all the year ; and they called themselves, as their title indicated, the least of all the disciples of the Church. King Louis XI. of France had heard of the many wonderful cures performed for the sick by St. Francis de Paula, and sent for him to come to him at Plessis-le-Tours, where he was dying. The saint felt that he had not been summoned in the right spirit, and refused to go, when Louis applied to Sixtus IV. for aid in the matter. At the command of the pope, Francis went ; and he was received at Amboise, by the dauphin and court, with all the honors possible. When he arrived at the castle, the king knelt to him, and prayed him to obtain from God the return of health and a longer life. Francis rebuked him, and reminding him that God alone could give life or death, and that submission to his will was man's first duty, he performed for him the last offices of religion. Francis was kept in France by Charles VIII. and Louis XII., and his influence was very great. The courtiers gave him the title of " Le Bon-homme," in derision of his mode of life ; but this became the title of his order in France, where his disciples became very popular, and were to the people "Les Bons-hommes" in every good sense of the term. Francis was godfather to Francis I., and they are frequently represented together in pictures. Before the Revolution the effigies of Francis de Paula were very common in France. His tomb was broken open by the Huguenots in 1562, and his remains burnt. He died at Plessis, and Louise d'Angoulême prepared his winding-sheet with her own hands. April 2, A. D. 1507.

St. Francis Borgia stands as the third among the saints in the Jesuit Order. He belonged to a family much less illustrious in their lives than in their rank. In youth he was surrounded with all that would seem to make life desirable and happy, — wealth, station, and power, — while he was fondly in love with his beautiful wife, and had a large family of promising children. But he was thoughtful and melancholy, and cherished in his heart deep religious feeling. Circumstances combined to strengthen these emotions. His friend Garcilasso de la Vega the poet died ; he was himself more than once brought near to death by severe sicknesses. At length, when the Empress Isabella died, it was his duty to raise the winding-sheet from her face at the moment the body was to be buried, and to swear to the identity of the remains. He did so, and took the oath,[1] and at the same moment made another vow to forsake the service of the kings of earth, and from that hour to serve only the King of Heaven. But this he could not fulfil literally at once. He was Governor of Catalonia, and administered the affairs of the province with great care and faithfulness ; but through the acquaintance of a Jesuit named Aroas, he became a disciple of Loyola, and corresponded with him. His wife died, and he then resolved that after providing for his children in the best manner, he would renounce the world and

[1] " Francis, not knowing the face, would only swear it was the body of the empress, because, from the care he had taken, he was sure no one could have changed it upon the road." — The Rev. ALBAN BUTLER.

every human affection. For six years he devoted himself to settling
his affairs, and then went to Rome and became an humble Jesuit.
He gave all his life and energy to perfecting the system of education
of his order. For seven years he was general of his society, being the
third who had held that high position. He died at Rome, and was
buried in the Gesu, near Loyola; but his grandson, the Cardinal Duke
of Lerma, removed his remains to Madrid. October 10, A. D. 1572.

St. Francis de Sales. This saint is famous for his religious
and devotional writings, which are held in great esteem by Protes-
tants as well as by those of his own church. He was also known as
very charitable, tolerant, and gentle towards those who disagreed
with him, as well as to those who lived wicked lives. When others
remonstrated against his charitable tenderness, he would reply,
"Had Saul been rejected, should we have had St. Paul?" He was
made Bishop of Geneva in 1602. He was very remarkable for his
personal beauty and the almost angelic expression of his face. January 29, A. D. 1622.

St. Francis Xavier was a Jesuit, the friend and disciple of Ignatius Loyola, and was sent by him as the leader of a band of missionaries to the Indies. He was of an illustrious family, and was born at
a castle in the Pyrenees. He studied at Paris. When young he was
gay and enthusiastic in his temperament, and it was not until after
many struggles that he was able to take the vow of obedience; but
having once done so, he was more ardent in the pursuit of his duties
than he had ever been in seeking the accomplishment of his own
desires and ends. He was thirty-five years old when he went to the
East, and most of the remainder of his life was spent in Japan. His
self-denial and sufferings were very great. He conferred the sacrament of baptism upon an almost innumerable host. He appointed
other teachers over their churches, and saw the crucifix erected in
many homes, as a token of the results of his labors, and of the
conversion of the heathen to the religion of Christ. He would have
hailed the martyr's death with joy; but his end, though a painful one,
was not brought about by the violence of his enemies. He attempted
to go to China. He had succeeded in reaching the island of Sancian,
where he was seized with fever and died. He suffered very greatly
for want of shelter and care. He regretted that he must die a natural
death, but at length experienced a willingness to depart in God's way,

and renounced his desire for martyrdom, since it was not according to the Divine will. His body was interred near the shore, where there is still a cross to mark the spot; but his remains were carried to Malacca and finally to Goa, where a magnificent church has been built to the honor of this great missionary saint. December 3, A. D. 1550.

St. Frediano of Lucca (*Lat.* S. Frigdianus). This saint was a native of Ireland. He was made Bishop of Lucca, to which place he had gone, in 560. The principal occurrence in his life which is represented in art is his turning the course of the river Serchio, when it threatened to deluge Lucca. This he did by drawing a harrow along the ground, and the river followed the course he thus marked out. His whole history is painted in a church at Lucca called by his name.

St. Gabriel (*Gr.* °Αγ. Γαβριήλ; *Lat.* S. Gabriel; *Ital.* San Gabriello, San Gabriele, L' Angelo Annunziatore; *Fr.* St. Gabriel). This saint, whose name signifies "God is my strength," is the second in rank among the archangels, or the seven who stand before God (Rev. viii. 2). His name is mentioned four times in the Bible (twice in Daniel, viii. 16 and ix. 21; twice in Luke, i. 19, 26), and always as a messenger bearing important tidings. First, he announces to Daniel the return of the Jews from their captivity, and then makes him understand the vision which shows forth the future of the nations; next he tells Zacharias of the child that should be born to his old age; and lastly he comes to tell the mother of our Lord that she is *the one* highly favored and blessed among women. These four authenticated acts make him of such importance as to command our deepest interest in all relating to him; and in addition to these, he is believed to have foretold the birth of Samson and that of the Virgin Mary. He is venerated as the angel who especially watches over childbirth. The Jews believe him to be the "chief of the angelic guards" and the keeper of the celestial treasury. The Mohammedans regard him as their patron saint, as their prophet declared him to be his inspiring and instructing angel. Thus is he high in the regard of Jews, Christians, and the followers of Islam. It is as the angel of the Annunciation that he is most frequently and beautifully represented. The spirit in which these pictures are painted has varied with the spirit in which the individual artist has contemplated the mystery. In the earlier ones both the angel and the Virgin are standing, and the manner of the Virgin is expressive of humility and of reverence for a superior being. She has been painted as kneeling; but after the thirteenth century *she* becomes the one to be exalted. She is from this time most frequently depicted as the *Regina angelorum;* and as his queen, Gabriel often kneels before her. His attributes are the lily; a scroll inscribed "Ave Maria, Gratia Plena;" a sceptre; and sometimes an olive branch, typical of the "peace on earth" that he announced. March 18.

St. Gaudentius of Novara was the bishop, and is now the patron saint, of that city.

St. Gaudenzio (*Lat.* S. Gaudentius) was one of the early bishops of Rimini. His effigy is found on its coins. He was scourged and then stoned to death by the Arians. He is patron saint of Rimini. October 14, A. D. 359.

St. Geminianus (*Ital.* San Geminiano). This saint was Bishop of Modena in the middle of the fifth century. So great was the fame of his miracles that he was sent for to go to Constantinople to heal the daughter of the emperor, who was possessed of an evil spirit. It is supposed to have been the Princess Honoria. (See Gibbon, 35th chapter.) When Modena was threatened with destruction by Attila, King of the Huns, it was spared on account of the intercession of Geminianus; and after his death he preserved the cathedral from destruction by a flood. He is represented on the coins of Modena, and honored as the patron saint and especial protector of that city.

St. Geneviève of Brabant. The story of this saint has furnished the subject for poems, plays, and pictures which are anything but religious in their character. But there are many representations in art of her romantic life and sufferings. She was the wife of Count Siegfried, who was led by his steward to believe her to be wanting in fidelity to himself and her marriage vows. He ordered her to be executed, but those charged with the task of putting her to death left her alone in the forest. She gave birth to a child, which was nursed by a white doe. A number of years having passed, her husband, while hunting, came to her abode. Explanations made plain her innocence. The steward was really put to death, while the wife was restored to her home and happiness. There is a picture by

Albert Dürer, which is sometimes called by the name of Geneviève of Brabant, but it is in truth the "Penance of St. John Chrysostom."

St. Geneviève of Paris (*Eng.*; *Ger.*; *Ital.* Santa Genoveva). This saint is essentially French, and is of very great importance and interest among those of mediæval times. The village of Nanterre was her birthplace, and during her childhood she tended a flock of sheep. When she was about seven years old, St. Germain spent a night at Nanterre. The inhabitants flocked to receive his benediction. When his eyes rested on the little Geneviève, he was made aware, by inspiration, of the sanctity of her character, and the glory for which God had chosen her. He talked with her; and with a manner which at her age showed her to be the especial child of God, she declared her wish to be the bride of Christ. The bishop hung round her neck a coin marked with the cross, and blessed her as one consecrated to God's service. From this time she felt herself separated from all worldly, and devoted to all heavenly interests. There are many wonderful stories told of her childhood. On one occasion her mother struck her in a fit of anger. She was struck blind, and remained so for two months, when Geneviève made the sign of the cross above the water with which she bathed her mother's eyes, and her sight was restored. Geneviève remained with her parents during their lives, and then went to a relative in Paris. Although she did not enter a convent, she vowed perpetual chastity at fifteen years of age. It was many years before God gave any public and unmistakable proof of his approbation of Geneviève. During this time, while some venerated her for the holiness of her life, others regarded her as a pretender and hypocrite. She was tormented, too, by demons, who, among other things, constantly blew out the tapers she had lighted for her nightly vigils. But she was able to relight them by faith and prayer. At length Attila threatened the destruction of Paris, and the people in their alarm would have fled from the city; but Geneviève addressed them, begged them to remain, and assured them that God would not allow this pagan to overcome his followers. According to her prediction, Attila suddenly changed the course of his march, probably by directing it to Orleans. And again, when Childeric took possession of Paris, and the people suffered from want of food, Geneviève took command of the boats which went to Troyes for aid; a tempest arose, which was calmed by her prayers, and the provisions they had received were brought safely to the sufferers. Childeric respected the saint; and Clovis, even before he thought of being a Christian, venerated Geneviève, and granted any requests she made of him. She influenced his own mind and that of his queen, Clotilde, so that the first Christian church was erected, and the pagan worship forbidden in the city of Paris. The church was that which is now known by her name. Ever after the miraculous manifestation of her power in the deliverance of Paris from Attila, her prayers were sought by all the people, whenever they were afflicted, and the miracles attributed to her intercession are both wonderful and numerous. One of these was the staying of a plague called the *mal ardent*. Until 1747 there was a little church called Ste. Geneviève des Ardents, which was on the site formerly occupied by the house of the saint. She was eighty-nine at the time of her death. She was buried beside King Clovis and his wife. St. Eloy made a magnificent shrine for the remains of the saint; but in the Revolution it was destroyed, and the relics burned in the Place de Grève. January 3, A. D. 509.

St. George of Cappadocia (*Lat.* S. Georgius; *Ital.* San Giorgio; *Fr.* St. Georges, le très-loyal Chevalier de la Chrétienneté; *Ger.* Der Heilige Jorg, Georg, or Georgius). The legend of this saint, as most frequently represented in art, makes him a native of Cappadocia. His parents were of the nobility, and Christians. He was a tribune in the army, and lived in the time of Diocletian. There is a disagreement as to the scene of his most wonderful conquest of the dragon. By some it is believed to have been Selene in Libya; by others, Berytus, or the modern Beyrout, of Syria; but the story is ever the same. Being on his way to join his legion, he came to a city whose inhabitants were in great terror on account of a terrible dragon who lived in a marsh near the walls. This fearful monster had devoured all the flocks and herds; and the people, having retired into the city, gave him daily two sheep until all they had were gone. Then, in order to prevent his approaching the city, they commenced to send out daily two children to be devoured by this insatiable monster. Terrible as this was, it was better than that he should come near them; for his breath poisoned the air for a great distance about him, and all who breathed it perished from its pestilential effects. The children were chosen by lot, and were less than fifteen years old. Now the king had a daughter, named Cleodolinda, whom he loved exceedingly. At length the lot fell to her. The king offered all he possessed, even to the half of the kingdom, that she might be spared; but the people said that as it was by his own edict that their children had been sacrificed, there was no reason for allowing him to withhold his own, and they threatened to take the princess by force, if she was not delivered to them. Then the king asked that she might be spared to him eight days longer. This was granted, and at the end of that time Cleodolinda went forth to the sacrifice, clothed in her royal robes, and declaring herself ready and willing to die for her people. She moved slowly towards the place where the dragon came daily for his victims, and the way was strewed with the bones of those who had already perished. Just then St. George came to the place; and seeing her tears he stopped to learn the cause of her sorrow. When she had told him, he said, "Fear not, for I will deliver you!" but she replied, "O noble youth! tarry not here, lest thou perish with me! but fly, I beseech thee!" Then St. George answered, "God forbid that I should fly! I will lift my hand against this loathly thing, and will deliver thee through the power of Jesus Christ!" Even as he spoke, the dragon approached them. Then the princess again entreated him, "Fly, I beseech thee, brave knight, and leave me here to die!" But St. George, making the sign of the cross, rushed to combat with the monster. The struggle was terrible, but at length the dragon was pinned to the earth by the lance of the brave knight. He then bound the dragon with the girdle of the princess; and giving it to her, she was able to lead the conquered beast like a dog. In this manner they approached the city. The people were filled with fear; but St. George cried out, "Fear nothing; only believe in the God through whose might I have conquered this adversary, and be baptized, and I will destroy him before your eyes." And in that day were twenty thousand people baptized. After this St. George slew the dragon and cut off his head. Then the king gave him great treasures; but he gave all to the poor, keeping absolutely nothing for himself, and he went on his way towards Palestine. This was the time of the publication of the Edict of Diocletian, which declared the persecution against the Christians. All who read it were filled with terror, but St. George tore it down and trod it into the dust. For this he was carried before the proconsul Dacian, and condemned to eight days' torture. He was first bound to a cross, and his body torn with sharp nails; next he was burned with torches, and then salt rubbed into his wounds. Seeing that all these horrible and devilish cruelties had no power to vanquish the spirit of the saint, Dacian sent for an enchanter, who invoked the aid of Satan, and then poisoned a cup of wine which St. George drank. Before doing so, however, he made the sign of the cross, and the poison had no effect on him. The magician was converted to Christianity by this miracle, and upon his declaring the fact, was immediately beheaded. St. George was next bound upon a wheel filled with sharp knives, but two angels descended from heaven and broke it in pieces. They then put him in boiling oil. Believing that he must be now subdued, he was taken by the judges to assist at the sacrifices in the heathen temple. Crowds came to witness his humiliation. But the saint knelt down and prayed, and instantly there came thunder and lightnings from heaven. The temple was destroyed; the idols were crushed; while the priests and many of the people perished. Now at last Dacian commanded him to be beheaded. He met death with joy and courage. The story of St. George bears great resemblance to those of Apollo, Bellerophon, and Perseus, while the destruction of the temple and his persecutors is very like that of the Philistines when they called Samson out of his prison-house to make sport for them. The Greeks give St. George the title of the GREAT MARTYR, and his veneration is very ancient in the East. In Europe he was but little honored until the Crusades, when the aid he obtained for Godfrey of Boulogne made Christian soldiers seek his patronage. When Richard I. made holy war, he placed his army under the protection of St. George, and from this time he has been patron saint of England. His feast was ordered to be kept through all England in 1222, and the Order of the Garter was instituted in 1330. April 23, A. D. 303.

St. Gereon, one of the commanders of the Theban legion. When St. Maurice and the greater part of the legion were at Aganum (now St. Maurice), Gereon with his command reached Cologne. Verus, the prefect, by order of the Emperor Maximin, commanded them to renounce Christianity. Upon their refusal, Gereon and many of his soldiers were put to death and thrown into a pit. The veneration of this saint extends back to the fourth century, but he is little heard of outside the part of Germany which was the scene of his sufferings.

Many of the representations of St. Gereon are in sculpture, and upon the stained glass in the oldest of the German churches.

St. Gervasius and **St. Protasius** (*Ital.* Gervasio e Protasio; *Fr.* St. Gervais et St. Protais). These were twin brothers who suffered martyrdom in the time of Nero. They were sent bound to Milan, together with Nazarius and Celsus. They were brought to Count Artesius, who bade them sacrifice to the idols. They refused; and Gervasius was condemned to be beaten to death with scourges loaded with lead, and Protasius to be beheaded. A man named Philip obtained their bodies and buried them in his garden, where they remained until the place of their burial was revealed in a vision to St. Ambrose. It happened after this wise. When Ambrose built the church at Milan (A. D. 387), the people were anxious that it should possess holy relics. While Ambrose was much engaged in thought of this, and very anxious to please his people, he went to the church of Sts. Nabor and Felix to pray; while there a trance came over him, and in it he beheld St. Paul and St. Peter; and with them were two young men, clothed in white and of wonderful beauty. It was revealed to Ambrose that these were two martyrs who had been buried near the spot where he was. Assembling his clergy, he made search, when the two bodies were found. They were gigantic in size. The heads were separate from the bodies, and in the tomb was a writing which told their story. These sacred relics were carried in procession to the basilica; and those sick ones who could touch them as they passed along the street were instantly healed. Among these was a man named Severus, who had been many years blind. As he touched these bones his sight was restored. This miracle was seen by so many of the people that it established beyond a question the great efficacy of these relics. St. Ambrose, as he laid them beneath the altar, blessed God and cried out, "Let the victims be borne in triumph to the place where Christ is the sacrifice : he upon the altar, who suffered for all; they beneath the altar, who were redeemed by his suffering." The enemies of Ambrose accused him of duplicity in this matter, and even said that Severus was bribed to play a part; but the authority of the father was sufficient to inspire confidence in spite of all, and the church was dedicated to SS. Gervasius and Protasius. Since the death of St. Ambrose this church, which is one of the most wonderful and famous in the world, is called Sant'

Ambrogio Maggiore. The veneration of these saints was introduced into France, where they became very popular, by St. Germain in 560. He carried some part of the relics to Paris. Many cathedrals and parish churches have been dedicated to them. It would be natural to expect their pictures to represent their vast size, but this is not the case. There are few Italian and many French paintings of them. June 19, A. D. 69.

St. Giles (*Gr.* Άγ. Γίλλος; *Lat.* S. Ægidius; *Ital.* Sant' Egidio; *Fr.* St. Gilles; *Sp.* San Gil) was an Athenian of royal blood. Some miracles which he performed — one of which was throwing his mantle over a sick man, and thus healing him — had gained for him the veneration of the people. St. Giles left his country and became a hermit. After long wanderings he came to a cave in a forest near the mouth of the Rhone, about twelve miles south of Nismes. Here he subsisted upon herbs and wild fruits and the milk of a hind. This gave rise to his attribute of a wounded hind; for it came to pass that as a party, said by some to be that of the King of France and by others the King of the Goths, were hunting, this hind was pursued by the dogs. It fled to the cave and nestled in the arms of the saint. A hunter sent an arrow after it; and when they came to look in the cave, they found the holy man wounded by the arrow. Their sorrow was great, and they entreated his forgiveness even on their knees. He resisted all their endeavors to draw him out of the cave, and there he soon died. Above this cave was built a magnificent monastery. A city sprung up about it bearing the name of the saint, and the counts of that district were called Comtes de Saint-Gilles. The church, which still remains upon the spot, is an extraordinary remnant of the Middle Ages. It is covered with bas-reliefs on the outside, and has a remarkable staircase in the interior. Queen Matilda dedicated a hospital, which she founded outside of London, to St. Giles. This was in 1117; and the name now belongs to an extensive parish. In Edinburgh, too, the parish church, founded in 1359, bears his name.[1] He is patron saint of Edinburgh, of Juliers in Flanders, and of the woodland everywhere. September 1, A. D. 725.

Glastonbury, Abbey of. The origin of this famous abbey is lost in antiquity; but the legend connects it with the introduction of Christianity into England. The wondrous story tells that when

---

[1] St. Giles Cathedral, Edinburgh, is one of the very few that escaped the fury of the so-called Reformers in Scotland.

Philip, who was one of the twelve Apostles, came to France, he sent Joseph of Arimathea with his son and eleven other disciples to Britain. King Arviragus so admired the beauty of their lives, and so appreciated the dangers which they had overcome in their long journey from Palestine, that he gave them an island called Avalon. Here they built a church by twining wands, and consecrated a place of burial. They limited their number to twelve, and lived in imitation of the Master and his disciples. By their preaching many Britons were converted. It is a wonderful old place. It is here King Alfred found a refuge from his Danish foes. Here King Arthur was buried; and here ever bloomed the "mystic thorn" at the feast of the Nativity. It was upon the strength of this legend that the kings of England claimed precedence of the kings of France in the religious councils of Pisa, Constance, Siena, and Basle. They declared that Joseph of Arimathea came to England in the fifteenth year after the assumption of the Virgin Mary, and that France received not the religion of Christ until the time of St. Denis; and that for this reason they did "far transcend all other kings in worth and honor, so much as Christians were more excellent than pagans."

Godfrey of Bouillon, Duke of Lower Lorraine, was born in Brabant about 1060. As the eldest son of the Count of Boulogne, he succeeded to the government of the duchy in 1076. Godfrey served with gallantry in the armies of Henry IV., and his fame was such that when the Crusades broke out he was appointed to the command of the principal army, and started for the Holy Land, with his brothers Eustace and Baldwin. The united armies numbered six hundred thousand men, but in two years were reduced to forty thousand. In the sieges of Nice and Antioch, and in all encounters with the enemy, Godfrey bore his full share, and at the taking of Jerusalem, in 1099, was proclaimed king. He declined this title, saying, "I will never accept a crown of gold where my Saviour wore a crown of thorns." He called himself the "Defender and Guardian of the Holy Sepulchre." A little later, Godfrey defeated the Saracens in the plain of Ascalon, thus possessing himself of all Palestine. He labored to organize a State, but died in July, 1100, justly lamented for his piety, valor, and kingly virtues. An equestrian statue of Godfrey de Bouillon stands in a square of Brussels. Tasso sang his praises in "Jerusalem Delivered;" and history declares him to have been of "first rank both in war and council."

St. Grata. See St. Adelaide.

St. Gregory, or **Gregory the Great** (*Lat.* S. Gregorius Magnus; *Ital.* San Gregorio Magno or Papa; *Fr.* St. Grégoire; *Ger.* Der Heilige Gregor; signification, "watchman"), was born at Rome in 540. His father, Gordian, was a senator. His mother, Sylvia, was a woman of remarkable character; and like many of the mothers of that time who bore sons destined to act a great part in the world, she had a vision, while he was but a baby in her arms, in which St. Antony revealed to her that this son should be the head of the Church on earth. When grown, he studied and practised law, and was prætor of Rome for twelve years. His character was, however, always deeply religious; and the piety of the mother seemed to have descended to, and become intensified in, the son. On the death of his father he devoted his wealth to religion and charity. He made his home on the Celian Hill a hospital and monastery, and dedicated it to St. Andrew. He then took a cell within it, and taking the habit of a Benedictine devoted himself to studies which fitted him for his duties in later life. This monastery is now the church of San Gregorio. When a fearful plague broke out in Rome, Gregory devoted himself to the nursing of the sick. One of the victims of the pestilence was Pope Pelagius. The people desired to have Gregory as his successor; but he shrank from the office, and even entreated the emperor not to assent to the wishes of the people. When finally his election was confirmed, he hid himself in a cave away from Rome. Those who sought for him were led by a celestial light about the place where he was hidden, and he was brought again to Rome. He soon proved that the choice of the people had been a wise one. He was the most humble of men, and was the first to call himself "servant of the servants of God." He reformed the Church music, composing what is called from him the Gregorian Chant. He showed a spirit of toleration and charity far in advance of his time; disapproved all persecution;[1] restored the synagogues of Terracina and Cappadocia to the Jews, from whom they had been taken; liberally redeemed captives out of his own means, and further, authorized the sale of the sacred vessels for their redemption; and was so moved

---

[1] St. Gregory said that conversions to the faith should not be forced, but won by meekness and charity.

at the sight of some wretched British captives who were to be sold in Rome that he sent missionaries to England. He had a special devotion to the souls in Purgatory; and set the example of a trental of masses, or masses on thirty successive days, for the faithful departed. St. Gregory always zealously asserted the obligation of celibacy among the clergy, extending this law to the subdeacons, who had before been ranked among the clergy of the minor orders. He felt the responsibilities of his office so much as to consider himself literally the father of each individual of the Church; and on one occasion he fasted, and interdicted himself from any sacerdotal function for several days, because a beggar had died in the streets of Rome. His charities were boundless. When a monk, a beggar asked alms at the monastery, and receiving something came again and again, until Gregory had nothing to give him but a silver porringer which Sylvia had sent to her son, and this he did not withhold. When pope, he had twelve poor men to sup with him each evening. One night he saw thirteen at his table, and calling his steward he demanded the reason of this. The steward replied, after counting, " Holy Father, there are surely twelve only !" Gregory said no more, but at the end of the meal he asked the uninvited one, " Who art thou?" and he said, " I am the poor man whom thou didst formerly relieve ; but my name is the Wonderful, and through me thou shalt obtain whatever thou shalt ask of God." Then Gregory believed him to be an angel, and some say, Christ himself. The painting of this legend is called the "Supper of St. Gregory." John the Deacon, who was his secretary, has left an account in which he declares that he has seen the Holy Spirit seated on his shoulder in the shape of a dove while he wrote. This explains why the dove is so frequently one of his attributes. "The Mass of St. Gregory," so often painted, is founded upon a legend that as the saint was officiating some one doubted the real presence in the elements. The saint prayed, and instantly a vision was revealed of the crucified Saviour, surrounded with all the instruments of his passion, upon the altar.

Another painting represents the miracle of the Brandeum. The Empress Constantia sent to Gregory, desiring a portion of the relics of St. Peter and St. Paul. Gregory replied that he dared not disturb the holy remains, and sent her the Brandeum, or a part of a

consecrated cloth which had enfolded the remains of St. John the
Evangelist. The empress, disappointed, rejected this gift with scorn.
Then Gregory, wishing to show that it was not so much the relics
themselves as the faith of the believer which worked the miracles,
placed the cloth upon the altar, and after praying pierced it with a
knife, and blood flowed from it as from a living body. A legend
popular in the Middle Ages, but quite unauthorized by the Church,
and contrary to Catholic faith and the Scriptures, — "out of Hell
there is no salvation," — recounts the manner in which St. Gregory
released Trajan from torment. It is said that on one occasion, when
that emperor was leading his soldiers to battle, he was stopped by
a poor widow who threw herself before his horse and demanded
vengeance for the death of her son, who had been killed by the son
of Trajan. The emperor promised that on his return he would attend to her request. "But, sire," replied the widow, "should you be
killed in battle, who then will do me justice?" "My successor,"
said Trajan. Then she replied, "What will it signify to you, great
emperor, that any other than yourself should do me justice? Is it
not better that you should do this good action yourself than leave
another to do it?" Then the emperor alighted, and listened to her
story, and finally gave his own son to her, and bestowed upon her a
large dowry. Now, as Gregory was one day thinking of this story,
he became greatly troubled at the thought that so just a man as this
should be condemned as a heathen to eternal torments, and he
entered a church and prayed most earnestly that the soul of the
emperor might be released from suffering. While still at prayer,
he heard a voice saying, "I have granted thy prayer, and I have
spared the soul of Trajan for thy sake; but because thou hast sup-
plicated for one whom the justice of God had already condemned,
thou shalt choose one of two things : either thou shalt endure for
two days the fires of purgatory, or thou shalt be sick and infirm for
the rest of thy life." This is given as the explanation of the great
weakness and the many infirmities suffered by Gregory; for he chose
the sickness in preference to the two days of purgatory. St. Gregory's health was always frail, but the last two years he lived he was
not able to leave his couch. His bed and a scourge with which he
kept his choristers in order are still preserved in the church of the
Lateran. March 12, A. D. 604.

St. Gregory Nazianzen (*Gr.* Ἀγ. Γρηγορέω Θεολόγος; *Lat.*
Sanctus Gregorius Nazianzenus; *Ital.* San Gregorio Nazianzeno;
Fr. St. Grégoire de Naziance; *Ger.* S. Gregor von Nazianz) was
born about 328. His father, St. Gregory, was Bishop of Nazianzum.
St. Nonna was his mother, and St. Gorgonia and St. Cesarea his
sisters. While a boy, he had a dream which in a great measure
influenced all his course in life. He thought there came to him
two celestial virgins of dazzling beauty. They took him in their
arms and kissed him. He asked who they were, and whence they
came; and one said, "I am called Chastity, and my sister here is
Temperance. We come to thee from Paradise, where we stand continually before the throne of Christ, and taste ineffable delights.
Come to us, my son, and dwell with us forever." When this was
said, they flew into heaven. He stretched out his arms to them and
awoke. This dream was to him like a direct command from God,
and he took vows of perpetual continence and temperance. He
studied in Athens, where St. Basil and Julian, who, though a Cæsar,
is only known as the Apostate, were his fellow-students. He was
not baptized until almost thirty years old. He devoted himself to
religious studies, and to austerities which he declared were ever
most repugnant to him; but their virtue was increased by this fact.
He was ordained priest by his father, became his conjutor, and succeeded to his bishopric in 362. He was invited to preach against
the Arians at Constantinople. The disputes ran very high, and
were carried on by all classes, and even by the women, who argued
in public as well as at home. Gregory was small in stature, and
every way insignificant in his appearance. At first he was stoned
by the Arians and Apollinarists when he attempted to speak; but
his earnest eloquence overcame all obstacles, and though he at
length gave up the bishopric of Constantinople, to which Theodosius had appointed him, intent thus to promote peace in the Church,
yet he had gained the respect of enemies and the confidence of
friends. Leaving Constantinople, he lived on a small estate of his
father's in great strictness and self-denial. St. Gregory Nazianzen is
the earliest Christian poet of whom we have any knowledge. In
his retirement he wrote hymns and lyrics which express all the struggles and aspirations of his naturally intense and imaginative nature.
May 9, A. D. 390.

St. Gudula (called in Flemish Sinte-R-Goelen, and in Brabant St. Goule or Ergoule) is the patroness of the city of Brussels. She was daughter of Count Wittiger. Her mother was St. Amalaberga, and St. Gertrude of Nivelle, her godmother. She was educated by the latter. There are many miracles told of her, but that of her lantern is the one best known and oftenest painted. It was her custom to go to the church of Morselle in the night, to pray. It was a long distance, and she carried a lantern. Satan was very envious of the influence she gained by her piety, and frequently put out her light, hoping that she might be misled. Whenever this was done, Gudula immediately relighted it by her prayers. January 8; about A. D. 712.

St. Guthlac of Croyland. The legend relates that "at the time of his birth a hand of ruddy splendor was seen extended from heaven to a cross which stood at his mother's door." Although this was thought to indicate future sanctity in the child, he grew up wild and reckless, and at the age of sixteen organized a band of robbers, and was their leader; but "such was his innate goodness that he always gave back a third part of the spoil to those whom he robbed." He lived thus eight years, when he saw the sinfulness of his life, and the remainder of it was devoted to penance and reparation. At the monastery of Repton he learned to read, and studied the lives of the hermits. He went at length to a wilderness, where he encountered evil spirits as numerous as those which tormented St. Anthony. St. Bartholomew was the chosen saint of Guthlac, and he often came to his rescue and drove the demons into the sea. The place of his retreat was a marsh. At first a little oratory was built, and at length a splendid monastery was raised on piles, and dedicated to St. Bartholomew. The marshes were drained, and labor and cultivation changed the appearance of the place, and put to flight the demoniac inhabitants of the former solitude. The ruins of Croyland Abbey cover twenty acres. The country is again neglected, and an unhealthy marsh. The remains of a beautiful statue said to be St. Guthlac may still be seen. St. Pega, the sister of St. Guthlac, gave to the monastery the whip of St. Bartholomew. April 11, A. D. 714.

St. Helena. It is admitted, by all authorities, that St. Helena was born in England; but the exact location of her birthplace is a matter of dispute and doubt. She married Constantius Chlorus ("the Pale"), and was the mother of Constantine the Great. When her son embraced Christianity, she was much distressed, and declared that it would have been better to be a Jew than a Christian. When she at length became a convert, her wonderful zeal and the great influence she had over the mind of her son conduced to the rapid growth and strength of the Church. In 326 she made a journey to Palestine; and when she arrived at Jerusalem, she was inspired with a strong desire to discover the cross upon which Christ had suffered. The temple of Venus stood upon the spot supposed to be the place of the crucifixion. She ordered this to be taken down, and after digging very deep, three crosses were found. There are two accounts given of the manner in which the true cross was selected. Some say the crosses were all applied to a sick person, — the first two without effect, while the third caused an instantaneous cure. Others say that they were carried to a dead person, and that at the application of the third, life was restored. Constantine erected a basilica upon the spot where the crosses were found, and it was consecrated September 13, A. D. 335. The following day was Sunday, and the Holy Cross was elevated on high for the veneration of the people. It is with the "Invention [Finding] of the True Cross," as it is called, that St. Helena is most frequently considered; but she did many other things which either in themselves or in their effects still speak of her active zeal for the Church. The Church of the Nativity at Bethlehem was erected by her in 327, and is the oldest church edifice in the world. August 18, A. D. 327.

Heliodorus. This narrative is found in the third chapter of the second book of Maccabees.[1] It is frequently illustrated in art, and is as follows. When Onias was high-priest at Jerusalem and all was prosperous there, a certain Simon, governor of the temple, became disaffected toward Onias on account of some trouble in the city. So he went to Apollonius, the governor of Cœle-Syria, and told him "that the treasury in Jerusalem was full of infinite sums of money, so that the multitude of their riches which did not pertain to the account of the sacrifices, was innumerable, and that it was possible to bring all into the king's hand." When Apollonius told

[1] The Catholic Church includes the Books of Maccabees among the inspired writings.

this to the king, he sent his treasurer Heliodorus, with commands to bring to him this money. When Heliodorus came to Jerusalem, he was courteously received by Onias; and when he told him what they had heard, and demanded if it was true that so much money was there, the high-priest told him that much money was indeed there, but that it was laid up for the relief of widows and orphans. Some of it belonged to Hircanus the son of Tobias, and it did not in truth belong to the treasury, as the wicked Simon had said. Onias said that the sum was four hundred talents of silver and about two hundred talents of gold, and "that it was altogether impossible that such wrong should be done unto them that had committed it to the holiness of the place, and to the majesty and inviolable sanctity of the temple, honored all over the world." But Heliodorus said that the king had given him commands that in any wise it should be brought into the treasury. So a day was set when he should receive the treasure. Now the whole city was in agony, and the priests prostrated themselves before the altars and entreated God that this should not be allowed, and called unto Him that the law which he had made should be kept, and the money preserved for those who had committed it to their care. "Then whoso had looked the high-priest in the face, it would have wounded his heart; for his countenance and the changing of his color declared the inward agony of his mind. For the man was so compassed with fear and horror of the body, that it was manifest to them that looked upon him what sorrow he had now in his heart. Others ran flocking out of their houses to the general supplication, because the place was like to come into contempt. And the women girt with sackcloth under their breasts, abounded in the streets, and the virgins that were kept in, ran, some to the gates, and some to the walls, and others looked out of the windows. And all holding their hands toward heaven made supplication. Then it would have pitied a man to see the falling down of the multitude of all sorts, and the fear of the high-priest being in such an agony. But in spite of all, Heliodorus went to the temple to execute his intentions. Now, as he was there present himself with his guards about the treasury, the Lord of spirits and the Prince of all power caused a great apparition, so that all that presumed to come in with him were astonished at the power of God, and fainted and were sore afraid. For there appeared unto them an horse with a terrible rider upon him, and adorned with a very fair covering, and he ran fiercely and smote at Heliodorus with his fore feet, and it seemed that he that sat upon the horse had complete harness of gold. Moreover, two other young men appeared before him, notable in strength, excellent in beauty, and comely in apparel, who stood by him on either side, and scourged him continually, and gave him many sore stripes. And Heliodorus fell suddenly unto the ground, and was compassed with great darkness; but they that were with him took him up and put him into a litter. Thus him, that lately came with a great train and with all his guard into the said treasury, they carried out, being unable to help himself with his weapons; and manifestly they acknowledged the power of God. For he by the hand of God was cast down, and lay speechless without all hope of life. But they praised the Lord that had miraculously honored his own place; for the temple, which a little afore was full of fear and trouble, when the almighty Lord appeared was filled with joy and gladness. Then straightway certain of Heliodorus' friends prayed Onias, that he would call upon the Most High to grant him his life, who lay ready to give up the ghost. So the high priest, suspecting lest the king should misconceive that some treachery had been done to Heliodorus by the Jews, offered a sacrifice for the health of the man. Now, as the high-priest was making an atonement, the same young men in the same clothing appeared and stood beside Heliodorus, saying, 'Give Onias, the high-priest, great thanks, insomuch that for his sake the Lord hath granted thee life. And seeing that thou hast been scourged from heaven, declare unto all men the mighty power of God.' And when they had spoken these words, they appeared no more. So Heliodorus, after he had offered sacrifice unto the Lord, and made great vows unto him that had saved his life, and saluted Onias, returned with his host to the king. Then testified he to all men the works of the great God, which he had seen with his eyes. And when the king asked Heliodorus who might be a fit man to be sent yet once again to Jerusalem, he said : 'If thou hast any enemy or traitor, send him thither, and thou shalt receive him well scourged, if he escape with his life; for in that place no doubt there is an especial power of God. For He that dwelleth in heaven hath his eye on that place and defendeth it, and he beateth and destroyeth them that come to hurt it.' And the things concerning Heliodorus and the keeping of the treasury fell out on this sort."

St. Henry of Bavaria was born in 972. He married Cunegunda, daughter of Siegfried, Count of Luxembourg. Both are saints, and both obtained that glory by their perfect and entire devotion to the Church. This was so marked a feature of Henry's character and reign that it caused a revolt among the princes of his empire, as they thought he had no right to lavish so much treasure in the service of religion. Henry was no less a soldier than a Christian. After defeating the seditious nobles, he restored to them their possessions and treated them as if nothing had occurred. When he went to war to subject and convert Poland and Sclavonia, he put himself and his army under the protection of SS. Laurence, George, and Adrian. He girded on the sword of the last-named, which had long been preserved in Walbeck Church. The legend relates that the three saints were visible, fighting by the side of Henry, and that through their aid he conquered. The church of Merseberg was built to commemorate this victory. He also fought in Italy, and drove the Saracens from Apulia. Henry had an especial veneration for the Virgin; and when on his expeditions, upon entering a place, always repaired first to some church or shrine dedicated to her. On one occasion, at Verdun, he was seized with such a disgust and weariness of his imperial life and duties that he desired to become a monk. The prior told the emperor that his first duty would be obedience. When Henry declared himself ready to obey, the prior commanded him to retain his office and discharge its duties. Henry and Cunegunda together founded and richly endowed the cathedral and convent of Bamberg in Franconia, as well as many other religious edifices in Germany, and also in Italy. After they had been united several years, during which time, by mutual consent, they lived in the strictest continence, Cunegunda was suspected of unfaithfulness to her husband. Henry believed in the purity of his wife, and she would have looked upon these reports as trials sent from heaven to test her patience, but she felt that her position demanded her justification, and she asked to be allowed the trial by ordeal. She walked over burning ploughshares uninjured. Henry tried to make amends to her by showing her the greatest respect and tenderness, but she preferred to retire to the cloister; to which he consented. Henry died in 1024, and was buried in the cathedral of Bamberg. His wife then took the Benedictine habit, and led a life of incessant prayer and labor, working with her hands for the poor and sick. She died in 1040, and was interred by the side of Henry. Festival of Henry, July 14. Cunegunda, March 3. For St. Henry, see also St. Laurence.

St. **Herman-Joseph** was a native of Cologne. His mother was very poor, but brought up her son piously. It was his custom every day, when on his way to school, to go to the church of St. Mary, and repeat his prayers before the image of Our Lady. One day, when an apple was all he had for his dinner, he offered it humbly to the Virgin; and the legend says that this so pleased "Our Blessed Lady, that she put forth her hand and took the apple and gave it to our Lord Jesus, who sat upon her knee; and both smiled upon Herman." When still young, Herman took the habit of the Premonstratensians. He had many beautiful visions, in one of which the Virgin descended from heaven, and putting a ring on his finger called him her espoused. From this vision he acquired the additional name of Joseph. April 7, A. D. 1236.

St. **Hermengildus** was the son of King Leovigild, and during the contest between the Catholics and Arians he was put to death by his father for relinquishing the Arian faith. He is one of the most famous Spanish martyrs. The *chef-d'œuvre* of Herrera is the apotheosis of this saint. He is carried into glory, while St. Isidore and St. Leander stand on each side, and the young son of Hermengildus gazes upwards as his father is borne to heaven. The saint holds a cross, and wears a cuirass of blue steel and a scarlet mantle. April 13, A. D. 586.

St. **Hilarion.** See St. Donato of Arezzo.

St. **Hilary** (*Ital.* Sant' Ilario; *Fr.* St. Hilaire) was Bishop of Poitiers. Although French, he is greatly reverenced in Italy, and is one of the patrons of Parma, where it is said a part of his relics repose. January 14, A. D. 363.

St. **Hilda of Whitby** was the great-granddaughter of King Edwin. She was abbess of Whitby, and celebrated for her piety and learning, and the excellent training which she gave all under her charge. Six bishops were elected out of the monastery of men, at Streaneshalch, which was under her jurisdiction. She attended a council held at her monastery. Her wisdom was so great that kings and princes sought her guidance. She was venerated by the people, and many wonderful miracles are attributed to her. Fossils having the shape of coiled serpents have been found which were believed to have been venomous reptiles changed by the prayers of St. Hilda. Bede thus tells of her death : " And in the year of the incarnation of Our Lord, 680, on the 17th of November, the abbess Hilda, having suffered under an infirmity for seven years, and performed many heavenly works on earth, died, and was carried into Paradise by the angels, as was beheld in a vision by one of her own nuns, then at a distance, on the same night : the name of this nun was then Bega ; but she afterwards became famous under the name of St. Bees." November 18, A. D. 680.

St. Hippolytus (*Ital.* Sant' Ippolito ; *Fr.* St. Hyppolyte ; *Gr.* Ἅγ. Ἱππόλυτος : signification, " one who is destroyed by horses," of which animal this saint is the patron). There is great obscurity in the legends of Hippolytus. He was a Roman soldier, and was appointed a guard over St. Laurence. He became a Christian from the influence of his prisoner, and his entire family were also converted. After the fearful martyrdom of St. Laurence, Hippolytus took the body and buried it. On account of this he was accused of being a Christian, which he denied not, but declared himself ready to meet any death rather than deny his Saviour. He saw nineteen of his family suffer death, among whom was his aged nurse, Concordia, who was so bold in declaring her faith that she was scourged to death, while the others were beheaded. Hippolytus was tied to the tails of wild horses, and thus torn to pieces. The Brescians claim that his relics repose in the convent of Santa Giulia. The legends also say that in the eighth century his remains were carried from Rome to the church of St. Denis, and on this account he is a popular saint in France. August 13, A. D. 258.

Holofernes. See Judith.

St. Hubert of Liége was a very gay nobleman. He was of Aquitaine, and lived at the court of Pepin d'Heristal. He participated in all the pleasures of the court, but was especially fond of the chase, and even hunted on the days appointed by the Church for fasting and prayer. As he hunted in the forest of Ardennes one day in Holy Week, there came to him a milk-white stag, with a crucifix between his horns. Hubert was overcome with awe and surprise. He became sensible of the wickedness of his life, and lived a hermit in the very forest where he had so often sought his amusement. There were bands of robbers, and large numbers of idolaters in and around the forest of Ardennes; and to them St. Hubert preached Christianity, and also introduced social reforms and civilization among them. At length he studied with St. Lambert, and became a priest. He was afterwards bishop of Liége. He requested that he might be buried in the church of St. Peter at Liége. Thirteen years after his death his remains were found to be perfect, and his robes unstained. The Benedictines of Ardennes desired to have his body, and it was removed to their abbey church about a century after his death. St. Hubert is patron of the chase and of dogs, and chapels are erected to him in the forests where the devout huntsman may pray. Bread blessed at his shrine is believed to cure hydrophobia. November 3, A. D. 727.

St. Hugh of Grenoble. This saint was Bishop of Grenoble at the time when St. Bruno founded the first Chartreuse. Hugh often retired to the monastery, and devoted himself to the life of the most humble and penitent brother. One of the miracles related as being performed by him is the changing of fowls into tortoises, when his Carthusian brethren could eat no flesh and could obtain no fish. It is said that Satan tempted Hugh forty years, by whispering continually in his ear doubts of God's Providence, on account of his permitting sin in the world. The saint fasted and did penance continually on account of this temptation, and it never obtained dominion over him sufficiently to weaken his faith in God. April 1, A. D. 1132.

St. Hugh, Bishop of Lincoln, was also a Carthusian. He was sent to England in 1126, and made Bishop of Lincoln. The cathedral, which had been destroyed by an earthquake, was rebuilt by St. Hugh. It is a fine specimen of the best Gothic architecture. Of all the munificent gifts of its founder, the only one remaining is the glass in one window, which is painted with scenes from his life. His proper attribute is a swan, typical of solitude, which was his delight. November 17, A. D. 1189.

St. Hugh, Martyr. The legend connected with this martyr relates that this child, who is represented as about three years old, was stolen by the Jews and crucified by them in ridicule of the

Saviour of the Christians, and in revenge for the cruelties which the Jews suffered in Christian countries. There are three other saints who have been canonized on account of having suffered the same martyrdom : St. William of Norwich, A. D. 1137 ; St. Richard of Pontoise, A. D. 1182 ; and St. Simon of Trent, A. D. 1472. The date of St. Hugh's death is in 1255, August 27.

St. Hyacinth belonged to the family of the Aldrovanski, one of the most noble in Silesia. He was educated in Bologna, and was distinguished not only for his intellectual superiority, but for his piety, and his prudence and judgment in everything he attempted to do. Soon after the completion of his studies, with his cousin Ceslas, he accompanied his uncle Ivo, who was Bishop of Cracow, to Rome. There they listened to the preaching of St. Dominick, which so moved the heart of Ivo that he besought the saint to send one of his order on a mission to his far-off and half-heathen country. But Dominick had no disciple to send, as all were engaged elsewhere. Then the young Hyacinth declared his intention to become a monk, and to preach to his ignorant and barbarous countrymen. Ceslas joined him, and they took the vows and the habit of the Dominicans in the church of St. Sabina at Rome. For forty years Hyacinth journeyed and preached in all the northern countries. It is said that his travels extended from Scotland to the Chinese boundaries. He founded various monasteries ; and it is related of him that, his convent in Kiov in Russia being sacked, he escaped, bearing the Pyx and the image of the Virgin, which he had taken from the altar. He reached the banks of the Dniester, pursued by the Tartars. The river was much swollen ; but being determined to preserve the precious objects from desecration by the pagans, he prayed to Heaven, and plunged into the river. The waters sustained him, and he walked over as on dry land. He died at his monastery in Cracow, to which he returned worn out by his labors and exposures. Anne of Austria, after her marriage, requested the King of Poland to send her some relics of St. Hyacinth. This he did, and they were placed in the Dominican Convent at Paris. From this time the saint became an object of veneration in France, where many pictures of him are seen. September 11, A. D. 1257.[1]

---

[1] St. Hyacinth, with his brother, St. Protus, is mentioned in the Liberian Calendar as having suffered martyrdom under Diocletian, A. D. 304.

St. Ignatius of Antioch (*Lat.* S. Ignatius; *Ital.* Sant' Ignazio; *Fr.* St. Ignace; *Ger.* Der Heilige Ignaz. His Greek title is θεοφόρος, "inspired"). Tradition says that this Ignatius is the same whom Jesus presented, when a child, to his disciples, with the words, "Whosoever shall receive one of such children in my name, receiveth me." He was a disciple of St. John the Evangelist, and the dear friend of Polycarp. It is also said that on account of his perfect purity of thought and life, he was permitted to hear the music of the angels, and that from the angelic choirs he learned the singing of God's praises in responses, which he introduced into his church after he was Bishop of Antioch. The Emperor Trajan, after one of his victories, commanded sacrifices to the gods in every province of his empire. The Christians refused to obey. Trajan came to Antioch, and sending for Ignatius charged him with the perversion of the hearts of his people, and promised him great favors if he would sacrifice in a pagan temple. But Ignatius scornfully refused, and said he would worship only the true and living God. Then Trajan asked how he could call Him living who had died upon a cross. But Ignatius spurned the idea of any God but the Lord, and Trajan commanded him to be imprisoned, and reserved for the amphitheatre at Rome. Ignatius rejoiced in his sentence, and set out on his journey with great courage. At Smyrna he saw Polycarp and other Christians, whom he encouraged to labor for the Church, and if need be to die for it. Arrived at Rome, on a feast day he was set in the midst of the amphitheatre. He addressed the people thus: "Men and Romans, know ye that it is not for any crime that I am placed here, but for the glory of that God whom I worship. I am as the wheat of his field, and must be ground by the teeth of the lions, that I may become bread worthy of being served up to him." According to one tradition he fell dead before the lions reached him, and his body was not touched by them. Another says that they tore him and devoured him, leaving only a few bones. Whatever remained of him was carried by his friends to Antioch; and it is said his relics were brought again to Rome, and placed in the church of St. Clement in 540, or near that time. February 1, A. D. 107.

St. Ignatius Loyola, who was the founder of the Order of the Jesuits, was in his youth a page in the court of Ferdinand the Catholic; and later, a brave and gay soldier. His family was one of

the most noble, and Ignatius was filled with pride of race, and was
vain of his handsome person. At Pampeluna, when thirty years old,
he was wounded in both legs; and the most torturing operations
which he endured in order to prevent lameness were in vain. While
confined by these sufferings, he read the Life of Christ and other
books, which resulted in his resolving to devote himself to the service
of the Blessed Mother of God, and that of her Son, whose soldier he
would be. As soon as possible he laid his sword and lance upon the
altar of Our Lady of Montserrat, and went to Manresa. Here he
was subject to great temptations, and Satan so tormented him with
doubts as to make him almost a maniac; but at length by celestial
visions he was restored to hope and confirmed in faith. He then
attempted to go to Jerusalem, but was prevented, and obliged to
remain in Spain. Not being allowed to teach on account of his
ignorance of theology, he submitted to a tedious course of study.
After a time he went to Paris, where he made the acquaintance of
five men who sympathized with his views, and who, with a few others,
formed themselves into a community under his direction. In addition to the usual monastic vows of poverty, chastity, and obedience,
they promised unreserved obedience to the pope, and to go to any
part of the globe whither he should send them. There were three
especial duties belonging to this order, which was called the "Company of Jesus:" first, preaching; second, the guidance of souls in
confession; and third, the teaching of the young. It was three years
before Ignatius obtained the confirmation of the order of which he
was the first General. He had many visions; he suffered great
temptations, and performed severe penances. Numerous miracles
have been wrought through his intercession. On his way to Rome,
it is said the Saviour appeared to him, bearing his cross and saying,
"Ego vobis Romæ propitius ero," and again an angel held before
him a tablet thus inscribed, "In hoc vocabitur tibi nomen." July
31, A. D. 1556.

St. Ildefonso or **Alfonso** (*Ger.* Der Heilige Ildephons). This
saint was one of the first Benedictines in Spain. He devoted himself
to the service of the Blessed Virgin, and wrote a book to prove her
perpetual virginity. He had two remarkable visions. In one St.
Leocadia, to whom he had vowed particular devotion, rose out of her
tomb to assure him of the favor of the Virgin, and of the approval of

his treatise in her praise. The saint wore a Spanish mantilla, and Ildefonso cut off a corner of it, which was preserved in her chapel at Toledo. Again, as he entered his church at midnight, at the head of a procession, he saw a great light about the high altar. All were alarmed save himself. Approaching, he beheld the Virgin seated on his ivory throne, surrounded by angels, and chanting a service. He bowed before her, and she said, "Come hither, most faithful servant of God, and receive this robe, which I have brought thee from the treasury of my Son." Then she threw over him, as he knelt, a cassock of heavenly texture, and the angels adjusted it. From that time he never occupied the throne or wore the garment. Archbishop Sisiberto died on account of his presumption in endeavoring to wear the robe and sit on the throne. Ildefonso was the archbishop, and is the patron saint of Toledo. January 23, A. D. 667.

Innocents, The Massacre of (*Ital.* Gli Innocenti Fanciulli Martiri, I Santi Bambini Martiri; *Fr.* Les Innocents; *Ger.* Die Unschuldigen Kindlein). These murdered infants are regarded with especial honor by the Church, as being the first Christian martyrs; and in a sense they are so. While we connect willingness to suffer for Christ with martyrdom, still it is true that unconsciously these children suffered for him, since it was on account of his birth that they were destroyed. They are represented with martyrs' palms. Sometimes they sustain the cross and the instruments of torture; again they surround the Madonna and Child, or are received into heaven by the Infant Saviour.

St. Isabella of France, who founded the convent at Longchamps, was sister to the saintly King Louis. She was educated with her brother by their mother, Blanche of Castile. She dedicated her convent to the "Humility of the Blessed Virgin," and gave to it all her dowry. As long as the convent existed, the festival of this saint was celebrated with great splendor. February 22, A. D. 1270.

St. Isidore the Ploughman (*Ital.* Sant' Isidoro Agricola; *Sp.* San Isidro el Labrador). The Spanish legend tells us that this saint could not read or write. His father was a poor laborer, and he himself was the servant of a farmer, named Juan de Vargas. Isidoro spent much time in prayer, and his master went one day to the field determined to forbid what he considered a waste of time. As he came near he saw two angels guiding the plough, while the saint knelt at his devotions near by. One day when his master thirsted, Isidore struck a rock with his goad, and pure water flowed out. He restored a child to life by his prayers, and performed various other miracles. May 10, A. D. 1170.

St. Isidore, Bishop of Seville, is styled the "Egregius Doctor Hispaniæ." His brother Leander, who preceded him in his bishopric, is called the "Apostle of the Goths," and they are both distinguished for their opposition to the Arian heresy. In Spanish pictures they are represented with Ferdinand of Castile and St. Hermengildus. In the church of St. Isidore, at Seville, is a magnificent picture (El Transito de San Isidoro), which represents him dying on the steps of the altar, having given all his property to the poor. Both these brothers are patron saints of Seville. April 4, A. D. 606.

St. Ives of Bretagne (*Ital.* Sant' Ivo ; on account of his profession, he is styled "Saint Yves-Helori, Avocat des Pauvres"). He belonged to a noble family, and from his mother, Aza du Plessis who conducted his early education, he derived his remarkable piety. As a boy he had an ambition to be a saint. He was but fourteen when he went to Paris, and here and afterwards at Orleans he devoted himself to legal studies. It has been said that lawyers have chosen him as their patron rather than pattern, as he was distinguished for his love of justice and its vindication under all circumstances. All through his years of study he gave many hours to religious duties, and especially to the labors of charity. He also at this time made a vow of celibacy. After returning home he studied theology. At the age of thirty he was made judge advocate. He always attempted to reconcile contending parties without resorting to law, and was always ready to plead for the poor without recompense. At length he entered the priesthood. Before assuming his priestly garments he gave those he had worn to the poor, and went out from the hospital where he had distributed them with bare head and feet. When a priest, he continued to be the Advocate of the Poor, and his double duties wore on his health. He died at the age of fifty. He is the patron of lawyers in all Europe. May 19, A. D. 1303.

St. James the Great (*Lat.* S. Jacobus Major ; *Ital.* San Giacomo, or Jacopo, Maggiore ; *Fr.* St. Jacques Majeur ; *Sp.* San Jago, or Santiago, El Tutelar). St. James, called the Major, the Great, or the Elder, is presented to us in two very different characters each being important and full of interest. First, in the Gospels as the brother of the Evangelist, and a near kinsman and favorite disciple of our Lord. He was much with Jesus, and present at many of the most important events in his life, such as his transfiguration and the agony in the Garden. Still, after the Saviour's ascension, nothing is told of him save that he was slain by Herod. But in his second character, as patron saint of Spain, we can make no complaint of the meagreness of the writings concerning him. The legends of him and his works would fill a volume; and he is said to have appeared after death at the head of the Spanish armies on thirty-eight different occasions. The Spanish legend, while it makes Santiago the son of Zebedee and a native of Galilee, does not represent him as a poor fisherman who followed that vocation for a livelihood, but as a nobleman's son who accompanied his father and brother in a boat, attended by servants, merely for pastime and sport. But so heavenly-minded was this young nobleman, that he was greatly attracted to Jesus, and chose to follow him in all his labors, witnessing his wonderful miracles and imbibing his spirit and teaching. After the ascension of Christ, James preached first in Judæa, and then, travelling as a missionary to bear the news of the Gospel to all the earth, came at last to Spain. Here he made few converts on account of the dreadful ignorance and idolatry of the people. At length, as he was standing one day on the banks of the Ebro, the Virgin appeared to him, and commanded him to build there a church under her patronage, assuring him that in the future this pagan land should devoutly worship her divine Son and honor herself. He obeyed; and having established the faith in Spain, he returned to Judæa, where he preached until his death many years after. The Jews were very bitter in their persecutions of James; and one Hermogenes, a sorcerer, especially opposed him. He sent one of his pupils, Philetus, to oppose him in argument. James signally defeated the Jew, and moreover converted him to the Christian Faith. This greatly enraged Hermogenes, who in revenge bound Philetus by his spells, and then told him to let his new teacher deliver him. Philetus sent his servant to James, who, when he heard his story, sent his cloak to his new disciple; and as soon as Philetus touched it he freed himself and went to James with haste. Hermogenes then sent a band of demons with orders to bind both

James and Philetus and bring them to him; but on the way they met a company of angels, who punished them severely. St. James then ordered the demons to bring Hermogenes bound to him. They obeyed, and besought him, as they laid the sorcerer at his feet, that he would be revenged for them and himself on a common enemy. But James assured them that his Master had taught him to do good for evil, and so released the prisoner. Hermogenes cast all his books into the sea, and entreated James to protect him from the demons who had been his slaves. The Apostle gave him his own staff; and from that time the persecutor became the earnest and faithful disciple, and preached the Faith with great fruit. At length the Jews were determined to destroy him, and sent to drag him before Herod Agrippa. His gentleness, and the miracles which he did on the way, so touched the soul of one of his tormentors that he begged to die with him. James gave him a kiss, saying " Pax vobis ; " and from this arose the " kiss of peace," which has been used as a benediction in the Church from that time.

The saint and his last convert were then beheaded. The legend of the dead body of James is far more wonderful than any of his life. His disciples took his body, but, not daring to bury it, put it on a ship at Joppa. Many accounts are given of this miraculous vessel. Some say it was of marble, but all agree that angels conducted it to Spain. In seven days they sailed through the Pillars of Hercules and landed at Iria Flavia, or Padron. They bore the body on shore and laid it on a large stone, which became like wax and received the body into itself. This was a sign that the saint desired to remain there. But the country was ruled by a very wicked queen, who commanded that they should place the stone on a car and attach wild bulls to it, thinking that they would dash it in pieces. But the bulls gently drew the car into the court of Lupa's palace. Then she was converted, and built a magnificent church to receive the body of James. Afterwards the knowledge of his burial-place was lost until the year 800, when it was revealed to a priest. The remains were removed to Compostella, which became one of the most famous of shrines, on account of the miracles wrought there. The Order of St. Jago was instituted by Don Alphonso for its protection, and was one of the most honorable and wealthy in all Spain. The fame of the shrine of Compostella spread over Europe, and in some years it was visited by a hundred thousand pilgrims. One of the most curious of the legends of this saint, and one frequently treated in art, is connected with three of these pious pilgrims. A German with his wife and son made a pilgrimage to the shrine of St. James, and lodged at Torlosa on the way. The son was a handsome youth, and the daughter of the Torlosa innkeeper conceived a wicked passion for him. He, being a virtuous young man, and moreover on a pious pilgrimage, repulsed her advances. She determined to revenge this slight to her charms, and hid her father's silver drinking-cup in his wallet. As soon as it was missed, she directed suspicion to the young pilgrim. He was followed, and the cup found in his sack. He was then taken to the judge, who sentenced him to be hung; and all that the family had was confiscated. The afflicted parents continued on their pilgrimage, and sought consolation at the altar of Santiago. On their return they stopped at the gibbet where their son had hung for thirty-six days. And the son spoke to them and said, "O my mother! O my father! do not lament for me; I have never been in better cheer. The blessed apostle James is at my side, sustaining me, and filling me with celestial comfort and joy." The parents, being amazed, hastened to the judge. He was seated at the table. The mother rushed in, and exclaimed, "Our son lives!" The judge mocked them, and said, "What sayest thou, good woman? Thou art beside thyself! If thy son lives, so do those fowls in my dish." He had hardly spoken when the two fowls, which were a cock and a hen, rose up feathered in the dish, and the cock began to crow. The judge called the priests and lawyers, and they went to the place of execution, and delivered the young man to his parents. The cock and hen thus miraculously resuscitated were placed under the protection of religious, and their posterity preserved for a long time. The most notable occasion upon which St. James appeared to lead the soldiers of Spain was in the year 939, when King Ramirez determined not to submit longer to the tribute of one hundred virgins, which was annually paid to the Moors. He defied Abdelraman to a battle which took place on the plain of Alveida, or Clavijo. After a furious contest the Christians were driven back. That night St. James appeared to Ramirez, and promised to be with him the following day, and give him the victory. The king related this to his officers, and also to his soldiers when they were ready for the field.

He recommended them to trust to the heavenly aid which had been promised. The whole army caught the spirit of their king, and rushed to battle. Immediately St. James appeared at their head on a milk-white charger, waving a white standard. He led them to victory, and sixty thousand Moors were left dead on the field. From that day "Santiago!" has been the Spanish war-cry. In early works of art St. James is usually, if not always, represented with the other Apostles, and may be known by his place, which is the third. But later he has been portrayed in all the different scenes of his life, and very frequently as a pilgrim of Compostella. In this character he bears the pilgrim's staff and wallet, the cloak and shell, while his hat is often on his shoulder. The most effective representation of this that I have seen is the statue by Thorwaldsen in the Church of Our Lady at Copenhagen. July 25, A. D. 44.

St. James Minor (*Fr.* St. Jaques Mineur; *Ital.* San Jacopo or Giacomo Minore; *Lat.* S. Jacobus Frater Domini; *Gr.* Ἀδελφόθεος, "brother of the Lord"). This saint has another most honorable title of "The Just." He was the son of Cleophas and Mary, the sister of the Virgin Mary; in reality cousin-german to the Saviour, but often styled "the Lord's brother." The epistle which he wrote beautifully speaks the piety and love for which he was venerated. He is distinguished as the first Christian Bishop of Jerusalem. The Jews threw him down from one of the terraces of the Temple; and as he fell his brains were beaten out with a fuller's club, which instrument of his death is his proper attribute in works of art. When the Apostles are all represented, St. James the Less is the ninth in order. The legends relate that James bore a striking resemblance to Jesus, so much so that they were at times mistaken for each other, and that it was this circumstance which made necessary the kiss of Judas. James made a vow that he would not eat bread from the time that he partook of the Last Supper until he should see Jesus raised from the dead. Soon after his resurrection the Saviour went to show himself to James, and asked for a table and bread. He blessed the bread, and gave it to James, saying, "My brother, eat thy bread; for the Son of man is risen from among them that sleep." May 1.

St. Januarius (*Ital.* San Gennaro; *Fr.* St. Janvier). This saint, who was Bishop of Benevento, came in the tenth persecution to

Naples with six of his disciples, to comfort and cheer the Christians. They were seized and thrown to the beasts of the amphitheatre, but these would not harm them. Januarius was then thrown into a fiery furnace, which hurt him not; and at last he was beheaded. He is represented as a bishop with the palm, and usually with Mt. Vesuvius in the distance; for he is the patron saint of Naples, and its protector from the fearful eruptions of the volcano. The miracle of the blood of Januarius is too well known to need description here. September 19, A. D. 305.

St. Jerome (*Lat.* S. Hieronymus; *Ital.* San Geronimo or Girolamo; *Fr.* St. Jérome, Hiérome, or Géroisme; *Ger.* Der Heilige Hieronimus). St. Jerome has universal importance and consideration on account of "The Vulgate," his translation of the New Testament into Latin, and also that which his wonderful piety and learning must inevitably command; but in the Catholic Church he is additionally venerated for his advocacy of the Virginal Life for men and women.[1] He was the son of Eusebius, a rich Dalmatian of Stridonium, and was born about 342. Being a scholar of more than usual promise, he was sent to Rome to complete his studies. There for a time he led a life of pleasure; but at length he became distinguished as a lawyer, and especially so on account of his eloquence in pleading his cause. At about thirty years of age he was baptized, and at the same time took a vow of celibacy. After having journeyed into Gaul, he went in 373 to the East, to gratify an insatiable desire to live among the scenes where Christ had dwelt. He became so enamoured of the hermit life, which was then so common in the Orient, that he retired to a desert in Chalcis, where he passed four years in study and seclusion. But this time was not without its recollections of another life, and longings for both the sins and pleasures of the past. He says: "Oh, how often in the desert, in that vast solitude which, parched by the sultry sun, affords a dwelling to the monks, did I fancy myself in the midst of the luxuries of Rome! I sat alone, for I was full of bitterness." But one thing which caused him severe trials was his love of learning and his appreciation of all that was elegant and beautiful in the ancient classics. This gave him a disgust for the crudeness of the Christian writers, and it was a fear-

---

[1] St. Benedict, however, is regarded as the father of Monasticism in the West.

ful struggle for him to master the Hebrew. All this appeared to him as great imperfection. He says that he fasted before he read Cicero, and he describes a vision which these mental struggles undoubtedly caused. He thought he heard the last trumpet sounded, and that he was commanded to appear before God for judgment. "Who art thou?" was the first question. Jerome replied, "A Christian." Then came a fearful reply : "'T is false ! thou art no Christian ; thou art a Ciceronian. Where the treasure is, there will the heart be also." After ten years of heart-rending temptation and struggle, of weary controversy and labors, he returned to Rome. Here he preached with all the enthusiastic eloquence he could command, against the luxury of the Roman clergy and laity, and maintained the necessity of extreme self-denial and abstinence. He especially influenced the Roman women, some of the most distinguished becoming converts to his preaching of Christ crucified, and ready to follow him in any self-sacrifice. Paula, a descendant of the Scipios and Gracchi, whose cell is shown in the monastery at Bethlehem, was perhaps the most celebrated of these converts, but Marcella is another name handed down to us with his. She is by some held to be the first who founded a religious community for women, while others give this high honor to St. Martha. Jerome remained but three years in Rome, when he returned to his monastery at Bethlehem. Here he died; and when he knew that death was approaching, he desired to be borne into the chapel, where he received the last rites of the Church, expiring soon after. He left many epistles and controversial writings, and the cell in which he wrote at Bethlehem is regarded with great veneration. The Jeronymites were distinguished for the magnificence of some of their churches and convents. The Escurial was theirs, as well as the Monastery of Belem, in Portugal, and that of St. Just, to which Charles V. retired when he gave up his throne. The proper attributes of St. Jerome are books, illustrative of his writings, and the lion, which is emblematic of the boldness and watchfulness of the saint ; but there is also a legend which accounts for the association of the lion with the holy man. One evening he was sitting at the gate of his monastery when a lion entered, limping, as if wounded. The monks fled, terrified, except Jerome, who went to meet the lion. The poor beast lifted his paw, and in it Jerome found a thorn, which he extracted, and then tended the wound till it was healed. The lion remained with the saint, and he made it the duty of the beast to guard an ass which brought wood from the forest. One day, while the lion slept, a caravan of merchants passed, and they stole the ass and drove it away. The lion returned to the convent with an air of shame. Jerome believed that he had eaten the ass, and condemned him to do the work of the ass, to which the lion quietly submitted, until the ass was again discovered by himself in the following manner: One day after his task was ended, he saw a caravan approaching, the camels of which (as is the custom of the Arabs) were led by an ass. The lion immediately saw that it was his stolen charge; and he drove the camels into the convent, whither the ass gladly led them. The merchants acknowledged the theft, and St. Jerome pardoned them for it. Hence the lion is so often associated with the saint; but its appropriateness as a type of his wilderness life and his zealous and vehement nature is a more satisfactory thought than the fanciful wildness of this legend can give. The introduction of the cardinal's hat into the pictures of this saint is a glaring anachronism, as there were no cardinals until three centuries later than that in which he lived. St. Jerome, as a penitent, is the subject of numberless pictures, and his Last Communion by Domenichino (Vatican) is one of the most celebrated of all pictures. St. Jerome is the special patron of students in theology. September 30, A. D. 420.

Jew, The Wandering. See Wandering Jew.

St. Joachim (*Ital.* San Gioacchino; *Fr.* St. Joakim) was the husband of Anna, and the father of the Blessed Virgin. He was of Nazareth, and his wife of Bethlehem, and both of the royal race of David. Joachim was rich, and an extremely devout man. He was childless; and it happened that on a certain feast-day when he brought his offering to the Temple it was refused by Issachar, the high-priest, who said, "It is not lawful for thee to bring thine offering, seeing that thou hast not begot issue in Israel." Joachim went away sorrowful; and searching the registers of Israel, he found that he alone, of all the righteous men, was childless. And he went away and would be seen by no one, and built a hut, and fasted forty days and nights, saying, "Until the Lord look upon me mercifully, prayer shall be my meat and my drink." And Anna mourned grievously for her barrenness and for the absence of her husband.

At length her handmaid, Judith, wished to cheer her, and tried to persuade her to array herself and attend the feast. But Anna repulsed her in such a way that Judith was angry, and told her mistress that she could wish her nothing worse than that which God had sent her, since he had closed her womb, that she could not be a mother. Then Anna arose and put on her bridal attire, and went forth to her garden, and prayed earnestly. And she sat beneath a laurel-tree, where a sparrow had a nest, and Anna said: "Alas! and woe is me! Who hath begotten me? Who hath brought me forth, that I should be accursed in the sight of Israel, and scorned and shamed before my people, and cast out of the temple of the Lord! Woe is me! to what shall I be likened? I cannot be likened to the fowls of heaven; for the fowls of heaven are fruitful in thy sight, O Lord! Woe is me! to what shall I be likened? Not to the unreasoning beasts of the earth; for they are fruitful in thy sight, O Lord! Woe is me! to what shall I be likened? Not to these waters; for they are fruitful in thy sight, O Lord! Woe is me! to what shall I be likened? Not unto the earth; for the earth bringeth forth her fruit in due season, and praiseth thee, O Lord!" And immediately she beheld an angel standing near her. And he said, "Anna, thy prayer is heard; thou shalt bring forth, and thy child shall be blessed throughout the whole world." And Anna replied, "As the Lord liveth, whatever I shall bring forth, be it a man child or maid, I will present it an offering to the Lord." And another angel came to tell her that Joachim was approaching; for an angel had also spoken to him, and he was comforted. Then Anna went to meet her husband, who came from the pasture with his flocks. And they met by the Golden Gate, and Anna embraced him, and hung on his neck, saying, "Now know I that the Lord hath blessed me. I who was a widow am no longer a widow. I who was barren shall become a joyful mother." Then they returned home together; and when her time was come, Anna brought forth a daughter, and she called her Mary, which in Hebrew is Miriam. March 20.

St. John the Baptist (*Ital.* San Giovanni Battista; *Fr.* St. Jean Baptiste; *Ger.* Johann der Täufer). In Scripture this saint, the herald of Christ, is presented in three characters; as Preacher, Prophet, and Baptist. Parts of his story are given by all the Evangelists, from the miraculous circumstances attending his birth to the awfully sinful horrors of his death. To these, tradition has added his miraculous deliverance from the assassins of Herod, by being enclosed with his mother in a rock, when she fled from the massacre with him in her arms. Art has represented him as leaving his home, while yet a child, to begin his desert life. Legends tell that the scene of his death was the royal fortified palace of Macheronta, near the Dead Sea, on the river Jordan; that he was buried at Sebaster, and that his head was brought to Europe in 453. He is venerated almost universally, and is the connecting link between the Old and New Dispensations, being the last prophet of the former and the first saint of the latter. The most ancient pictures represent him as meagre and wasted, with unshorn beard and hair. This would seem the true way; but often in later times he is made beautiful, and even dressed in rich mantles which cover the garment of camel's hair. When painted as the Messenger, he wears the hairy garment, and bears a cup, a reed cross, and a scroll with the inscription, "Vox clamantis in deserto," or "Ecce Agnus Dei!" The Greek signification of "Messenger" is "Angel;" and this is rendered in Byzantine art by painting him with wings. As a witness to the divinity of Christ, he is represented at various ages. He is introduced into Holy Families in this character in many different positions, all expressive of worship to the Holy Child. He is patron of all who are baptized, and also patron saint of Florence. In baptisteries he is very frequently represented in sculpture. In the historical pictures of this saint, which easily explain themselves, there is but one peculiarity to be noticed. That to which I refer is the representation of the legend that Mary prolonged her visit to Elizabeth until the birth of the child. In these pictures Mary usually receives or holds the babe, and is known by the glory about her head. The Greek legends say that his death took place two years before that of Christ, and that he descended to Hades to remain until the Saviour's death should give him deliverance. He bore to the departed spirits the tidings of the approaching redemption, at which they all rejoiced, while the devils were filled with fearful rage. Nativity of St. John the Baptist, June 24.

St. John the Evangelist (Greek title, θεολόγος, "Word of God;" *Lat.* S. Johannes; *Ital.* San Giovanni Evangelista; *Fr.* St. Jean, Messire St. Jehan; *Ger.* Der Heilige Johann). More is known of this "disciple whom Jesus loved" than of the other Evangelists. He was son of Zebedee, and brother of James the Great. His life seems to have been almost inseparable from that of the Master, ever after his call to follow him. He saw the Transfiguration. He leaned on the bosom of Our Lord at the Last Supper. He stood by the cross, and received the charge of Jesus concerning the Virgin Mary, and he laid the body of the Saviour in the tomb. He went with Peter through Judæa, to preach the Gospel, after the death of Mary. He then went to Asia Minor, living chiefly at Ephesus, and founding the seven churches. During the persecution of Domitian he was taken, bound, to Rome; and the Catholic traditions tell that he was thrown into a caldron of boiling oil without injury. The scene of this miracle was outside the Latin Gate, and the chapel of San Giovanni in Olio commemorates the event. Being afterwards accused of magic, he was exiled to Patmos, where he is believed to have written his Revelation. Upon the death of Domitian, he was allowed to return to his church at Ephesus. Here, when ninety years old, he is said to have written his Gospel. He died at Ephesus, at the age of one hundred and twenty years.[1] The Greek tradition is that he died without pain, and immediately arose again without change, and ascended to heaven to rejoin Jesus and Mary. The legends of the life and miracles of this saint are extremely interesting. St. Isidore relates that at Rome an attempt was made against the life of John, by poisoning the sacramental cup. When he took the cup, the poison came forth in the form of a serpent, and he drank the wine unhurt, while the poisoner fell dead at his feet. It is said to have been done by order of Domitian. Another account says that he was challenged to drink of a poisoned cup, in proof of the authority of his mission, by Aristodemus, the high-priest of Diana at Ephesus, and that while John was unhurt, the priest fell dead. Clement of Alexandria relates that when John was first at Ephesus, he took under his care a young man of great promise. When he was taken away to Rome he left this youth to the care of a bishop. But the young man became dissipated in his life, and at length was the leader of a band of robbers. When John returned, he asked of the bishop an account of his charge; and when he knew the truth, he blamed the

---

[1] The tradition that he never died exists, but has no ground in Catholic belief.

unfaithful guardian, and suffered great grief on account of the young man. He then went in search of his ward; and when he reached his abiding-place, the captain of the robbers tried to avoid his old friend. But John prevailed on him to listen to his words. As John talked to him, he tried to conceal his hand, which had committed many crimes. But John seized it, and kissing it, bathed it with his tears. He succeeded in reconverting the robber, and reconciled him to God and to himself. Again, two rich young men sold their possessions to follow the Apostle. Afterwards they repented, seeing which John sent them to gather stones and fagots, and changed these to gold, saying, "Take back your riches, and enjoy them on earth, as you regret having exchanged them for heaven." When John returned to Ephesus from Patmos, he met a funeral procession as he approached the city. When he asked whose it was, and heard it was Drusiana's, he was sad; for she had been rich in good works, and John had dwelt in her house. He ordered the bearer to put down the bier, and he prayed earnestly to God, who restored the woman to life; she arose, and John returned with her, and dwelt again in her house. Two wonderful miracles are related of John, as being performed after his death. King Edward the Confessor reverenced John next to the Saviour and the Virgin Mother. One day he attended a mass in honor of St. John; and, returning, he met a beggar, who asked him an alms in the name of God and St. John. The king drew from his finger a ring, and gave it to the man, unknown to any one beside. When Edward had reigned twenty-four years, two Englishmen, who had been pilgrims to the Holy Land, met on their return a man, also in the garb of a pilgrim. He asked them of their country, and said, "When ye shall have arrived in your own country, go to King Edward, and salute him in my name. Say to him that I thank him for the alms which he bestowed on me in a certain street in Westminster; for there, on a certain day, as I begged of him an alms, he bestowed on me this ring, which till now I have preserved, and ye shall carry it back to him, saying that in six months from this time he shall quit the world, and come and remain with me forever." Then the pilgrims said, "Who art thou, and where is thy dwelling-place?" And he replied, "I am John the Evangelist. Edward, your king, is my friend, and for the sanctity of his life I hold him dear. Go now, therefore, deliver to him this message and this ring, and I will pray to God that ye may arrive safely in your own country." Having said this, St. John gave them the ring, and vanished out of their sight. Then thanking God for this glorious vision, the pilgrims kept on their way, and went to King Edward, and delivered the ring and the message. He received them gladly, and entertained them as royal guests. He also made preparations for death, and gave the ring to the Abbot of Westminster, to be forever preserved as a holy relic. This legend is represented in sculpture in the chapel of Edward the Confessor. Again, in A. D. 425, when the Empress Galla Placidia returned to Ravenna from the East, she encountered a fearful storm. She vowed to St. John; and being safely landed, she built in his honor a splendid church. After it was done she was greatly desirous of having some relics of the saint to consecrate the sanctuary. One night as she prayed earnestly, the saint appeared to her; and when she threw herself down to kiss his feet, he vanished and left his sandal in her hand, — a relic long time preserved. The church of Galla Placidia at Ravenna, though greatly changed, yet remains; and on it may be traced, in sculpture, both the storm, and the empress making her vow, and the miracle of the slipper. St. John is represented in art as an evangelist, an apostle, and a prophet. The Greeks represented him, whether apostle or evangelist, as an old, gray-bearded man; but in Western art he is never beyond middle age, and often young. As a prophet, and the instrument of the Revelation, he is an aged man, with flowing beard. The scene is a desert with the sea, to represent Patmos, while the eagle is beside him. His proper colors are a blue or green tunic, with red drapery; and his attributes, beside the eagle, are the pen and book, and the cup either with the serpent or the consecrated wafer, which latter typifies the institution of the Eucharist. Sometimes the eagle has a nimbus or glory. This figures the Holy Ghost, as the Jews made the eagle a symbol of the spirit. When the Baptist and Evangelist are introduced in the same picture, as frequently occurs, the latter may be known from his more youthful look as well as by the above attributes. When associated with the other Apostles, he is distinguished by his youth and flowing hair, or by his nearness to the Saviour, and frequently by some token of peculiar love in the position or aspect of the Master. On great occasions, at the church of the Santa Croce, at Rome, a cup is exhibited as that from which John,

11

by command of Domitian, drank poison without injury. December 27, A. D. 99.

St. John Capistrano was a Franciscan friar, who after the capture of Constantinople by the Turks, was sent out to preach a crusade for the defence of Christendom. At the siege of Belgrade, in 1456, when Mohammed was repulsed by the Hungarians, this saint was seen, with his crucifix in hand, in the midst of the battle encouraging and leading on the soldiers. He died the same year, and in 1690 he was canonized. His attribute is the crucifix, or the standard with the cross. A colossal statue of him is on the exterior of the cathedral at Vienna. He has a Turk under his feet, while he bears in one hand a standard, and in the other a cross. October 23, A. D. 1456.

St. John Chrysostom (*Lat.* S. Johannes Chrysostom; *Ital.* San Giovanni Crisostomo, San Giovanni Bocca d' Oro; *Fr.* St. Jean Chrysostome). This saint is always called by his Greek appellative, which signifies, "of the golden mouth." He was born at Antioch in 344. He was of an illustrious family. His father died while he was still young, and his mother, Arthusia, remained a widow that she might devote herself entirely to her son. At twenty he had won renown by the eloquence of his pleas, for he was an advocate, but he greatly desired to retire from the world as a hermit. The entreaties of his mother prevented this until he was about twenty-eight, when in spite of all he fled to the wilderness near, and led a life of such rigor as to destroy his health and oblige him to return to Antioch. Soon after this, Flavian ordained him a priest; and tradition declares that at the moment of his ordination a white dove descended on his head. This signified his especial inspiration from the Holy Spirit; and truly thereafter, he seems, as a Christian orator, to have been assisted of God. Only Paul is ranked above him. He saved the people of his native city by his eloquence, when they had so offended the Emperor Theodosius that he had threatened them with dreadful punishment. So much was he beloved at Antioch, that when chosen Patriarch of Constantinople he had to go away secretly before the people could interfere to retain him. At Constantinople he lived a life of humble self-denial, but entertained the stranger and the poor with kind hospitality. His enthusiasm, his poetic imagination, his elegant scholarship, added to his great earnestness, caused him to speak as

one inspired ; and he preached so fearlessly against the irregularities of the Empress Eudoxia, of the monks, and all the customs
of the court, that he was banished from the city. The people
obliged the emperor to recall him ; but again he was inexorable in
his denunciations, and again was sent into exile. His guards treated
him so cruelly that he perished from exposure and fatigue. He
was sixty-three years old, and had been bishop ten years. It was
thirty years after his death when his remains were removed to
Constantinople, and the Emperor Theodosius, advancing as far as
Chalcedon to meet them, fell prostrate on the coffin and implored
the forgiveness of the saint in the names of Arcadius and Eudoxia,
his guilty parents. St. John Chrysostom died September 14, A. D.
407. The Greeks keep his festival November 13, and the Latin
Church, January 27.

St. John Gualberto (*Ital.* San Giovanni Gualberto ; *Fr.* St.
Jean Gualbert, or Calbert) was born at Florence. His family was
rich and noble, and he received an education befitting his rank. He
had but one brother, Hugo, whom he passionately loved. While John
was still young, Hugo was slain by a gentleman with whom he had a
quarrel. John, with the consent and encouragement of his parents,
determined to pursue the murderer to the death. It happened that
on Good Friday, at evening, as John left Florence for his father's
country-house, he took the road which leads to the church of San
Miniato-del-Monte. In ascending the hill he met his brother's assas-
sin, and drew his sword to kill him, feeling that a just God had thus
delivered his enemy into his hand. The wretched man fell on his
knees, imploring mercy. He extended his hand in the form of a cross,
and reminded John that Jesus had died on the cross praying for
pardon for his murderers. John felt himself moved by a great struggle ; and the conflict between his desire for revenge and his wish to
act as a Christian was so great that he trembled from head to foot.
But at length, praying to God for strength, he lifted his enemy ; and
embracing him, they parted. John, overpowered with emotion, had
scarcely strength to enter the church, where he knelt before the
crucifix at the altar. Here he wept bitterly, and all the horror of
the crime he had been about to commit was vividly impressed on his
mind. He prayed for pardon ; and as he raised his eyes to the face
of Jesus, he beheld the holy head bowed in sign of forgiveness. This

miracle completed the great change already begun in him, and he determined to leave the world. He took the Benedictine habit, and entered the monastery of San Miniato. When the abbot died, John was elected to succeed him; but he would not accept the office, and leaving the convent, retired to the Vallombrosa, in the Apennines, about twenty miles from San Miniato. At first he had but two companions in his retreat, but the fame of his sanctity attracted numbers to him; and thus originated the Order of Vallombrosa, of which this saint was the founder. They adopted the Rule of St. Benedict, but revived some of the severities which had fallen into disuse, and instituted others, especially that of silence. The pope confirmed this new order, and before the death of the saint twelve houses were filled with his followers, in different places. The Church of the Trinità at Florence belonged to them, and in it is preserved the miraculous crucifix before which John knelt on that memorable Good Friday night. The ruins of the monastery of Salvi, near Florence, which was of the Vallombrosa, show by their extent what its importance must have been. John was most strict in his humility and simplicity, and was so shocked at the way in which his disciples at Moscetta embellished their convent that he prophesied some fearful punishment for them. Shortly after, an inundation destroyed a large part of their buildings. He was also distinguished for his determined opposition to the practice of simony, by which many ecclesiastics dishonored the Church in his time. Pietro di Pavia had purchased the archbishopric of Florence. He was a man of notoriously bad character. John denounced him publicly. Pietro sent soldiers to burn and pillage San Salvi, and several monks were murdered. Still Gualberto would not be silent; and it is probable that his order would have been destroyed by the powerful wickedness of Pietro, had not one of the monks, called Peter Igneus, demanded the ordeal by fire. He stood the test triumphantly, and the archbishop was deposed. Several miracles, like that of multiplying the food when the monks were in want, are attributed to this saint. The Vallombrosians had fine libraries and many works of art, before they were despoiled. These pictures are now scattered in galleries. Cimabue painted his famous Madonna for them, and Andrea del Sarto his Cenacolo. Gualberto meeting the murderer is represented in a little tabernacle which has been erected on the spot where the encounter took place. July 12, A. D. 1073.

St. John de Matha (*Sp.* San Juan de Mata) was a native of Faucon, in Provence. He was born in 1154, and his parents were of noble family. Like so many saints, he was consecrated to God by his mother, whose name was Martha. He was a student in the University at Paris, and after becoming famous for his piety was ordained a priest. The first time he celebrated the mass he had a vision of an angel, whose hands crossed over each other rested on the heads of two slaves who knelt on each side of him. On the breast of the white robe which the angel wore, was a cross of red and blue. Felix de Valois, another holy man, was a friend of the saint; and when John had told him the vision, and that he regarded it as an intimation from heaven that he was to labor for the relief of prisoners and captives, the two determined to found a new order having this labor for its object. It was called "The Order of the Holy Trinity for the Redemption of Captives." John and Felix went to Rome for the confirmation of their work, and were most kindly received; for the pope had also had a vision of an angel with two captives chained, one of whom was a Moor, the other a Christian, which taught that all races and religions were to be benefited by this new brotherhood. The parent institution of the order was that of Cerfroy, but they were called Mathurins, and had a monastery in Paris near the street still called by their name. At Rome they were given the church and convent on Monte Celio, so beautifully situated, and from the ancient barque in front of it called Santa Maria della Navicella. Having obtained followers and money, John sent his disciples, and went himself to various places in Africa and Spain, and exchanged and ransomed prisoners and brought them home. This was a most noble work; for no class of Christians so needed assistance as those who had been made prisoners and then slaves during the fierce wars of those times. He had delivered hundreds, when, being about to sail with one hundred and twenty slaves, the infidels became furious and tore up his sails and broke his rudder. But he used his mantle and those of his disciples as sails, and praying God to be his pilot, the ship was quietly wafted to Ostia. But the health of the saint was so feeble that he was not able to go even to Paris, and after two years of suffering he died at Rome. February 8, A. D. 1213.

St. John Nepomuck (*Ital.* San Giovanni Nepomuceno; *Ger.* Heil. Johannes von Nepomuk; *Sp.* San Juan Nepomuceno). This saint was the confessor of the good and beautiful princess Joan of Bavaria, who was unfortunately married to the cruel Wenceslaus IV. of Germany. John knew there was no earthly recompense for such woes as his empress endured, and he earnestly endeavored to so lead her religiously that she might suffer with patience the hardness of her life. At length Wenceslaus commanded him to reveal the confession of the empress. This the saint refused to do, and imprisonment and torture failed to break his silence. At length the empress by prayers and tears obtained his release. She dressed his wounds and nursed him with her own hands. Then he returned to court and preached as usual; but, knowing the uncertainty of his life, he first chose the text, "Yet a little while and ye shall not see me." He endeavored to prepare himself and all who heard him for death. Not long after, as he approached the palace, the emperor saw him from the window, and being seized with one of his tempers, he ordered him to be brought before him. Again he demanded the confession of the empress. The saint kept perfect silence. Then the emperor commanded the guards to throw him over the parapet of the bridge into the Moldau. The legend relates that, as he sank, five stars hovered over the spot, which, when the emperor saw them, so distracted him that he fled and hid for some time in the fortress of Carlstein. The empress greatly mourned, and the people carried his body in procession to the Church of the Holy Cross. When Prague was besieged in 1620, it is believed that St. John Nepomuck fought with his people. The empress did not long survive her faithful friend and confessor. He was a canon regular of St. Augustine. He is patron saint of bridges and running water in Austria and Bohemia. His statue stands on the bridge at Prague on the very spot whence he was thrown down. Five stars are his proper attribute. Sometimes he has his finger on his mouth; sometimes a padlock on his mouth or in his hand in token of silence. He is patron of discretion and silence, and protector against slander. May 16, A. D. 1383.

St. John and St. Paul were brothers and Roman officers in the service of Constantia. They were put to death by Julian the Apostate. Their church on the brow of the Cœlian Hill is on the spot where their house stood, which is one of the most lovely in ancient Rome. It has existed since 499. The church at Venice which bears their name was built by colonies from the convent of St. John and St. Paul at Rome. It is filled with most interesting monuments, but none exist in honor of these saints. In art they are always represented together, and their attributes are the military dress with the sword. June 26, about 362.

St. Joseph (*Lat.* S. Josephus; *Ital.* San Giuseppe; *Fr.* St. Joseph; *Ger.* Der Heilige Josef). Joseph was always honored among the saints, but signally so since the sixteenth century. The great honor which God conferred upon him in selecting him to be the guardian of the Virgin and her Divine Son is sufficient proof that he was a holy man. The Scripture account leads us to conclude that he was gentle and tender as well as just. He was of the lineage of David and the tribe of Judah, — a carpenter, and dwelt in Nazareth. This is the sum of the positive knowledge we have of him. Legends are the source of all other opinions concerning him. In these there is great difference regarding his age. Many think that he was a widower when he espoused Mary.[1] In early art he was made very old, and some monks averred that he was more than fourscore at the time of his marriage to Mary. In later years he has been represented of mature middle-age, strong and able to fulfil the duty of providing for his charge. One attribute of age has however been handed down from the earliest time, the crutch or cane, and is seldom omitted. The legend of the marriage of Mary and Joseph is given in the Protevangelion and History of Joseph, in these words: "When Mary was fourteen years old, the priest Zacharias (or Abiathar, as he is elsewhere called) inquired of the Lord concerning her, what was right to be done; and an angel came to him and said, 'Go forth and call together all the widowers among the people, and let each bring his rod (or wand) in his hand; and he to whom the Lord shall show a sign, let him be the husband of Mary.' And Zacharias did as the angel commanded, and made proclamation accordingly. And Joseph the carpenter, a righteous man, throwing down his axe, and taking his staff in his hand, ran out with the rest. When he appeared before the priest, and presented his rod, lo! a dove issued out of it, — a dove dazzling white as snow, and after settling on his head, flew toward heaven. Then the high-priest said to him, 'Thou art the person chosen to take the Virgin of the Lord, and to keep her for

---

[1] St. Jerome asserts that he was always virgin.

Him.' And Joseph was at first afraid, and drew back, but afterward he took her home to his house, and said to her, 'Behold, I have taken thee from the Temple of the Lord, and now I will leave thee in my house, for I must go and follow my trade of building. I will return to thee, and meanwhile the Lord be with thee and watch over thee.' So Joseph left her, and Mary remained in her house." Jerome makes a difference which artists have followed. He relates that among the suitors for Mary was the son of the high-priest, and that they all deposited their wands in the Temple over night. Next morning, Joseph's rod had blossomed. The others, in their disappointment, broke their wands and trampled on them; while one, Agabus, who was of noble race, fled to Mt. Carmel and became an anchorite. In many pictures the espousals take place in the open air, and various places outside the Temple, having no appearance of the sacrament of marriage. This is explained by the fact that among the Jews marriage was a civil contract rather than a religious ceremony. Joseph's next appearance, in the legends, is on the journey to Bethlehem. The way, so long and weary to the suffering Virgin, is described, and the Protevangelion tells that "when Joseph looked back, he saw the face of Mary, that it was sorrowful, as of one in pain; but when he looked back again she smiled. And when they were come to Bethlehem there was no room for them in the inn, because of the great concourse of people. And Mary said to Joseph, 'Take me down, for I suffer.'" Another legend relates that Joseph sought a midwife, but when he returned with her to the stable Mary was sitting with her infant on her knees, and the place was filled with a light far brighter than that of noonday. And the Hebrew woman in amazement said, "Can this be true?" And Mary replied, "It is true: as there is no child like unto my son, so there is no woman like unto his mother." Four times God sent angelic messengers to guide Joseph in the execution of his important mission. First, he assured him of the purity of Mary, and that he need fear nothing in taking her to wife. The legends say that after waking from this vision, he "entreated forgiveness of Mary for having wronged her even in thought." The second dream commanded him to flee into Egypt. The pictures of the Flight, and of the Repose, which is an incident of the flight, represent the watchful care of Joseph. The duration of the sojourn in Egypt is differently given,

and ranges from two to seven years. The third vision told Joseph
to return to Judæa, and a fourth guided him on the journey. After
the return to Nazareth, Joseph is associated only with a quiet, indus-
trious life, and the training of his foster-son to the trade of a carpenter. The time of Joseph's death is also a disputed point. Some
assert that it occurred when Jesus was eighteen years old, while some
make it nine years later. One of the most interesting accounts of
this event is found in an Arabian history of Joseph the Carpenter.
Jesus is supposed to relate it to his disciples. He tells that Joseph
acknowledged him as the "Redeemer and Messiah," and speaks thus
of Mary : "And my mother, the Virgin, arose, and she came nigh
to me and said, 'O my beloved Son, now must the good old man die!'
And I answered, and said unto her, 'O my most dear mother, needs
must all created beings die ; and Death will have his rights, even over
thee, beloved mother : but death to him and to thee is no death, only
the passage to eternal life ; and this body I have derived from thee
shall also undergo death.'" Then after giving an account of the
death scene, he says, "I and my mother Mary, we wept with them,"
alluding to the sons and daughters of Joseph who were about him
weeping. Then follows an account of a struggle between good and
bad spirits for the soul of Joseph ; but at last Gabriel comes to clothe
it with a robe of brightness and bear it to heaven. On account of
this triumphant end, Joseph came to be invoked as the patron of
death-beds. His death is often represented in family chapels which
are consecrated to the dead. The 20th of July had been observed
in the East with great solemnity as the anniversary of Joseph's
death for many years before he was popular in the West. It was the
custom to read publicly homilies upon his life and death ; and many
of them are very curious and ancient, dating from the fourth century
in some cases. There is great significance in the different modes of
representing this saint, and in the attributes given him. He regards
Mary with veneration mingled with tender care and thoughtfulness.
In the pictures of the Nativity, the Adoration of the Magi, and in
many Holy Families, he is in an attitude of quiet and contemplative
admiration ; and while treated with dignity is never made an important
point in the picture. In the flight, and in the repose in Egypt, he is
the care-taker and guide, and the importance of his trust is made apparent. He sometimes holds the Infant, or bears him in his arms,

in token of his high office of providing for him; and at the same time
carries a lily, the emblem of chastity, or his budded rod, in token of
the purity of the relation between himself and Mary.   Sometimes he
gathers dates, leads the ass which bears the Virgin and Child, and
carries the wallet and staff of the pilgrim.   When he kneels before
the Infant and presents a flower, it is an act of homage on the part
of the saint.   His dress should be a gray tunic and a saffron-colored
mantle.   March 19.

St. Jovita or Giovita.   See St. Faustinus.

St. Juan de Dios was the founder of the Order of the Hospitallers, or Brothers of Charity; in fact, he may be said to be the
founder of the same class of institutions in all countries; — of
our own hospitals and asylums for the poor, the "Maisons de
Charité" of France, the "Barmherzigen Brüder" of Germany, the
"Misericordia" of Italy, and the "Caritad" of Spain.   He was the
son of poverty, born in Monte-Mayor, Portugal, in 1495.   He had
no education, but was piously reared by his mother.   When Juan
was but nine years old, he was so charmed by the stories of a priest
who was entertained by his parents, and who had travelled far and
wide, that he went away with him without the knowledge of his
family.   The priest for some reason left him utterly alone in Oropesa,
a village of Castile.   He entered the service of a shepherd, where he
remained until he entered the army.   He was reckless and dissipated
as a soldier, and yet at times was greatly moved by recollections
of the piety of his mother and the lessons of his childhood.   He met
with many adventures, and narrowly escaped death from wounds and
accidents.   Being set to guard some booty taken from the enemy, he
fell asleep, and the prize was carried off.   His commanding officer
ordered him hanged on the spot; but after the rope was around his
neck, a superior officer who chanced to pass, released him on the condition that he should leave the camp.   He returned to his old occupation in Oropesa; but his restless mind gave him no peace, and in
1532 he joined the troops raised for the Hungarian war.   At the
end of the strife, he returned to his native place, making a pilgrimage
to Compostella on his way.   Here he was so seized with remorse,
when he learned that his parents had died of grief for his desertion
of them, that his reason was impaired.   Having no money, he became
the shepherd of a rich lady near Seville.   Here he gave much time

to meditation and prayer, and determined to do some good in order to atone as much as possible for his past sins. He remembered the sad and wretched condition of the poor, and of captives and prisoners, of whom he had seen many during his wanderings. At length he determined to devote himself to their relief, and even, if possible, to be a martyr. He went to Gibraltar, and there saw a Portuguese noble, who, with his family, was exiled to Ceuta, in Africa. He entered the service of these distressed people. They suffered much from sickness and poverty, and Juan became their only support. He hired himself as a laborer, and toiled for them until they received aid from other sources. Then returning to Spain he travelled about, selling religious books and pictures, and doing all in his power for the poor until he was told in a vision, "Go, thou shalt bear the cross in Granada." The miraculous bearer of this message was a radiant child who held a pomo-de-Granada (pomegranate) in his hand. Juan came into Granada at the time of the celebration of St. Sebastian's festival. He was already much excited in mind; and the exhortations of the famous preacher, St. John of Avila, roused in him such sorrow for his sins that he seemed as one bereft of his senses. He was taken to a mad-house, and, as the custom was, scourged every day until the blood flowed freely from his wounds. The same preacher referred to was filled with pity for him, and by patient attendance restored him to reason and liberty. John obtained a little shed for his home, and here founded the first Hospital of Charity; for he began the practice of bringing here the most wretched ones he could find, and of begging for their support. At first he could provide for but two or three, but would himself lie outside on the ground for the sake of sheltering an additional one. Soon he succeeded in obtaining a large circular building, in the centre of which was kept a great fire; and here he often gathered two hundred homeless wretches. He gave up the idea of martyrdom, and devoted himself with wonderful zeal to the relief of the misery about him. He made no rules for any order, and does not appear to have contemplated the establishment of one, and yet he "bequeathed to Christendom one of the noblest of all its religious institutions." In France he has the title of "le bienheureux Jean de Dieu, Père des Pauvres." His proper attributes are the pomegranate and cross. Often he is painted with a beggar kneeling before him. "The Charity of San Juan de Dios," painted by Murillo for the Church of the "Caritad" at Seville, represents him staggering beneath the burden of a dying beggar, whom he is bearing through a storm to his hospital. It is said that few behold this picture without tears. March 8, A. D. 1550.

St. Juan de la Cruz. He is mentioned by Mr. Stirling as "a holy man who was frequently favored with interviews with our Saviour, and who, on one of these occasions, made an uncouth sketch of the Divine apparition, which was long preserved as a relic in the convent of the Incarnation at Avila." He was the first barefooted Carmelite, and is famous for his terrible austerities and penances. He was the ally of St. Teresa in all her reforms, and is frequently represented with her. Books with the titles of his writings are often introduced into his pictures. November 24, A. D. 1591.

Judas Iscariot (*Ital.* Giuda Scariota; *Fr.* Judas Iscariote). The silence of the Gospel concerning the life of Judas before he became a disciple is more than filled by the legends of the Middle Ages. They relate that he was of the tribe of Reuben, and that his mother dreamed before his birth that he would murder his father, commit incest with his mother, and betray his God for money. Horrified at this prospect, his parents determined that he should not live to fulfil such prophecies; so they put him in a chest and threw it into the sea, but the chest was washed on shore, and the child taken by a certain king and reared as his son. This king had a son whom Judas hated from the natural ugliness of his disposition. At length he killed him in a quarrel, and fled to Judæa and was employed as a page by Pontius Pilate, who was attracted by the comeliness of his person. In course of time, he fulfils the dreadful prophecies regarding his parents, and at length learns from his mother the secret of his birth. He is filled with horror of himself, and having heard of the power of Christ to forgive sins, he seeks to become his follower. Jesus receives him, knowing all. Judas now adds avarice to his other vices, and becomes so completely corrupt as to fit him for the awful destiny foreshadowed for him. The bribery, betrayal, repentance, and death follow according to the Scripture account. His repentance is in some cases most vividly portrayed. Remorse is made a real person, who seizes and torments him until he invokes Despair, who brings to him all kinds of implements of death and bids him choose from them. He is represented, too, with an imp upon his shoulder, figuring the Satan that entered into him. The Mohammedans believe that Christ ascended alive into heaven, and that Judas was crucified in his likeness. But his death has been variously represented in art. Those who have painted him as hanging with his bowels gushing out have seemingly made a mistake. The more reasonable version is, that having hanged himself he fell, and from the fall he "burst asunder." One tradition is that he was found hanging, and thrown over the parapet of the Temple and dashed in pieces. Expression has been given to the wildest imaginations concerning him. An old miniature makes demons toss his soul from hand to hand like a ball. The horror of this restlessness is a fearful thought. The "bursting asunder" was considered a special judgment, in order that his soul should escape from his bowels, and not be breathed out through the lips that had betrayed Christ. The idea is represented by a demon taking the soul, in the usual form of a little child, from the bowels. The ugliness of person and expression given to Judas in pictures appeals to our feeling, although not in harmony with the legend; and it does not seem that such a man would have been allowed in the company of the twelve. The proper color for him is a dirty yellow. At Venice the Jews were formerly compelled to wear hats of this Judas color, while in Spain and Italy malefactors and galley slaves are clothed in it.

St. Jude. See St. Simon.

Judith and Holofernes. In the seventeenth year of the reign of Nabuchodonosor, King of Nineveh, he went out to battle with King Arphaxad of Ecbatane; and he sent to all the people round that they should join his army and help him to conquer the Medes. But the people scorned the commands of Nabuchodonosor, and did not join his army. Then was he wroth, and he swore to destroy those nations which would not acknowledge him for the king of the whole earth. So he sent Holofernes, who was the chief captain of the army of the Assyrians, and gave him commands to go forth and destroy the cities and exterminate the people who had scorned his authority. Holofernes did so; and when he came to the city of Bethulia, he sat down before it to besiege it. He was advised not to attack the city, which was so high up in the mountains as to be almost impregnable, but to seize the fountain outside the city and thus cut off their water, so that the people of Bethulia would fall dead in their own streets from thirst. Holofernes received this advice, and seized the fountain. Now, when all the water in the city was gone, the women and children began to drop with faintness, and the men were ready to perish; then came they to Ozias, the chief of the city, and they said, "It is better that we deliver us up to the Assyrians than that we die thus;" and Ozias reasoned with them that God would deliver them, but they would not hearken. Then Ozias said, "Let us wait five days; and if God does not send rain to fill our cisterns, neither deliver us in any other way, then we will deliver us up to the enemy." Now there was in Bethulia a widow, Judith, and she was exceeding beautiful and very pious. She had been a widow three years and four months, and she had "fasted all the days of her widowhood, save the eves of the Sabbaths and the eves of the new moons, and the feasts and the solemn days of the house of Israel." She was, moreover, very rich in lands and servants, cattle and money, and beautiful apparel and jewels. Now she was thought very wise, and her opinion greatly esteemed. She did not approve of the decision of the people, and told Ozias and the other chief men that they had done wrong; that God was not a man that his counsels should be limited or a time set for him to deliver them; and she said she would go forth out of the city with her waiting-woman, and that before the time they had promised to deliver up the city should come, God would give their enemies into her hand. So she went, and prayed God to be with her, to allow her to sway the heart of Holofernes by the pleasant words she would speak and by the sight of her beauty. Then she put off her widow's garments, and she dressed herself in the apparel which she wore in the days of Manasses her husband; she plaited her hair, and put a tire upon it, "and she took sandals upon her feet, and put about her her bracelets and her chains and her rings and all her ornaments, and decked herself bravely, to allure the eyes of all men that should see her." And when she had taken wine and figs and bread and parched corn, she put them in a bag and gave to her waiting-woman, and they proceeded to the gate of the city; and Ozias and all who saw her wondered at her great and dazzling beauty. So went she forth; and when she was come to the camp of Holofernes, those who saw her admired her greatly, and they took her to their captain with great honor. Now, when Holofernes saw her, from that moment he desired to have her; but he questioned her of herself, and why she had thus come. Then she told him that her people were wicked in that they did not submit to his command, and that to this sin they were about to add that of drinking the wine which had been kept for the use of the Temple, and that she, foreseeing the destruction which must come for all this sin, had sought his presence. She added that she would remain with him, going out every night into the valley to pray; and that when the wicked designs of her people were accomplished she would tell him, and then he could go forth with his army and conquer them without difficulty. So she remained, and Holofernes offered her food; but she said, "I will not eat thereof, lest there be an offence; but provision shall be made for me of the things that I have brought." And when he said, "If thy provision should fail?" she answered, "As thy soul liveth, my lord, thine handmaid shall not spend those things that I have, before the Lord work by mine hand the things that he hath determined." So he gave her a tent; and she and her waiting-woman dwelt there, going out every night into the valley. Now on the fourth day Holofernes made a feast for his own servants, and called none of his officers to it. And he sent Vagao, the eunuch who had charge of all that he had, to invite Judith to this feast; and she arose and decked herself and went. "Now, when Judith came in and sat down, Holofernes his heart was ravished with her, and his mind was moved, and he desired greatly her company; for he waited a time to deceive her, from the day that he had seen her." Then Holofernes urged her to eat and drink, which she did, such things as her maid prepared for her; and she said, "I will drink now, my lord, because my life is magnified in me this day, more than all the days since I was born." Holofernes took great delight in her, and drank much more wine than he had ever drank at any time before in one day. At last, when evening was come the servants retired, and Vagao shut the tent, and Judith was alone with Holofernes, and he was drunk with the wine. Then Judith, praying to God to assist her, took down his sword which was at his head, and she took hold of the hair of his head and said, "Strengthen me, O Lord God of Israel, this day." And she smote him twice upon his neck, and took away his head. Then she pulled down the canopy, and went forth and gave the head to her maid, who put it in her meat-bag, and they went forth into the valley, as was their custom. But now they kept on till they came to Bethulia; and Judith called to the watchman when they were still afar off. And when her voice was heard, all the city hastened to hear what news she might bring. And she commanded them to praise God, and showed them the head of Holofernes and the silken canopy. Then Judith gave an order that they should hang the head on the highest part of the wall, and when the morning should come every man should take his weapon and go forth as if to battle; then the Assyrians would go to the tent of Holofernes, and fear should fall upon them, and they would flee before the men of Bethulia. And it was all as she said. Now, when Vagao knocked at the door of the tent, he had no answer, — he went not in, for he thought that Holofernes had slept with Judith, — but when he could hear no one he entered, and found the body from which the head had been cut away. Then was the Assyrian camp filled with dismay, and they fled into every way of the plain and of the hill country. And the children of Israel fell upon them, and smote them, and chased them beyond Damascus. And the tent of Holofernes with all its rich appointments was given to Judith; and the men of Bethulia spoiled the camp of the Assyrians. Then Judith sang a song of triumph; and she went to Jerusalem, and gave the tent and all its belongings to the sanctuary, and they feasted there for three months. And Judith lived to be one hundred and five years old; but she would not marry, though many desired her. And the people of Israel esteemed her according to her worth; and when she died they of Bethulia mourned her seven days, and buried her by the side of her husband, Manasses.

St. Julia (*Fr.* Ste. Julie; *Ital.* Santa Giulia) was a noble virgin, who is often represented with the Brescian saints. She was martyred at Corsica, and her relics carried to Brescia, where a church and convent were dedicated to her. She is painted young, lovely, and richly attired. She died in the fifth century. May 22.

Julian the Apostate. Julian, Flavius Claudius, Emperor of Rome, nephew of Constantine the Great. Famous for his attempt to re-establish paganism. Born at Constantinople in 331, died of a wound received in battle near Ctesiphon, when fighting against Sapor, King of Persia, being thirty-two years old. When young, he was kept in obscurity by his cousin Constantius, from jealousy. He was first taught by Christian bishops, and was then a pupil of the school at Athens, and intimately associated with men distinguished for wonderful piety and learning. His defenders plead that he revolted from the Church on account of its intolerance of philosophy. But if he hated intolerance, how must he have hated himself; for he persecuted those he called persecutors, and became a fanatic in his opposition to religion. For the legend of his death, see St. Mercurius.

St. Julian Hospitator (*Ital.* San Giuliano Ospitale; *Fr.* St. Julien l'Hospitalier) was a count, and lived in great state. He hunted and feasted continually. One day, as he pursued a deer it turned on him and said, "Thou who pursuest me to the death shalt cause the death of thy father and thy mother!" He stopped affrighted, and resolved to flee from his parents in order not to fulfil the prophecy. So he went into a far country. The king of this country received him kindly, and gave him a rich and lovely widow for his wife, with whom he lived so happily as to forget his home and the prophecy. But his father and mother had put on the attire of pilgrims, and set out to find their son. Now, while Julian was absent at court, they arrived at his house, and Basilissa, his wife, showed them every kindness, and put them in her own bed to sleep. The next morning, while she was gone to church to thank God for having brought them to her, Julian returned. He entered his chamber, and in the dim light saw two people in bed, and one of them a bearded man. Seized with furious jealousy, he drew his sword and slew them both. Rushing out, he met his wife. Astonished, he asked who was in his bed, and hearing the truth was as one dead. He then wept bitterly, and exclaimed, "Alas! by what evil fortune is this, that what I sought to avoid has come to pass? Farewell, my sweet sister! I can never again lie by thy side, until I have been pardoned by Christ Jesus for this great sin!" But she replied, "Nay, my brother, can I allow thee to depart, and without me? Thy grief is my grief, and whither thou goest I will go." So they travelled till they came to a stream swollen by mountain torrents, in which many who tried to cross were drowned. Here Julian built a cell for himself and a hospital for the poor; and he constantly ferried the travellers over the river without reward. At length, one stormy night in winter, when it seemed that no boat could cross the stream, he heard a sad cry from the opposite bank. He went over, and found a youth who was a leper dying from

12

cold and weariness. In spite of his disease he carried him over and bore him in his arms to his own bed, and he and Basilissa tended him till morning, when the leper rose up, and his face was transformed into that of an angel, and he said, "Julian, the Lord hath sent me to thee; for thy penitence is accepted, and thy rest is near at hand." And he vanished from sight. Then Julian and his wife fell down, and praised God for his mercies; and soon they died, for they were old, and full of good works. He is patron saint of ferrymen and boatmen, of travellers and of wandering minstrels. His dress should be that of a hermit; his attribute a stag, which may be distinguished from that of St. Hubert by the absence of the crucifix between the horns. January 9, A. D. 313.

St. Julian of Rimini was of Cilicia; and but little is known of him beyond the fact that he endured a prolonged martyrdom with unfailing courage. Of this St. Chrysostom writes. He is represented as young and graceful, but melancholy. He is richly dressed, and carries the palm, the standard of victory, and the sword. March 16.

Julian. There are twelve saints of this name; but the two given above are the most important, and most frequently represented in art.

St. Justa, or Justina, and St. Rufina, patronesses of Seville. These were the daughters of a potter of Seville. They sold earthenware, and gave away all they made after supplying their bare necessities. Some women went to buy of them vessels to be used in the worship of Venus. The saints answered that they would sell nothing for that purpose; whereupon the women broke all their ware, and the populace seized them and bore them to the prefect. But first, the saints destroyed the image of Venus. They were condemned to the torture. Justa died on the rack, and Rufina was strangled. The Giralda is their especial care, and it was believed that this beautiful tower was preserved by them in the terrible thunder-storm of 1504. They are sometimes painted as *muchachas* (or of the humbler class), and sometimes beautifully attired. They always bear palms and *alcarrazas*, or earthen pots. July 19, A. D. 304.

St. Justina of Antioch. See St. Cyprian. September 26, A. D. 304.

St. Justina of Padua (*Lat.* Sancta Justina Patavina Urbis Protectrix; *Ital.* Santa Giustina di Padova; *Fr.* Ste. Justine de Padoue) was a daughter of King Vitalicino, who was a Christian, and brought up his child in the same faith. After the death of her father she was accused before the Emperor Maximian, who ordered her death by the sword. She opened her arms, was pierced through the bosom, and died. She is patroness of Padua and Venice ; and in the former city there is a sumptuous church in her honor, which was founded in 453, and rebuilt in the sixteenth century. Her proper attribute is the sword transfixing her bosom. Sometimes the unicorn, which belongs to Justina of Antioch, is also given to this saint, which causes confusion between the two. The unicorn attending a female is also the emblem of chastity; when it accompanies Justina of Padua, the Venetian costume, or Venice itself, or else St. Mark in the distance, will usually decide ; but when the female is alone or with a company of martyrs and the unicorn, it is Justina of Antioch. October 7, A. D. 303.

St. Lambert of Maestricht (*Ital.* San Lamberto ; *Fr.* and *Ger.* Lambert, Lanbert, or Landbert). This name signifies, "illustrious with landed possessions." He was Bishop of Maestricht, but was exiled and recalled in 677. It is said that when an acolyte he carried burning coals in the folds of his surplice to kindle the incense ; this typifies his fervor. The cause of his death is given in two ways. One account is that two brothers who had robbed the church of Maestricht were slain without the knowledge of the bishop, and their kinsmen in revenge entered the house of Lambert, and murdered all within. He was killed with a dart or javelin. The other story is that, having boldly reproved Pepin d'Heristal for his love of his mistress, the beautiful Alpaïde, the grandmother of Charlemagne, one of her relatives entered his dwelling and slew him. His attributes are the palm and javelin September 17, A. D. 709.

Lamech. There is a Jewish tradition that after Lamech became blind, he was hunting in a forest where Cain had concealed himself, and mistaking the vagabond for a wild beast, he slew him with an arrow, and afterwards killed his son, Tubal-Cain, who had pointed out to him the thicket in which Cain had been. This is said to explain Gen. iv. 23, "For I have slain a man to my wounding, and a young man to my hurt." This legend has been illustrated in an engraving by Lucas von Leyden, and in sculpture in the cathedrals at Amiens and Modena as well as in the Campo Santo at Pisa.

Last Supper (*Ital.* Il Cenacolo, La Cena; *Fr.* La Cène; *Ger.* Das Abendmahl Christi). This subject occupies a most important place in art when illustrating the history of Christ as the Redeemer. It has been treated in two distinct modes, — first, as a mystery, the institution of the Sacrament of the Eucharist; again as illustrative of the detection and exposure of Judas. Keeping this distinction in mind will help to explain the differences in treatment of the various artists, and will influence the judgment in deciding points connected with them; as what seems irreverent and out of place in a religious and devotional picture is quite admissible in one that is barely historical.

St. Laurence (*Lat.* S. Laurentius; *Fr.* St. Laurent; *Ital.* and *Sp.* San Lorenzo; *Ger.* Der Heilige Laurentius, or Lorenz). Historically, but little is known of this saint. Even the time and place of his birth are matters of doubt; but that he existed, and was martyred according to the general belief, is undoubtedly true. His legend relates that he was a Spaniard, and a native of Osca, or Huesca, in Aragon, where his parents are honored as SS. Orientius and Patienza. He went to Rome when quite young, and by his exemplary life so pleased Sixtus II., then Bishop of Rome, that he made him his archdeacon, and gave the treasures of the Church into his care. When Sixtus was condemned to death as a Christian, St. Laurence clung to him, and desired to accompany him, saying, among other things, " St. Peter suffered Stephen, his deacon, to die before him; wilt thou not also suffer me to prepare thy way?" Sixtus assured him that in three days he would follow him, and that his sufferings would be far the greatest, because, being younger and stronger, he could longer endure. He also commanded Laurence to distribute the property of the Church to the poor, so that the tyrant should never possess it. So Laurence took the treasures, and sought through all Rome for the poor; and he came at night to the Cœlian Hill, where dwelt Cyriaca, who was a devout widow, who often concealed the persecuted Christians and cared for them. She was sick, and St. Laurence healed her by laying his hands on her, and also washed the feet of the Christians in the house, and gave them alms. Thus from house to house he dispensed his charities, and prepared for his hastening martyrdom. The tyrant, learning that the treasures were in his hands, ordered him to be brought to the tribunal. He was required to tell where the treasures were; but this demand he refused, and was put into a dungeon under the care of Hippolytus, whom he converted to Christianity with his whole family, so that they were baptized. Being questioned again by the prefect concerning the treasures, he promised that in three days he would show them. The time arriving, he gathered the poor ones to whom he had given aid together, and showed them to the tyrant, saying, "Behold, here are the treasures of Christ's Church!" The prefect then ordered him to be tortured until he should tell what he wished to know. But no horrors could subdue the saint; and the prefect ordered him to be carried by night to the baths of Olympias, which were near the villa of Sallust, and a new torment inflicted on him, which was that he should be stretched on an iron bed made of bars like a gridiron, and roasted over a fire kindled beneath. This was done; and all who saw were filled with horror of the tyrant who could conceive such cruelty, and condemn so gentle and comely a youth to such suffering. But Laurence was still unsubdued, and cried out, "Assatus sum; jam versa et manduca" ("I am done or roasted; now turn me and eat me"). And all were confounded by his endurance. Then he looked to heaven, and said, "I thank thee, O my God and Saviour, that I have been found worthy to enter into thy beatitude!" and so he died. The prefect and executioners went away, and Hippolytus took the body and buried it in the Via Tiburtina. For this the tyrant commanded him to be tied to the tail of a wild horse, and so he was martyred. Soon after, this prefect, as he sat in the amphitheatre, was seized with pangs of death, and cried out to St. Laurence and Hippolytus, as he gave up the ghost. In Rome six churches have been dedicated to St. Laurence; in Spain, the Escurial; in Genoa, a cathedral; and in England, about two hundred and fifty churches, besides many others in all Christendom. St. Laurence is connected with the death of the Emperor Henry II. by the following legend. One night, as a hermit sat in his hut he heard a sound as of a host rushing past. He opened his window, and called out to know who they could be. The answer came, "We are demons. Henry the Emperor is about to die at this moment, and we go to seize his soul." The hermit then begged that on their return they should tell him the result of their errand. This they promised, and after a time that same night they came again and knocked at the window. When the hermit questioned of their success, the fiends swore that all had gone ill; for they arrived just as the emperor expired, and were about to seize his soul when his good angel came to save him. After a long dispute the Angel of Judgment (St. Michael) laid his good and evil deeds in the scale, and the latter descended and touched the earth, and the victory was to the demons, when, lo! the roasted fellow (for so he wickedly called the saint) appeared, and threw into the other scale the holy cup, which changed the balance and defeated the fiends. But the demon had avenged himself by breaking the handle off the cup, and this he gave the hermit. In the morning the hermit hastened to the city and found Henry dead, and one handle gone from the cup he had given the Church, and this had disappeared in the night. St. Laurence is usually painted in the rich dress of an archdeacon, bearing the palm and *la graticola*, or gridiron. But sometimes he carries a dish full of money, and the cross, to signify his office of treasurer to the Church, and also of deacon, for deacons bore the cross in processions. The gridiron varies in form and size. Sometimes it is embroidered on his robe, suspended round his neck, or borne in his hand; and again he puts his foot on it in triumph. Patron of Nuremberg, the Escurial, and Genoa. August 10, A. D. 258.

St. Lazarus (*Lat.* and *Ger.* same as *Eng.*; *Fr.* St. Lazare; *Ital.* San Lazarro; *Sp.* San Lazaro, Lazarillo: signification, "God will help"). This saint is venerated as the first bishop of Marseilles. When seen in any pictures other than those of his resurrection, he wears, in common with many other saints, the bishop's dress; but as he is most frequently associated with Mary and Martha, he is not easily mistaken. In rare instances a bier is seen in the background. September 2.

St. Leander. February 27, A. D. 596. See St. Isidore.

St. Leocadia was a native of Toledo. She was thrown into prison during the persecution of Diocletian. While there she was told of the death of St. Eulalia, who was her friend, and she earnestly prayed that death might reunite them. Her prayer was soon answered, and she died in prison. Another legend relates that she was thrown down from a height of rocks, and a chapel was built on the spot where she fell, and in it she was buried. When St. Ildefonso had written his treatise defending the doctrine of the perpetual virginity of the Mother of God, angels rolled the stone from the tomb of St. Leocadia, and she went to St. Ildefonso to tell him of the approbation of his work in heaven. Before she could disappear he cut a piece from the mantilla which she wore, and this relic was preserved as one of the Church treasures. She is patroness of Toledo, and her statue surmounts the gate (Puerta del Cambron). She is seen only in Spanish pictures. December 9, A. D. 304.

St. Leonard (*Lat.* S. Leonardus; *Ital.* San Leonardo; *Fr.* St. Léonard, or Lionart: signification, "brave as a lion") was a courtier of the court of King Theodobert, and was much beloved by the king for his cheerfulness and amiability. He was a Christian, and especially delighted in visiting and relieving prisoners and captives; and oftentimes the king pardoned those for whom he pleaded. At length, weary of the court, he retired to a desert near Limoges, and became a hermit. One day, as the king and queen, with all the court, rode to the chase, the queen was seized with the pains of child-bearing, and seemed likely to die. The spot where they were was near the house of Leonard; and he, hearing of this distress, came and prayed for the queen, and she was soon safely delivered. Then the king gave St. Leonard a portion of the forest, and he founded a religious community, but he would never accept any office above that of deacon. His dress is that of a Benedictine or of a deacon, and his attribute a chain. Sometimes he bears a crosier as founder of a community, and often slaves or captives are near him. November 6, A. D. 559.

St. Leopold of Austria (*Ger.* Der Heilige Leopold, Luitpold, or Leupold: signification, "bold for the people"). Leopold, Margrave of Austria, was born in 1080. At twenty-six he married Agnes, widow of Frederic, Duke of Suabia. She bore him eighteen children, and eleven of them were living at his death. He founded the splendid monastery of Kloster-Neuberg, on the Danube. The legend relates that soon after his marriage he stood with Agnes on the balcony of his palace of Leopoldsberg. They regarded the extensive view before them, with Vienna near by; and hand in hand, they vowed to build and endow an edifice for the service of God in gratitude to Him who had blest their love. Just at that moment the wind lifted, and bore away the bridal veil of Agnes. Eight years from this time, when hunting in a forest near by, Leopold found this veil on a tree. He remembered his vow, ordered the forest cleared, and built the monastery of Kloster-Neuberg. A flourishing town was built around it, and some of the finest vineyards in Austria were here. The whole life of Leopold was that of a virtuous and just man. He is one of the patron saints of Austria, and is represented in armor. Sometimes he has a rosary in his hand. November 15, A. D. 1136.

St. Lieven, or **Livin,** was a poet and a Benedictine missionary. He was born in Ireland, and educated in the schools of that country, famous in those days for their superiority. While pursuing his labors near Ghent, he was cruelly martyred. His tongue was pulled out, and then his head cut off. The mother of St. Brice had been his hostess, and both she and her son were killed with St. Lieven. He had written a hymn in honor of St. Bavon, within whose church at Ghent he was buried; and there his relics still repose. He is sometimes painted holding his tongue with tongs. Rubens painted this martyrdom with terrible truthfulness. November 12, A. D. 656.

St. Lioba. This saint was the most distinguished companion of St. Walburga. She was a poet, and very learned for the time in which she lived. Charlemagne and his Empress Hildegarde were very fond of Lioba, and would gladly have kept her with them as a companion and counsellor, but she preferred her convent life. She was buried at Fulda by the side of St. Boniface. September 28, A. D. 779.

St. Longinus (*Ital.* San Longino; *Fr.* St. Longin, Sainct Longis). This saint is known as being the "first fruits of the Gentiles." He is said to be the centurion who pierced the Saviour's side. The legend relates that soon after this act he touched his eyes with his blood-stained hands, and instantly the weakness of sight or blindness from which he had long suffered was cured. He then sought the Apostles, and was baptized. After this he preached in Cæsarea, and converted numbers; and being commanded to sacrifice to the pagan deities, he refused. Longinus was desirous of the martyr's crown, and assured the governor, who was blind, that after his own death the governor's sight should be restored. Upon this he was beheaded, and immediately the governor was healed, and became a Christian. This legend is repudiated by the Church, but the knowledge of it explains the importance given to the centurion in many works of art. His dress is that of a Roman soldier, and his attribute a spear or lance. He has been patron saint of Mantua since the eleventh century, when his relics were said to have been brought to that city. His statue is under the dome of St. Peter's in Rome, because tradition says that his lance or spear is still among the treasures of the Church. March 15, A. D. 45.

St. Lorenzo Giustiniani was a Venetian of noble family. He was born in 1380, and from his youth was enthusiastic in his piety. Quirina, his mother, though young and beautiful, remained a widow that she might devote herself to her son. At nineteen he believed that he was called to a religious life by a miraculous vision. His family desired him to marry, but he retired to the cloister of San Giorgio-in-Alga. He came to his mother's palace to beg, "per i poveri di Dio." She filled his wallet, and hid herself in her chamber. He became so distinguished for his piety that he was made Bishop of Castello. When the patriarchate of Grado was removed to Venice, Lorenzo was the first to fill the office. The people so revered him that they believed his prayers had saved them from war, famine, and plague; and his memory received general and enthusiastic homage long before he was canonized by Alexander VIII. September 5, A. D. 1455.

St. Louis Beltran, or **Bertrand** (*Ital.* San Ludovico Bertrando), was born at Valencia. He became a celebrated Dominican, and was a missionary. He lived in the sixteenth century. He was a friend of St. Teresa. Feeling called to preach to the heathen, he went to Peru; but he declared that he encountered greater trials from the wickedness of the Christians than from the ignorance of the heathen. He has no especial attribute; but Peruvians or Peruvian scenery often determines his personality. Espinosa placed himself and his family under the care of this saint during the plague in Valencia in 1647; and in consideration of their protection from harm he painted a series of pictures, and placed them in the chapel of the saint in the convent of San Domingo at Valencia. October 9, A. D. 1581.

St. Louis Gonzaga, or **St. Aloysius**, was born in 1568. He was the oldest son of the Marchese di Castiglione. He entered the Society of Jesus when not yet eighteen years old. He became eminently distinguished for his learning, piety, and good works, and died at Rome in 1591 of fever, which he contracted while nursing the sick. He has no particular attribute, but his youth distinguishes him from most saints of his order. A. D. 1591.

St. Louis, King of France (*Lat.* S. Ludovicus Rex; *Ital.* San Luigi, Rè di Francia). Son of Louis VIII. and Blanche of Castile. Born in 1215 at Poissy. The holiness of Louis, his talents and virtues, combined to make him respected and beloved by all; and even Voltaire said of him, "Il n'est guère donné à l'homme de pousser la vertu plus loin!" The Franciscans claim that he put on their habit before embarking on his first crusade, and that in it he died. He was a great collector of relics, for which he had an extreme veneration. Baldwin II. secured his aid by surrendering to him the crown of thorns; and when it was brought from Constantinople Louis carried it from Sens to Paris, bareheaded and barefooted. Having also a piece of the "True Cross," he built the beautiful chapel, La Sainte Chapelle, in honor of these precious relics. In 1247, being very sick, he lay in a trance for hours. When he awoke he exclaimed, "La Lumière de l'Orient s'est répandue du haut du ciel sur moi par la grâce du Seigneur, et m'a rappelé d'entre les morts!" He then called the Archbishop of Paris, and in spite of all remonstrance from his priests and friends he commanded the cross of the crusade to be affixed to his dress. The archbishop obeyed with tears and sobs. As soon as his health allowed, he sailed for Egypt. His wife and brothers went also; and his army of fifty thousand men embraced the flower of the French nobility. After many disasters, Louis was made prisoner. But his zeal never cooled, and he regarded all his soldiers who perished as martyrs of a noble type. When ransomed, he spent three years in Palestine, and returned to France, where he remained sixteen years. He was a wise ruler, and repaired his losses and enlarged his kingdom. At the end of this time he set out on a second crusade. Those whom he left as children when he went at first, now made his army. After more trials by disease and suffering, he died in his tent, lying upon ashes, and wearing the dress of a penitent. A portion of his relics were taken to Palermo, and placed in the church of Monreale. The remainder were laid in St. Denis, but did not escape the destroyers in the first revolution. His proper attributes are the crown of thorns, his kingly crown and sword. August 25, A. D. 1270.

St. Louis of Toulouse (*Ital.* San Ludovico Vescovo) was the nephew of the last-named saint, son of the King of Naples and Sicily. Like his kingly uncle-saint, he was piously reared by his mother. When he was but fourteen, his father, being made prisoner by the King of Aragon, gave Louis and his brothers as hostages. He became wearied of everything but religion, and in 1294, when he was made free, he gave all his royal rights to his brother Robert, and became a monk of the Order of St. Francis. He was then twenty-two years old. Soon he was made Bishop of Toulouse; and he set out, barefooted and clothed as a friar, to take his new office. He went into Provence on a charitable mission, and died at the castle of Brignolles, where he was born. He was first buried at Marseilles, then removed to Valencia, where he was enshrined. His pictures represent him as young, beardless, and of gentle face. He has the fleur-de-lys embroidered on his cope or on some part of his dress. The crown which he gave away lies at his feet, while he bears the mitre of a bishop. August 19, A. D. 1297.

Sœur Louise de la Miséricorde, who was first the lovely Louise de la Vallière, was never canonized as a saint, except in the hearts of those to whom her sorrow and suffering, her repentance and charities, have made her martyr and saint. She became a Carmelite nun at thirty years of age, in 1674. She commanded Le Brun to paint "Mary Magdalene Renouncing the World," as an altar-piece for her convent. It has been thought a portrait of her; but many believe that another Magdalene by the same artist, which is in Munich, is probably the best likeness of La Vallière.

St. Lucia (*Eng.* St. Lucy, or Luce; *Fr.* St. Luce, or Lucie). When Diocletian was emperor and Pascasius was governor of Sicily, this saint dwelt in Syracuse. She was a noble and virtuous maiden. Her mother was named Eutychia. Lucia, without the knowledge of her mother, had made the vow of chastity; but her friends had her betrothed to a rich young man who was not a Christian. Eutychia being ill, her daughter persuaded her to visit Catania to pay her devotions at the shrine of St. Agatha. While Lucia knelt beside the tomb she had a vision of the saint, who addressed her thus, "O my sister handmaid of Christ," and assured her that her mother was healed, and that, as Catania had been blessed by Agatha, so Lucia should obtain the favor of Heaven for Syracuse. Now, when her mother was healed, Lucia persuaded her to allow that she should remain single, and wished her dowry to give to the poor. Her mother feared lest she should be a beggar before she died, and hoped to die soon if Lucia thus distributed her wealth. But the daughter so entreated and argued that at length Eutychia consented willingly. Then Lucia gave to the poor all she had. This so enraged the young pagan to whom she was betrothed that he accused her to Pascasius as a Christian. She was taken to this cruel governor, who ordered her to sacrifice to the gods; and when she would not, he condemned her to be taken to a vile place and treated with indignity. She assured him that he could not make her sin, although he could control her body; for that was not sin to which the mind did not consent. Then the tyrant in fury commanded her to be taken away; but when they tried they could not move her. Then they fastened ropes to her, and pulled her, but still she remained fixed. All the magicians and sorcerers were brought, but their spells had no power on her. Then they kindled a great fire about her; but she prayed that these heathens might be confounded, and the fire did not harm her. At this Pascasius was so enraged that a servant, in order to please him, murdered her by piercing her throat with a poniard. Her body was buried by the Christians on the very spot where she died; and not long after a church was erected there, and dedicated in her name. This legend, which is one of the most ancient, does not speak of the loss of her eyes, but more modern ones relate the following additional story. There dwelt in Syracuse a youth, who having seen her but once was so enamoured of her that he took every means to woo her, and constantly protested that it was her wonderfully beautiful eyes which so haunted him and possessed his soul that he could not rest. Whereupon Lucia, considering the Scripture saying, "If thine eye offend thee, pluck it out," took out her eyes and sent them to the young man on a dish, with this message, "Here hast thou what thou hast so much desired; and for the rest, I beseech thee, leave me now in peace." The young man was so affected by this that he became a convert to Christianity and an example of virtue and chastity. But Lucia did not remain blind; for as she was one day praying, her eyes were restored and were more beautiful than at first. The legend advises those who doubt this to consult the writings of various learned men, where they will find these facts related. There is another legend which makes the loss of her eyes a part of her martyrdom, but there is little authority for this. Her attributes are a light, which is the signification of her name; her eyes on a dish, with or without an awl by which they were bored out; and a poniard as the instrument of her death. Sometimes light proceeds from wounds in her neck, and again she is being pulled by men and oxen, with no effect. In her apotheosis an angel carries her eyes to heaven, while others bear the saint. Patroness of Syracuse; protectress against all diseases of the eye; patroness of the laboring poor. December 13, A. D. 303.

St. Ludmilla was the grandmother of St. Wenceslaus, or Wenzel, who is venerated in the north of Germany. Ludmilla was converted by the preaching of St. Adelbert, and she educated her grandson in the Christian faith. His brother Boleslaus was a pagan, and instructed by his mother, Drahomira. Bohemia at length became divided between Christians and pagans; and Boleslaus and his mother determined to kill Ludmilla, who protected the Christians. They hired assassins who strangled her with her veil when she was praying in her oratory. Wenceslaus was then persuaded to visit his mother, and was slain by his brother when he too was in the act of paying his devotions at the altar. Ludmilla was the first martyr saint of Bohemia. September 16, A. D. 927.

St. Luke (*Lat.* S. Luca; *Ital.* San Luca; *Fr.* St. Luc). We are told but little of St. Luke in the Gospel. It would seem that he was not converted until after the Ascension of our Lord. He was a disciple of Paul, and was with him until his death. Some say he was crucified at Patras, and others that he died a peaceful death. That he was a physician may be inferred from the fact that Paul speaks of him as "Luke, the beloved physician;" but the general belief that he was an artist rests on Greek traditions, and can only be traced to the tenth century. A picture of the Virgin found in the Catacombs with an inscription to the import that it is "one of seven painted by Luca," is regarded as a confirmation of this belief concerning the Evangelist Luke.

Tradition relates that he carried always with him two portraits, one of the Saviour and the other of Mary. He made many converts by displaying these faces, which inspired those who saw them with devotion. Moreover, in his hands, they became the instruments of miracles. In the church of Santa Maria, in Via Lata at Rome, a small chapel is shown as that in which Luke wrote his Gospel and multiplied images of the Virgin, which it was his delight to do. From these legends he has been chosen the patron saint of artists and academies of art. He is often represented as painting the Virgin. His attributes are the ox, given him because he wrote especially of the priesthood of the Saviour, and the ox is the emblem of sacrifice; the book, signifying his writings, and a portrait of the Virgin placed in his hand. Sometimes the ox has wings; and again the head of an ox is placed on the figure of a man as a symbol of this Evangelist. In the church of San Domenico and San Sisto at Rome, there is a tablet which is inscribed thus: "Here at the high altar is preserved that image of the most blessed Mary which being delineated by St. Luke the Evangelist, received its colors and form divinely. This is that image with which St. Gregory the Great (according to St. Antonine), as a suppliant, purified Rome; and the pestilence being dispelled, the angel messenger of peace, from the summit of the castle of Adrian, commanding the Queen of Heaven to rejoice, restored health to the city." Another picture in the Ara Cœli claims to be the one which was thus honored. Both of them are dark and far from beautiful; and if they are the work of St. Luke, I would much prefer the *word-picture* of Mary which he gives in his Gospel to those of his brush. October 18.

St. Lupo. See St. Adelaide.

St. Macarius (of Alexandria) was one of the most famous hermit saints of Egypt. He is represented in the great fresco by Pietro Laurati in the Campo Santo at Pisa. He is in the centre, looking down at a skull which he touches with his staff. This is explained by the following legend: As Macarius was wandering among the Egyptian tombs he saw a skull of a mummy. He turned it over, and asked to whom it belonged. It answered, "To a pagan." He then said, "Where is thy soul?" And the skull replied, "In hell." Macarius then said, "How deep?" "The depth is greater than the distance from heaven to earth," answered the skull. Then Macarius asked, "Are there any deeper than thou art?" and the skull replied, "Yes, the Jews are deeper still." And again the hermit said, "Are there any deeper than the Jews?" "Yes, in sooth!" replied the skull; "for the Christians whom Jesus Christ hath redeemed, and who show in their actions that they despise his doctrine, are deeper still!" January 2, A. D. 394.

Madonna, La, or **Our Lady** (*Fr.* Notre Dame; *Ger.* Unsere liebe Frau; *Eng.* The Virgin Mary; *Lat.* Virgo Gloriosa, Virgo Sponsa Dei, Virgo Potens, Virgo Veneranda, Virgo Prædicanda, Virgo Clemens, Virgo Sapientissima, Sancta Virgo Virginum; *Ital.* La Vergine Gloriosa, La Gran Vergine delle Vergini; *Fr.* La Grande Vierge; *Gr.* Θεοτόκη).

Taking the legends connected with the life of Mary in order, the first is the legend of *Joachim and Anna* (*Ital.* La Leggenda di Sant' Anna Madre della Gloriosa Vergine Maria, e di San Gioacchino). See St. Joachim.

The next historical picture is *The Nativity of the Blessed Virgin* (*Fr.* La Naissance de la S. Vierge; *Ital.* La Nascità della B. Vergine; *Ger.* Die Geburt Maria). As tradition tells that Joachim and Anna were "exceedingly rich," the room in which the birth is represented is usually rich in furniture and decorations. A glory sometimes surrounds the head of the child. Most artists have also painted attendants, and a number of friends and neighbors who have come to rejoice with St. Anna that her prayers are answered and a child born to her, while she herself reclines on her bed and receives the attentions of the handmaidens and the congratulations of her friends. September 8.

The Presentation of the Virgin (*Ital.* La Presentazione, ove nostra Signora piccioletta Sale i gradi del Tempio; *Ger.* Die Vorstellung der Jungfrau im Tempel, Joachim und Anna weihen ihre Tochter Maria im Tempel). The legend says: "And when the child was three years old, Joachim said: 'Let us invite the daughters of Israel, and they shall take each a taper or a lamp, and attend on her, that the child may not turn back from the temple of the Lord.' And being come to the temple, they placed her on the first step, and she ascended alone all the steps to the altar; and the high-priest received her there, kissed her, and blessed her, saying, 'Mary, the Lord hath magnified thy name to all generations, and in thee shall be made known the redemption of the children of Israel.' And being placed before the altar, she danced with her feet, so that all the house of Israel rejoiced with her, and loved her. Then her parents returned home, blessing God because the maiden had not turned back from the Temple." There are various pictures of the life of Mary in the Temple. She is represented as instructing her companions, as spinning, and as embroidering tapestry. She is sometimes attended by angels; and tradition declares that her food was supplied by them, and that Mary had the privilege, which none other of her sex ever had, of going into the Holy of Holies to pray before the ark of the covenant. Presentation of B. V. November 21.

The Marriage of the Virgin (*Ital.* Il Sposalizio; *Fr.* Le Mariage de la Vierge; *Ger.* Die Trauung Mariä). When fourteen years old, Mary was told by the high-priest that it was proper for her to be married. But she replied that her parents had dedicated her to the service of the Lord. Then the high-priest told her of a vision he had had concerning her, and she submitted herself to the Lord's appointment with sweet humility. The manner in which her husband was selected is told in the legend of St. Joseph. In the representations the Virgin is attended by a train of maidens, and the disappointed suitors are often seen. The priest joins her hand to that of Joseph, or Joseph is placing the ring on her finger. Joseph frequently carries his blossomed wand, while the other suitors break or trample on theirs. The cathedral of Perugia is said to contain among its relics the nuptial ring of the Blessed Virgin. The return of Joseph and Mary to their house is also a subject of art; and Luini represents them as walking hand in hand, Joseph regarding her with veneration, and she looking down, modestly serene. January 23.

The Annunciation (*Fr.* La Salutation Angélique, L'Annonciation; *Ger.* Die Verkündigung, Der englische Gruss; *Ital.* L'Annunciazione, La B. Vergine Annunziata). In addition to the Gospel account of this event, artists have been influenced by legends. One relates that as Mary went forth at evening to draw water, she heard a voice which said, "Hail, thou that art full of grace!" but she could see no one. Being troubled, she returned to her house and her work, which is said to have been purple and fine linen. St. Bernard relates the event in this wise: Mary was studying the book of Isaiah, and as she read the verse, "Behold, a Virgin shall conceive and bear a son," she thought within herself, "How blessed the woman of whom these words are written! Would I might be but her handmaid to serve her, and allowed to kiss her feet!" And instantly the angel appeared to her, and in her the prophecy was fulfilled. The time is sometimes just at evening, in reference to which belief that hour has been consecrated as the "Ave Maria." But others believe it to have been midnight, and that Christ was born at the same hour the following December. The place is usually within the house and rarely by a fountain, as the legend presents it. Sometimes Gabriel flies in from above, or is borne by a cloud. Sometimes he walks, but is always young, beautiful, and yet thoughtful in look. He has wings, and in the early pictures full drapery. He either bears the lily (Fleur de Marie), or it is in some other part of the picture. Sometimes he has the olive, typical of peace, or a sceptre with a scroll inscribed "Ave Maria, gratia plena!" Very rarely he has the palm. The Holy Spirit, as a dove, is sometimes poised over the head of Mary, sometimes hovers toward her bosom, or enters the room through the window. A less agreeable introduction is that of the Eternal Father above the sky, surrounded by a glory and sending forth celestial light. The spirit or sentiment of the picture depends in a great measure upon the age in which it was painted. Before the fourteenth century Mary is usually represented as humble and submissive, as if listening to the mandate of God, and that from the lips of a superior being. But after that time the increased veneration of the faithful to the Virgin pictures her as she was, — the superior being; and her aspect befits the "Regina angelorum." The work-basket, typical of the industry of Mary, is seldom omitted; and to express her temperance, a dish of fruit and a pitcher of water are frequently introduced. There are certain mystical or allegorical representations of the Annunciation difficult to be understood. One represents a unicorn taking refuge in the bosom of the Virgin : an angel near by winds a hunting-horn, while four dogs crouch near him. Its signification is given thus in an ancient French work. The fabulous unicorn, who with his single horn was said to wound only to free the part wounded from all disease, is an emblem of Jesus, the great physician of souls. The four dogs represent Mercy, Truth, Justice, and Peace, as the four considerations which influenced the Saviour to undertake the salvation of men. The remainder of the explanation is so peculiar that no translation can give the exact idea. It is thus : "Mais comme c'étoit par la Vierge Marie qu'il avoit voulu descendre parmi les hommes et se mettre en leur puissance, on croyoit ne pouvoir mieux faire que de choisir dans la fable, le fait d'une pucelle pouvant seule servir de piége à la licorne, en l'attirant par le charme et le parfum de son sein virginal qu'elle lui présentoit — enfin l'ange Gabriel concourant au mystère étoit bien reconnoissable sous les traits du veneur ailé lançant les lévriers et embouchant la trompette." Another mode of representation is that of Mary, standing with her hands folded over her breast and her head bowed. She is beneath a splendid portico. Gabriel kneels outside and extends the lily. Above, the Padre Eterno appears and sends forth the Saviour, who is in the form of the Infant Christ bearing his cross, who floats downward toward the earth, preceded by the Holy Spirit in the form of the Dove. These ideal pictures usually, if not always, date earlier than the seventeenth century. March 25.

The Visitation (Fr. La Visitation de la Vierge ; *Ital.* La Visitazione di Maria ; *Ger.* Die Heimsuchung Mariä). This scene, which represents the meeting of Mary and Elizabeth, is also called "The Salutation of Elizabeth." This picture is not easily mistaken, however painted ; sometimes the scene is in the garden of Zacharias, where the legend relates that Mary often retired to meditate upon the great honor God had bestowed upon her. It is told that one day while in this garden the Virgin touched a flower which before had no perfume, but since that time its odor is delicious. Again the two favored women meet at the entrance of the dwelling of Elizabeth. She is of course much older than Mary, but should not be feeble and wrinkled. Her manner befits one who recognizes the Mother of her Lord, with glad humility, but shows also a certain dignity, since she herself is appointed by God to an exalted motherhood. Zacharias and Joseph as well as servants are frequently introduced, and sometimes the ass on which Mary has ridden. Zacharias is robed as a priest, and Joseph as a traveller. Sometimes Elizabeth kneels as if to make more impressive her words, "And whence is this to me, that the mother of my Lord should come to me?" July 2.

The Nativity (Fr. La Nativité ; *Ital.* Il Presepio, Il Nascimento del Nostro Signore ; *Ger.* Die Geburt Christi). An ancient legend relates that about the same time that Cæsar Augustus decreed "that all the world should be taxed," he was warned by a sibyl of the birth of Jesus. The pictures and sculptures representing this legend are not improperly considered in connection with those of the Nativity, to which they so distinctly point. The legend relates that the emperor consulted the sibyl Tiburtina, to know if it were right that he should accept the divine honors which the Senate had decreed to him. The sibyl, after meditating some days, took the emperor alone, and showed him an altar. Above this altar the heavens opened, and he saw a beautiful virgin bearing an infant in her arms, and he heard a voice saying, "This is the altar of the Son of the living God." Then Cæsar Augustus erected on the Capitoline Hill an altar, and inscribed it "Ara primogeniti Dei." The church called the Ara-Cœli stands on the same spot as that on which the altar was built; and in it is a bas-relief representing this legend, to which a very great antiquity is attached by the Church. There are other paintings of the same subject. The Nativity, when treated as an historical event, is represented in a stable, at midnight, and in winter. The earlier pictures give Mary an appearance of suffering, but from the fourteenth century it is not so. Sometimes she kneels by the child, or points to the manger in which he lies, or bending over him is bright with the light which comes from the child, and which, according to the legend, illuminated the place with supernatural light. Joseph is sitting, or leaning on his staff, and frequently holds a taper or other light to show that it is night. The angels who sang the "Gloria in Excelsis" were at first represented as three, but in later pictures their number is larger, as of a chorus. The ox and the ass are invariably seen. The old monks had various ideas associated with these animals. They regarded them as the fulfilment of prophecy (Habakkuk iii. 4), and as typical of the Jews and Gentiles, — the ox representing the former and the ass the latter; and one old writer relates that they warmed the heavenly babe with their breath. Sometimes the ass is with open mouth, as if proclaiming in his way the light that had come to enlighten the Gentiles. The shepherds are frequently in the background. • When treated as a mystery, the Virgin adores the child who is her son and her God. It is sometimes difficult to distinguish between this and a "Madre Pia," but usually something is introduced to denote the Nativity. The babe lies in the centre with his finger on his lip, as if to say, "Verbum sum," and looks upward to the angels, who in the heavens sing his glory. His hand sometimes rests on a wheat-sheaf, emblem of the bread of life. Mary kneels on one side, and Joseph, if present, also kneels; and often angels adore and sustain the child.

When other figures are introduced, they are saints, or votaries for whom the picture was painted. December 25.

The Adoration of the Shepherds (*Fr.* L'Adoration des Bergers; *Ger.* Die Anbetung der Hirten; *Ital.* L'Adorazione dei Pastori). The shepherds present their offerings of fruits, lambs, or doves, and with uncovered heads show their devotion with rude simplicity. Women, dogs, and sheep sometimes accompany them; and there is a legend that the Apostles Simeon and Jude were of their number. Sometimes the child sleeps, and the Virgin or Joseph raises the covering to show him to the shepherds. When angels scatter flowers, they are those gathered in heaven.

The Adoration of the Magi (*Ger.* Die heilige drei Königen; Die Anbetung der Weisen aus dem Morgenland; *Ital.* L'Adorazione de' Magia; L'Epifania; *Fr.* L'Adoration des Rois Mages). This picture, while it makes one of the historical series in the life of the Virgin, has another deep interest in the consideration that it is the expression of the Epiphany, — of the manifestation to the Gentiles of God made man. The legend follows the Scripture account, and the reasonable inferences to be deduced from it, more closely than many others. It is that these Magi were not men who knew the arts of magic, but wise princes of some eastern country. The prophecy of Balaam had been held in remembrance by their people, "I shall see him, but not now; I shall behold him, but not nigh: there shall come a Star out of Jacob, and a sceptre shall rise out of Israel," and when they saw a star differing from those which as learned astronomers they had studied, they recognized it as the star of the prophecy, and at once followed whither it led. It has been said that the star when first seen had the form of a child bearing a sceptre or cross. The wise men said farewell to their homes and friends, and took numerous attendants for their long journey. After many perils, the climbing of mountains, the crossing of deep streams, and many difficulties, they came to Jerusalem. On inquiry for the King they sought, they were directed to Bethlehem, and asked by Herod to bring him news on their return of where the child could be found, that he too might worship him. At length the star stood still over the lowly place where Jesus was. No matter how different may have been their previous imaginations from the reality they found, their faith was equal to the demand upon it; and they bowed down, thus giving themselves first, and then presented the gold, which signified that Jesus was king; the frankincense, that he was God; and the myrrh, that he was suffering man, and must yield to death. In return for their gifts Christ gave them charity and spiritual riches in place of gold; perfect faith for their incense; and for myrrh truth and meekness of spirit. The Virgin gave them, as a precious memorial, one of the linen bands in which she had wrapped the divine child. Being warned in a dream, they returned not to Herod, but went another way. There is a legend that their homeward journey was made in ships; and in a commentary of the fifth century on the Psalms it is said that when Herod found that they had escaped from him "in ships of Tarsus," he burned all the vessels in the port. But however they returned, the legend relates that the star guided them to the East as it had led them from it, and they reached their homes in safety. They never again assumed their former state, but in imitation of their new sovereign they gave their wealth to the poor, and went about to preach the new gospel of peace. There is a tradition that after forty years, when St. Thomas went to the Indies, he met there these wise men and baptized them; and afterwards, as they continued to preach, they went among barbarians and were put to death. Long after, their remains were found, and the Empress Helena had them removed to Constantinople. During the first Crusade they were carried to Milan, and lastly the Emperor Barbarossa placed them in the cathedral at Cologne, where they remain in a costly shrine whereat many wonderful miracles have been wrought. The names of these three "Kings of Cologne," as they are often called, are Jasper, or Caspar, Melchior, and Balthasar. In the pictures they are of three ages: the first, Jaspar, very old, with gray beard; Melchior of middle age; and Balthasar always young, and sometimes a Moor or black man, to signify that he was of Ethiopia, and that Christ came to redeem all races. Sometimes this idea is manifested by making Balthasar's servant black. Their costumes, attendants, and various appointments vary with the time in which the pictures were painted, and with the nationality of the artist. Now they have all the usual paraphernalia of royalty as seen in the continental capitals; again the knowledge acquired in the Crusades was employed, and all about them is Oriental in style; and elephants, leopards, and even monkeys are introduced into the scene. The holy child is sometimes held by his mother, and sometimes sits alone, but usually raises his hand as if in blessing. In early days Joseph was seldom present; but as devotion to him increased in the Church, he was more frequently made an actor in this scene: he sometimes only looks on quietly; again he receives the treasure, and in some instances the Magi seem to congratulate him. The various modes of representing this inexhaustible subject would if described fill a volume. January 6.

The Purification of the Virgin; *The Presentation of Christ in the Temple* (*Ital.* La Purificazione della B. Vergine; *Ger.* Die Darbringung im Tempel). The Virgin, after the birth of her son, complied with all the requirements of the law, and the scene in the Temple is sometimes called the Purification, but more frequently it is regarded as referring especially to the Saviour; and many representations present the prophecy of Simeon as the important event in the scene. It is also considered as the first of the seven sorrows of the Virgin; and the words, "Yea, a sword shall pierce through thy own soul also," may well have saddened the heart of Mary, and given her a warning of all the glorious sorrows which were before her. The legend of Simeon is so closely connected with this scene as to be better given here than elsewhere. Two hundred and sixty years B. C., Ptolemy Philadelphus requested the high-priest of the Jews to send him scribes and interpreters to translate for him the Hebrew Scriptures, so that he might place them in his library. Six learned Rabbis from each tribe were sent, seventy-two in all; and among them Simeon, who was full of learning. His portion was the book of Isaiah; and when he came to the sentence, "Behold a Virgin shall conceive," he feared the translation might offend the Greeks, and after much consideration he rendered it a *young woman*, but when it was written, an angel effaced it, and wrote the word *Virgin* as it should be. Then Simeon wrote it again and again, and every time it was changed. When this was done three times, he was confounded; and as he meditated on this, it was revealed to him that the prophecy should not only be fulfilled, but that he "should not see death till he had seen the Lord's Christ." So he lived until these things came to pass, and then he was led to the Temple on the very day when this Virgin Mother came to present there her Divine Son. And there it was that he exclaimed, when his prophecy was ended, "Lord, now lettest thou thy servant depart in peace according to thy word." Anna the prophetess has her part in this picture. She prophesied of him who should bring redemption to Israel, but she did not take the child; from this she has been regarded as an image of the synagogue, which had prophesied much of the Messiah, but failed to embrace him when he came. This picture is frequently called the *Nunc Dimittis*, which is its title in Greek art. February 2.

The Flight into Egypt (*Ital.* La Fuga in Egitto; *Fr.* La Fuite de la Sainte Famille en Égypte; *Ger.* Die Flucht nach Aegypten). There are various legends connected with this journey of the Holy Family which have been illustrated by artists. One is that when, escaping, and fearing lest they should be overtaken by the officers of Herod, they came to a place where a man was sowing wheat. Mary said to him, "If any shall ask you whether we have passed this way, ye shall answer, 'Such persons passed this way when I was sowing this corn.'" And then, by a miracle of the infant Jesus, the corn grew in one night so as to be fit for the harvest. Next day the officers did indeed come; and the man, who was cutting his wheat in great wonder and thankfulness, answered as he had been instructed, and the pursuers turned back. Another legend relates that the Holy Family encountered a band of robbers, of which there were large numbers in that country in those days. One of the robbers was about to attack them when another said, "Suffer them, I beseech thee, to go in peace, and I will give thee forty groats, and likewise my girdle." This offer the first robber accepted. The second then took the travellers to a safe place, where they passed the night. The Virgin said to him, "The Lord God will receive thee to his right hand, and grant thee pardon of thy sins!" And this was done; for (according to the legend) these were the two thieves who were crucified with Jesus, and the merciful one was the same who went with Christ to Paradise. Another popular incident of this journey in legendary writings is that the palm-tree bent its branches at the command of the child, to shade the Blessed Virgin. It is also related that a tree which grew at the gate of Heliopolis and was venerated as the home of a god, bowed itself at the approach of the Saviour, and that all along the route of the Holy Family, wherever there were idols, these fell on their faces and were broken in fragments. This is assented to by religious

authorities as well as by writers of legends. There are many ways of
representing the three travellers on this remarkable journey, but all
are easily recognized.   There are a few in which they are either embarking or are in a boat crossing one of the streams or lakes which in-
tercepted the course of their journey. Sometimes an angel assists the
Virgin to enter, and sometimes steers the boat. See, also, St. Joseph.

The Repose of the Holy Family (*Ital.* Il Riposo ; *Ger.* Die Ruhe
in Aegypten ; *Fr.* Le Repos de la Sainte Famille). The subject of
this picture is really an incident of the Flight ; but it is not found
in very early art, — rarely, if at all, before the sixteenth century.
When other figures than those of the Virgin and child with Joseph
are introduced, it is not a *Riposo*, but a *Holy Family*. The legend
states that the Holy Family reposed beneath a sycamore grove near
the village of Matarea, and that near the same village a fountain
sprang forth miraculously for their refreshment. This gave a religious interest to the sycamore, and the Crusaders brought it to Europe ; and this same " Fountain of Mary " was shown me by the Arab
guides, a few miles from Cairo. Mary is sometimes painted dipping
water, and again washing linen in this fountain, which the legend
also tells that she did.   In pictures of the Repose, angels often
minister to the comfort of the travellers, in various ways and with
beautiful propriety. There is a wild ballad legend, which probably
originated in the East, which gives an account of the meeting of Mary
and a Zingara, or gypsy. The gypsy crosses the palm of the child
and tells his future, according to their customs. Her prophecy of
all his sufferings quite overcomes the Virgin ; but the Zingara con-
soles her with the assurance of the redemption of mankind through
all these sorrows, and ends by asking forgiveness of her sins, instead
of the usual gold or silver piece the gypsies love so well. This affords a fine subject for art, and has been painted. When the Holy
Family are seen as on a journey, and the Saviour represented as
walking, it is the return from Egypt that is intended.

The Holy Family (*Fr.* La Sainte Famille ; *Ital.* La Sacra Famiglia,
La Sacra Conversazione). From the return to Nazareth until Jesus
is twelve years old, the Gospels record no events of the life of the
Virgin or her Son.   Under the title of Holy Family, there are hundreds of pictures representing the imaginary life of these exalted
ones, whose every act was full of interest to all the world. The

simplest form is that of two figures, the Virgin and Child; and frequently she is nursing the babe, sometimes kisses him, or amuses him with playthings, and again watches him asleep, and ponders in her heart upon her wonderful child; which last are called "Il Silenzio," or "Le Sommeil de Jésus." Where there are three figures it is generally St. John who is added, but sometimes St. Joseph makes the third. Four figures include either St. John and St. Elizabeth or more rarely St. Joseph and St. John. Five figures include all who have been named, and Zacharias sometimes makes the sixth. More than these are unusual, although there are pictures in which large numbers surround the Holy Family proper, and are supposed to represent the relatives of the Saviour, especially those who were afterwards to be his disciples and followers. But any description of these pictures would fill volumes. Many of them are designated by some prominent peculiarity, and bear such names as "La Vierge aux Cerises," "La Vierge à la Diadème," "La Vierge à l'Oreiller Verd," "La Madonna del Bacino," "Le Ménago du Menuisier," "Le Raboteur," etc.

The Dispute in the Temple (*Ital.* La Disputa nel Tempio; *Fr.* Jésus au milieu des ¯Docteurs). While this is the representation of a very important act in the life of Jesus, it is quite as frequently made one of the series from the life of the Virgin. And in regarding these pictures it will aid one to consider whether it is the wonderful knowledge of Jesus or the grief of Mary which is the more forcibly portrayed.

The Death of Joseph (*Ital.* La Morte di San Giuseppe; *Fr.* La Mort de St. Joseph; *Ger.* Josef's Tod). See St. Joseph.

The Marriage at Cana in Galilee (*Ital.* Le Nozze di Cana; *Fr.* Les Noces de Cana; *Ger.* Die Hochzeit zu Cana). Although Jesus performed his first miracle at this marriage feast, it was not a favorite subject in early art. It is accounted greatly to the Virgin's honor that this miracle was done at her request. His answer, that his hour had not yet come, and his performing the miracle immediately after, is construed to mean that although the period had not fully arrived for the use of his power, still, out of regard to his mother and her wishes, the power was put forth. In some pictures the bride is dressed as a nun about to make her vows; and an ancient legend declared that this was the marriage of St. John the Evangelist with Mary Magdalene, and that immediately they separated, and led chaste and austere lives, devoting themselves to Christ's service. After this marriage the Virgin is scarcely mentioned in the Gospels until the time of the Crucifixion.

In the Rosary two scenes from the Passion of Our Lord make two of the mystical sorrows : the *Procession to Calvary*, or "Il Portamento della Croce," and the *Crucifixion*. It was in the Via Dolorosa, through which Christ bore his cross, that Mary is said to have fainted at the sight of his sufferings, and this incident is frequently a subject of painting. The celebrated "Lo Spasimo di Sicilia" of Raphael represents Mary as "Notre Dame du Spasme," or "du Pâmoison," as the French call the mournful festival which they keep in Passion Week to commemorate this event. The Italians call these representations "Il Pianto di Maria," or "La Madonna dello Spasimo." But in all these pictures and those of the Crucifixion, Mary is a prominent figure. There has been much said and written upon the impropriety of representing the Virgin as too greatly overcome with her grief, as it is thought to detract from the grandeur of her character ; and it would seem that although the time had come when Simeon's prophecy was fulfilled, yet her heaven-given patience and hope should have sustained her, and she should have endured where any other mother might have fainted.[1] The legend relates that in the *Descent from the Cross*, when Joseph of Arimathea and Nicodemus removed the nails from the hands of the Saviour, St. John took them away secretly, that Mary might not see them ; and while Nicodemus drew forth those which held the feet, Joseph so sustained the body that the head and arms of Jesus hung over his shoulder. Then Mary arose, and kissed the bleeding hands of her beloved Son, and clasping them tenderly, sank to the earth in anguish ; and this action is usually represented in pictures of the Descent from the Cross. In the *Deposition*, or the act of laying down the body of Christ, the Virgin supports her Son, or bends tenderly over him. In older pictures she is fainting here, which does not meet with the same censure from critics in this case as in the Procession to Calvary. The Virgin is also seen in the representations of the *Entombment*, although this is not painted in the series of the Life of the Virgin ; and in this, as in the others, her sorrow is often expressed by fainting. The next subject in course is, *John*

---

[1] "Now, there *stood* by the Cross of Jesus, his Mother." — John xix. 25.

conducting the Virgin to his Home, which, beautiful as it is, did not appear in works of art until the seventeenth century, so that it is not frequently seen. Although not recorded in Scripture, the traditions tell that Jesus appeared first of all to his mother, and the story is thus told: After all was finished, Mary retired to her chamber, and waited for the fulfilment of the promise of Christ's resurrection. And she prayed earnestly: "Thou didst promise, O my most dear Son, that thou wouldst rise again on the third day. Before yesterday was the day of darkness and bitterness; and behold, this is the third day. Return then to me, thy mother. O my Son, tarry not, but come!" And while she prayed, a company of angels surrounded her, and they waved palms, and joyously sang the Easter hymn, "Regina Cœli lætare, Alleluia!" Then Christ entered, bearing the standard of the cross, and followed by the patriarchs and prophets whom he had released from Hades. All knelt before Mary, and thanked her because their deliverance had come through her. But she greatly desired to hear the voice of Jesus, and he raised his hand in benediction, saying, "I salute thee, O my mother!" And she fell on his neck, exclaiming, "Is it thou, indeed, my most dear Son?" Then he showed her his wounds, and bade her be comforted since he had triumphed over death and hell. Then Mary on her knees thanked him that she had been his mother, and they talked together until he left her to show himself next to Mary Magdalene. The representations of the Apparition of Christ to the Virgin are in the most matter-of-fact style, and poorly portray the spirit of this beautiful legend. The *Ascension of Christ* is the seventh of the mystical sorrows of the Virgin, for by it she was left alone. The legends say that she was present, and gazing at the departing Saviour, prayed, "My Son, remember me when thou comest to thy kingdom. Leave me not long after thee, my Son!" Mary, when represented in the pictures of the *Descent of the Holy Ghost*, is placed in the centre or in front, as Regina et Mater Apostolorum. It has been objected that as Mary was Wisdom, or the Mother of Wisdom, she needed no accession of understanding. But if the testimony of Scripture is taken, it would seem proper that she should be represented here (Acts i. 14 and ii. 1). There is no authoritative record of the life of Mary after the ascension of Jesus; but there are many legends which speak of circumstances of her life, and a very curious one of her death and assumption. One which has been the subject of pictures is the Communion of Mary, in which she receives the Sacrament from the hand of St. John. The traditions relate that when the persecution began at Jerusalem, the Virgin went with St. John to Ephesus, accompanied by Mary Magdalene; also, that she dwelt on Mt. Carmel in an oratory which the prophet Elijah had built, and from this she became the patroness of the Carmelites, and the sixteenth day of July is set apart by the Church as that of the Blessed Virgin Mary of Mt. Carmel.

The Death and Assumption of the Virgin (*Lat.* Dormitio, Pausatio, Transitus, Assumptio, B. Virginis; *Ital.* Il Transito di Maria, Il Sonno della Beata Vergine, L'Assunzione; *Fr.* La Mort de la Vierge, L'Assomption; *Ger.* Das Absterben der Maria, Mariä Himmelfahrt). Sometimes these two events are represented together, the death making the lower, and the apotheosis the upper portion of the picture. But so many circumstances of the legend are portrayed in these pictures that they cannot be well understood without a knowledge of it. It is thus given by Mrs. Jameson in the "Legends of the Madonna :" "Mary dwelt in the house of John upon Mt. Sion, looking for the fulfilment of the promise of deliverance; and she spent her days in visiting those places which had been hallowed by the baptism, the sufferings, the burial and resurrection of her divine Son, but more particularly the tomb wherein he was laid. And she did not this as seeking the living among the dead, but for consolation and for remembrance. And on a certain day the heart of the Virgin, being filled with an inexpressible longing to behold her Son, melted away within her, and she wept abundantly. And, lo! an angel appeared before her clothed in light, as with a garment. And he saluted her, and said, 'Hail, O Mary! blessed by Him who hath given salvation to Israel! I bring thee here a branch of palm gathered in Paradise; command that it be carried before thy bier in the day of thy death; for in three days thy soul shall leave thy body, and thou shalt enter into Paradise, where thy Son awaits thy coming.' Mary, answering, said : 'If I have found grace in thy eyes, tell me first what is thy name; and grant that the Apostles, my brethren, may be reunited to me before I die, that in their presence I may give up my soul to God. Also, I pray thee that my soul, when delivered from my body, may not be affrighted by any spirit of darkness, nor any evil angel be allowed to have any power over me.' And the angel said, 'Why dost thou ask my name? My name is the Great and the Wonderful. And now doubt not that all the Apostles shall be reunited to thee this day; for He who in former times transported the prophet Habakkuk from Judæa to Jerusalem by the hair of his head, can as easily bring hither the Apostles. And fear thou not the evil spirit; for hast thou not bruised his head, and destroyed his kingdom?' And having said these words, the angel departed into heaven; and the palm branch which he had left behind him shed light from every leaf, and sparkled as the stars of the morning. Then Mary lighted the lamps and prepared her bed, and waited until the hour was come. And in the same instant John, who was preaching at Ephesus, and Peter, who was preaching at Antioch, and all the other Apostles, who were dispersed in different parts of the world, were suddenly caught up as by a miraculous power, and found themselves before the door of the habitation of Mary. When Mary saw them all assembled round her, she blessed and thanked the Lord; and she placed in the hands of St. John the shining palm, and desired that he should bear it before her at the time of her burial. Then Mary, kneeling down, made her prayer to the Lord, her Son, and the others prayed with her; then she laid herself down in her bed, and composed herself for death. And John wept bitterly. And about the third hour of the night, as Peter stood at the head of the bed, and John at the foot, and the other Apostles around, a mighty sound filled the house, and a delicious perfume filled the chamber. And Jesus himself appeared, accompanied by an innumerable company of angels, patriarchs, and prophets; all these surrounded the bed of the Virgin, singing hymns of joy. And Jesus said to his mother, 'Arise, my beloved, mine elect! come with me from Lebanon, my espoused! receive the crown that is destined for thee!' And Mary, answering, said, 'My heart is ready; for it was written of me that I should do thy will!' Then all the angels and blessed spirits who accompanied Jesus began to sing and rejoice. And the soul of Mary left her body, and was received into the arms of her Son; and together they ascended into heaven. And the Apostles looked up, saying, 'O most prudent Virgin, remember us when thou comest to glory!' and the angels who received her into heaven sung these words, 'Who is this that cometh up from the wilderness leaning upon her Beloved? She is fairer than all the daughters of Jerusalem.' But the body of Mary remained upon the earth; and three among the virgins prepared to wash and clothe it in a shroud; but such a glory of light surrounded her form, that though they touched it they could not see it, and no human eye beheld those chaste and sacred limbs unclothed. Then the Apostles took her up reverently, and placed her upon a bier, and John, carrying the celestial palm, went before. Peter sung the 114th Psalm, 'In exitu Israel de Egypto, domus Jacob de populo barbaro,' and the angels followed after, also singing. The wicked Jews, hearing these melodious voices, ran together; and the high-priest, being seized with fury, laid his hands upon the bier, intending to overturn it on the earth; but both his arms were suddenly dried up, so that he could not move them, and he was overcome with fear; and he prayed to St. Peter for help, and Peter said, 'Have faith in Jesus Christ and his Mother, and thou shalt be healed;' and it was so. Then they went on, and laid the Virgin in a tomb in the Valley of Jehoshaphat. And on the third day Jesus said to the angels, 'What honor shall I confer on her who was my mother on earth, and brought me forth?' And they answered, 'Lord, suffer not that body which was thy temple and thy dwelling to see corruption; but place her beside thee on thy throne in heaven.' And Jesus consented; and the Archangel Michael brought unto the Lord the glorious soul of our Lady. And the Lord said, 'Rise up, my dove, my undefiled, for thou shalt not remain in the darkness of the grave, nor shalt thou see corruption;' and immediately the soul of Mary rejoined her body, and she arose up glorious from the tomb and ascended into heaven, surrounded and welcomed by troops of angels, blowing their silver trumpets, touching their golden lutes, singing and rejoicing as they sung, 'Who is she that riseth as the morning, fair as the moon, clear as the sun, and terrible as an army with banners?' (Cant. vi. 10.) But one among the Apostles was absent; and when he arrived soon after, he would not believe in the resurrection of the Virgin (and this Apostle was the same Thomas who had formerly been slow to believe in the resurrection of the Lord); and he desired that the tomb should be opened before him, and when it was opened it was found to be full of lilies and roses. Then Thomas, looking up to heaven, beheld the Virgin bodily, in a glory of light, slowly mounting towards the heaven; and she, for the assurance of his faith, flung down to him her girdle, the same which is to this day preserved in the cathedral of Prato. And there were present at the death of the Virgin Mary, besides the twelve Apostles, Dionysius the Areopagite, Timotheus, and Hierotheus; and of the women, Mary Salome, Mary Cleophas, and a faithful handmaid whose name was Savia." The French legend gives Mary Magdalene and Martha among those who witnessed the Virgin's death. The full illustration of this legend requires seven different scenes; namely, (1) The Angel announces her Death, and presents the Palm; (2) She takes leave of the Apostles; (3) Her Death; (4) The Bearing to the Sepulchre; (5) The Entombment; (6) The Assumption; (7) The Coronation in Heaven. Frequently two or three of these scenes are represented together; as, the Death below, and the Assumption above, and sometimes the Coronation above all. The angel who announces the death frequently presents a taper to the Virgin. It is customary to place a blessed taper in the hand of one dying. The death of the Virgin is sometimes called the Sleep (Il Sonno della Madonna), as in early times a belief existed that she only slept before her assumption. This belief has since been declared heretical. There are two modes of treating the Assumption : one represents the assumption of the soul, and in-this Christ receives the spirit, standing near the death-bed of the Virgin. The other portrays the union of the soul to the body, when it rises from the tomb, and leaving earth and all earthly things, the Mother soars to meet the Son, and to share his glory and his throne for-evermore. She is represented in a mandorla, or aureole, crowned or veiled (sometimes both), her dress spangled with stars, and surrounded by angels. These are the more ideal or devotional pictures. The strictly historical ones have the wondering Apostles, the doubting Thomas, and the blossoming tomb below ; while Mary, "quasi aurora consurgens" is borne towards heaven. The *Legend of the Holy Girdle* belongs properly to the consideration of the pictures of the Assumption of the Virgin. It is of Greek origin, and relates that St. Thomas, when about to go to the far East, gave the girdle to one of his disciples for safe keeping. The girdle remained for a thousand years guarded from profane eyes, and was in the possession of a Greek priest, to whom it had descended from a remote ancestry. He had one daughter, dearly beloved, to whom he gave the care of the sacred girdle. It happened that Michael of Prato, who had gone on the

Crusade of 1096, had remained in Jerusalem after the war was ended, and lodged in the house of this priest. He loved the daughter, too, and wished to marry her, but the father would not consent. Then the mother assisted the lovers to be married, and gave them the precious girdle as a dowry. They fled, and embarked for Tuscany. They landed at Pisa, and sought the home of Michael at Prato, bearing always with them the casket which held the sacred relic. Michael so venerated his treasure, and so feared lest he should be robbed of it, that he every night lighted a lamp in honor of it, and besides placed it beneath his bed for safety. Now, although he did this without knowing that thus he was wanting in respect to so holy a relic, it displeased his guardian angel, who every night lifted him out of his bed, and laid him on the bare earth. At length Michael fell sick, and knowing that he was near death he delivered the girdle to Bishop Uberto, commanding him to preserve the girdle in the cathedral of Prato, and ordain that from time to time it should be shown to the people. This injunction Uberto obeyed, and he carried the girdle in a solemn procession to the church. There it remained until 1312, when an attempt was made to carry it away and sell it to Florence. This attempt was discovered, and Musciatino, the would-be thief, was put to death. Then the people of Prato erected a shrine for the safe keeping of the girdle; and the chapel containing it is painted to represent all the circumstances of this legend.

The Coronation of the Virgin is not always easily distinguished from the allegorical picture called the "Incoronata." When the historical scene is intended, the last of the life of Mary, the death-bed, the tomb, the Apostles, and weeping friends are seen on the earth, while above the Saviour crowns his Mother, or she is seated beside him on his throne.

Having thus briefly considered the historical pictures of Our Lady, the mystical, allegorical, or strictly devotional ones remain. These are : — `

The Virgin Alone (*Lat.* Virgo Gloriosa; *Ital.* La Vergine Gloriosa; *Fr.* La Grande Vierge). Pictures representing the Virgin Mary alone, and placing her before us as an object of religious veneration, are painted in a variety of ways, and to illustrate the different attributes which are accorded to her by the Church. When she stands alone, with saints or apostles apparently subordinate to her, she is THE WOMAN; the MOTHER OF HUMANITY, a second Eve; and the VIRGIN OF VIRGINS. When she has a book, she is the representation of HEAVENLY WISDOM, — Virgo Sapientissima. When she has a sceptre, or wears a crown over her veil, or is enthroned alone, she is the QUEEN OF HEAVEN, — Regina Cœli. When represented as above, and surrounded by worshipping angels, she is QUEEN OF ANGELS, — Regina Angelorum. When veiled, with folded hands, and a face full of purity, sweetness, and all imaginable beauty, she is the MADONNA, the BLESSED VIRGIN, — Santa Maria Vergine.

L'Incoronata, — The Coronation of the Virgin (Lat. Coronatio Beatæ Mariæ Virginis; *Ital.* Maria Coronata dal divin suo Figlio; *Fr.* Le Couronnement de la Sainte Vierge; *Ger.* Die Krönung Mariä). This picture is entirely different in its spirit and object from the historical coronation of the Virgin before described. That picture makes the closing scene in the life of Mary, and, as before remarked, has the Apostles, the tomb of flowers, and the death-bed to distinguish it. But the intent of the devotional coronation is to represent the Virgin as the type or emblem of the Spiritual Church. She is received into glory and exalted above all created beings, angels and men, as the Espoused, the Bride of Christ, — the CHURCH. Frequently the Saviour has an open book with the inscription, "Veni, Electa mea, et ponam te in thronum meum," etc., — "Come, my Chosen One, and I will place thee upon my throne." Many chapels are dedicated to the Virgin in this character, "Capella dell' Incoronata." The dress of the Virgin is most beautiful, and frequently embroidered with suns, moons, and golden rays, recalling the "woman clothed with the sun," which John describes (Rev. xii. 1). When Mary holds the child and is crowned, it is not a coronation, but a representation of her as the Mother of God.

Our Lady of the Immaculate Conception (Lat. Regina sine labe originali concepta; *Fr.* La Conception de la Vierge Marie; *Ital.* La Madonna Purissima; *Sp.* Nuestra Señora sin pecado concebida, La Concepcion; *Ger.* Das Geheimniss der unbefleckten Empfängniss Mariä). This picture is unknown in the early days of art, but has been almost miraculously multiplied since the beginning of the seventeenth century, when Paul V. instituted the office for the commemoration of the Immaculate Conception of the Virgin, and forbade

14

teaching or preaching the opposite belief. The question had been in agitation a decade of centuries,[1] and in the fifteenth century the Sorbonne had declared in its favor. The Immaculate Conception of the Mother of God was defined as an article of faith by Pope Pius IX. in 1854. The model for the Virgin in this representation is the woman of the Apocalypse. She is young, about twelve or fourteen; her robe of white, with blue mantle; her hands folded as if in prayer; her beauty, "all that painting can express;" the sun, a vivid light, about her, the moon beneath her, and a starry crown above her head. Sometimes the same idea of the Madonna Purissima is represented by the head alone. It is painted very young, with white vesture and flowing hair. Before the definition of the doctrine of the Immaculate Conception, there was another mystical representation of Mary, which might be confounded with those of the Madonna Purissima. It is the embodiment of the idea that the redemption of the human race existed in the mind of the Creator before the beginning of the world. And this is expressed by the Virgin surrounded by the same attributes as in the Conception, and sometimes setting her foot on the serpent. Mary, made thus a second Eve, is sometimes painted as an accompaniment to the picture of Eve holding the apple. The date of the picture will decide the question between these subjects. December 8.

The Mater Dolorosa (*Ital.* La Madre di Dolore, L'Addolorata; *Fr.* Notre Dame de Pitié, La Vierge de Douleur; *Sp.* Nuestra Señora de Dolores; *Ger.* Die Schmerzhafte Mutter). There are three distinct modes of representing the "Mourning Mother," to whom the afflicted of the Catholic world address their prayers, feeling that she has felt the deepest pangs of earthly sorrow. As the *Mater Dolorosa*, she is alone, seated or standing, and frequently only a head or half figure; of middle age, with bowed head, clasped hands, sorrowful face, and streaming eyes. Often the bosom is pierced with one, and sometimes with seven swords. As the *Stabat Mater*, she stands on the right of the crucifix while St. John is on the left. The whole figure expresses intense sorrow. She is usually wrapped in a dark violet or blue mantle. *La Pietà*, the third Sorrowing Mother, when strictly rendered, consists only of the Virgin and the dead Christ. Occa-

---

[1] Though, for the honor of her Son, the Immaculate Conception of the Blessed Virgin was generally believed from the beginning.

sionally lamenting angels are introduced. This representation has been varied in every possible way which could express sorrow, resignation, tenderness, love, and dignity. But usually the Son is in the arms, on the lap, or lying at the feet of the Mother.

The Virgin of Mercy, Our Lady of Succor (*Ital.* La Madonna di Misericordia; *Fr.* Notre Dame de Miséricorde; *Sp.* Nuestra Señora de Gracia; *Ger.* Maria Mutter des Erbarmens). This picture represents the Virgin as the Merciful Mother of Humanity. In it she sometimes stands with outstretched arms, crowned or veiled; her ample robe extended by angels, over kneeling votaries and worshippers. Sometimes these embrace all ranks and ages, and again those of some particular order who seek her aid. But these instances are rare, as she usually bears the child in her arms, signifying that from her maternity itself a large portion of her sympathy is derived. In pictures of the Day of Judgment, the Virgin is also represented as Our Lady of Mercy. She is on the right hand of the Saviour, while John the Baptist kneels on the left. Mary is usually a little lower than the Saviour, but has been represented in ancient pictures seated by his side. She appears as a mediator and intercessor for mercy, whatever her position. In one instance this inscription is painted beneath her: "Maria Filio suo pro Ecclesia supplicat."

The Virgin and Child Enthroned (*Lat.* Sancta Dei Genitrix, Virgo Deipara; *Ital.* La Santissima Vergine, Madre di Dio; *Fr.* La Sainte Vierge, Mère de Dieu; *Ger.* Die Heilige Mutter Gottes). The very title of these pictures, which are numberless, explains their signification. They are devotional, and represent the mother and child in various positions, and with such differences of expression and sentiment as must inevitably result from the vast number of artists who have treated this subject. Its beauties are inexhaustible as they are indescribable, and there are few hearts that have not been filled with emotion and admiration by some of these representations of what is purest and holiest in woman.

In addition to the Madonnas already mentioned, there are numerous votive Madonnas both public and private. Their titles usually indicate the objects for which they were painted, as those painted for the Carmelites, which are called "La Madonna del Carmine." Others denote especial acts, as "La Madonna della Vittoria," or deliverance from dangers, such as pestilence, floods, fire, and tempests, as the "Madonna di San Sebastiano," which was an offering of the city of Modena against the plague. Family votive Madonnas usually bear the name of those who offer them, as the "Madonna di Foligno," which was presented by Sigismund Conti, of Foligni, in fulfilment of a vow made when in danger from a severe storm. There is scarcely a church or a religious institution of the Catholic Church which does not possess at least one votive Madonna.

The Mater Amabilis (*Ital.* La Madonna col Bambino; *Fr.* La Vierge et l'enfant Jésus; *Ger.* Maria mit dem Kind). This is the representation of the Virgin as THE MOTHER alone; and its exquisite beauty and feeling, when painted as it should and may be, is only to be *felt*, it cannot be *told*. Here "she is brought nearer to our sympathies. She is not seated in a chair of state with the accompaniments of earthly power; she is not enthroned on clouds, nor glorified and star-crowned in heaven; she is no longer so exclusively the VERGINE DEA, nor the VIRGO DEI GENITRIX; but she is still the ALMA MATER REDEMPTORIS, the young and lovely and most pure mother of a divine Christ. She is not sustained in mid-air by angels; she dwells lowly on earth, but the angels leave their celestial home to wait upon her." A version of this Madonna is styled the "Madre Pia," and represents the Virgin as acknowledging the divinity of her Son. The spirit of these pictures is the same as that of some Nativities where the Virgin adores the babe, but the accessories determine the difference between them. And lastly there are the Pastoral Madonnas, in which numerous persons, such as the relatives of the Virgin or St. Joseph, the saints and holy personages, are introduced as participating with the Virgin in the adoration of the child.

La Madonna della Sedia. The pretty and poetical legend of this famous picture relates that centuries ago there dwelt among the Italian hills a venerable hermit, whom the people called Father Bernardo. He was renowned for wisdom and holiness, and many visited him for advice and consolation. He often remarked that though his solitude was deep, yet he was not entirely alone, for he had two daughters, one that spoke to him and one that was dumb. Now the first was the daughter of a vine-dresser, named Mary, who dearly loved the old man and often brought him little presents of such things as would add to his comfort; while she cheered him with loving words and caresses. But his dumb daughter was a "brave old oak," that grew near his hut and sheltered it with its branches. This tree old Bernardo greatly loved, and in the heat of summer he brought water to its thirsty roots, and tended and talked to it as if it could hear and feel. At morning and evening he fed the birds which lived in its branches, and in return was cheered by their songs. Many times some woodman had desired to cut down this oak, but the prayers of the old man deterred him from the deed. There came at last a terrible winter when the mountains were laden with heavy snow, and then the sun shone warm, and fearful freshets came down like torrents, and swept away flocks and trees and even hamlets in their course. After the worst had subsided, Mary and her father went to see how it had fared with the good hermit, fearing that he had perished. But his dumb daughter had saved his life; for when the thaw came on he had sought the roof of his hut, but he was soon convinced that there was no safety for him there; and as he lifted his eyes in prayer it seemed that the limbs of the oak beckoned him to come to them. Then he climbed with confidence among its branches, and there he stayed three days. While below him his hut and everything else was swept away, still his dumb daughter stood firm. But he only had a few dry crusts to eat; and when Mary arrived he was fainting and ready to die from cold and exposure. Then this talking daughter comforted him, and took him to her home until his hut could be rebuilt. And now with great fervor-Bernardo thanked God for his preservation, and called down blessings upon his two children who had both been instruments in his deliverance; and he prayed God to distinguish them in some way from the other works of his hand. Years passed on, and the hermit was laid to rest; his hut was in ruins forever, and the oak was converted into wine-casks for Mary's father. One day, one of these casks was in an arbor where Mary, now a wife and mother, sat with her two boys. As she pressed her baby to her breast and watched the elder one at play, she thought of the old hermit, and wondered if his blessing would ever be fulfilled in her or these children. Just then the older child ran towards her with a stick to which he had fastened a cross; and at the same time a young man approached, whose large dreamy eyes were such as feast on beauty, but his air was that of one restless and weary. And so he was; for he had long been seeking a model which could be used to assist him in painting a picture of the Blessed Virgin and her Son which floated before his vision, just real enough to haunt his thoughts continually, and just unreal enough to refuse to be rendered by his brush. This was Raphael Sanzio d'Urbino. Now at last, as he gazed on Mary, the wish of his heart was realized. But he had only a pencil! On what could he draw? Just then the smooth cover of the huge wine-cask presented itself to him, and eagerly he drew upon it the outlines of Mary and her babe. This he took away with him, and rested not till with his very soul he had painted his wondrous "Madonna della Sedia." Thus was the blessing and desire of the old monk realized, and together his two daughters were distinguished for all time.

St. Marcella is represented with Lazarus and his sisters. All that is known of her is that she accompanied these saints from the East, wrote the life of Martha, and announced the Faith in Sclavonia.

St. Marcellinus. See St. Peter Exorcista.

St. Margaret (*Ital.* S. Margarita; *Fr.* Ste. Marguerite; *Ger.* Die Heilige Margaretha; *Gr.* Ἁγ. Μαργαρίτης: signification, "a pearl"). This saint was the daughter of a pagan priest of Antioch. She was a delicate child, and was therefore sent to a nurse in the country. This woman was a Christian, and brought Margaret up in her own faith. She was seen one day by Olybrius, who was governor of Antioch; and her beauty so impressed him that he commanded she should be brought to his palace, and he determined to marry her if he should find that she was free born. But Margaret declared herself a Christian, to the great horror of the governor and her relatives. The latter deserted her, and Olybrius attempted to subdue her by torments of so fearful a nature that he could not endure the sight of her agony. Still she yielded not. She was then imprisoned, and in her dungeon Satan appeared to her in the shape of a hideous dragon, and endeavored to confound her with fear. But Margaret held up a cross and he fled from her; or (as another legend teaches) he swallowed her, and instantly burst asunder, and she remained unhurt. He then came in the form of a man, to tempt her still further; but she overcame him, and placed her foot upon his head, and compelled him to confess his vile purpose and to answer her questions. Again she was taken before the governor and tortured; but her firmness was so great that she not only remained true to Christ herself, but she converted many who witnessed her devotion, so that in one day five thousand converts were baptized. Then it was determined that she should be beheaded; and as they led her away to death she prayed that in memory of her deliverance from the womb of the dragon, all who called on her in childbirth should be safely delivered, and a heavenly voice assured her that her prayer should be granted.

The attributes of Margaret are the palm and the dragon. She is young and girlish, and is thus easily distinguished from St. Martha, who also has the dragon. Sometimes she has pearls around her head, and rarely the daisy or marguerite, which is so named in memory of her. She is especially the type of maiden innocence and humility.

> "Si douce est la Marguerite."

In the picture by Lucas v. Leyden, she is rising from the back of the dragon, while a piece of her robe remaining in his mouth indicates that he had swallowed her. She is the patroness of women in child-birth, and patroness of Cremona. July 20, A. D. 306.

St. Margaret of Cortona, whose church is on the highest part of the hill upon which that city is built, was the Magdalene of that locality. She was born in Alviano in Tuscany. Her mother died when she was still in infancy, and the cruelty of a step-mother and the unkindness of her father drove her to desperation, and she led an evil life for several years. One of her lovers was assassinated when returning from a visit to her. A little dog which was with him returned to Margaret, and attempted to lead her to the body of his master, by pulling at her robe and piteously whining. Wondering at length that her lover returned not, she went with the dog, and was horrified to find the murdered body of him she sought. She was overcome with terror and repentance, and went to her father's house. But the step-mother persuaded her father to refuse to admit her. She then retired to a vineyard near by, and here in her lonely wretchedness she was tempted to return to her sinful life. But she prayed God to be to her more than all earthly friends could be, and while so praying she had a revelation that her prayer was answered, and she was directed to go to the Franciscan convent at Cortona. This she did, and entering barefooted and with a cord about her neck, she threw herself before the altar and begged to be admitted to the order as a humble penitent. She was refused this privilege until she should prove her penitence by a more worthy life. But at length she took the habit of St. Francis in 1272. Tradition relates that as she knelt one day before the crucifix, Christ bowed his head in answer to her prayers, and from that time she was held in great reverence by the people of Cortona. She is painted young and beautiful, her dress not always that of the nun, but usually with the cord for a girdle, which indicates the Third Order of St. Francis. Her attribute is a dog, which is seldom omitted. February 22, A. D. 1297.

Santa Maria Maddalena de' Pazzi was of the noble Florentine family whose name she bears. She was a Carmelite nun. Her life was one of extreme sanctity and humility, yet comparatively uneventful. May 27, A. D. 1607.

Maria Maggiore, Santa. This splendid church at Rome is said to owe its origin to a vision related in a legend called that " of the Snow," — in Italian, "della Neve." Giovanni Patricio, a Roman who was rich and childless, prayed the Virgin to direct him how he should dispose of his wealth. On the 5th of August, A. D. 352, Mary came to him in a dream, and commanded him to build a church in her name on the spot where he should find snow the next morning. His wife and the Pope Liberius each had the same vision ; and early next day they all went to the Esquiline, where they found miraculous snow, in spite of the heat of the season. Liberius traced upon it, with his crosier, the plan of the church, and here the church was built. Murillo painted two beautiful pictures of this legend, called, in Spanish, S. Maria la Blanca.

St. Marina. The sad story of this saint presents a touching illustration of self-sacrifice and unbounded humility, for which she was greatly revered. Her father was an Eastern hermit ; and when he first went to the desert he so longed for his daughter whom he had left, that he dressed her in male attire, and charged her never to reveal her sex. He then took her with him to his retreat, and there she grew up as Brother Marinus. She was frequently sent to the shores of the Red Sea with a wagon and oxen to get supplies for the monks. The man to whom she went had a daughter who was found to be with child, and who wickedly accused Marinus of being her seducer. Marina did not deny the charge, and the abbot ordered her to be scourged and driven out of the walls of the monastery; and the wicked woman came with her child, and putting it in the arms of Marina, said, " There, as you are its father, take care of it." Then Marina cared for the child. She remained outside the gate of the convent and begged a support, which was given her with many insults, as to a vile sinner. But when she died and the truth was discovered, there was great mourning on account of all she had endured, and she was honored for her humility. She is represented with the dress of a monk and the face of a beautiful woman, with a child in her arms. June 18. Eighth century.

St. Mark (*Lat.* S. Marcus; *Ital.* San Marco Evangelista; *Fr.* St. Marc; *Ger.* Der Heilige Marcus). This Evangelist was not an apostle, but a convert and beloved disciple of St. Peter, according to the tradition of the Catholic Church. He journeyed with Peter even to Rome, where he wrote his Gospel; and many believe it to have been dictated by St. Peter. He went afterwards to preach in Egypt, and after spending twelve years in Libya and the Thebais, he founded the church at Alexandria. On account of his miracles the heathen accused him of being a magician; and at length, when celebrating the feast of their god Serapis, they seized St. Mark and dragged him through the streets with cords until he died. Then immediately there fell a storm of hail, and a tempest of lightning came with it which destroyed his murderers. The Christians buried his remains, and his tomb was greatly venerated. But in A. D. 815 some Venetian merchants despoiled the tomb of its sacred relics, and took them to Venice, where the splendid cathedral of San Marco was erected over them. There are many legends of this saint which have afforded subjects for representations in art. One day as he walked in Alexandria, it is said that he saw a poor cobbler who had wounded his hand so severely with an awl that he could no longer support himself. St. Mark healed the wound, and the man, who was called Anianus, was converted and afterwards became Bishop of Alexandria. The famous legend of the preservation of Venice is thus related: It was on the 25th of February in 1340. The waters had been rising for three days; and on this night there was a fearful storm, and the height of the water was three cubits more than ever before. An old fisherman with difficulty reached the Riva di San Marco with his little boat, and determined to wait

there for the ceasing of the tempest. But there came to him a
man who entreated him to row him over to San Giorgio Maggiore.
After great persuasion, the fisherman, believing it to be the will of
God, consented. Having arrived at San Giorgio, the stranger landed
and commanded the fisherman to await his return. The former came
back bringing with him a young man, and told him to row again to
San Niccolo di Lido. The fisherman doubted his ability to do this;
but his passengers assured him he might row boldly, and strength
would be given him. They came at last to San Niccolo di Lido, where
the two men landed. When they returned to the shore there was a
third one also. They ordered the fisherman to row beyond the two
castles. When they came to the sea, they saw a barque filled with
frightful demons rapidly approaching. These were coming to over-
whelm the city with water. Then the three men in the boat made
the sign of the cross and bade the demons depart. Instantly the
barque vanished, the sea became calm, and the waters began to
subside. Then the men commanded the boatman to land them at
the places whence they had come. He did so, but in spite of the
great wonder he had seen he demanded of the third that he should
pay him. Then the man replied : "Thou art right; go now to the
Doge and to the Procuratori of St. Mark ; tell them what thou hast
seen, for Venice would have been overwhelmed had it not been for
us three. I am St. Mark the Evangelist, the protector of this city ;
the other is the brave knight St. George ; and he whom thou didst
take up at the Lido is the holy bishop St. Nicholas. Say to the
Doge and to the Procuratori that they are to pay you ; and tell them
likewise that this tempest arose because of a certain schoolmaster
dwelling at San Felice, who did sell his soul to the devil and afterwards hanged himself." The fisherman answered that his story
would not be believed. Then St. Mark took from his finger a ring,
and gave it to the man, saying, "Show them this, and tell them
when they look in the sanctuary they will not find it." And he
disappeared. The next morning the fisherman did as he had been
commanded. It proved as he had been told, and the ring was not
found. Then the man was paid, a procession was ordained with
great solemnity, and the citizens gave thanks to God and the three
saints for their miraculous deliverance. The fisherman received a
pension, and the ring was given to the Procuratori, who replaced it

in the sanctuary. Another legend relates that a certain slave whose master resided in Provence, persisted in going to the shrine of St. Mark to pray, for which he was condemned to be tortured. As the sentence was about to be executed, St. Mark descended to save his votary. The executioners were confounded, and the instruments of torture broken and made unfit for use. The tradition which makes St. Mark the amanuensis of St. Peter is frequently illustrated in paintings. The attribute of St. Mark is the lion, either with or without the wings, but generally with them. This enables one to distinguish him from St. Jerome, who has the lion unwinged. He often wears the robes of a bishop. April 25, A. D. 68.

St. Martha (*Ital.* Santa Marta, Vergine, Albergatrice di Christo; *Fr.* Ste. Marthe, la Travailleuse). St. Martha is highly venerated on account of having persuaded her sister Mary to listen to the words of Jesus, thus becoming the instrument of her conversion. The old story in "Il Perfetto Legendario" goes on to say of this, "Which thing should not be accounted as the least of her merits, seeing that Martha was a chaste and prudent virgin, and the other publicly contemned for her evil life; notwithstanding which, Martha did not despise her, nor reject her as a sister, but wept for her shame, and admonished her gently and with persuasive words, and reminded her of her noble birth, to which she was a disgrace, and that Lazarus, their brother, being a soldier, would certainly get into trouble on her account. So she prevailed, and conducted her sister to the presence of Christ; and afterwards, as it is well known, she lodged and entertained the Saviour in her own house." The Provençal legends relate that Martha was the first who founded a convent for her own sex, and the first one after the Blessed Virgin who consecrated her virginity to God. While Mary Magdalene made converts in Marseilles, Martha made known the Faith at Aix. In those days there was a fearful dragon who inhabited the river Rhone, and ravaged the country by night. He was called the Tarasque, and on the scene of his life the city of Tarascon now stands. Now Martha sprinkled this monster with holy water and bound him with her girdle, and then he was speedily killed by the people. When after many years of labor, death approached, she desired to be borne to some spot where she could see the sun in the heavens. She wished the story of the Passion of Our Lord to be read to her; and as she died she said,

"Father, into thy hands I commend my spirit." Her attribute is a dragon; and she may be known from St. Margaret by the pot of holy water, while the latter has the cross. St. Martha also bears sometimes a cooking utensil. Patroness of cooks and housewives. June 29, A. D. 84.

St. Martial was Bishop of Limoges. St. Valérie, or Valère, was a beautiful virgin who was converted by his teaching. She refused to listen to the addresses of the Duke de Guyenne. This so enraged the duke that he "luy fit trancher la teste, couronnant sa virginité d'un martyre bien signalé, car à la venuë d'un chacun elle prit sa teste, et la porta jusques au pied de l'Autel ou S. Marcial disoit la messe; le bourreau, la suivant pas-à-pas, mourut dans l'Eglise, après avoir clairement protesté qu'il voyoit les anges à l'entour de son corps." This legend is illustrated in the cathedral of Limoges. She is represented with a streak around the neck. Her festival is December 10.

St. Martin of Tours (*Lat.* S. Martinus; *Ital.* San Martino) was one of the most popular saints of the Middle Ages. He was born at Saberia, in Pannonia, in the time of Constantine the Great; and tradition relates that on one occasion the Empress Helena, who was the daughter of a wealthy lord of Caernarvonshire, prepared for him a supper with her own hands, and waited on him while he ate it, like the humblest servant; and at the end gathered up the crumbs, esteeming them more precious than any meal she could eat at the emperor's board. From a child St. Martin was of a religious disposition, but he became a soldier before he was baptized. In the army he won the love and respect of his comrades, by the great excellences of his character and the purity of his life. He was especially noted for his benevolence and charity to the poor. The winter of 332 was so severely cold that large numbers perished in the streets of Amiens, where the regiment of St. Martin was quartered. One day he met at the gate a naked man, and taking pity on him he divided his cloak (for it was all he had), and gave half to the beggar. That night in a dream Jesus stood before him, and on his shoulders he wore the half of the cloak that Martin had given the beggar. And he said to the angels who attended him, "Know ye who hath thus arrayed me? My servant Martin, though yet unbaptized, hath done this." Then Martin was immediately baptized; being at the time twenty-three years old. At forty years of age, he desired to leave the army that he might devote all his time to God's service. Then the legend tells that Julian the Apostate, now emperor, accused him of cowardice, saying that he wished to be dismissed to avoid a coming battle. But Martin replied, he would be set naked in the front of the fight, armed only with the cross, and not fear to meet the enemy. Then the emperor commanded men to guard him and see that this was done; but before the time of battle peace was made, and it was not attempted. After leading a religious life for years he was made Bishop of Tours in 371. He did many miracles, healing the sick, and even restoring to life the son of a poor widow. One day, as he celebrated mass in his cathedral, he asked his deacon to clothe a naked beggar before him. The deacon did not comply readily, and St. Martin took off his priestly robe and gave it to the wretched man; and while he officiated at the altar a globe of fire was seen above his head, and as he elevated the Host, his arms (being exposed on account of the absence of the garment) were covered, by a miracle, with chains of gold and silver, which angels fastened upon them. His evenness of temper was an especial virtue, and he was never angry, neither spoke he ever unkindly. In spite of all, he was often greatly tempted, and Satan one day ridiculed him because he so soon received the sinful who repented. St. Martin replied, " O most miserable that thou art! if thou also couldst cease to persecute and seduce wretched men, if thou also couldst repent, thou also shouldst find mercy and forgiveness through Jesus Christ!" It is due to the wonderful energy of St. Martin that paganism was rooted out of that portion of Gaul in which he ruled the Church. He destroyed temples, demolished the images of the gods, and was impervious to all the threats and dangers which he incurred by so doing. The demons whom he thus disenthroned often appeared to him, sometimes in hideous forms and again with all the beauty of Venus; but he overcame all fear and all temptation, and steadfastly served God. At length he wearied of the people who thronged about him, and he built himself a cell away from Tours, between the rocks and the Loire. From this the monastery of Marmoutier arose. St. Martin not only opposed heathenism, he battled against blind superstition as well. There was near Tours a chapel where the people venerated a martyr, as they believed; but Martin thought them mistaken. He went and stood on the sepulchre, and prayed that it might be revealed to him if any martyr rested there. Soon a dark form appeared, and told St. Martin that he was a robber whose soul was in hell, and whose body rested beneath him, where he stood. Then the saint destroyed the chapel and altar, as he did those of the pagans. He was once invited to sup with the emperor. The cup was passed to Martin, before his majesty drank, with the expectation that he would touch it to his lips, as was the custom. But a poor priest stood behind Martin, and to the surprise and admiration of all, the saint presented the full goblet to him, thus signifying that a servant of God deserved more honor, however humble his station, than any merely earthly potentate. From this legend he has been chosen the patron of all innocent conviviality. It is said that on an occasion when St. Martin sought an interview with the Emperor Valentinian, his majesty did not rise from his chair as the saint approached, whereupon the chair took fire beneath him, and necessity compelled him to do what reverence had no power to effect. This unique legend has been represented in art. St. Martin died after being bishop more than thirty years, and many heard the songs of the angels who bore him to Paradise. From the time of his death he has been an object of extreme veneration. In art he is usually represented with a naked beggar at his feet. A goose when introduced alludes to the season of his feast, which occurs at the time when geese are eaten, and is called, in England, Martinmas-tide. In France this festival was kept like the last day of the Carnival, — a time of feasting. November 11, A. D. 397.

St. Martina was a Roman virgin. A church dedicated to her stands at the foot of the Capitoline Hill. It is on the left as we descend to the Forum from the Ara Cœli. Here from very ancient times there was a chapel where the people venerated this saint, who was martyred in the time of Alexander Severus. In 1634, when repairing this chapel, a sarcophagus was discovered built into the foundations, which contained the body of a young woman, while the head was in a separate casket. This, being regarded as the body of the saint, called the attention of all Rome to the place, and even the pope was filled with enthusiasm at the discovery. Cardinal Francesco Barberini undertook to rebuild the church, and Pietro da

Cortona very solemnly dedicated his talents to the work of adorning the same. The church was given to the Academy of Painters, and consecrated to St. Luke, their patron. It now bears the name of "San Luca e Santa Martina." Pietro da Cortona left all his fortune to the chapel of St. Martina, which he himself had painted. She is represented as young and beautiful, with different instruments of torture, signifying the manner of her death. January 30.

St. Mary of Egypt (*Ital.* Santa Maria Egiziaca Penitente; *Fr.* Ste. Marie l'Egyptienne, La Gipesienne, La Jussienne). The legend of this Mary Egyptiaca is much older than that of Mary Magdalene. It was in a written form, and fully believed in the sixth century; for a very ancient tradition stated that a female hermit had dwelt for years in Palestine, and there died. The legend as now given rests on the authority of St. Jerome, and relates that a woman named Mary, whose wickedness far exceeded that of the Magdalene, dwelt in Alexandria. After seventeen years of abandonment to sin, in the year 365, as she walked one day near the sea, she saw a vessel about to depart well filled with pilgrims. On inquiry she found that they were going to Jerusalem to keep the feast of the true cross. She was seized with anxiety to go also, but had no money to pay her passage. Then she sold herself to the sailors and pilgrims, and so accomplished the journey. Arriving at Jerusalem, she thought to enter the church with the others; but when she reached the entrance some invisible power held her so that she could not go in, and as often as she tried to cross the threshold, so often was she driven back. Then a sense of all her sins came over her, and she was overcome with sorrow, and prayed to God for grace and pardon; whereupon the restraining power was taken away, and she entered the church on her knees. She then bought three loaves of bread and went into the desert, even beyond Jordan. Here she remained in deepest penitence. She drank only water, and subsisted on roots and fruits, and her three loaves, which were constantly renewed by a miracle. Her clothing wore out and dropped from her; then she prayed God to clothe her, and her prayer was answered, for her hair became a cloak about her, or, as others say, a heavenly robe was brought her by an angel. She had lived thus forty-seven years when she was found by Zosimus, a priest. She begged him to keep silence concerning her, and to return at the end of a year and bring with him the Blessed Sacrament, that she might confess her sins and receive communion before her death. Zosimus complied with her desires and returned to her in a year. He was not able to cross the Jordan, and Mary was miraculously assisted to cross to him. After receiving the Sacrament she requested him to leave her again to her solitary life, and to return at the end of another year. When the year was passed and he went again to meet her, he found her lying dead, with her hands folded as in prayer. And upon the sands these words were written : "O, Father Zosimus, bury the body of the poor sinner, Mary of Egypt! Give earth to earth, and dust to dust, for Christ's sake !" When he endeavored to do this, he found he had not sufficient strength, for he was an old man. Then a lion came and assisted him, digging with his paws ; and when the body of Mary was in the grave the lion went quietly away and Zosimus returned home, praising God for the mercy he had shown to the penitent woman. She is represented in art as old, worn, and wasted, with long hair, and three loaves of bread in her hand. When united with Mary Magdalene, the contrast of age, appearance, and dress is very striking. The pictures of her penance are sometimes mistaken for the Magdalene ; but if the vase, skull, and crucifix are wanting, it is the Mary of Egypt. A chapel in the church of St. Merry in Paris is painted with scenes from her life. April 9, A. D. 433.

St. Mary Magdalene (*Lat.* S. Maria Magdalena ; *Fr.* La Madeleine, La Sainte Demoiselle pécheresse ; *Ital.* Santa Maria Maddalena ; *Sp.* Santa Maria Magdalena). The writings which would fill volumes, the numberless sermons which have exhausted the talents of the preachers and the patience of the hearers, the learned arguments of tongue and pen, and the wild, imaginative legends which have each and all essayed to give and establish the truth about this saint, have left her, in the heart of the world, what the Gospel alone and unaided makes her, — the *first* sinning and repenting woman forgiven through the love of Jesus, a glorious beacon of hope, shining down through all ages, silently saying to all other Magdalenes, "Go and sin no more." It has never been decided whether she was differently spoken of as "Mary of Bethany," the "woman who was a sinner," and she "out of whom Jesus cast seven devils," or whether she was but one of these ; but the legend, as it is generally represented in Western art, is as follows : Mary Magdalene was the daughter of noble, if not royal parents, and the sister of Martha and Lazarus. Syrus, their father, had vast riches, and at his death these were divided equally among the three. The castle of Mary, called Magdalon, was in the district of Magdala on the shore of the sea of Tiberias. Lazarus was by profession a soldier. Martha was virtuous and discreet; but Mary, giving herself up to luxury and idleness, became at length so wicked as to be called "THE SINNER." Martha, loving her sister and filled with sorrow by her sinful life, continually rebuked her, and finally persuaded her to listen to the teachings of Jesus. The seven evil spirits which Jesus cast out were the seven deadly sins, to which she had been subject before her conversion. The entertainment of the Saviour at the house of Martha, the supper at the house of Simon the Pharisee, the devotion of Mary to Jesus, and the scenes connected with his death and resurrection, are given in the legend as in the Gospels. It then adds that after the ascension of Christ, Lazarus and his sisters with their handmaid Marcella, Maximin who had baptized them, and the blind man to whom Jesus had given sight, called Cedon, were placed in a boat with no rudder to steer and no oars nor sails to speed them, and set adrift. This was done by the heathen. They were carried by winds and waves to a harbor which proved to be that of Marseilles. The people of that place were also heathen, and they refused to give the castaways food or shelter. Then these found a resting-place in the porch of a temple, and Mary began to tell of Christ and to urge the people to forsake their idols; and both the sisters did such miracles that many were converted and baptized. When Maximin was dead, Lazarus was made first bishop of Marseilles. But Mary desired to live in solitude, and retired to a frightful wilderness, where she lived thirty years a life of penitence and sorrow for the sins she never ceased to regret and bewail. It was supposed she was dead ; but at length a hermit whose cell was in the same desert as her own saw a miraculous sight which disclosed the truth that she still lived. It appears that often in her hunger and exhaustion angels had ministered to her, and during the last years of her life they bore her, every day, up into regions where she could hear celestial harmonies, and see the glory prepared for those who repent and believe in God. It was this daily ascension that the hermit saw; and he hastened to the city to relate the wonderful vision. Legends disagree concerning the place and manner of her death. Some relate that it occurred in the desert, where angels watched over her and cared for her, while others say she died in a church, after receiving the last sacraments from St. Maximin. The scene of her solitary penance is said to be the site of the monastery of La Sainte Beaume, or the Holy Cave, between Marseilles and Toulon. In the thirteenth century some remains, believed to be those of St. Lazarus and St. Mary Magdalene, were found about twenty miles north of Toulon, at a place called St. Maximin. Here a church was built in 1279 by Charles, Count of Provence, brother of St. Louis, King of France. A few years later, Charles was made prisoner by the King of Aragon; and he ascribed the praise of his liberation to Mary Magdalene, who was his chosen protectress. Many miracles were wrought through her intercession, one of which has been frequently represented in pictures. A certain prince of Provence came to Marseilles with his wife to sacrifice to the pagan gods. They listened to the instructions of Mary, and were persuaded to leave the service of the idols. One day the husband told Mary of his strong desire to have a son. Mary asked him if he would believe if his prayer were heard. He promised that he would believe. Not long after, this prince decided to go to Jerusalem to see St. Peter, and to ascertain if what Magdalene told him agreed with the preaching of that saint. The wife determined to go also, but he said, " How shall it be possible, seeing that thou art with child, and the dangers of the sea are very great ?" But she so entreated him that he granted her request, and they departed. After a day and night had passed, a terrible storm arose. The pains of childbirth came upon the woman, and in the midst of the tempest the babe was born and the mother died. The sailors wished to throw the body into the sea, believing that the storm would not cease while it remained in the ship; but the prince persuaded them with entreaties and money to retain it awhile. Soon they arrived at an island, where he laid his wife on the shore, and placing the babe on her breast he covered them with his cloak and wept bitterly, and said, " O Mary Magdalene ! to my grief and sorrow didst thou come to Marseilles ! Why didst thou ask thy God to give me a son only that I might lose both son and wife together ? O Mary Magdalene ! have pity on my grief, and if thy prayers may avail, save at least the life of my child !" Then he proceeded to

Jerusalem, and remained there two years. He was instructed by St. Peter, and saw the places which had been hallowed by the life and death of the Saviour. Now on his return he landed at the island where he had left the body of his wife, that he might weep at her last resting-place. Who can tell his surprise when he saw his child running about on the shore? And when the infant saw the strange man he was afraid, and hid beneath the cloak that covered his dead mother. Then when the father approached, the mother also opened her eyes and smiled, and put out her arms to embrace her husband. Then did the prince greatly rejoice, and they all returned to Marseilles, and threw themselves at the feet of the Magdalene and were baptized. There are legends (though never accepted by the Church) which relate that an attachment existed between St. John the Evangelist and Mary Magdalene; and even that the feast which Jesus attended at Cana of Galilee was on the occasion of the marriage of these two saints. Donatello's famous statue, carved in wood, stands above her altar in the baptistery in Florence. It represents her as the wasted, sorrowing penitent, and is strangely in contrast with the loveliness of many representations of her. Her proper attribute is the jar of ointment. This signifies either the ointment which she brake upon the feet of the Saviour, or that which she prepared for the anointing of his crucified body. It varies in size and form; is usually either in her hand or standing near her, though sometimes borne by an attending angel. The colors of the dress of the Magdalene are red, expressing love; violet, penitence and mourning; and blue, constancy. Sometimes she wears a violet tunic and red mantle. Some Spanish pictures represent her with dark hair; but it should be luxuriant, fair, and golden. Patroness of frail and penitent women; of Provence and Marseilles. July 22, A. D. 68.

St. Mary the Penitent (*Ital.* Santa Maria Penitente; *Fr.* Ste. Marie, la Pénitente). This Mary was the niece of the hermit Abraham, and her life was mostly spent in the deserts of Syria. She too was a sinner and became a penitent, to whose prayers God granted miraculous answers. Her father had large riches and lived in splendor. When he died, the daughter was carried to her hermit uncle to be religiously instructed. She was seven years old when taken to the desert. Abraham built a cell close to his own and opening into it by a window, and there placed the child. Here he taught her to pray, to sing praises, to recite psalms, and to despise the pleasures of the world. Thus Mary lived until she was twenty years old. At this time there came a young hermit to the cell of Abraham to receive his instructions. The beauty of the face which he beheld by chance through the window, and the music of the voice which chanted holy praises so near him, inflamed his heart with love for the maiden; and he tempted her to sin, forgetting his vows. When she at length reflected on what she had done, she so feared her uncle that she fled from his sight, and went to a remote place, where for two years she lived a shameless life of sin. Now on the very night that she fled, Abraham dreamed that a hideous dragon came to his cell and found there a white dove and took it away with him. When he awoke the dream troubled him. Again when he slept he saw the same dragon; and he crushed its head with his foot, and took the dove from its maw and put it in his bosom. Then the dove came to life, and spreading its wings, flew to heaven. Then the hermit knew that this dream referred to his beloved Mary. He took his staff and went forth, seeking her through all the land. After a long time he found her; and when she was overcome with shame and sorrow he encouraged her, and promised himself to do penance for her. Then she cried out, "O my father! if thou thinkest there is hope for me, I will follow thee whithersoever thou goest, and kiss thy footsteps which lead me out of this gulf of sin and death!" Then he comforted her, and leaving behind all her jewels and gay attire, she returned with him to the cell in the desert. Here she ministered to her aged uncle, and lived a life of contrition and penance. For many years after his death she still continued the same life; and so great was the virtue of her prayers that the sick who were brought to her were cured when she prayed. When she died she was borne by angels to paradise. Conversion of Mary the Penitent, October 29.

St. Matthew (*Lat.* S. Matthœus; *Ger.* Der Heilige Matthäus; *Fr.* St. Matthieu; *Ital.* San Matteo). Among the Evangelists St. Matthew holds the first place on account of having written his Gospel first. In representations of the disciples he is the seventh or eighth. He has not been a popular subject of art. The Scripture account tells only that his name was Levi, and his office that of tax-gatherer; a Hebrew by birth. When Christ called him, he immediately left all else to obey; and he also made a great feast in his house, at which Jesus with his disciples sat with publicans and sinners — to the horror of the Jews. After the separation of the Apostles, Matthew preached twenty-three years in Egypt and Ethiopia. At the capital of Ethiopia he was honorably entertained by that eunuch whom Philip had baptized. He raised the son of the King of Egypt from the dead, and cured his daughter, called Iphigenia, of leprosy, and placed her at the head of a society of young maidens, dedicated to the service of God. A heathen king determined to take her away from this community; for which impiety, his palace was burned, and he became a leper. When this saint was in Ethiopia a terrible fear was over the people, on account of two skilful magicians who put many under their spells, and afflicted them with dreadful diseases. St. Matthew overcame these sorcerers, and ended their power by baptizing the people. All this is related in the "Perfetto Legendario." The manner of his death is doubtful. The Greek legend says he died a peaceful death, but the Western traditions declare that he suffered martyrdom in the time of Domitian. His proper attributes are the purse, when represented as an Apostle ; the pen and book, with an attendant angel, when the Evangelist. The angel holds the inkhorn or the book, or points to heaven, or dictates. Greek pictures of his death show him dying peacefully, while an angel swings a censer ; other representations give the martyrdom by the sword. September 21, A. D. 90.

St. Matthias (*Ital.* San Mattia ; *Fr.* St. Mathias ; *Lat.* S. Matthæus) was the last apostle, chosen to take the place made vacant by the treachery of Judas. St. Denis relates that he was selected by the Apostles on account of a beam of divine splendor which pointed to him. This has been represented in art. He preached in Judæa, and was martyred by the Jews. His attribute is a lance or an axe. February 24.

St. Maurelio, or **Maurelius**, was the first bishop, and is the patron saint of Ferrara and Imola. His image is on the coins of Ferrara. He was beheaded.

St. Maurice (*Lat.* S. Mauritius ; *Ital.* San Maurizio ; *Ger.* Der Heilige Moritz ; *Fr.* St. Maurice). The legend of St. Maurice and the Theban Legion is one of the most ancient of all legends, and has been so received as to have almost the importance of a strictly historical fact. The Theban Legion was so called because levied in the Thebaïd. It was composed of 6,666 men, all of whom were Christians. It was commanded by Maurice, who was of illustrious descent. This legion was so characterized by valor, piety, and fidelity, that it had received the title of *Felix*. When Maximin was about to enter Gaul, he ordered this legion to accompany him thither. When they had passed the Alps the legion was divided : a part went to the Rhine, and the remainder halted on the banks of Lake Geneva. Here Maximin ordered a great sacrifice to the gods, with all the games and festivities which accompanied the pagan rites. There, Maurice and his soldiers separated themselves from the army, and pitched their camp at a place now called St. Maurice, but then Agamum. Maximin then made it known that the purpose of his expedition was the extermination of the Christians, and threatened the Theban Legion with his vengeance if they did not join in the sacrifices. They steadfastly refused to do so, or to assist in the persecution of the Christians. Then Maximin commanded the men to be decimated. Those to whom the lot fell rejoiced in being thus chosen to testify to their faith, and those who were left were still so determined that they were decimated the second time. Even when the third summons came, Maurice replied, "O Cæsar ! we are thy soldiers, but we are also the soldiers of Jesus Christ. From thee we receive our pay, but from him we have received eternal life. To thee we owe service, to him obedience. We are ready to follow thee against the barbarians ; but we are also ready to suffer death, rather than renounce our faith or fight against our brethren." Then Maximin commanded that the rest of the army should surround these men, and murder every one with the sword. He was obeyed, — not one was left alive. But some were trampled to death, some hanged, and some shot with arrows. Maurice knelt down and was beheaded. At Cologne, and in other places, many more who belonged to the Theban Legion suffered martyrdom. Savoy, Piedmont, and parts of Germany abound in these soldier saints. The name of Maurice signifies "a Moor," and he is represented as one in some pictures. He is dressed in armor, and bears the standard and the palm. In Italian pictures he wears a red cross on his breast, which is the badge of the Sardinian Order of St. Maurice. September 22, A. D. 286.

　　St. Maurus was the son of a Roman senator, and was placed under the care of St. Benedict at Subiaco, when only twelve years old. He became one of the most famous disciples of his great master. At one time Maurus expressed his satisfaction at the death of one Florentius, who had attempted to poison St. Benedict, and had committed many crimes which disgraced his office (for he was a priest); this expression so shocked his teacher that he commanded him to atone for his sin by a severe penance. After the death of Benedict, Maurus introduced the Benedictine Order into France, and founded the monastery of St. Maure-sur-Loire (then called Glanfeuil), where he died. His attribute is the book or censer. January 15, A. D. 584.

St. Mercuriale was the first Bishop of Forli in the second century. His attribute is a dragon, representing sin, which the saint had vanquished. He is patron saint of Forli.

St. Mercurius (*Gr.* Ἅγ. Ἑρμῆς: signification, "God's messenger"). The representations of this saint belong especially to Greek art. He was an officer whom Julian the Apostate put to death on account of his Christian faith. When Julian afterwards fought against the Persians, St. Basil had a vision in which he saw a woman seated on a throne and surrounded by angels. To one of these she said, "Go forthwith, and awaken Mercurius, who sleepeth in the sepulchre, that he may slay Julian the Apostate, that proud blasphemer against me and against my Son!" As soon as the vision had passed, Basil went to the tomb of Mercurius, but neither the body nor the armor which had been buried with him were in the tomb. But the next day the body of the saint and all the armor was as before, except that the lance was stained with blood. "For on the day of battle, when the wicked emperor was at the head of his army, an unknown warrior, bareheaded, and of a pale and ghastly countenance, was seen mounted on a white charger, which he spurred forward; and brandishing his lance, he pierced Julian through the body, and then vanished as suddenly as he had appeared. And Julian being carried to his tent, he took a handful of the blood which flowed from his wound, and flung it into the air, exclaiming with his last breath, '.Thou hast conquered, Galilean! Thou hast conquered!' Then the demons received his parting spirit. But Mercurius, having performed the behest of the Blessed Virgin, re-entered his tomb, and laid himself down to sleep till the Day of Judgment."

St. Methodius. See St. Cyril.

St. Michael (*Lat.* S. Michael Angelus; *Fr.* Monseigneur St. Michel; *Ital.* San Michele, Sammichele; ʿΑγ. Μιχαήλ). St. Michael, whose name signifies "like unto God," or Michael the Archangel, is regarded as the first and mightiest of all created spirits. He it was whom God commissioned to expel Satan and the rebellious angels from heaven. His office now is believed to be twofold, — including that of patron saint of the Church on earth, and Lord of the souls of the dead; presenting the good to God, and sending the evil and wicked away to torment. It is believed to have been St. Michael who appeared to Hagar (Gen. xxi. 17), to Abraham to forbid the sacrifice of Isaac (Gen. xxii. 11); who brought the plagues on Egypt, led the Israelites on their journey, contended with Satan for the body of Moses (Jude 5), put blessings instead of curses in Balaam's mouth (Num. xxii. 35), was with Joshua at Jericho (Josh. v. 13), appeared to Gideon (Judges vi. 11), brought the pestilence to Israel (2 Sam. xxiv. 16), destroyed the Assyrian army (2 Chron. xxxii. 21), delivered the three Hebrew children from the fiery furnace (Dan. iii. 25), and sent Habakkuk to feed Daniel in the lion's den (Bel and the Dragon, 32). The legends also relate that St. Michael appeared to the Blessed Virgin to announce to her the time of her death, and that he received her soul and bore it to Jesus. And again, during the sixth century, when a fearful pestilence was raging in Rome, St. Gregory advised that a procession should be made, which should pass through the streets singing the service which since then has been called the Great Litanies. This was done for three days, and on the last day, when they came opposite to the tomb of Hadrian, Gregory beheld the Archangel Michael hovering over the city; and he alighted on the top of the Mausoleum and sheathed his sword, which was dripping with blood. Then the plague was stayed, and the Tomb of Hadrian has been called the Castle of Sant' Angelo from that day, and a chapel was there consecrated, the name of which was Ecclesia Sancti Angeli usque ad Cœlos. St. Michael is also said to have appeared to command the building of two churches. The first was on the eastern coast of Italy, and was called the church of Monte Galgano. The legend relates that in the fifth century there dwelt in Siponto a man named Galgano, who was very rich in herds which were pastured on the mountain. At one time a bull strayed away, and Galgano took his servants and went to find him, and when seen he was on the very summit of the mountain, near the mouth of a cave. Galgano was angry with the bull, and ordered a servant to kill him; but the arrow came back to the bosom of him who sent it, and killed him instantly. Then Galgano, being troubled, sent to the bishop to know what he should do. Then the bishop fasted and prayed for three days, at the end of which time St. Michael appeared to him and told him that the spot where the bull had been seen was especially sacred to him, and he could not permit it to be violated by blood, and he commanded that a church should be built there under his patronage. When they entered the cave they found a stream of water running from the rock, which cured all manner of diseases; and three altars were already built there, and one was covered with a rich cloth embroidered in crimson and gold. So the fame of this vision spread through all Europe, and the church which was there built became a place of pilgrimage. Again, in the reign of Childebert II., St. Michael appeared to St. Aubert, Bishop of Avranches, and commanded that a church should be built on the summit of a rock in the Gulf of Avranches, in Normandy. This rock is inaccessible at high water, and has been celebrated as an impregnable fortress. The bishop was also told that a bull would be found concealed there and a spring of pure water, and the church should be made to cover as much ground as the bull had trampled. St. Aubert considered this as but a dream; but it was repeated again and again, and the third time the Archangel pressed his thumb upon the head of the bishop and left there a mark which never disappeared. After this a small church was built which was afterwards replaced by a magnificent abbey, begun by Richard, Duke of Normandy, and completed by William the Conqueror. Mont-Saint-Michel became one of the most celebrated places of pilgrimage, as it is one of the most picturesque in scenery; but this legend seems only a poor repetition of that of Monte Galgano. From this time St. Michael was greatly venerated in France. He was selected as patron saint of the country and of the order which St. Louis instituted in his honor. An old French writer also makes him the angel of good counsel, and says, " Le vrai office de Monseigneur St. Michel est de faire grandes révélations aux hommes en bas, en leur donnant moult saints conseils," and particularly "sur le bon nourissement que le père et la mère donnent à leurs enfans." St. Michael is always represented as young and beautiful. As patron of the Church Militant he is "the winged saint," with no attribute save the shield and lance. As conqueror of Satan, he stands in armor, with his foot upon the Evil One, who is half human or like a dragon in shape. The angel is about to chain him or to transfix him with the lance. But the treatment of this subject is varied in many ways, all however easily recognized. As lord of souls St. Michael is unarmed; he holds a balance, and in each scale a little naked figure representing the souls; the *beato* usually joins the hands as in thankfulness, while the rejected one expresses horror in look and attitude. Frequently a demon is seizing the falling scale with a Plutonic hook or with his talons. In these pictures the saint is rarely without wings. When introduced in pictures of the Madonna and Child he presents the balance to Christ, who seems to welcome the happy soul. Whether with or without the balance, he is always the lord of souls in pictures of the death, assumption, or glorification of the Blessed Virgin; for tradition says that he received her spirit and cared for it until it was reunited to her body and ascended to her Son. The old English coin called an angel was so named because it bore the image of this archangel. September 29. Apparition of St. Michael, May 8.

St. Miniato, or Minias. The Florentine legend relates that this saint was an Armenian prince who belonged to the Roman army and served under Decius. When that emperor was encamped outside the city of Florence, Miniato was denounced as a Christian and condemned to be thrown to the beasts of the amphitheatre. A panther was first set upon him, but the saint was delivered from him in answer to his prayers. He was then hanged, put in boiling oil, and stoned without being destroyed; for an angel descended to comfort him, and clothed him in a garment of light. Finally he was beheaded. It is said that this occurred in 254. He is represented dressed as a prince with a scarlet robe and a crown. His attributes are the palm, the lily, and javelins.

St. Modwena was an Irish virgin who had power to heal diseases. King Egbert had a son who was epileptic, and no physician of his court could heal him. Now the king, hearing of the power of Modwena, sent his son over seas to her with many and rich gifts.

The virgin refused the presents, but she healed the sick boy. Then the king sent for her to come to England. He was surprised at her learning and piety; and he built for her a convent at Polesworth, in Warwickshire, and gave his daughter Edith into her care. This Edith of Polesworth, as she is called, became a holy nun, and was canonized. St. Modwena is represented in the black habit of a Benedictine nun, with a white veil; in one hand a crosier, as first abbess of her monastery, and in the other a book. July 5, A. D. 1387.

St. Monica (*Fr.* Ste. Monique) was the mother of St. Augustine and a Christian, while his father was a heathen. Monica was sorely troubled at the dissipated life of her young son; she wept and prayed for him, and at last sought the advice and aid of the Bishop of Carthage. He dismissed her with these words: "Go in peace; the son of so many tears will not perish." At length she had the joy to behold the baptism of St. Augustine by the Bishop of Milan, in which city it took place. She is venerated as the great patroness of the Augustinian nuns. She is represented in many of the pictures illustrative of the life of St. Augustine. Her dress is a black robe, with veil or coif of white or gray. In one picture in Florence she is seated on a throne and attended by twelve nuns or saints. May 4, A. D. 387.

Moses, The Patriarch. There are some legends concerning Moses so entirely outside all connection with the Scripture account of him, that the pictures which are painted to represent them are quite incomprehensible without the traditions. According to these the daughter of Pharaoh Valid went to the Nile in order to heal some disease from which she suffered, by the use of its waters. And when Thermutis (for so she was called) touched the babe, she found she was immediately well. One legend relates that the king had seven daughters, all of them lepers, and that all were made whole by the touch of the infant; and that therefore the king allowed them to rear the child in the palace. But art represents the first version; and the legend goes on to say that Thermutis, having no children, grew so fond of the boy that she desired that he should succeed to the throne of Egypt. Now, when the child was three years old, she brought him to the king, who caressed him, and sportively placed the crown on his head. Moses pulled it off, and dashed it to the ground, it is said, because it was engraved with the figures of idols, which even then Moses abhorred; again it is said that it was the covering of the king's beard that he pulled off and threw down. But be it as it may, those who stood by looked upon it as a bad omen, and advised the king that the boy should be slain; but others said he was too young to know right from wrong; while others still thought there was something very uncommon in the babe. Then the third counsellor said, "Let a ruby ring and a burning coal be set before him; if he should choose the ring it will show that he knows right from wrong, and so let him be slain; but if he choose the coal it will show he is too young to distinguish the right, and so let him live." Then this was done; and the ring was the king's signet, which was large and shining. Then at first the child reached out for the ring; but the angel Gabriel, who took the form of one of the attendants, turned his hand aside, so that he took the coal and put it into his mouth, and his tongue was so burned that he could never speak distinctly while he lived, but his life was spared. This appears in art from the fourteenth century.

St. Nabor and **St. Felix.** Little is known of these two saints beyond the fact that they were Christians, and were martyred on account of their faith in the reign of Diocletian. They suffered at Milan, and were buried by a Christian named Philip. A chapel was built over their remains, and it was in this church that St. Ambrose prayed when he had the vision which led to the discovery of the relics of SS. Gervasius and Protasius. They are represented in art both in armor and in secular costume. July 12.

St. Narcissus. See St. Afra of Augsburg.

St. Natalia. See St. Adrian.

St. Nazarius (*Ital.* San Nazaro). See St. Celsus.

St. Neot was the preceptor as well as the kinsman of King Alfred. He was a very learned monk of Glastonbury. It is said that he journeyed to Rome seven times. He is described as "humble to all, affable in conversation, wise in transacting business, venerable in aspect, severe in countenance, moderate even in his walk, upright, calm, temperate, and charitable." He dwelt at one time in a wild solitude in Cornwall. He died in 878. Two towns in England bear his name. His attributes are the pilgrim's staff and wallet. October 28.

St. Nereus (*Ital.* San Nereo).   See St. Achilleus.

St. Nicaise (*Lat.* S. Nicasius) was bishop of Rheims, and was famed for the success of his preaching.   When Rheims was besieged in 400 by the Vandals, St. Nicaise went forth to meet them, attended by his clergy and singing hymns.   A barbarian soldier struck off the upper part of his head; but still the saint marched on and continued to sing, until after a few steps he fell dead.   He is represented in his bishop's robes, carrying a part of his head, upon which is the mitre.   December 14.

St. Nicholas of Myra (*Lat.* S. Nicholaus; *Ital.* San Niccolo or Nicola di Bari; *Ger.* Der Heilige Nicolaus, or Niklas).   Very little of historical fact is known of this saint.   There was a bishop of this name much venerated in the East as early as the sixth century; a church was dedicated to him in Constantinople about A. D. 560; in the Greek Church he ranks next to the great Fathers.   He began to be reverenced in the West in the tenth century, and since the twelfth has been one of the most popular of all saints in Russia, as well as in Italy, and in all Catholic Europe.   But what history does not tell is more than supplied by tradition.   The stories of St. Nicholas are numberless, and many of them have been treated in art.   According to these legends Nicholas was born of illustrious Christian parents, after they had been many years married without having children; and it was thought that this son was given by God as a reward for the alms which they had bestowed upon the Church and the poor, as well as for the prayers they had offered.   Their home was in Panthera, a city of Lycia in Asia Minor.   The very day of his birth this wonderful child arose in his bath, and joining his hands, praised God that he had brought him into the world.   And from the same day he would take the breast only once on Wednesday and Friday; thus knowing how to fast from the time that he knew hunger.   On account of his holy dispositions his parents early dedicated him to the service of the Church.   While still young, Nicholas lost both father and mother; and he regarded himself as but God's steward over the vast wealth of which he was possessed.   A certain nobleman of Panthera, who was very rich, lost all his property, and became so destitute that he could not provide for his three daughters, and he feared that he should be driven to sacrifice their virtue for money to keep them from starvation.   The daughters were filled with grief, and having no bread knew not where to look for aid. Now Nicholas heard of this, and resolved to relieve them. So he took a good sum of gold, and tied it in a handkerchief, and went to the house by night to try how he could give it to them and not be himself seen. As he lingered near the dwelling, the moon shone out brightly and showed an open window. Then Nicholas threw the gold inside the house and hastened away. The money fell at the feet of the unhappy father; and with it he portioned his eldest daughter, and she was married. Again Nicholas did the same, and the second daughter received this sum. But now the nobleman resolved to watch, in order to know who was thus kind to him; and when Nicholas went the third time, he seized him by his robe, saying, "O Nicholas! servant of God! why seek to hide thyself?" Then Nicholas made him promise that he would tell no man. This was but one of the many charities which he did in Panthera. At length he determined to go to Palestine. On the voyage a sailor fell overboard and was drowned, but St. Nicholas restored his life; and when a storm arose, and they were about to perish, the sailors fell at his feet and implored him to save them; and when he prayed the storm ceased. After his return from Palestine Nicholas dwelt in the city of Myra, where he was unknown, and he lived in great humility. At length the Bishop of Myra died; and a revelation was made to the clergy to the effect that the first man who should come to the church the next morning would be the man whom God had chosen for their bishop. So when Nicholas came early to the church to pray, as was his custom, the clergy led him into the church and consecrated him bishop. He showed himself well worthy of his new dignity in every way, but especially by his charities, which were beyond account. At one time a dreadful famine prevailed in his diocese; and when he heard that ships were in the port of Myra laden with wheat, he requested the captains to give him a hundred hogsheads of wheat out of each vessel. But they dared not do this; for the grain was measured at Alexandria, and would be again measured at Constantinople, where they were to deliver it. Then Nicholas said that if they obeyed him, it would happen by the grace of God that their cargoes should not be diminished. So they complied; and when they were arrived at the granary of the emperor they found as much wheat in their ships as when they left Alexandria. And moreover that which

they gave St. Nicholas was miraculously increased; for he fed the
people so that they had enough to eat, and still sufficient remained
to sow their fields for the next year. During this time of hunger,
as St. Nicholas was travelling through his diocese, he did one of his
greatest miracles. He slept in the house of a man who was a most
loyal son of Satan; for in this time of want he was accustomed to
steal children, to kill them and serve them up as meat to those who
stopped at his inn. Now Nicholas no sooner had this abominable
dish placed before him than he knew what it was, and understood
the horrible wickedness of the man. Then he accused the host, and
went to the tub where the children were salted down, and made the
sign of the cross over it, when, lo! three children rose up whole and
well. All the people were struck dumb at this miracle, and the three
children were restored to their mother, who was a widow. At one
time Constantine sent certain tribunes to put down a rebellion in
Phrygia. On their journey they stopped at Myra, and Nicholas
invited them to his table; but as they were about to sit down, he
heard that the prefect of the city was preparing to execute three
innocent men, and the people were greatly moved thereat. Then
Nicholas hastened to the place of execution, followed by his guests.
When they arrived the men were already kneeling, with their eyes
bound, and the executioner was ready with his sword. St. Nicholas
seized the sword and commanded the men to be released. The
tribunes looked on in wonder, but no one dared to resist the good
bishop. Even the prefect sought his pardon, which he granted after
much hesitation. After this, when the tribunes went on their way,
they did not forget St. Nicholas; for it happened that while they
were absent in Phrygia their enemies poisoned the mind of Constantine against them, so that when they were returned to Constantinople
he accused them of treason and threw them into prison, ordering
their execution on the following day. Then these tribunes called
upon St. Nicholas, and prayed him to deliver them. That same
night he appeared to Constantine in a dream, and commanded him
to release those whom he had imprisoned, and threatened him with
God's wrath if he obeyed not. Constantine not only released them,
but he sent them to Myra to thank St. Nicholas, and to present him
with a copy of the Gospels which was written in letters of gold and
bound in covers set with pearls and rare jewels. Also certain sailors

who were in danger of shipwreck on the Ægean Sea called upon
Jesus to deliver them for the sake of St. Nicholas; and immediately
the saint appeared to them, saying, " Lo, here I am, my sons! put
your trust in God, whose servant I am, and ye shall be saved." And
the sea was calm, and he took them into a safe harbor. Now, the
fame of these miracles so went abroad through the world, that since
that time those who are in peril invoke this saint and find aid in
him. And so his life was spent in doing all manner of good works;
and when he died it was in great peace and joy, and he was buried
in a magnificent church in Myra. The miracles attributed to St.
Nicholas after his death are quite as marvellous as those he did
while yet alive. A man who greatly desired to have a son made a
vow that if this wish were realized, the first time he took his child
to church he would give a cup of gold to the altar of St. Nicholas.
The son was granted, and the father ordered the cup to be made; but
when it was finished it was so beautiful that he decided to retain it for
his own use, and he had another less valuable made for St. Nicholas.
At length he went on the journey necessary to accomplish his vow,
and while on the way he ordered the little child to bring him water
in the cup which he had taken for himself. In obeying his father,
the boy fell into the water and was drowned. Then the father
repented sorely of his covetousness, and repaired to the church of
St. Nicholas and offered the second cup; but when it was placed upon
the altar it fell off and rolled on the ground, and this it did the second
and third time; and while all looked on amazed, behold, the drowned
child stood on the steps of the altar with the beautiful cup in his
hand; and he told how St. Nicholas had rescued him from death and
brought him thither. Then the joyful father made an offering of both
cups, and returned home full of gratitude to the good St. Nicholas.
This story has often been told in prose and poetry, as well as represented in art. Again, a Jew of Calabria, having heard of all the
wonderful deeds of St. Nicholas, stole his image from the church and
set it up in his house. Whenever he left his house he put the care
of his goods in the hands of the saint, and threatened that if anything
should befall them in his absence he would chastise the saint on his
return. One day the robbers came and stole his treasures. Then
the Jew beat the image and cut it also. That night St. Nicholas
appeared to the robbers all wounded and bleeding, and commanded

them to restore what they had stolen; and they, being afraid at the vision, did as he bade them. Then the Jew was converted by this miracle and was baptized. Another rich Christian merchant who dwelt in a pagan country had an only son who was made a captive, and was obliged to serve the king of the country as cupbearer. One day, as he filled the king's cup, he remembered that it was St. Nicholas' day, and he wept. Then the king demanded the cause of his grief; and when the young man told him, he answered, "Great as is thy St. Nicholas, he cannot save thee from my hand!" And instantly the palace was shaken by a whirlwind, and St. Nicholas appeared and caught the youth by the hair, and set him in the midst of his own family with the king's cup still in his hand. And it happened that the very moment when he came there was that in which his father was giving food to the poor, and asking their prayers for his captive son. It is necessary to keep these traditions in mind when regarding the pictures of St. Nicholas; for in two different pictures there appears a boy with a cup, so that it is important to distinguish them by the accessories. Sometimes it is a daughter who is rescued from captivity. The tomb of St. Nicholas was a famous resort for pilgrims for centuries. In 807 the church was attacked by Achmet, commander of the fleet of Haroun Al Raschid. But the watchfulness of the monks prevented him from doing any harm; and putting to sea, he and his whole fleet were destroyed in punishment for their sacrilegious attempt. The remains of the saint rested in Myra until 1084, although several attempts were made by different cities and churches to possess themselves of these holy relics. At length, in the year mentioned, some merchants of Bari who traded on the coast of Syria resolved to obtain these remains, of which they had heard so great wonders. At this time Myra was desolated by the Saracens, and the ruined church was guarded by three monks. The remains were taken without difficulty and carried safely to Bari, where a splendid church was erected for their resting-place. The Venetians, however, claim that they have the true relics of St. Nicholas, brought home by Venetian merchants in 1100. But the claims of Bari are generally acknowledged, and the saint is best known as St. Nicholas of Bari. In Greek pictures he is dressed like a Greek bishop, with no mitre, the cross in place of the crosier, and the emblems of the Trinity embroidered on his cope. In Western art he has the bishop's dress, the mitre, the cope very much ornamented, the crosier, and jewelled gloves. His attributes are three balls, which are on the book, at his feet, or in his lap. They are said to represent the three purses of gold which he threw into the window of the poor nobleman; or three loaves of bread, emblematic of his feeding the poor; or again, the persons of the Trinity. The first interpretation is the most general. He is chief patron of Russia, patron of Bari, Venice, and Freiberg, as well as of many other towns and cities, numbers of them being seaport places. He is protector against robbers and losses by violence. He is patron of children and school-boys in particular; of poor maidens, of sailors, travellers, and merchants. December 6, A. D. 326.

St. Nicholas of Tolentino was born in the little town of St. Angelo, near Fermo, in 1239. His parents had prayed earnestly to St. Nicholas for a son; and as they believed that this son was given to them through the intercession of this saint, they named him Nicholas, and dedicated him to the service of the Church. At an early age he took the habit of an Augustine friar; and so great was the austerity of his life that it has been said that "he did not live, but languished through life." He was successful as a preacher, and his miracles and visions are numberless. He never allowed himself to taste animal food; and when he was very weak he refused a dish of doves that his brethren brought him, and waved his hand above the dish, when the doves rose up and flew away. Tradition relates that at the hour of his birth a brilliant star shot through the heavens from Sant' Angelo, where he was born, and rested over the city of Tolentino, where he afterwards lived. In the year 1602 a plague visited the city of Cordova; and according to the legend the governor caused the image of St. Nicholas of Tolentino to be carried through the city, in solemn procession, on the day which was observed as the festival of that saint. Father G. de Uavas, bearing a crucifix, met the procession, when the figure of Christ stooped from the cross and embraced that of St. Nicholas, and immediately the plague was stayed. He is also represented in art as restoring a child to life, and doing many other miracles. He is painted in the black habit of his order, with a star on his breast; he often bears a crucifix wreathed with lilies, typical of the purity and austerity of his life. September 10, A. D. 1309.

St. Nilus of Grotta Ferrata (*Ital.* San Nilo ; *Fr.* St. Nil le jeune). St. Nilus was connected with many interesting events in Roman history in life, and since his death is associated with art in an interesting manner. He was a Greek, born near Tarentum. It was not until after the loss of his wife, whom he loved devotedly, that he embraced a religious vocation. He took the habit of the Greek Order of St. Basil, and was soon made the superior of his community on account of his worth and learning. The chances of war drove him to the west of Italy ; and he fled to the convent of Monte Cassino at Capua, which was of the Benedictine Order. He was received with great kindness, and a small convent assigned to him and his followers by the abbot. At this time Capua was governed by Aloare, who was the widow of the Prince of Capua, and reigned in the name and right of her two sons. This wicked mother had influenced her children to murder their cousin, who was a powerful and worthy nobleman. Now she was seized with the agony of remorse, and sought St. Nilus to confess her crime, and entreated absolution at his hands. He refused this, except upon condition that she should give up one of her sons to the family of the murdered man, to be dealt with as they saw fit.[1] This she would not consent to do. Then St. Nilus denounced her unforgiven, and told her that what she would not give, Heaven would soon exact of her. She offered him large sums of money, and begged him to pray for her ; but he threw down her money in scorn and left her. Not long after this the younger son killed the elder in a church, and for this double crime of fratricide and sacrilege he was put to death by command of Hugh Capet. Nilus afterwards went to Rome, and lived in a convent on the Aventine, where large numbers of sick people visited him, and he did many and great miracles. Among others, his cure of an epileptic boy forms a subject for art. Crescentius was consul at this time, and had set up Philagatus, Bishop of Placentia, as anti-pope, against Gregory V., with the title of John XVI. Then Otho III. came to Rome to expel the anti-pope, and laid siege to the castle of St. Angelo, to which Crescentius had retired. After a short siege the castle was given up on honorable terms ; but not heeding

---

[1] This incident is not mentioned in the Rev. Alban Butler's sketch of the saint ; and the pledge exacted of the mother comports not with the Christian spirit.

these, Otho ordered that Crescentius should be thrown headlong
from the walls, and Stephanie, his wife, given up to the outrages
of the soldiers. So great was the influence of Nilus in Rome at this
time, that he interceded, to good effect, with both Pope and Emperor,
in behalf of the anti-pope, claiming that he should be treated with
mildness, as he was a bishop. The saint then left Rome, and went
first to a cell near Gaeta, but soon after to a cave near Frascati,
called the Crypta, or Grotta Ferrata. Otho went on a pilgrimage to
Monte Galgano. When returning, he visited Nilus, and on his knees
besought his prayers. He offered to erect a convent and endow it
with lands, but this Nilus refused; and when Otho demanded what
boon he could grant him, the saint stretched out his hand, and replied,
" I ask of thee but this : that thou wouldst make reparation for thy
crimes before God, and save thine own soul!" Soon after Otho
returned to Rome he was obliged to fly from the fury of the people,
and was poisoned by Stephanie, the widow of Crescentius. When
St. Nilus died, he desired his brethren to bury him immediately, and
to keep secret the place where they laid him. This they did; but
his disciple, Bartolomeo, built the convent which Nilus had not
wished to do, and received the gifts he had refused. The magnificent
convent and church of San Basilio of Grotta Ferrata was built, and
St. Nilus is regarded as its founder. The rule is that of St. Basil,
and the priests say mass in Greek, but they wear the Benedictine
habit as a dependency of Monte Cassino. The finest Greek library
in all Italy was here, and is now in the Vatican; and Julius II.
changed the convent to a fortress. In 1610 Domenichino was
employed by Cardinal Odoardo Farnese to decorate the chapel of
St. Nilus, which he did, with paintings from the life of the saint.
September 26, A. D. 1002.

St. Norbert (*Ital.* San Norberto, Fondatore de' Premostratesi ;
Ger. Stifter der Prämonstratenser-Orden). This saint was a relative
of Henry IV. He was born at Cologne, and early dedicated to the
Church. But he led a dissolute life as a young man. At last, as he
was one day riding, he was overtaken by a tempest, and a ball of fire
fell from heaven and, exploding at the feet of his horse, sank into the
earth. He was terrified when he reflected upon what his state would
have been had he been killed by it, and he resolved to lead a different life from that time. He bestowed his money on the poor, and

determined to be a missionary. He only reserved a mule to carry the sacred utensils for the altar and the vestments, and ten marks of silver. He dressed himself in skins, with a cord as a girdle, and thus he went forth to preach. After preaching for some years there were many who desired him to form a community, and lead them in a life of austerity and severe discipline. He prayed to the Blessed Virgin for direction, and she pointed out to him a spot called Pré-montré (Pratum Monstratum), in the valley of Coucy, where he should establish his monastery. The Virgin also directed what habit his monks should wear; that it should be a coarse black tunic, with a white woollen cloak, in imitation of angels, who are clothed in white; and a four-cornered cap of white also, but in form like the beret of the Augustinian canons. The rule was that of Augustine in extreme severity. St. Norbert was made Bishop of Magdeburg, and before his death his order embraced twelve hundred souls. According to the legend, one day when he had consecrated the holy wine, and was about to drink it, he saw a large and poisonous spider in the cup. For a moment he hesitated; but he reflected that he could not spill the consecrated wine, — it would be sacrilege; so he drank it, and remained unharmed. This was considered a miraculous recompense of his faith, and is often represented in art. When at Antwerp, there was one Tankelin who preached most heretical doctrines, saying that the sacraments were unnecessary, the priesthood a cheat, and a community of wives as well as goods the true doctrine. St. Norbert confronted this heretic, opposed him, and triumphed over him with great honor. He wears in pictures the dress of an archbishop, with mitre, crosier, and cope. Sometimes he bears the sacramental cup, over which is a spider. He also has, in some instances, a demon at his feet, representing the sin and error which he had overcome. May 6, A. D. 1134.

St. **Omobuono** was a citizen saint of Cremona. He was a merchant, and married to a good and prudent wife; so, though a saint, he was not monk or priest.[1] From his youth all his affairs prospered greatly, and his wealth was equalled only by his charity. He not only fed and clothed but he comforted the poor, and tried to encourage the erring ones to repent and lead virtuous lives. His wife often feared lest his generosity should make his children poor, but his

---

[1] Sanctity, even in a heroic degree, is attainable in every state of life.

money seemed to be miraculously increased; and it is related that being on a journey with his family, he gave all the wine and bread he had provided for their use to some poor pilgrims whom he met; but when he took his wine-flasks to a spring and filled them with water, most excellent wine was poured from them, and his bags were filled with bread by angels. He died peacefully while kneeling before a crucifix in the church of St. Egidio, just as the choir sang the "Gloria in Excelsis." He is represented clothed in a loose tunic and a cap, both of which are trimmed with fur. He usually distributes alms to the poor; wine-flasks stand near him.

St. Onuphrius (Onofrio, Honofrio, Onuphre) was a hermit. He went out from Thebes and passed sixty years in the desert, during which time he never uttered a word except in prayer, nor saw a human face. His clothing was of leaves, and his hair and beard were uncut. He was thus seen by Paphnutius, who when he first saw him was filled with fear, believing him to be some strange wild beast; but when he saw that it was a man, he fell at his feet filled with reverence for his sanctity. Then Onuphrius recounted all he had endured in his solitude: how he had been tempted; had suffered from cold, heat, hunger, thirst, and sickness; and how God had sent angels to comfort, strengthen, and minister unto him. Then he begged Paphnutius to remain with him, as he was near to death. It was not long before he died, and Paphnutius covered his remains with one half of his cloak. Then he had a revelation that he should go into the world and make known the wonderful life and merits of him who had died. Many convents where silence and solitude are especially practised are placed under the protection of this saint. Tasso died and is buried in the convent of St. Onofrio in the Trastevere in Rome. St. Onuphrius is represented as meagre and old: a stick in his hand, and a branch with leaves twisted about him. In many old pictures he looks more the beast than the man. Sometimes money is lying at his feet to signify his scorn of it. June 12.

Ordeal. The trial by ordeal was used for the decision of cases where the oath of the accused person was not considered worthy of reliance. It was called the great purgation. The word *ordeal* is from two Saxon words, — *or*, great; and *deal*, judgment. There were three tests used in these trials: (1) By red-hot iron; this the person held in the hand, or walked on barefoot. (2) By boiling water; the person dipped the hand to the wrist or the arm to the elbow, and took out a stone. (3) By cold water, or compelling persons to swim; this was chiefly used for detecting witches, and was also employed not only by judges, but at length by the people and especially by foresters, to discover criminals. These tests had their origin among the northern nations, but were condemned at Rome, whenever any notice of them reached there. Where certain bishops sanctioned these trials, examples are recorded of God's favor shown to the good faith and piety of the innocent; as, for instance, in the case of the monk Peter, surnamed Igneus, at Florence, in 1067.

St. Oswald. This king, being moved with a desire to live a truly Christian life, asked that a teacher might be sent to instruct him and his people. The first man who was sent was severe in disposition, and had no success with the unlearned. Then Aidan came, and by means of his mildness and great discretion, he had much influence with the king and his people. Aidan was afterwards prior of Melrose. According to the legends, it happened that as Oswald sat at dinner one Easter Day with Aidan by his side, he was told that there were those at his door who begged for bread. Now there was before him a silver dish filled with delicate and savory meat. Oswald told the servant to give the beggars the meat, and then to break the dish and divide it among them. Then Aidan took his right hand, saying, "May this hand never wither!" And his prayer was granted; for at Oswald's death his heathen enemies cut off his head and hands, and set them on stakes; but his head was taken to the church of Lindisfarne, and buried in St. Cuthbert's tomb, between the arms of that saint: his right hand was carried to Bamborough Castle, where it was a long time preserved, free from decay. At one time Oswald was driven from his throne by Cadwallader. At length he determined to regain his kingdom. He raised an army; and when in sight of his enemies he ordered his men to make a large wooden cross, and himself helped to place it in the ground. Then he cried out, "Let us all kneel down and beseech the living God to defend us from the haughty and fierce enemy, for he knows that we have undertaken a just war for the safety of our nation." And when they fought, Oswald was victorious. The greatest proof of his charity of heart is shown in the fact that as he died he prayed for those who killed him. "May God have mercy on their souls, as Oswald said when he fell," was a proverb for many years in England. And the legend tells that " in the place where he was killed by the pagans, fighting for his country, infirm men and cattle are healed to this day ; nor is it to be wondered at, that the sick should be healed in the place where he died, for whilst he lived he never ceased to provide for the poor and infirm, and to bestow alms on them and assist them." His remains were carried to Bardney in Lincolnshire by Osthrida, and afterwards to St. Oswald's in Gloucestershire by E. Heda, the daughter of King Alfred. He is dressed as a king, in his pictures; he wears a crown and carries a cross. August 5, A. D. 642.

St. Ottilia was the blind daughter of the Duke of Alsace. Her father, who was a pagan, commanded that on account of her infirmity she should be left out, and exposed to death. Her nurse then fled to a monastery with the child. Then Erhard, a bishop of Bavaria, was told in a vision that he should go to a certain monastery, where he would find a little girl of noble birth who was blind. He was commanded to baptize her and call her name Ottilia, and promised that her sight should be given her. All this was done according to the vision. Her father repented of his wickedness before his death, and gave her all his wealth. Then Ottilia, knowing that for his cruelty her father was tormented in purgatory, determined to deliver him by prayers and penance. She built a convent at Hohenburg, of which she was abbess, and there she gathered one hundred and thirty nuns. She is represented in the black Benedictine habit. Her attributes are the palm or crosier, and a book upon which are two eyes. She is patron saint of Alsace, and especially of Strasburg. She is also protector of all who suffer with diseases of the eye. December 13, A. D. 720.

St. Pancras (*Ital.* San Pancrazio; *Fr.* St. Pancrace). This saint, when only fourteen years old, died a martyr's death. He boldly defended the Christians and their faith before Diocletian, and was beheaded. His remains were buried by Christian women. His church at Rome, near the gate which bears his name, was built in the year 500. French kings formerly confirmed their treaties in his name ; for he was regarded as the avenger of false swearing, and it was believed that all who swore falsely in his name were immediately and visibly punished. May 12, A. D. 304.

St. Pantaleon of Nicomedia (*Ital.* San Pantaleone; *Gr.* Ἅγ. Πανταλέων) was born (according to tradition) at Nicomedia in Bithynia. He was remarkable for his personal beauty and elegant manners, on account of which, after completing the study of medicine, he became the favorite physician of the Emperor Galerius Maximian. The father of Pantaleon was a pagan, and his mother a Christian; but at the heathen court the son forgot all the instructions that his mother had carefully given him. At length he heard a priest, Hermolaus, preach, and was converted. When the persecution broke out, he knew he could not conceal himself, and he prepared to suffer a cruel martyrdom. He went about to the sick and needy, and well earned the title of the " all-merciful," which is the Greek signification of his name. When accused before the emperor, he was condemned to be beheaded, together with the aged and venerable Hermolaus, who was apprehended at the house of Pantaleon. The latter was bound to an olive-tree, and as soon as his blood flowed to the roots of the tree it burst forth with leaves and fruit. He is especially venerated at Venice. There have been some who doubted his existence, and believed his name to have been derived from the war-cry of the Venetians, — Pianta Leone (Plant the Lion)! But Justinian erected a church under his patronage in Constantinople, and he was celebrated in the Greek Church at that time when Venice would have been more likely to introduce his veneration from the East than to have originated it in any other way. Patron of physicians. He is represented as young, beardless, and handsome. As a martyr he is bound to an olive-tree, with his hands nailed to it above his head, a sword at his feet. Without observation he might be mistaken for St. Sebastian. When he is painted as patron, he wears the physician's robe and bears the olive or palm, or both. July 27. Fourth century.

St. Patrick (*Lat.* S. Patricius) was the son of Christian parents. He was carried a captive to Ireland when a boy, and tended the herds of his master. He was greatly moved at the ignorance and heathenism of the people about him; and when at last he made his escape and returned to his home, he had visions in which it appeared that the children of Ireland not yet born stretched forth their hands to him and cried for salvation. Patrick resolved to become a missionary, and prepared himself for his labor. He received his mission from Pope Celestine, and returned to Ireland. He labored there forty years. He gained many disciples, and preached with the greatest success. He baptized the kings of Dublin and Munster, and the seven sons of the King of Connaught. Having found Ireland under the spiritual sway of the Druids, he left it Christianized ; with schools which became famous, and sent forth many learned scholars. The familiar story of the expulsion of the reptiles from Ireland, by this saint, has the meaning of many other legends and allegories, and figures probably the triumph of good over evil. He died and was buried at Down, in the province of Ulster. His resting-place is still venerated by the people, and his remains were preserved many years; but his church at Down was destroyed in the reign of Henry VIII., and such relics of him as remained were scattered either by the soldiers of Elizabeth or by those of Cromwell. When represented as bishop, he wears the usual dress with the mitre, cope, and crosier, while a neophyte regards him with reverence. As the Apostle of Ireland he should wear a hooded gown and a leathern girdle. The staff, wallet, standard with the cross, and the Gospel are all his proper attributes. Serpents are represented as running from him at the motion of his crosier. March 17, A. D. 464.

St. Paul (*Lat.* S. Paulus; *Ital.* San Paolo; *Sp.* San Pablo; *Fr.* St. Paul; *Gr.* Ἅγ. Παῦλος). St. Paul and St. Peter occupy the first place among the Apostles. St. Peter more especially represented the converted Jews, and St. Paul the Gentiles ; together they represent the Universal Church. There are few legends connected with St. Paul, but the scenes of his life as given in the Gospel have furnished inexhaustible subjects for the illustrations of art. St. Paul is so often represented with St. Peter that it is necessary to be able to distinguish the one from the other. Augustine and other early writers allude to portraits of St. Paul as existing in their time ; and it is supposed that the traditionary picture of him which is so strictly followed had its origin in those portraits. He is small of stature, with high forehead, sparkling eyes, and aquiline nose. His hair and beard are brown, and the latter long and flowing. Later artists have varied the head of St. Paul more than that of St. Peter, but the most ancient pictures are exact in these particulars. When the two Apostles are together, their proper place is on each side of the Saviour, or of the Virgin enthroned. Their pictures should be placed on each side the altar, or of the arch over the choir. The dress is the same for both, — a blue tunic and white mantle in Greek pictures, a blue or green tunic and yellow mantle in later works of art. Paul bears the sword in a double sense, signifying his spiritual warfare and the manner of his death. He also has a book or scroll, and sometimes twelve rolls, representing his epistles. When he leans on his sword, it is his death which is represented; when he holds it aloft, it signifies the "good fight" which he fought. If two swords are given him, both the manner of his death and that of his life are signified. The events in the life of this Apostle are so well known to all that they are easily recognized in art. The church called "San Paolo delle Tre Fontane," near Rome, is built over three fountains which are said to have sprung up at the three places where the head of St. Paul fell and bounded, after being cut off by the executioner. It is said that the fountains vary in the warmth of the water, — the first, or the one where the head fell, being the hottest; the next, or that of the first bound, cooler; and the third still cooler, — but probably time has equalized the temperature, for I could not distinguish the difference. Formerly a magnificent monastery existed here; but three old churches and ruins, with a few sickly-looking monks, are the only remains of its former splendor. The body of St. Paul was interred where the church of San Paolo-fuori-le-mura stands, between the Ostian Gate and the Aqua Salvias; but traditions relate that they were removed with those of St. Peter to the Catacombs, and laid in the same tomb, during the reign of Heliogabalus. Two hundred years later the Oriental Christians endeavored to possess themselves of them; but the Western Christians contended for them with success, and they removed them to the church of the Vatican, and placed them together in a magnificent shrine. St. Peter and St. Paul, June 29. Conversion of St. Paul, June 30. See also St. Peter.

St. Paul. Hermit. See St. Anthony.

St. Paul and **St. John.** See St. John and St. Paul, brothers.

St. Paula (*Gr.* Ἁγ. Παῦλα) was a noble Roman matron, a pupil and disciple of St. Jerome. Though descended from the Scipios and the Gracchi, and accustomed to luxurious self-indulgence, she preferred to follow her saintly teacher to Bethlehem and devote herself to a religious life. The church dedicated to St. Jerome at Rome is said to be upon the spot where the house of Paula stood, in which she entertained that holy man during his stay in Rome, A. D. 382. She studied Hebrew in order to understand the Scriptures better. She built a monastery, an hospital, and three nunneries at Bethlehem. Her daughter St. Eustochium was with her. The rule for these convents was very strict, and her own austerities so severe that she was reprimanded for them by St. Jerome. Her granddaughter Paula was sent to her at Bethlehem to be educated, and succeeded her as superior of the monastery. The elder Paula died making the sign of the cross on her lips, and was buried in the church of the Holy Manger, where her empty tomb is now seen near that of St. Jerome. Her relics are said to be at Sens. January 26, A. D. 404.

St. Paulinus of York was sent from Rome to England in 601, to assist St. Augustine in his mission. He became the first Primate of York, where he founded the cathedral. Wordsworth gives a word-picture of him thus : —

> "Of shoulders curved, and stature tall,
> Black hair and vivid eye, and meagre cheek,
> His prominent feature like an eagle's beak."

By the preaching of Paulinus, Coifi, the Druid and high-priest of Thor, was converted. King Edwin had renounced idolatry, and given Paulinus license to preach. When the king asked Coifi who would destroy the idols, the priest answered, " I ! for who can more properly than myself destroy those things which I worshipped through ignorance ! " It was not lawful for the high-priest to ride, except on a mare, or to bear arms ; but now he asked Edwin to give him a horse and a sword. This was done, and he rode to the temple and thrust his spear in, and commanded the temple and idols to be burned. Paulinus is often seen in pictures of St. Augustine. October 10, A. D. 644.

St. Perpetua was one of the martyrs who suffered at Carthage during the persecution of Severus. This saint manifested miraculous fortitude in submitting to her fate. She was tossed by a wild cow in the amphitheatre, but was not quite killed, and after great tortures was put to death in the spoliarium, or place where the wounded were despatched by the gladiators. She had a vision of a narrow ladder which reached to heaven, beset with spikes, and a dragon lay at the bottom, on whose head she must tread in order to mount the first step. One scene from her life, represented in modern art, is her farewell to her infant child. There are many incidents in her story which would be most interesting subjects for the artist, that as yet remain without representation. In her pictures a cow stands by her side or near her. March 7, A. D. 203.

St. Peter (*Lat.* S. Petrus; *Ital.* San Pietro or Piero; *Fr.* St. Pierre; *Sp.* San Pedro: signification, "a rock"). St. Peter and St. Paul are so associated in history that it is quite impossible to separate them in our minds, or entirely to do so in descriptions of them; and in works of art they are constantly associated. St. Peter is a strong man, old, with gray hair, and curling, silvery beard, a broad forehead, and an expression of courage and confidence. Sometimes he is bald; there is a legend that the Gentiles shaved his head in mockery, and that from this originated the tonsure of the priests. His dress is a blue tunic and white mantle in the oldest pictures and mosaics, but in later art it is a blue or green tunic with a yellow mantle. In the earliest pictures Peter bears only a scroll or book, and there is nothing to distinguish him from Paul except the difference in the head and features. The keys are not assigned as his attribute until the eighth century. He has usually two keys, one golden and one silver; they are interpreted as signifying his power to bind and to loose; or again, one as the key of heaven, the other of hell, when the first is of gold and the second iron, and sometimes a third is added to express dominion over earth also. When the traditional differences in the two men are well represented, the contrast is marked and impressive. In some early representations, from the middle to the end of the fourth century, Peter bears a cross and stands on the left of Christ, with Paul on the right. This cross is said to be the emblem of the death he should die. When St. Peter and St. Paul occur together in strictly devotional pictures, they are represented as the founders of the Universal Church. The Church reveres St. Peter as its visible head, and St. Paul as the Apostle of the Gentiles. When St. Peter is represented in company with all the Apostles, he frequently has a fish, which is the symbol of his early avocation; but if the fish is given him when alone, it is symbolical of Christianity and the Sacrament of Baptism. When represented as the Head of the Church, he is seated on a throne, one hand raised in benediction, while in the other he holds keys, and often a book or scroll inscribed "Thou art Peter, and on this rock have I built my Church." Sometimes he wears the papal tiara. When another saint without attributes is seen with Peter, it is Mark, who was his interpreter and amanuensis at Rome; and a tradition relates that St. Mark's Gospel was written after the dictation of Peter. The historical pictures, or those which represent scenes in the life of Peter, are of great interest and almost numberless, but all easily recognized. Of the legendary pictures those connected with Simon Magus are important. The story is, that Simon was a magician of great fame among the Jews. He did wonderful things at Jerusalem, and greatly astonished the people; but the miracles of Peter far excelled the inventions of the sorcerer. Then Simon endeavored to buy from the Apostles the secret by which these miracles were done. These offers much enraged Peter, who rejected them with great indignation. Simon then threw away his wand, and casting his books into the Dead Sea, he fled to Rome, where he became a favorite of Claudius, and again of Nero. Peter also came to Rome, and afterwards Paul. Simon asserted that he was a god and could raise the dead. Peter and Paul challenged him to prove his skill before the emperor. His arts failed; and not only then, but many times he was vanquished by the Apostles. At last Simon attempted to fly to heaven in the sight of the emperor and all Rome. He was crowned with laurel and supported by demons, and thus precipitated himself from a tower. He appeared to float in the air for a time; but Peter knelt and commanded the demons to let go their hold of him, when he fell to the earth, was severely hurt, and died a few days later in rage and confusion. This legend[1] is not without solid foundation in history, as there existed a Samaritan magician by that name who assumed to be God. Irenæus calls him the father of all heretics. He carried about with him a beautiful woman called Helena, who was, he said, the first conception of his divine mind. He presented her as being the resuscitation of

---

[1] It rests on the testimony of Christian Fathers, as Sts. Justin, Ambrose, Cyril, of Jerusalem, Augustine, Philastrius, Isidore of Pelusium, Theodoret, etc.; and of the pagan writer, Dion Chrysostomus.

Helen of Troy. In the church of St. Francesca Romana at Rome, there are two stones let into the wall, bearing a double depression, made, it is said, by St. Peter's kneeling on them when Simon Magus was attempting his heavenward flight. Another legend relates that, after the burning of Rome, Nero accused the Christians of having fired the city. This was the origin of the first persecution. The Christians besought St. Peter to save himself by flight, which he at length consented to do. He departed by the Appian Way, and when about two miles from the city he met a vision of Our Saviour. Peter exclaimed, "Lord, whither goest thou?" Looking sadly upon him, Christ replied, "I go to Rome to be crucified a second time." Peter understood this as a warning that he ought to return to Rome, which he did. This is called the "Domine, quo vadis?" when illustrated. In the little church erected on the spot sanctified by this miracle, is shown a slab containing footprints, said to be those made by the feet of Christ, as he talked with Peter. After Peter's return to Rome he preached and labored as usual, until he was seized with St. Paul and thrown into the Mamertine Prison. Here the centurions who guarded them, Processus and Martinian, and many prisoners, were converted. When St. Peter wished to baptize them and there was no water, he prayed to God and a fountain sprung up from the stone floor, which may still be seen. It was not long till the two Apostles were martyred. The traditions disagree in regard to the place where St. Peter suffered. According to one, he was crucified with his head downward in the courtyard of a military station on the summit of Mons Janicula, where the church of San Pietro in Montorio now stands; but according to another, his crucifixion took place in the Circus of Caligula, at the foot of the Vatican. The legends make St. Peter the keeper of the entrance to Paradise. The church of San Pietro in Vincoli at Rome was built by Eudoxia, wife of Valentinian III., and in it were preserved the chains with which St. Peter was bound at Jerusalem. The chains are preserved in a bronze tabernacle in the sacristy, and are shown to the people on the festival of St. Peter in Vinculis on the first of August. St. Peter and St. Paul, June 29.

St. Peter of Alcantara was not canonized until 1669. According to the legend, he walked on the sea by faith. In a picture in the Munich Gallery, he not only walks himself, but a lay brother goes with him, whom Peter seems to encourage by pointing to heaven. October 19, A. D. 1562.

St. Peter Exorcista and **Marcellinus** (*Ital.* SS. Pietro e Marcellino). These saints are always represented together. According to the legend, they were imprisoned during the last persecution of Diocletian. Their jailer, Artemius, had a daughter, Paulina, who was sick. Peter promised to restore her to health if Artemius would believe in God. Then Artemius ridiculed him, saying, "If I put thee into the deepest dungeon, and load thee with heavier chains, will thy God then deliver thee?" Then Peter told him that it mattered little to God whether he believed or not; but that Christ might be glorified, he desired that it should be done. And it was so; and in the night Peter and Marcellinus, dressed in shining white garments, came to Artemius in his own chamber. Then he believed, and was baptized with all his family and three hundred others. When the saints were to die, it was ordered that the executioner should take them to a forest three miles from Rome, in order that the Christians should not know of their burial-place. So when they were come to a solitary place and the executioner pointed it out as the spot where they were to die, they themselves cleared a space, and dug their graves, and died encouraging each other. They are represented in priestly habits, bearing palms. June 2, about 304.

St. Peter Martyr. St. Peter the Dominican (*Ital.* San Pietro, or Pier, Martire; *Fr.* St. Pierre le Dominicain, Martyr). This saint is esteemed next to St. Dominick by his order. He was born at Verona about 1205. His parents were of the heretical sect called Cathari, but Peter went to a Catholic school. He was beaten at home for reciting the creed. St. Dominick found him a zealous disciple, when at Verona, and he persuaded him to unite with his order at the early age of fifteen. Peter was a successful preacher, and addressed himself earnestly to the conversion of the Cathari. He was made Inquisitor General under Pope Honorius III. The Cathari hated him, and hired assassins who watched that they might kill him in a forest where they knew he would pass unaccompanied, save by a single monk. When he appeared one of the murderers struck him down with an axe. They then pursued and killed his attendant. When they returned to St. Peter he was reciting the Apostles' Creed, or, as others say, was writing it on the ground with his blood, when the assassins completed their cruel work. Fra Bartolomeo painted the head of his beloved Jerome Savonarola as St. Peter Martyr. He is represented in the habit of his order, and bears the crucifix and palm. His more peculiar attribute is either the axe stuck in his head, or a gash from which the blood trickles. April 28, A. D. 1252.

St. Peter Nolasco (*Sp.* San Pedro Nolasco) was a convert of St. John de Matha. When young, he enlisted in the crusade against the Albigenses. He was the son of a noble of Languedoc, and became the tutor of the young King James of Aragon, or Don Jayme el Conquistador. But being much moved at the consideration of the sufferings of captives, he founded a new order called "The Order of Our Lady of Mercy" (Nuestra Señora de la Merced). At first the order was military, consisting of knights and gentlemen; and the king placed himself at their head, and gave them his arms as a device or badge. The order was very popular, and soon extended itself on all sides. Peter Nolasco was the superior, and spent his life in expeditions to the provinces under the Moors, from which he brought back hundreds of redeemed captives. In time the order changed its character from that of a military to that of a religious institution. According to tradition, when Peter was old, he was taken from his cell by angels, and borne to and from the altar where he received the Holy Eucharist. He is represented as old, with a white habit and the shield of King James on his breast. January 13, A. D. 1258.

St. Peter Regalato. This saint appears in the later Italian and Spanish pictures of the Franciscans, to which order he belonged. He was especially distinguished for his sublime gift of prayer. March 30, A. D. 1456.

St. Petronilla (*Fr.* Ste. Pernelle) was the daughter of St. Peter. When at Rome with him, she was deprived of the use of her limbs by sickness. One day, when some of his disciples sat at dinner with the Apostle, they asked why it was that when he healed others his own child remained helpless. Peter replied that it was good for her to be ill; but, that the glory of God should be manifest, he commanded her to rise and serve them. This she did, and when the dinner was over lay down helpless as before. Years after,

17

when she had become perfected by suffering, she was made well in answer to her earnest prayers. Now Petronilla was very beautiful, and a young noble, Valerius Flaccus, desired to marry her. She was afraid to refuse him, and promised that if he returned in three days he should carry her home. She then earnestly prayed to be delivered from this marriage; and when the lover came with his friends to celebrate the marriage, he found her dead. Flaccus lamented sorely. The attendant nobles bore her to her grave, in which they placed her crowned with roses. May 31.

St. Petronius was bishop of Bologna, and distinguished himself by his zeal against the Arian heresy. He was a Roman of an illustrious family. His pictures are confined to Bologna; and there is in that city a beautiful church dedicated in his name. He is represented in episcopal robes, with mitre and crosier. He has a thick black beard in an ancient representation, but generally is without it. His attribute is a model of Bologna, which he holds in his hand. October 4, A. D. 430.

St. Philip (*Ital.* San Filippo Apostolo; *Fr.* St. Philippe). St. Philip was born at Bethsaida. Beyond the fact that he was the first called to follow the Saviour, little is told of him in the Gospel. After the ascension of Christ he preached in Scythia twenty years. Then going to Hieropolis in Phrygia, he found the people worshipping a huge serpent or dragon, whom they thought to be a personification of Mars. Then Philip took pity on their ignorance. He held up the cross and commanded the serpent to disappear. Immediately it glided from beneath the altar, and as it moved it sent forth so dreadful an odor that many died, and among them the son of the king; but Philip restored him to life. Then the priests of the serpent were so wroth with the Apostle that they crucified him, and when he was fastened to the cross they stoned him. The Scriptures state that Philip had four daughters who did prophesy (Acts xxi. 9). St. Marianne, his sister, and his daughter St. Hermione, are martyrs in the Greek Calendar. St. Philip is represented as a man of middle age, scanty beard, and benevolent face. His attribute is a cross which varies in form, — sometimes a small cross in his hand; again a high cross in the form of a T, or a staff with a small cross at the top. It has three significations: it may represent the power of the cross which he held before the dragon; or his martyrdom; or his mission as a preacher of the cross of Christ. Patron of Brabant and Luxembourg. May 1.

St. Philip, Deacon (*Gr.* 'Αγ. Φίλιππος). It is necessary to distinguish him from the Apostle. It was Philip the deacon, who baptized the chamberlain of Queen Caudace. This baptism has been beautifully illustrated in art. June 6.

St. Philip Benozzi (*Ital.* San Filippo Beniti, or Benizzi) stands at the head of the Order of the Servi, or Serviti, at Florence. He was not the founder of the order, not having joined it until fifteen years after its establishment, but he is its principal saint. The history of the origin of this order is full of interest, and an outline of it may be given in few words. It originated about the year 1232. Seven rich Florentine nobles, in the prime of life, were accustomed to meet every day in the Chapel of the Annunziata to sing the Ave, or evening service in honor of the Blessed Virgin, whom they especially venerated. They became so well known for these pious acts that the women and children cried out as they passed, "Behold the servants of the Virgin !" ("Guardate i Servi di Maria!") At length they resolved to dispense their goods to the poor and forsake the world. They retired to Monte Senario, about six miles from Florence, where they built huts, and lived for the service of the Virgin. Their first habit was plain white in honor of the immaculate purity of Mary; but one of the number was warned in a vision that they should change it to black, in remembrance of her " maternal sorrow and the death of her Divine Son." These men, being allied to the proudest families of Florence, drew much attention to their order, and the city became proud of them. St. Philip Benozzi had studied medicine at the Universities of Paris and Padua, and was a very learned man; but after receiving his degrees and commencing the practice of surgery in Florence, he became greatly wearied and oppressed with the sight and knowledge of human suffering. One day, as he listened to the service in the chapel of the Annunziata, he was impressed by the words, "Draw near, and join thyself to the chariot." He went home full of thought upon these words, and when he slept he had a vision of the Virgin seated in a chariot, and she told him to draw near and join her servants. Then he retired to Monte Senario; but such was his modesty that it was long before the brethren understood the extent of his learning. He distinguished himself as a preacher, but far more as a peacemaker, for he did much to reconcile the then opposing factions of Tuscany. He obtained the confirmation of his order, and preached with great success through Italy and France. He was General of his order at the time of his death. The pictures of Andrea del Sarto in the cloisters of the Annunziata at Florence have still further immortalized this saint. These were painted after his beatification by Leo X., A. D. 1516; but his canonization did not take place until 1671. August 23, A. D. 1285.

St. Philip Neri (*Ital.* San Filippo Neri), the founder of the Order of the Oratorians, was a Florentine, and born in 1515. His father was of one of the oldest Tuscan families, and a lawyer. When eighteen years of age, Philip went to Rome, and became a tutor in a noble family. By his intellect, eloquence, and purity of character, he became very influential in the religious movements of his time. He was the intimate friend and almoner of St. Charles Borromeo, and in this capacity did much good. He was ever employed in works of charity, and gathered about him young men, members of the nobility and of the learned professions, who went about reading and praying with the sick and needy, founding and visiting hospitals, and doing various charities. They were bound by no vows, and were not secluded from the world. They called themselves Oratorians, and from them arose the Pères de l'Oratoire of France.[1] St. Philip Neri was the spiritual adviser of the Massimi family; and it is related that when the son and heir of Prince Fabrizio Massimi died of a fever, St. Philip came into the chamber where the family were lamenting over his dead body. Philip laid his hand on the head of the boy, and called his name; he opened his eyes and sat up. Philip then said, "Art thou unwilling to die?" "No," replied the boy. "Art thou resigned to yield thy soul to God?" "I am." "Then go," said Philip; and the boy sank back and expired with a sweet smile upon his face. On the 16th of March the Palazzo Massimi at Rome is dressed for a festival in honor of this event, and services are held in the chapel, at which sometimes the Pope officiates. A picture illustrative of this miracle is in the church of S. Maria della Vallicella, which

---

[1] Also, the Oratorians of England, of whom the late Frederic Wilfrid Faber, poet and ascetic writer, was, and Cardinal Newman is, a devoted member.

was given to the Oratorians when their order was confirmed. In this church a chapel was dedicated to St. Philip Neri, and a mosaic copy of Guido's picture of this saint was placed there by Nero de' Neri of Florence. The bed, the crucifix, the books, and other relics of the saint are preserved in the oratory. May 26, A. D. 1595.

St. Phocas of Sinope (*Ital.* San Focà). This saint lived in the third century. He had a cottage and garden near the Gate of Sinope, in Pontus. His cottage was open to all who needed shelter and lodging, and the produce of his garden was distributed to the poor after his own slight wants were supplied. As he sat at supper one night, some strangers knocked at his door. He asked them to enter, gave them water to wash, and set food for them. Later in the evening they told him they had been sent to find Phocas, who had been accused as a Christian, and they had been commanded to kill him wherever he should be found. The saint betrayed no emotion, and gave them a chamber in which to sleep. When all were at rest, he went to his garden and made a grave among the flowers he loved. In the morning he announced that Phocas was found. The guests rejoiced, and said, "Where is he?" But when he answered, "I am he," they were unwilling to betray their host. Then he said, "Since it is the will of God, I am willing to die in his cause." Then they beheaded him on the border of the grave, and buried him. This saint is represented only in Byzantine art. He is in the garb of a gardener, and has a spade as his attribute. Patron of gardens and gardeners. July 3, A. D. 303.

St. Placidus was the son of Tertullus, a Roman Senator, who placed this child under the care of St. Benedict, at Subiaco, when only five years of age. Placidus was sent by his superior to preach in Sicily when he was still quite young. According to tradition his sister Flavia and two young brothers joined him, and they dwelt in a convent near Messina. This was attacked by brigands, who massacred Placidus and Flavia, with thirty of their companions. The later Benedictine writers do not believe the account of this massacre. He is represented in the black habit of his order, or with the rich dalmatica above a black tunic. The palm is his attribute. January 15, A. D. 584.

Plautilla, though not a canonized saint, is seldom omitted in representations of the martyrdom of St. Paul. According to the legend,

she was a Roman matron, and one of the converts of St. Peter and
St. Paul. She placed herself on the way by which she knew that
St. Paul would pass to his martyrdom, in order to see him for the
last time. When he came, she besought him to bless her, and wept
greatly. Then Paul seeing her faith asked her to give him her veil,
that he might bind his eyes with it when he was beheaded, and
promised that he would return it to her after his death. Then all
who heard mocked at this promise, but Plautilla gave him the veil;
and after his death St. Paul did indeed appear to her, and gave her
again the veil, which was stained with his blood.

St. Potitus of Pisa (*Ital.* San Potito). See St. Ephesus.

St. Praxedes and **St. Pudentiana** (*Ital.* Santa Prassede e Santa
Pudenziana; *Fr.* Ste. Prassède et Ste. Potentienne). When St. Peter
came to Rome, he dwelt in the house of Pudens, who was a patrician of
great wealth. Not long after the coming of the Apostle, Pudens and
Sabinella, his wife, with Novatus his son, and his two daughters,
Praxedes and Pudentiana, were all converted and baptized. Soon
after, the parents and brother died; and the sisters, left alone, inherited
all the riches of the family. They had houses and public baths at
the foot of the Esquiline. Then began the first great persecution,
in which St. Peter perished. Now the sisters determined to devote
themselves to the relief and care of the suffering Christians and to
the burying of the bodies of such as were slain. They had the assistance of a holy man named Pastorus, who was devoted in their service.
They shrank from nothing that came in the way of their self-imposed
duties. They sought out and received into their houses such as were
torn and mutilated by tortures. They visited and fed such as were
in prison. They took up the bodies of the martyred ones which
were cast out without burial, and carefully washing and shrouding
them, they laid them reverently in the caves beneath their houses.
All the blood they collected with sponges, and deposited in a certain
well. Thus boldly they showed forth the faith which was in them;
and yet they escaped persecution and martyrdom, and died peacefully
and were buried in the cemetery of Priscilla. Pastorus wrote a history
of their deeds and virtues. Their house, which was made holy not
only by their lives but by the preaching of St. Peter, was consecrated
as a place of Christian worship by Pope Pius I. Their churches are
among the interesting remains of ancient Rome. In the nave of the

church of Santa Prassede is a well in which she was said to have put the blood of those who suffered on the Esquiline, while the holy sponge is preserved in a silver shrine in the sacristy. In the church of St. Pudentiana there is a well, said to contain the relics of three thousand martyrs. These sisters are pictured as richly draped, and the sponge and cup are their especial attributes. July 21 and May 19, A. D. 148.

St. Prisca. The church of this saint, at Rome, on the Aventine, is supposed to occupy the spot on which stood the house of Aquila and Priscilla, where St. Peter lodged ; which site was thought to be also that of the Temple of Diana, founded by Servius Tullius. And here is shown the font in which St. Peter baptized the earliest converts in Rome, and among others St. Prisca. According to the legend, she was a virgin of illustrious family, and was exposed to the beasts of the amphitheatre when but thirteen years of age. A fierce lion, who was let loose upon her, humbly licked her feet, to the joy of the Christians. She was then beheaded, and an eagle watched over her body until it was buried. She is represented bearing a palm with the lion beside her, and sometimes the eagle, thus being honored by the kings of both beasts and birds, as the legend remarks. The name of St. Prisca is retained in the Anglican calendar, January 18, A. D. 275.

St. Procopius was King of Bohemia. He relinquished his crown and became a hermit. Many years passed without his being known ; but at length, as a certain Prince Ulrich was hunting, he pursued a hind, which fled for safety to the arms of St. Procopius, and so the saint was discovered. On account of the similarity of the attribute, his pictures are sometimes mistaken for those of St. Giles. July 8, A. D. 303.

St. Proculus is the military patron of Bologna. In the time of the tenth persecution a cruel man named Marinus was sent to Bologna to enforce the edict of the emperor. Proculus was so filled with indignation, which might perhaps be called holy, that he entered the house of Marinus and killed him with an axe, which axe is the attribute given the saint in art. He sometimes carries a head in his hands, which may be either that of Marinus or his own.[1]

St. Protasius of Milan. See St. Gervasius.

[1] This legend of St. Proculus is among the unauthorized legends.

St. Pudentiana (*Ital.* Santa Pudenziana; *Fr.* Ste. Potentienne). See St. Praxedes.

Quattro Coronati, or the Four Crowned Brothers. According to tradition these were four Christian brothers, workers in wood and stone, who dwelt in Rome in the time of Diocletian. They refused to employ their art in fashioning gods or building temples for them, and for this suffered martyrdom. Some were scourged, some beheaded, and some put in iron cages and cast into the sea. The "Cinque Martiri" were also of the same trades, and their fate the same. The names of the Coronati are given as SS. Carpophorus, Severus, Severianus, and Victorianus. The church dedicated to them is on that part of the Cœlian Hill which extends from the Lateran to the Coliseum. It is said that their remains were found here during the fourth century. Their title of Coronati alludes to the crown of martyrdom. The five martyrs (I Cinque Martiri) are honored at the same time and place with the Coronati, and they are represented in art with the implements of their trade; — the mallet, chisel, square, and rule, bearing palms and wearing crowns. November 4, A. D. 400.

St. Quintin was the son of Zeno. He became converted, and gave up a high command which he held in the Roman army in order to preach. He labored especially in Belgium and at Amiens. He was accused before the prefect Rictius Varus, and suffered death by being impaled on an iron spit. This instrument of his torture is his attribute, which is not always represented. October 31, A. D. 287.

St. Quirinus was a soldier in the army of Aurelian. He became a Christian, and preached so openly as especially to exasperate his officers, who were pagans. His martyrdom was extreme in cruelty. His tongue was first taken out and thrown to a hawk. He was then dragged to death by horses. He is represented in armor, with a horse and a hawk and a shield, with nine balls as well as the martyr's palm.

St. Quirinus, Bishop of Sissek in Croatia. He was martyred by being drowned with a millstone about his neck. One of the eight guardian saints of Austria. June 4, A. D. 309.

St. Radegunda was the daughter of the King of Thuringia, Berthaire, and the wife of Clothaire V. of France, who first carried her captive with all her family, and afterwards married her. This queen was devoted to prayer and almsgiving, and often wore beneath her royal garments a robe of penitential hair-cloth. One day, as she walked in her garden, she heard the prisoners, who were separated from her only by a wall, weeping and imploring pity. She thought of her own sorrows in the past, and she prayed earnestly for them, not knowing how else to aid them; and as she prayed their fetters burst asunder and they were freed from captivity. Later in life Radegunda took the religious habit, and founded a monastery at Poitiers. She is represented with the royal crown, and beneath it a long veil. A captive kneels before her with his broken fetters in his hand. August 13, A. D. 587.

Ragnar Lodbrog. See St. Edmund.

St. Ranieri (*Ital.* San Ranieri; *Fr.* St. Regnier). The whole life of this saint was full of poetry and mystery. He was born in or about the year 1100. His family was that of the Scaccieri of Pisa. In his youth an eagle appeared to him bearing in his beak a blazing light, and said, "I come from Jerusalem to enlighten the nations." But Ranieri lived a life devoted to pleasure. At length, as he one day played the lyre surrounded by beautiful damsels, a holy man passed by who turned and looked on Ranieri; and there was so 'much of sorrow in his gaze that the young man threw down his lyre and followed the man of God, bewailing and weeping his own sins and his wasted life. Soon he embarked for Jerusalem, where he took off his own garments and wore the schiavina, or slave-shirt, and this he wore ever after for personal humiliation. He lived the life of a hermit, in the deserts of Palestine, for twenty years. During this time he had numerous visions. On one occasion he felt his vows of abstinence to be almost more than he could keep. He then had a vision of a golden vase set with precious stones and full of oil, pitch, and sulphur. These were kindled to fire, and none could quench the flames. Then there was put into his hands a small ewer of water, and when he turned on but a few drops the fire was extinguished. This vision he believed to signify the human passions, by the pitch and sulphur; but the water was the emblem of temperance. He then determined to live on bread and water alone. His reverence for water was very great; and most of his miracles were performed through the use of it, so that he was called San Ranieri dell' Acqua. But when he tarried with a host who cheated his guests by putting water in his wine, the saint did not hesitate to expose the fraud; for he revealed to all present the figure of Satan sitting on one of the wine-casks in the form of a huge cat with the wings of a bat. He did many miracles after his return to Pisa, and made converts by the sanctity of his life and example. When he died, many miraculous manifestations bore witness to his eminent holiness. All the bells in Pisa were spontaneously tolled, and the Archbishop Villani, who had been sick in bed for two years, was cured to attend his funeral. At the place in the Requiem Mass where it is the custom to omit the "Gloria in Excelsis," it was sung by a choir of angels above the altar, while the organ accompanied them without being played by any perceptible hands. The harmony of this chant was so exquisite that those who heard it thought the very heavens were opened. He was buried in a tomb in the Duomo. After the plague in Pisa in 1356, the life of this saint was painted in the Campo Santo by Simone Memmi and Antonio Veneziano. These frescos are most important in the history of art, and consist of eight scenes from the life of St. Ranieri: (1) His Conversion; (2) He embarks for Palestine; (3) He assumes the Hermit's Dress; (4) He has many Temptations and Visions in the Desert; (5) He returns to Pisa; (6) He exposes the Fraud of the Innkeeper; (7) His Death and Funeral Obsequies; (8) His Miracles after Death. July 17, A. D. 1161.

St. Raphael, the Archangel (*Lat.* S. Raphael; *Ital.* San Raffaello; *Fr.* St. Raphael; *Ger.* Der Heilige Rafael: signification, " the medicine of God "). Raphael is considered the guardian angel of humanity. He was sent to warn Adam of the danger of sin and its unhappy consequences.

> " Be strong, live happy, and love ! but first of all
> Him whom to love is to obey, and keep
> His great command ; take heed lest passion sway
> Thy judgment to do aught which else free-will
> Would not admit ; thine, and of all thy sons
> The weal or woe in thee is placed ; beware ! "
>
> *Milton.*

He was the herald who bore to the shepherds the "good tidings of great joy which shall be for all people." He is especially the protector of the young, the pilgrim, and the traveller. In the Scripture [1]

---

[1] The Church includes the Book of Tobias among the inspired writings.

his watchful care of the young Tobias during his eventful journey is typical of his benignity and loving condescension towards those whom he protects. His countenance is represented as full of benignity. Devotional pictures portray him dressed as a pilgrim, with sandals; his hair bound with a diadem or a fillet; the staff in his hand, and a wallet or *panetière* hung to his belt. As a guardian spirit he bears the sword and a small casket or vase, containing the "fishy charm" (Tobit vi. 6) against evil spirits. As guardian angel he usually leads Tobias. The picture of Murillo in the Leuchtenberg Gallery represents him as the guardian angel of a bishop who appears as a votary below. September 12.

St. Raymond (*Sp.* San Ramon). On account of the circumstances of his birth this saint is styled Nonnatus. He belonged to the Order of Mercy, and labored for the captives among the Moors. By the Mahometans, among whom he was long a captive for the ransom of his Christian brethren, his lips were bored through with a red-hot iron and fastened with a padlock. He later was made a cardinal, and the General of his order. He presided at a chapter held at Barcelona. Pope Gregory IX. and King James of Aragon assisted at his funeral obsequies. August 31, A. D. 1240.

St. Raymond of Peñaforte was born at the castle belonging to his family at Peñaforte in Catalonia. He was allied to the royal house of Aragon, and his family were of Barcelona. He early entered upon a religious life, and became a model in his zealous devotion to the Church and his charity to the poor. He assumed the Dominican habit, and was the third General of that order. His zealous preaching against the Moors was thought to be the first cause of the final expulsion of the infidels from Spain. A miracle which he is said to have performed, and which is attested to in the bull of his canonization, is related thus: Raymond was the spiritual director of King James of Aragon (el Conquistador). This king was an accomplished gentleman, and did not incline to allow his confessor to interfere with his pleasures. Now he was greatly in love with a beautiful woman of his court from whom Raymond vainly attempted to separate him. The king summoned the priest to attend him to Majorca, but he refused to go unless the lady remained behind. James affected to comply, but the lady accompanied him in the dress of a page. Raymond soon discovered the deceit, and remonstrated severely with the king, who was very angry. The priest threatened to return to Spain, but James forbade any vessel to leave the port, and passed sentence of death upon any who should aid Raymond to go away. St. Raymond then said, "An earthly king has deprived us of the means of escape, but a Heavenly King will supply them." Then walking up to a rock which projected into the sea, he spread his cloak on the waters, and setting his staff upright and tying one corner of the cloak to it for a sail, he made the sign of the cross, and boldly embarked in this new kind of vessel. He was wafted over the surface of the ocean with such rapidity that in six hours he reached Barcelona. This miracle was attested to by five hundred persons, who saw him land at Barcelona and take up his cloak perfectly dry from the water and wrap it round him, and then with great humility retire to his cell. Don Jayme, overcome by this miracle, repented of his obstinacy and afterwards governed his kingdom and his life by the advice of St. Raymond. He is represented in the habit of his order, and kneels on his mantle while he is borne over the sea, or else the miracle is represented in the background. January 23, A. D. 1275.

St. **Regulus** was an African bishop. He fled from his diocese in the time of the contentions between the Arians and the Catholics. He came to Tuscany, and lived the life of an anchoret. In the invasion of Totila he was beheaded. According to tradition he took up his head and proceeded two stadia, when he sat down. Being found thus by two of his disciples, he gave them his head, and they buried him there with great reverence and (what is not strange) with *unspeakable awe.*

St. **Reparata** was a virgin of Cesarea in Cappadocia. In the persecution under Decius she was martyred, though only twelve years old. As she died her spirit was seen to issue from her mouth in shape like a dove, and to fly to heaven. This saint was for six hundred years the chief patroness of Florence, and the Duomo was dedicated in her name; but it was re-dedicated to Santa Maria-del-Fiore. She is represented in various colored robes, and bears the crown, palm, book, and a banner with a red cross on a white ground.

St. **Roch** (*Lat.* S. Rochus; *Ital.* San Rocco; *Fr.* St. Roch or Roque) was the son of noble parents. Montpelier, in Languedoc, was his birthplace. When he was born, there was a small red cross

on his breast. His mother interpreted this as a sign that he should
be consecrated to God's service, and she educated him with great care.
The saint too was of the same mind; but he inclined to follow the
example of Jesus, — to go about doing good, — in preference to that
of many holy men, who flee from the world to serve God. His parents died when he was less than twenty years old, and left him vast
estates. He sold all, and gave the money to hospitals and to the
poor. He then went on foot to Rome in the garb of a pilgrim.
When he arrived at Aquapendente, a terrible plague was raging there.
St. Roch offered to attend the sick in the hospitals. He was especially successful in his care of the plague-stricken, and it appeared
that some peculiar blessing attended him; so prevalent was this idea
that, considering his youth and gentleness, the people were ready to
believe him an angel, and he himself was not without the thought
that a special blessing was on his efforts. He then went to Cesena
and Rimini, where he labored in the same manner; and then he arrived at Rome in the midst of a fearful pestilence, and for three years
more devoted himself to the most hopeless cases. He constantly
prayed that God might find him worthy to die as a martyr to
this care for others. Years passed thus, and he went from city to
city, wherever he heard of any dreadful disease and suffering. At
length at Piacenza he was himself struck down by an unknown
epidemic then raging there. One night he sank down in the hospital,
weary with nursing, and fell asleep. When he awoke he found himself plague-stricken with a horrible ulcer on his thigh, the pain of
which compelled him to shriek aloud. He feared lest he should
disturb others, and crawled into the street; but he was not allowed
to remain there. He then dragged himself to a wood outside the
city, and lay down to die. But a little dog which had attended him
in all his wanderings now cared for him, and brought him every day
a loaf of bread. According to the legend, an angel also dressed his
wound and cared for him; but this is questioned, and it is stated
that a man named Gothard did this for him; but be this as it may,
as soon as the saint was able he set out for his home. When he
arrived at a little village near Montpelier, where the land belonged
to his estates, and the people were the vassals of his family, no one
knew him, and they regarded him so suspiciously that they took him
before the judge as a spy. The judge was his uncle, but even he did

not recognize him, and condemned him to be imprisoned. St. Roch regarded all this as the will of God, and said nothing, desiring that all should be as Providence should direct. So he was cast into a dungeon. There was no one to plead for him, and he adhered to his resolve of silence; thus he remained five years. One morning when the jailer went to his cell it was filled with a glory of light, and the prisoner lay dead with a paper beside him, which told his name, and these words also: "All those who are stricken by the plague, and who pray for aid through the merits and intercession of St. Roch, the servant of God, shall be healed." Then the judge, when he saw this paper, wept and was filled with remorse. The saint was honorably buried midst the prayers of the whole city. Nearly a century elapsed before St. Roch was heard of outside his native city, where he was held in the greatest possible veneration. But at the time of the great church council at Constance, the plague broke out in that city, and priests and people were in consternation, when a German monk, who had been in France, advised that the power of St. Roch should be tested in this emergency. His counsel was followed, and the image of the saint was borne through the city accompanied by a solemn procession, with prayers and litanies. Then the plague ceased, and to this the increased veneration of St. Roch may be traced. Towards the close of the fifteenth century the Venetians, who were especially exposed to the plague from their commercial intercourse with the East, resolved to possess, if possible, the relics of St. Roch. The men appointed to accomplish the purpose went to Montpelier as pilgrims. They succeeded in carrying away the sacred remains, and were received with joy by all Venice, from the Doge down to the poorest beggar. Then the splendid church of San Rocco was built under the auspices of a society which already existed in Venice for the care of the sick, and which had been formed under his protection. In this society many of the nobility enrolled themselves. Many votive pictures are seen of this saint, in which he is represented as interceding for the sick person, who is introduced in the painting. In devotional pictures, St. Roch is represented as a man in middle age, of refined and delicate features, with an expression of benevolence and kindness. He is dressed as a pilgrim, with the cockle-shell on his hat, the staff in his hand, and the wallet at his side. With one hand he points to the plague spot on his side, or lifts his robe to show it. His dog also attends him. Patron of all who are in prison ; of all sick persons in hospitals, but especially of those afflicted by the plague. August 16, A. D. 1327.[1]

St. Romain, whose whole history is painted on the windows of the cathedral of Rouen, was bishop of that city in the time of Clovis I. He is considered as the great apostle of Normandy, for he preached there with remarkable zeal and overthrew paganism. The Seine at one time so overflowed its banks as to threaten the destruction of the city. St. Romain commanded the waters to retire, but of the slime and mud which remained a poisonous dragon was born, called by the French "la Gargouille." This monster spread consternation all along the shores of the river. Then the saint, by the aid of a wicked murderer, went forth and slew the beast. From this time it was the privilege of the chapter of Rouen to pardon a criminal condemned to death ; and this was so until the time of the Revolution. February 28, A. D. 639.

St. Romualdo was born at Ravenna, of the noble family of the Onesti, about the year 956. He was trained like other young noblemen, and loved the chase ; but often as he rode on the hunt in the forests of Ravenna, he was soothed and charmed by the beauty of the scenery, and would slacken his pace, and become absorbed in the thought of the quiet peace of those who dwelt alone with Nature. Then he would breathe a prayer, and return to his busy life of pleasure. But his father, Sergius, was a man of very different mettle. He was proud and self-willed, and could brook no opposition. Having disagreed with a relative concerning the succession of a certain pasture, he challenged him to combat and slew him. Romualdo was present at the time, and was so overpowered with horror that he believed it his duty to expiate his father's crime. He retired to a monastery near Ravenna, Sant' Apollinare in Classe, and assumed the habit of the Benedictines. But his enthusiastic and sensitive temperament suffered much from the irregularities of certain monks ; and he conceived the idea of establishing new monastic institutions, according to the pure spirit which he felt should control them, and of reforming the old ones and raising them to the same standard. Henceforth his life was a continuous battle. He

---

[1] There are no authentic acts of the life of St. Roch.

was hated and reviled by unworthy monks everywhere, and even his
life was in danger from the bitterness of their enmity to him. But
he scorned all danger, and despised all persecution, and fought most
bravely by prayer and labor for the cause he had undertaken to
maintain. His first monastery was founded near Arezzo in the
Apennines; in a glen called Campo-Maldoli, from the name of the
family to whom it belonged. From this the new order was called
that of the Camaldoli. The members of this order are consecrated
to perpetual service to God; they strictly practise solitude, silence,
and contemplation; they do not even eat together, but every one
lives in a separate hut with his own garden, in order to comply
with the requirements for manual labor. The Camaldolesi are among
the most severe of all monks, and are, in fact, hermits in societies.
According to the legend, the color of the habit of his order was
changed in this wise: Not long before his death the saint fell asleep
beside a fountain not far from his cell, and he beheld a vision of a
ladder reaching from earth to heaven, on which the brethren of his
order ascended by twos and threes, and all dressed in white. So he
immediately changed the color, which had been black; and white has
ever since been worn by the Camaldolesi. Thirty years after his
secession from his first convent he had become famous throughout
the north of Italy, and had communities of reformed monks number-
ing hundreds. He is represented with a loose white habit, and a full
beard which falls to his girdle; he leans upon a crutch. February 7,
A. D. 1027.

St. Romulo (*Lat.* S. Romulus) was a noble Roman, whom,
according to the legend, St. Peter sent to preach to the people of
Fiesole, which was then a most important Etruscan city. After thus
being the apostle he became the first bishop of Fiesole. He was at
length accused before the prætor, as a Christian, and was sentenced
to suffer death. This was in the time of Nero. After suffering the
most cruel tortures, he was slain with a dagger. The old cathedral
of Fiesole is dedicated to St. Romulo. He is represented in the
episcopal robes, and bears the palm. July 23.

Santa Rosa di Lima was born at Lima in Peru, and is the only
canonized female saint of the New World. She was distinguished by
her extreme hatred of vanity. The severities of her life, also, were
very great. She was especially beautiful in her complexion; hence

her name. She rejected many suitors, and at last destroyed her great charm with a compound of pepper and quicklime. When her mother commanded her to wear a wreath of roses, she so arranged it that it was in truth a crown of thorns. Her food was principally bitter herbs. She was a model of filial devotion, and maintained her parents by her labor after they had become poor, toiling all day in her garden, and all night with her needle. She took the habit of the Third Order of St. Dominick. The Peruvian legend relates that when Pope Clement X. was asked to canonize her, he refused, exclaiming, "India y Santa! así como llueven rosas!" ("India and saint! as likely as that it should rain roses!") Instantly a shower of roses commenced in the Vatican, and did not cease till the Pope acknowledged his mistaken incredulity. Stirling's "Artists of Spain," thus speaks of Santa Rosa: "This flower of Sanctity, whose fragrance has filled the whole Christian world, is the patroness of America, the St. Teresa of Transatlantic Spain." In a picture by Murillo, she is represented with a thorny crown; holding in her hand the figure of the Infant Saviour, which rests on full-blown roses. August 30, A. D. 1617.

St. Rosa di Viterbo was a member of the Third Order of St. Francis. She lived in the thirteenth century, and was remarkable for the influence she exercised in Viterbo, as well as for her extensive charities and the eloquence of her speech. She lived a life of great austerity. She is now the patroness of that city, to which while living she was a benefactress. She is represented in a gray tunic, with knotted girdle, and a chaplet of roses. May 8, A. D. 1261.

St. Rosalia of Palermo, whose statue towers upon the summit of Monte Pellegrino, overlooking the Mediterranean, and cheering the mariners, who consider her their protectress, was a Sicilian virgin of noble birth. When scarcely sixteen years old, she withdrew from her home and friends secretly, and lived in a cave in Monte Pellegrino, near the summit. She had rejected many suitors, and longed for the solitude where nothing could distract her mind from the service of God. She died without having been discovered; and twice after she had ascended to her heavenly bridegroom, she interceded for Palermo and saved it from the ravages of the pestilence. At length her remains were discovered lying in her cave; and such was the purity of this unsullied virgin that they remained uncorrupted even in death. Her name was inscribed above her in the rock, and on her head was a crown made of the roses of Paradise, and placed there by angels. Her cave has become a chapel to which pilgrims resort. She is usually represented reclining in her cave, which is bright with celestial light; angels crown her with roses, and she holds a crucifix upon her breast. Again, she is seen standing and inscribing her name upon the rock. She wears a brown tunic, sometimes ragged, and her hair is loose about her. September 4, A. D. 1160.

Rosary, The. The beads used by Catholics and called by this name are so often represented in art that an explanation of their use and signification will not be out of place. The use of beads to assist the memory in regard to the number of prayers recited is of very ancient date and of Eastern origin. They were employed by the ancient anchorites, and also by the Benedictines before their use became general in the Church. The rosary in its present accepted form was instituted by St. Dominick. He invented a new arrangement of the beads, and dedicated it to the Blessed Virgin. The festival of the Rosary was instituted by Gregory XIII. after the battle of Lepanto, A. D. 1571; and from this time it became popular as a subject of art, and there are large numbers of pictures which relate to its institution. A complete rosary has one hundred and fifty small beads and fifteen larger ones. The latter represent the Paternosters, and the former the Ave-Marias. The large beads divide the rosary into fifteen decades, each one consisting of ten Ave-Marias, preceded by a large bead, or Pater-noster, and all concluded with a Gloria Patri. Five decades make a chaplet, which is a third part of a rosary. To these beads a crucifix is added. The "Mysteries of the Rosary" consist in the assigning of a certain event in the life of the Virgin or in the life of the Saviour to each decade. There are five joyful mysteries, which are, — the Annunciation, the Visitation, the Nativity, the Purification, and Christ found in the Temple; five dolorous or sorrowful mysteries, — Our Lord in the Garden of Gethsemane, the Flagellation, Christ Crowned with Thorns, the Procession to Calvary, and the Crucifixion; five glorious mysteries, — the Resurrection, the Ascension, the Descent of the Holy Ghost, the Assumption of our Lady, and her Coronation. The rosary in the hand or about the person of a saint signifies that they obtained aid " per intercessione dell' Sacratissimo Rosario." When held before the Madonna, it indicates that by the use of it she is to be honored ; in short, the rosary was intended to excite and assist devotion in various ways, and its representations illustrate the same idea. Festival of the Rosary, first Sunday in October.

St. Rufina. See St. Justina of Seville.

St. Sabina, to whom a church is dedicated at Rome, was a noble matron who suffered martyrdom during the reign of Hadrian. The church, which dates from the early part of the fifth century, is said to occupy the site of her house, and the altar-piece represents a soldier dragging the saint up the steps of a temple, with a sword in his hand. With her Seraphia, a Greek slave, who had converted Sabina, was also executed. Her attribute is the palm. August 29, second century.

Santa Casa. This is the title given to the house in which the Blessed Virgin was born at Nazareth. According to the legend, this house was threatened with profanation or destruction at the time of the invasion of the Saracens, when four angels took it and bore it over sea and land to the coast of Dalmatia; but there it was not safe, and the angels again removed it to a spot near Loretto ; but here the brigands invaded it, and it was again removed to the spot where it now remains, — said to have been done in 1295. The Madonna di Loretto is represented as holding the Infant Saviour, and seated upon the roof of a house which is borne by four angels. Loretto became one of the most celebrated places of pilgrimage, and many chapels have been dedicated to Our Lady of Loretto.

St. Scholastica. Very little is known of this saint. She was the sister of St. Benedict, and followed him to Monte Cassino, and there gathered about her a small community of nuns. Benedict visited her but once every year. At one time, when he arose to take leave of her, she begged him to remain longer, and when he refused she bent her head and prayed that God would interfere to detain her brother with her. Then immediately a furious storm arose, and he was forced to remain for several hours. This was their last parting ; for two days after St. Scholastica died, and Benedict saw her soul ascend to heaven in the form of a dove, while he was praying in his cell. She is represented in a black habit, with a dove at her feet or pressed to her bosom, and a lily in her hand. February 10, about 543.

St. Sebald is one of the most distinguished among the early German saints, and is especially venerated in Nuremberg. The legends relate that he was the son of a Danish king, and left England with St. Boniface. His name in English is Seward, Siward, or Sigward. He travelled through the north of Germany, preaching as a missionary, and at last lived permanently in Nuremberg. While he dwelt in a cell not far from the city, he went there almost daily to teach the poor. He was in the habit of stopping to rest in the hut of a cartwright. One day, when it was very cold, he found the family in the hut nearly frozen, and they had no fuel. Then Sebald commanded them to bring in the icicles which hung from the roof and use them to feed the fire. They obeyed, and were thus miraculously warmed. Again the saint desired fish for a fast-day, and sent the same cartwright to buy it. Now the Lord of Nuremberg had commanded that no person should buy fish until the castle was supplied; so the poor man was punished by having his eyes put out. But St. Sebald restored his sight. His wonderful shrine in the church at Nuremberg was made, according to its inscription, by Peter Vischer and his five sons. These sons with their families all dwelt with the father Peter, and shared alike his labors, his rewards, and his fame. It was commenced in 1508, finished in 1523, and remains undisturbed. The saint is represented, in his statue by Peter Vischer, as a pilgrim with shell in hat, rosary, staff, and wallet. He holds in his hand a model of his church. About A. D. 770.

St. Sebastian (*Lat.* S. Sebastianus; *Ital.* San Sebastiano or Bastiano; *Fr.* St. Sébastien; *Sp.* and *Ger.* Sebastian). The legend of this saint, though very old, has the advantage of being better authenticated by history than many antique traditions. Sebastian was descended from a noble family which had been honored with high offices in the empire. He was born at Narbonne, and when still quite young was made commander of a company of the Prætorian Guards, and was thus always near the emperor, Diocletian, with whom he was an especial favorite. Now Sebastian was secretly a Christian, and while from this very fact he conscientiously fulfilled all his duties to the emperor, he also protected the Christians, and endeavored to make converts; and in this last he was very successful

Among those whom he had thus influenced were two young soldiers, of noble family, called Marcus and Marcellinus. They were accused as Christians and condemned to the torture; this they firmly endured, and were led out for execution. Then their families, their wives and children, besought them to recant and live. That which the tortures could not effect, these prayers and tears were about to do, — they wavered; then Sebastian, regardless of himself, rushed forward and eloquently exhorted them that they should not betray their Redeemer. So earnest was he, and so great was his power, that the two soldiers went boldly to their death, while their friends, many of the guards, and even the judge himself, were also converted and secretly baptized. Now Sebastian's time had come; but before his public accusation, the emperor so loved him that he sent for him to see if privately he could not influence him to save his life. And he said, "Have I not always honored thee above the rest of my officers? Why hast thou disobeyed my commands, and insulted my gods?" Then answered the young saint, with courage, but also with meekness, "O Cæsar, I have ever prayed, in the name of Jesus Christ, for thy prosperity, and have been true to thy service; but as for the gods whom thou wouldst have me worship, they are devils, or, at best, idols of wood and stone." After this, Diocletian ordered that Sebastian should be bound to a stake, and shot to death with arrows, but that it should be inscribed on the stake that he had no fault but that of being a Christian. Then the archers did their duty, and he was left for dead, being pierced with many arrows. At night, Irene, the widow of one of his friends who had been martyred, came with her companions to take his body away to burial. And, lo! it was found that he was still alive, for none of the arrows had entered a vital part. Then Irene took him home, and carefully tended him until he was well again. When his friends saw him they begged that he would fly from Rome and save his life; but Sebastian went to the palace and stood where he knew the emperor must surely see him, and he pleaded for certain condemned ones, and plainly told the emperor of his cruelty and wickedness. Then Diocletian, being amazed, exclaimed, "Art thou not Sebastian?" And he said, "I am Sebastian, whom God hath delivered from thy hand, that I might testify to the faith of Jesus Christ and plead for his servants." Then was Diocletian doubly infuriated; and he commanded that Sebastian should be taken to the circus and beaten to death with clubs, and his body thrown into the Cloaca Maxima, and thus hidden from his friends. But in spite of all this, a lady named Lucina, who was a Christian, found means to obtain his remains, and they were laid with reverent care in the Catacombs at the feet of St. Peter and St. Paul. Apollo was the heathen god who it was believed afflicted men by the plague; and he it was whom men invoked against it, and the arrow was the emblem of pestilence. It would seem that from the association of the arrow with St. Sebastian the belief arose that he was especially powerful to obtain aid against this curse; for there are, according to tradition, many cities which have been saved from the plague by his intercession. A century after the great plague in the time of Gregory the Great, another fearful pestilence ravaged Rome. In the church of San Pietro-in-Vincoli is an ancient mosaic of St. Sebastian, and on a tablet the following inscription in Latin: "To St. Sebastian, Martyr, dispeller of the pestilence. In the year of salvation 680, a pernicious and severe pestilence invaded the city of Rome. It was of three months' duration, — July, August, and September. Such was the multitude of the dead, that, on the same bier, parents and children, husbands and wives, with brothers and sisters, were borne out to burial-places, which, everywhere filled with bodies, hardly sufficed. In addition to this, nocturnal miracles alarmed them; for two angels, one good and the other evil, went through the city; and this last, bearing a rod in his hand, as many times as he struck the doors so many mortals fell in those houses. The disease spread for a length of time, until it was announced to a holy man that there would be an end of the calamity, if, in the church of St. Peter ad Vincula, an altar should be consecrated in the name of Sebastian the Martyr; which thing being done immediately, the pestilence, as if driven back by hand, was commanded to cease." From this time Sebastian became the universal patron against pestilence, which honor he has shared in later years with St. Roch. The pictures of St. Sebastian are innumerable and unmistakable. He is young, beautiful, without drapery, bound to a tree, and pierced by arrows. He looks to heaven, whence descends an angel with palm and crown. He is the favorite saint of Roman women, and indeed of the women of all Italy. January 20, A. D. 288.

St. Secundus, especially venerated at Asti, is one of the saints of the Theban legion. See St. Maurice.

Seven Joys, The, and **The Seven Sorrows of the Blessed Virgin,** are often represented in series of pictures. The subjects of the seven joys are: (1) The Annunciation; (2) The Visitation; (3) The Adoration of the Magi; (4) The Presentation in the Temple; (5) Christ found by Mary, disputing with the Doctors; (6) The Assumption; (7) The Coronation. The seven sorrows represent: (1) The Prophecy of Simeon; (2) The Flight into Egypt; (3) Christ lost by his Mother; (4) The Betrayal of Christ; (5) The Crucifixion (only St. John and the Virgin present); (6) The Taking down from the Cross; (7) The Ascension of Christ, leaving Mary on earth.

Seven Sleepers of Ephesus, The (*Ital.* I Sette Dormienti; *Fr.* Les Sept Dormants, Les Sept Enfants d'Ephèse; *Ger.* Die Sieben Schläfer). This tradition is of great antiquity. Gibbon says it can be traced to within fifty years of the time of the miracle it relates. There is scarcely a written tongue in which it is not found. Syriac, Latin, and Scandinavian relate it, and the writer of the Koran has given it a place. In the time of the persecution of Decius there dwelt in Ephesus seven young men who were Christians. Their names were Maximian, Malchus, Marcian, Dionysius, John, Serapion, and Constantine. Having refused to offer sacrifice to the gods, they were accused before the tribunal. They fled to Mt. Cœlian and hid in a cave. They were pursued and discovered. Then it was ordered that great stones should be rolled against the mouth of the cave, and they should thus be left to die of starvation. They resigned themselves to this dreadful fate, and embracing each other went to sleep. Time rolled on until one hundred and ninety-six years had passed. Then, in the reign of Theodosius, a heresy arose denying the resurrection of the dead. The emperor, greatly afflicted at this, retired to his palace, and dressed himself in sackcloth, and sprinkled ashes on his head; and God for his sake restored these seven sleepers. For a certain man of Ephesus went to Mt. Cœlian to build him a stable, and he discovered this cavern and rolled the stones away. When the light entered there, the sleepers awoke, and thought they had slept but for a night. Then it was determined that Malchus should venture into Ephesus to obtain food. He went with fear and caution, and was surprised to find the gates of the city surmounted by crosses. Then when he entered within the walls he heard the name of Christ, which he had been accustomed to sigh forth only with his breath, boldly spoken everywhere. He believed himself in a dream. He entered a baker's shop, and in payment for his loaf he offered a coin of the time of Decius. He was regarded with great astonishment, and suspected of having robbed some hidden treasure. When accused he knew not what to say, and he was dragged to the bishop with contumely and reproaches. When the bishop had' talked with him, the truth was discovered. Then went out the emperor, the governor, the bishop, and hosts of the people, and the six other sleepers were found in the cave. Then when the emperor was come, one of them said, "Believe in us, O Emperor! for we have been raised before the Day of Judgment, in order that thou mightest trust in the resurrection of the dead!" Then they all bowed their heads and gave up the ghost. Representations of this legend are very common among works of art of the thirteenth and fourteenth century, in glass, miniatures, and sculpture. They are usually extended in their cave side by side. Their names are inscribed above their heads, and they have the martyr's palm. June 27.

Sibyls, The, were prophetesses, who foretold the coming of Christ to the Gentiles as the prophets did to the Jews. They are, in the art of the Latin Church, what the sages of antiquity were to the Greeks, and are, in fact, a kind of witnesses to the truth of Christianity. It may be shown that the Church made use of the witness of the sibyls by an extract from the hymn "Dies Iræ," said to have been written by Pope Innocent III. It is translated thus in the English version of the Missal : —

> "The dreadful day, the day of ire,
> Shall kindle the avenging fire
>   Around the expiring world ;
> And Earth, as Sibyl said of old,
> And as the prophet king foretold,
>   Shall be in ruin hurled."

Their origin was obscure ; they were regarded as holy virgins, who lived in caves and grottos. They were believed to have the power to read the future, and were interrogated by their votaries upon important matters, and their answers were considered authoritative.

Varro, who wrote about one hundred years B. C., gives their number as ten, and their names as taken from the localities of their habitations: The Sibylla Persica from Persia; the Sibylla Libyca from Libya; the Sibylla Delphica from Delphi; the Sibylla Erythræa from Erythræa; the Sibylla Cumana from Cumæ; the Sibylla Samia from Samos; the Sibylla Cimmeria from the Black Sea; the Sibylla Tiburtina from Tivoli; the Sibylla Hellespontina from the Hellespont; the Sibylla Phrygia from Phrygia. Two others called the Agrippa, or the Hebraica, and the Europa were added in later times, as well as others seldom referred to. Sometimes the Queen of Sheba is represented as one of these wonderful beings. There have been serious disagreements in the opinions of the Fathers of the Church regarding the sibyls and the worth of their prophecies. Some of the early Fathers considered them agents of Beelzebub, while others, including St. Jerome and St. Augustine, believed them to be inspired of God. The two most interesting traditions of the sibyls in this connection are those of the Cumæan and Tiburtine Sibyls, who appeared to King Tarquin and the Emperor Augustus. The first, the Cumæan, presented herself to Tarquin with nine books which she desired to sell him. They contained Sibylline Oracles. Tarquin refused her request. She went away and burned three of them and returned with six. Again he refused; again she burned three, and again returned with the three remaining. Then Tarquin sought the advice of the soothsayers, and they assured him that the destinies of the world depended upon the preservation of these oracles. So they were bought, and for centuries after were consulted on all great emergencies of the Roman nation. They were preserved in the Capitol under the care of priests, but during the wars of Marius and Sylla they perished. Then messengers were sent far and wide all through the empire to collect the scattered Sibylline leaves, and as many as were found were again carefully preserved. The idea of the ancient Romans, as recorded by Tacitus and Suetonius, that those who should rule the world should come out from Judæa, is believed to have been derived from these Sibylline leaves. Again, when the Roman Senate decreed divine honors to Augustus, he consulted the Tiburtine Sibyl whether he ought to receive them. She replied that it was more becoming for him whose power was declining to go away from her silently, for a Hebrew child would be born who would reign over the gods themselves; or that a king would come from heaven whose kingdom would never end. Another version relates that the heavens were opened, and a vision of the Virgin with the Infant Saviour in her arms, standing on an altar, was shown him, and a voice was heard saying, "Hæc ara filii Dei" (This is the altar of the Son of God). The emperor adored the vision, and reported it to the Senate. And in remembrance of it he erected upon the Capitol an altar inscribed "Ara primogeniti Dei." On this spot stands the church of Santa Maria in Capitolio, or the "Ara cœli." A passage of Virgil, who wrote forty years B. C., is also quoted as proving that the advent of Christ was foretold in Sibylline prophecy. It is thus translated : "The last age of the Cumæan song now approaches; the great series of ages begins again; now returns the Virgin (Astræa), now return the Saturnian kingdoms, now a new progeny is sent from high heaven. Be but propitious, chaste Lucina, to the boy at his birth, through whom the iron age will first cease, and the golden age dawn on the whole world." The Sibyls do not appear in the earliest art. They were not represented in the Catacombs. In the fourteenth century the vision of Augustus was employed as a symbol of the appearing of the star to the Magi, or the manifestation of Christ to the Gentiles. They were employed in the cyclical decorations of churches with the prophets. Often they were about the principal entrance, or, if inside, near the door; their position being typical of their having been "forerunners of the Lord." Their number varies. In the Eastern Church there is but one "*la sage Sibylle.*" They should be recognized by their scrolls; but the inscriptions have been so varied that they are not always guides. The sibyls of Michael Angelo, on the ceiling of the Sistine Chapel, are too well known to need any description; and it has been said that these representations are "the highest honor that art has rendered to the sibyls." Their various attributes, dress, and age, as nearly as it is possible to give them, are as follows : —

The Sibylla Persica was supposed to be a daughter-in-law of Moses. She predicted the coming of the Messiah. She is old; and her attributes are a serpent beneath her feet, and a lantern in her hand.

The Sibylla Libyca prophesied the manifestation of Christ to the Gentiles. She is twenty-four years old, and bears a lighted torch.

The Sibylla Erythræa is the prophetess of Divine vengeance. She predicted the Trojan War; in this character she holds a naked sword. But it is also said that she foretold the Annunciation, and in this representation she has a white rose. She is old.

The Sibylla Delphica. Her attributes are a horn, or the crown of thorns.

The Sibylla Samia. Attributes, a reed, or a cradle. She lived, it is supposed, in the time of Isaiah.

The Sibylla Cimmeria prophesied the Crucifixion. She is eighteen years old, and has a cross or a crucifix.

The Sibylla Cumana is fifteen years old; and her attribute is a manger, she having foreseen the Nativity in a stable.

The Sibylla Hellespontina prophesied the Incarnation and also the Crucifixion. Her attributes are the crucifix and a budding rod.

The Sibylla Phrygia prophesied the Resurrection. Attributes, a banner and a cross.

The Sibylla Tiburtina symbolizes the mocking and the flagellation of Christ. She is dressed in skins, and bears a rod.

The Sibylla Agrippa. Attribute, a scourge; fifteen years old.

The Sibylla Europa prophesied the Massacre of the Innocents. Attribute, a sword; fifteen years old. Sometimes all the sibyls have books in which they read; or they bear torches or lanterns; and some have a sun on the head.

St. Sigismond of Burgundy (*Ital.* San Gismondo) was the son of Gondubald and the cousin of St. Clotilda, wife of Clovis, King of France. Gondubald was an Arian, and had murdered the parents of Clotilda. Sigismond was a devout Catholic; but he fell into grievous sin by putting to death his eldest son on the accusation of his second wife, who hated and falsely accused the son of her predecessor. Sigismond later was seized with remorse, and sorely repented his crime. He prayed that his deserved punishment might be inflicted in this world rather than in the next, and his prayer was granted; for Chlodomir, the barbarous king of the Franks, invaded his kingdom, took him prisoner, and finally drowned him in a well at Columelle, four leagues from Orleans. His body was at length found, and removed to the convent of St. Maurice. In a chapel dedicated to St. Sigismond, in Cremona, Francesco Sforza was married to Bianca Visconti; and in witness of his love and gratitude he adorned this chapel with great beauty. St. Sigismond is represented in the splendid altar-piece, by Giulio Campi. He is patron saint of Cremona. May 1, A. D. 525.

Simeon, The Prophet. See the Madonna. The Presentation in the Temple.

St. Simon Zelotes, or The Zealot; St. Jude, Thaddeus, or Lebbeus (*Ital.* San Simone, San Taddeo; *Fr.* St. Simon le Zélé, St. Thaddée; *Ger.* Judas, Thaddäus). St. Simon is surnamed the Canamæan, or Canaanite, and Zelotes, or the Zealot, to distinguish him from St. Peter, and from St. Simeon, the brother of St. James the Less. The name "Canamæan" has, in Syro-Chaldaic, the same meaning which the word "Zelotes" bears in Greek. St. Luke translated it; but the other Evangelists retained the original name, for Canath, in Syro-Chaldaic, or modern Hebrew, signifies "zeal." St. Jude is distinguished from the Iscariot by the surname of Thaddeus, and also by that of Lebbeus. He was brother to St. James the Less, also to St. Simeon of Jerusalem, and a certain Joses; all of whom were kinsmen of Christ, their mother being the sister of the Blessed Virgin. St. Jude wrote a Catholic, or general, epistle to all the churches of the East. We have no authentic record of the labors of these Apostles, nor of the manner of their martyrdom. It is thought that St. Simon was sawn asunder, and St. Jude killed with a halberd. They therefore bear the saw and halberd as their attributes. They are sometimes represented as young, and again as old, according to the tradition which the artist follows. In Greek art, Jude and Thaddeus are different persons, Jude being young and Thaddeus old. They have rarely been represented as members of the Sacra Famiglia, and when so introduced have their names in the glories about their heads. Both saints are honored on October 28.

St. Siro, or Syrus, whose statue is in the cathedral of Pavia, was first bishop of that city, and governed the church fifty-six years. His effigy appears on the coins of Pavia.

St. Stanislas Kotzka, a young Polish nobleman, was among the earliest pupils of the Jesuits. He was distinguished for his piety as a child. His mother educated him until he was fourteen, when he went to Vienna. He entered the Society of Jesus through the influence of Francis Borgia. He died at Rome when but seventeen. Once he fell sick at Vienna, and being apparently near death,

desired the Viaticum. The landlord, a Lutheran, would not suffer it
to be brought publicly to the house, whereupon the saint seemed
in a vision to receive communion at the hands of an angel. He is
represented in art on a couch with an angel at his side. He is one
of the patron saints of Poland, and as such his attribute is the lily.
November 13, A. D. 1589.

St. Stephen, Protomartyr (*Lat.* S. Stephanus; *Ital.* San Ste-
fano; *Fr.* St. Étienne; *Ger.* Der Heilige Stefan). Little has been
added to the Scripture account of this holy deacon by tradition or
the fancy of his votaries. His name is significant of faith, devotion,
zeal, and enduring love; it commands the veneration of the world,
standing as it does at the head of the great and "noble army of
martyrs." He was chosen deacon during the first ministry of Peter,
and did great wonders and miracles. He was falsely accused of
speaking blasphemously of the Temple and the Jewish law. For
this he was condemned to death, and stoned by the people outside
of the gate at Jerusalem, now called by his name. The legend concerning his relics relates that it was not known for four hundred years
what had become of his body. Then a certain priest of Carsagamala in
Palestine, named Lucian, had a vision in which Gamaliel, the same
who had instructed Paul in all the learning of the Jews, appeared to
him, and revealed the burying-place of Stephen. Gamaliel himself
had taken up the body and had placed it in his own sepulchre, where
he had also interred Nicodemus and other holy men and saints. This
dream or vision was repeated a second and third time. Then Lucian,
with the sanction of the bishop, dug in a garden that had been
pointed out, and found the relics of St. Stephen, and their wonderful
sanctity was proved by many miracles. They were first placed in the
church of Sion at Jerusalem; then carried by Theodosius to Constantinople; and lastly by Pope Pelagius to Rome, where they were
deposited in the same tomb with those of St. Laurence. The legend
adds that when the sarcophagus was opened to receive these sacred
remains, St. Laurence moved to the left, thus giving the honorable
right hand to St. Stephen. On this account St. Laurence is called
by the populace of Rome "Il cortese Spagnuolo" ("the courteous
Spaniard"). St. Stephen is represented as young and beardless,
in the dress of a deacon. The dalmatica is square and straight at
the bottom, with large sleeves and heavy gold tassels hanging from

the shoulders; it is crimson and richly embroidered. He has the palm almost always, and the stones are his special attribute, and when given to him it is impossible to mistake him; but when they are left out, he is like St. Vincent. December 26.

St. Stephen of Hungary was the son of Duke Geysa. His father and mother were baptized late in life by St. Adelbert, the Northumbrian missionary. They gave their son the name of the Protomartyr. Stephen was thus the first Christian king of Hungary. He found his country in ignorance and heathenism; he not only Christianized it, but he subdued other pagan nations about him and brought them also into the Church. He sent to Rome requesting the pope to grant him the title of king and to give him his benediction. The pope sent him a crown, and a cross to be borne before his army. Maria Teresa was crowned with this diadem, which was preserved at Presburg. St. Stephen married the sister of St. Henry, called Gisela. No child survived him, and his son St. Emeric is associated with him in the veneration of the Hungarians. He is represented in armor with his crown. As apostle of Hungary he bears the standard with the cross and the sword. September 2, A. D. 1038.

Sudarium. See St. Veronica.

St. Susanna was the daughter of Gabinius, brother of Pope Caius, and nearly related to the Emperor Diocletian. She was remarkable for her beauty, but more so for her learning. Diocletian desired her as a wife for his adopted son Maximus. She had made a vow of chastity, and refused even this tempting offer. Then Diocletian desired his empress, Serena, to try her influence with the maiden. But Serena was herself a Christian, and sympathized with Susanna in her determination. At length Diocletian became exasperated at her firmness, and sent an executioner who killed her in her own house. Her attributes are the sword and palm. August 11, A. D. 290.

Susanna. The illustrations of the history [1] of Susanna are often seen among works of art; indeed, "Susanna at the Bath" is seen at least once in almost every picture gallery of any size. She was of Babylon, the daughter of Chelcias, and of exceeding beauty. She

---

[1] The Catholic Church includes the Book of Daniel, in which this history is given, among the inspired writings.

was married to Joacim, a very rich man, and greatly respected; and unto his house all the Jews resorted. There was a fair garden adjoining this house, and there Susanna was often seen walking with her maids. Now there were two judges, elders of the people, and both wicked men, who came each day to Joacim's house; and they both desired to possess Susanna, for her beauty had inflamed their hearts. So it happened that one day, when all the people departed at noon, they departed also, but they both returned and went into the garden to watch for Susanna; and when they met there, being surprised, they each questioned the other of what he sought. Then they acknowledged their wicked purposes, and agreed together that they would hide, and wait for the coming of the woman. Then came Susanna with two maids, and it was warm, and she thinking the garden empty save of herself, sent her maids to bring oil and washing balls, that she might bathe there. So they left her to bring these things, and they shut the door of the garden, as she had also told them. Then the two judges laid hold of her, and they told her their wicked designs upon her, and they said, "If you consent not unto us, we will accuse you, and say that we saw a young man with you here, and the doors were shut, and the maids sent away." Then Susanna sighed, and said, "I am straitened on every side: for if I do this thing, it is death unto me; and if I do it not, I cannot escape your hands. It is better for me to fall into your hands and not do it, than to sin in the sight of the Lord." Then she cried out, and the elders cried out against her, and they opened the door, and the servants of the house rushed in; then the elders declared against her, and all were sorrowful, "for there was never such a report made of Susanna." Now the next day, when all the people were assembled, these elders came; and they called for Susanna, and Joacim was there, and his wife came with her children, and her parents and friends. Then the elders made accusation against her that they had seen her with the young man, and that he had escaped, but her they had retained. And they compelled her to raise her veil, and expose her beauty to the people. Now the assembly believed the accusation, and she was condemned to death, and all her friends were weeping and filled with grief; but she raised her eyes to heaven, and cried, "O everlasting God! that knowest the secrets, and knowest all things before they be; thou knowest that they have borne false witness against me, and behold, I must die, whereas I never did such things as these men have maliciously invented against me." Then the Lord heard her cry, and there arose a young man called Daniel, and cried out, "I am clear from the blood of this woman." Then the people asked the meaning of his words, and he declared that it was not just to condemn a daughter of Israel without examination, and he begged them to return again to the place of judgment. So they returned; and Daniel desired that the elders might be separated that he might question first one, and then the other. And it was so; and taking them separately, Daniel asked them of the place where they had seen that of which they accused Susanna. And they contradicted each other; for one said it was beneath a mastic tree, and the other said the tree was an holm. Then Daniel said that having thus lied, they could not be trusted, and the whole accusation was false, and he desired that they might be punished for their false witness according to the law of Moses. So they were put to death, even as they had intended to kill Susanna. Then the family of the woman and Joacim, her husband, rejoiced greatly because there was no dishonesty found in her, and Daniel from that day forth had great reputation in the sight of the people.

St. Swidbert, who was a Benedictine monk, left England to lead the life of a missionary in Friesland and the Duchy of Berg. He built a large monastery in Kaiserwerdt (about six miles below Dusseldorf) on the Rhine. He is represented as a bishop holding a star, which probably signifies the rising light of the Gospel which he preached to the pagans. March 1, A. D. 713.

St. Swithen was associated with St. Neot in educating Alfred the Great. He was Bishop of Winchester. It is told of him that when superintending the building of a bridge near Winchester, a poor woman complained to him that a workman had broken the eggs in her basket, whereupon St. Swithen made the eggs whole. He went to Rome with Alfred. He desired that his body should be buried with the poor people, outside the church, "under the feet of the passengers, and exposed to the droppings of the eaves from above." When the clergy attempted to remove his body to a more honorable tomb inside the church, there came on a storm of rain, which prevented their doing so; and this continued forty days until the project was abandoned. It would seem that there could have been no necessity for suffering from want of rain in Winchester in those times. St. Swithen is represented as a bishop. July 2, A. D. 862.

St. Sylvester, Pope (*Ital.* San Silvestro; *Fr.* St. Silvestre). He is represented in pontifical robes, with the plain mitre, or the triple tiara, with the book and crosier as bishop. His proper attribute is the bull, which crouches at his feet; his dress distinguishes him from St. Luke, who has the ox. Sometimes he holds the portraits of St. Peter and St. Paul. December 31, A. D. 335.

For legends, see Constantine, Emperor.

St. Teresa (*Ital.* Santa Teresa, Fondatrice dei Scalzi; *Fr.* Ste. Thérèse de Jésus des Carmes-Déchaussés; *Sp.* La Nuestra Serafica Madra Santa Teresa de Jesus). The father of this saint was Don Alphonso Sanchez de Cepeda, and her mother was named Beatrix. She herself is called Teresa d'Avila, on account of the place of her birth, which was Avila, in Castile. She was born March 28, 1515, and was one of twelve brothers and sisters. Her father was exceedingly pious, and her mother extremely romantic. Under these two influences the character of the saint was formed. Among her brothers was one of ardent temperament, sympathetic with her own, whom she dearly loved. They especially delighted in reading the lives of the saints and martyrs, and they conceived a passionate desire to obtain the crown of martyrdom themselves. When but eight or nine years of age, they sought to go into the country of the Moors, hoping to be taken and sacrificed by the infidels. They were disappointed in this project, and then resolved to become hermits, but were prevented from thus pleasing themselves. But they bestowed all their pocket-money in alms; and whenever they played with other children, they always took the characters of monks and nuns, — walked in processions and sang hymns. When Teresa was twelve years old, her mother died. During her girlhood she seems to have forgotten her religious impressions, and to have given herself up to dress and pleasure, pride of position, and self-love. She ardently longed to be loved, and admired. Her father saw the dangers which surrounded her, and placed her in a convent, commanding that she should be strictly secluded from the world. Again her religious nature was aroused, and she felt that a convent was her only haven of peace and safety. A marriage which was disagreeable had been proposed to her. The conflict between her differing tastes and inclina

19

tions was so serious that she fell ill. Again, on her recovery, the struggle was renewed, and a second time she was prostrated by sickness. All this shows the extreme sensitiveness and ardor of her nature. At length the writings of St. Jerome decided her to lead a religious life. Her father consented; but again her mental sufferings on parting from her family nearly cost her her life. She entered the convent of Carmelites at Avila at the age of twenty. Here her mind became more settled, though not at rest, and her health was long enfeebled. She herself writes that for twenty years she did not find the repose for which she had hoped. But she adds, "At length God took pity on me. I read the 'Confessions of St. Augustine.' I saw how he had been tempted, how he had been tried, and how he had at length conquered." From this time there was a change in her life and feeling. About the year 1561 Teresa set her mind upon reforming the Order of Mount Carmel. From the people of Avila she obtained money, and there she founded her convent. She dedicated it to St. Joseph, whom she had chosen for her patron saint. When she entered her convent she had but eight nuns with her; before her death there were thirty convents established according to her rule. She met with great difficulties, but she overcame them; and during the later years of her life she travelled from convent to convent, promulgating the reformed rules of her order, and settling all points of difficulty. Her labors were not for nunneries alone; she also effected changes in monasteries, and indeed founded fifteen convents for men. It was she who made the Carmelites go barefoot or sandalled. Hence arises the term "Barefoot Carmelites." In Italy they are called "Scalzi" ("the Unshod") and also "Padri Teresiani." St. Teresa wrote many essays and exhortations for her nuns; some mystical and poetical writings, and a history of her life, at the command of her spiritual directors. She never recovered the perfect use of her limbs after the repeated sicknesses of her youth, and with years her infirmities increased. She was attacked with her last illness at the palace of the Duchess of Alva. She desired to be removed to her own convent of San José. In her last moments she repeated the text from the Miserere, "A broken and contrite heart, O Lord, thou wilt not despise." Her shrine at Avila in the church of her convent is a very holy place, and many pilgrims visit it. The nuns of the convent always sit on the steps and not on the seats of the choir, because there is a tradition that the angels occupied these seats whenever St. Teresa attended mass. She is represented kneeling; and a flame-tipped arrow pierces her breast, — a symbol of the fervor of Divine love which possessed her soul. Sometimes she is gazing upwards towards the holy dove, a symbol of inspiration, — a divine gift never claimed by St. Teresa. Philip III. chose her for the second patron saint of Spain, ranking her next to Santiago. The Cortes confirmed his choice. October 15, A. D. 1582.

St. Thecla (*Ital.* Santa Tecla; *Fr.* Ste. Thècle; *Ger.* Die Heilige Thekla). Although more especially honored by the Greeks, Thecla has also been accepted and reverenced in the Latin Church. St. John pronounced the book called the "Acts of Paul and Thecla" to be spurious; but in the earliest days of the Church it was thought the highest praise of any woman to compare her to St. Thecla. The legend relates that when St. Paul preached in the house of Onesiphorus at Iconium, Thecla could hear his sermons in her own house, by sitting at the window, and she became so entranced by what she heard that she would not turn her head or leave the window for any purpose. Now she was betrothed to Thamyris, who loved her with great devotion. Her mother, Theoclea, sent for the youth, and told him how intent the maiden was upon the words of Paul; that she would neither eat nor drink, and seemed to care for nothing but what she heard from the Apostle. Then Thamyris also entreated her with words of love, but she would not heed him. Then he complained to the governor, and the governor imprisoned Paul, until he should have time to hear him in his own defence. But Thecla went to the prison, and bribed the turnkey with her earrings, and the jailer with a silver looking-glass, and so gained admission to Paul. She sat at his feet and listened to his instructions, and kissed his chains in her delight. When the governor heard all this, he commanded that Paul should be scourged and driven out of the city, and that Thecla should be burned. So the young people of the city gathered wood for the burning of Thecla, and she was brought naked to the stake, where her beauty moved the hearts of all, and even the governor wept at the thought of the death she was to suffer. But when the fire was kindled, although it was very large, the flames did not touch her, and she remained in the midst of it uninjured. At length the fire was extinguished, and she made her escape. Then Paul took her to Antioch, where she was again accused before the governor, who condemned her to be thrown to the beasts of the amphitheatre. When this sentence was known, it created great indignation, and the people cried out, saying, "The judgments declared in this city are unjust." But Thecla submitted without reproaches, only asking of the governor that her chastity might be respected until the time of her martyrdom. Now, when the time arrived, the amphitheatre was crowded with spectators. Thecla was deprived of her garments, and a girdle fastened about her waist, and the beasts were let in upon her. Murmurs of rage and disapprobation arose from the populace. The women cried out, "O unrighteous judgment! O cruel sight! The whole city ought to suffer for such crimes!" and a woman named Trissina wept aloud. But a fierce lioness bounded towards Thecla, and when she reached her lay down at her feet; all the bears and the lions also stretched themselves out as if asleep. Then the governor called Thecla and asked, "Who art thou, woman, that not one of the beasts will touch thee?" And Thecla replied, "I am a servant of the living God, and a believer in Jesus Christ his Son." And the governor ordered that her garments should be brought, and saying to her, "Put on thy apparel," he released her. Then Trissina took Thecla to her own home. But Thecla desired much to see Paul, and determined to go in search of him. Trissina gave her much money and clothing for the poor, in order that Paul might be aided in his work. Thecla found him at Myra in Lycia, where he preached and labored for the conversion of the people. Thecla returned to Iconium, and after years spent in the service of Christ, she was led by the Spirit to retire to a mountain near Seleucia, where she lived in solitude and was beset with great temptations. While she lived in this mountain, she wrought many miraculous cures; so that when the sick were brought to her cave they were healed, and the physicians of Seleucia were of no account. Then they consulted and said, "This woman must be a priestess of Diana. It is by her chastity she does these cures. If we could destroy that, her power would be overthrown." So they sent evil men to do her violence. And Thecla ran from them, praying for aid from Heaven; and lo! a great rock opened before her, leaving a space large enough for her to enter; and when she went in, it closed and she was seen no more, but her veil, which one of the men had seized, remained in his hand. The legend adds : " Thus suffered the blessed virgin and martyr Thecla, who came from Iconium at eighteen years of age, and afterwards, partly in journeys and travels, and partly in a monastic life in the cave, lived seventy-two years, so that she was ninety years of age when the Lord translated her." Thecla is honored as the first female martyr in the Greek Church. St. Martin of Tours greatly venerated her, and greatly promoted devotion to her in the Latin Church. She is represented in brown or gray drapery, and bears the palm. Wild beasts are about her. Patroness of Tarragona. September 23. First century.

St. Theodore (*Lat.* S. Theodorus ; *Ital.* San Teodoro ; *Ger.* Der Heilige Theodor). This is a warrior saint. He held a high rank in the army of Licinius. He was converted to Christianity, and set on fire the temple of Cybele. Some legends state that he was burned alive ; others, that he was beheaded. He is represented in armor, with a dragon beneath his feet. He was patron saint of Venice before St. Mark. There is another St. Theodore sometimes represented in Greek art, called St. Theodore of Heraclea. He is painted as an armed knight on horseback. The Venetian saint is represented in the more ancient pictures as young and beautiful, and often in company with St. George. January 11, A. D. 300.

St. Theonestus was one of the saints of the Theban Legion. See St. Maurice.

St. Theophilus (*Gr.* Ἁγ. Θεόφιλος ; *Lat.* S. Theophilus ; *Ital.* and *Sp.* San Teofilo ; *Ger.* Der Heilige Theophilus, Gottlieb ; *Fr.* St. Théophile : signification, "a lover of God "). See St. Dorothea.

St. Thomas (*Ital.* San Tommaso ; *Sp.* San Tomé) was a Galilean fisherman ; he is called Didymus, the twin, and is the seventh in the ranks of the Apostles. From the Scripture his character appears to be affectionate and self-sacrificing : " Let us go also, that we may die with him." But so great was his incredulity that he has always been remembered for that rather than for his other characteristics. According to tradition he travelled very far into the East ; founded a church in India, and met the three Magi, whom he baptized. The legend, called that of " La Madonna della Cintola," relates that when the Virgin ascended to heaven, Thomas was not present with the other Apostles. Three days later, when he returned, he could not believe their account, and desired her tomb to

be opened.   It was empty; then the Virgin, that he might be satisfied, dropped her girdle to him from the heavens.   (See also the
Madonna; the Assumption.)   According to another legend, when
Thomas was at Cæsarea, he had a vision in which Christ appeared
and told him that Gondoforus, the king of the Indies, had sent his
provost to find an architect to build him a palace more gorgeous
than that of the Roman Emperor.   And Jesus desired St. Thomas to
go and undertake this labor.   Then Thomas went, and Gondoforus
gave him much treasure, and commanded the building of the magnificent palace, and went to a distant country and remained two
years.   Thomas built no palace, but gave all the riches with which
he had been intrusted to the poor and sick.   When the king returned he was very wroth, and ordered that St. Thomas should be
cast into prison, and reserved for a terrible death.   Now at this time
the brother of the king died, and four days after his death he sat
upright, and spoke to the king, saying, " The man whom thou wouldst
torture is a servant of God : behold, I have been in Paradise, and
the angels showed to me a wondrous palace of gold and silver and
precious stones ; and they said, ' This is the palace that Thomas
the architect hath built for thy brother, King Gondoforus.'   The
king ran to the prison to liberate Thomas.   Then the Apostle said,
" Knowest thou not that those who would possess heavenly things
have little care for the things of this earth ?   There are in heaven
rich palaces without number, which were prepared from the beginning of the world for those who purchase the possession through
faith and charity.   Thy riches, O king, may prepare the way for
thee to such a palace, but they cannot follow thee thither."   According to tradition the Portuguese found at Meliapore an inscription,
saying that Thomas was pierced with a lance at the foot of a cross
which he had erected in that city, and that his body had been removed to Goa in 1523.   When represented as an Apostle, his
attribute is the builder's rule or square.   As a martyr, he bears
the lance.   The two principal scenes in which he is represented,
" The Incredulity of Thomas " and the " Madonna della Cintola," are
easily recognized.   Patron of Portugal and Parma.   December 21.

St. Thomas à Becket, St. Thomas of Canterbury (*Lat.* S.
Thomas Episc. Cantuariensis et Martyr ; *Ital.* San Tommaso Can-
tuariense ; *Fr.* St. Thomas de Cantorbéri).   Mrs. Jameson, in her

"Legends of the Monastic Orders," gives a summary of the principal events in the life of this saint, which is at once so concise and so comprehensive that I cannot do better than to quote it : "The whole of his varied life is rich in materials for the historical painter, offering all that could possibly be desired, in pomp, in circumstance, in scenery, in costume, and in character. What a series it would make of beautiful subjects, beginning with the legend of his mother, the daughter of the Emir of Palestine, who, when his father, Gilbert à Becket, was taken prisoner in the Crusade, fell in love with him, delivered him from captivity, and afterwards followed him to England, knowing no words of any Western tongue, except 'Gilbert' and 'London,' with the aid of which she found him in Cheapside ; then her baptism ; her marriage ; the birth of the future saint ; his introduction to the king ; his mission to Rome ; his splendid embassy to Paris ; his single-handed combat with Engleran de Trie, the French knight ; the King of England and the King of France at his bedside, when he was sick at Rouen ; his consecration as archbishop ; his assumption of the Benedictine habit ; his midnight penances, when he walked alone in the cloisters bewailing his past sins ; his washing the feet of the pilgrims and beggars ; his angry conference with the king ; their reconciliation at Friatville ; his progress through the city of London, when the grateful and enthusiastic people flung themselves in his path, and kissed the hem of his garment ; his interview with the assassins ; his murder on the steps of the altar ; and finally, the proud king kneeling at midnight on the same spot, submitting to be scourged in penance for his crime." His martyrdom made him a saint ; it gives him also a place in art. When he was made archbishop he ceased to be chancellor, and became a different man, especially in his relations to Henry II. He maintained his rank as spiritual father of the king and people with great determination. Henry was at last desperate at the continued opposition of the courageous priest, and in a moment of more than usual temper exclaimed, "Of the cowards that eat my bread, is there none that will rid me of this upstart priest ?" This was enough, — as powerful as a death-warrant, — and four Normans, attendant upon the king, bound themselves by oath to murder the archbishop. They went to Canterbury ; and from the time of their appearance before him, he divined their awful errand. At first they were not armed ;

he spoke to them with great spirit, and declared that he feared not their swords, and would die sooner than retract what he had said or done. This enraged them, and they rushed out to summon their followers. Then was heard the singing of the Vespers, and his friends urged Becket to go into the church as a place of safety. He ordered the cross of Canterbury to be borne before him, and passed through the cloister into the church. His friends barred the gates behind him, but he commanded them to be reopened, saying that God's house should never be fortified as a place of defence. As he ascended the steps of the choir, the four knights with twelve attendants, all armed, burst into the church. "Where is the traitor?" demanded one of the number. All was silent. "Where is the archbishop?" asked Reginald Fitzurse. Then Becket replied, "Here I am; the archbishop, but no traitor! Reginald, I have granted thee many favors; what is thy object now? If thou seekest my life, let that suffice; and I command thee, in the name of God, not to touch one of my people." He was then told that he must absolve the Archbishop of York and the Bishop of Salisbury, whom he had excommunicated. "Till they make satisfaction, I will not absolve them," he firmly answered. "Then die!" said Tracy. The first blow aimed at his head was broken in its force by his cross-bearer, so that he was but slightly wounded. Feeling the blood on his face, he bowed his head, and said, "In the name of Christ, and for the defence of his Church, I am ready to die." The assassins then wished to remove him from the church, in order to lessen the horrible sacrilege they were committing; but Becket said, "I will not stir; do here what you please, or are commanded." He added, "I humbly commend my spirit to God, who gave it;" and instantly he was struck down, and was soon dead; but so many blows were lavished on him that his brains strewed the pavement before the altar. His monks buried him in the crypt at Canterbury. According to tradition, as they bore him to the tomb, angels were heard singing the beginning of the Service of the Martyrs, "Lætabitur justus." The monks were for a moment amazed; they ceased their funeral hymn; then, as if inspired, they joined their voices with the angelic hymn, and bore the great bishop in triumph to his grave. In due time he was canonized. His remains were enclosed in a splendid shrine, and votaries from all parts of the world made pilgrimages to the scene of his martyrdom. But later, the power of the kings of the earth burned his relics, and threw the ashes into the Thames. Thomas à Becket was fifty-two years old when he was martyred. He is represented as a bishop, with the crosier and the Gospels in his hand ; as a martyr, he is without the mitre and a sword or axe is struck into his head, or the blood trickles from a wound over his face. December 29, A. D. 1170.

St. Thomas Aquinas (*Ital.* San Tommaso di Aquino, Dottore Angelico) was born at Belcastro in the year 1226. His father was Count of Aquino, Lord of Loretto and Belcastro. Thomas was grand-nephew of Frederick I., and a kinsman of the emperors Henry VI. and Frederick II. The sweetness of temper for which as a child he was remarkable, he preserved through life. When ten years old, the teachers at Monte Casino declared they could instruct him no further, so great was his learning. His mother, the Countess Theodora, desired that he should have a private tutor, but his father placed him at the University of Naples. His own inclination and his mother's counsels kept him free from the temptations around him. At seventeen he assumed the Dominican habit at Naples. His mother hastened to persuade him not to take the final vows. Fearing he could not resist her appeals, he fled towards Paris : but his brothers, Landolfo and Rinaldo, seized him near Acquapendente; they tore off his monk's habit, and took him to his father's castle of Rocca-Secca. Then his mother came ; and when her entreaties would not prevail, she had him guarded, and allowed no one to see him save his two sisters, who were instructed to persuade him to give up the idea of a religious life. The result was that Thomas so influenced his sisters that they sympathized with him, and aided him to escape. He was lowered from a window in a basket ; some monks waited for him below, and not a long time elapsed before he took his final vows. He was as eminent for his humility, and the simplicity of his manners, by which he concealed his acquirements, as for his learning. He was surnamed Bos, the Ox. On one occasion when it was his duty to read in the refectory, the superior corrected him, and told him to read a word with a false quantity. St. Thomas knew that he was right and the superior wrong, but he did as directed instantly. Being told that he should not have yielded, he replied, "The pronunciation of a word is of little importance, but humility and obedience are of the greatest." Pope Clement IV. desired to make him an archbishop, but he declined all preferments.   He was the most learned man of his time [1] in the Church.   Being sent on a mission to Naples, he was taken ill at Fossa-Nova, on his journey.   He was carried to a Cistercian abbey, where he died.   Before extreme unction was administered to him, he requested to be laid on ashes on the floor.   He is represented in the Dominican habit.   His attributes are : a book or books ; the pen or inkhorn ; the sacramental cup, on account of his having composed the Office of the Blessed Sacrament ; on his breast a sun, and sometimes an eye within it ; frequently he looks up at a dove, or writes.   March 7, A. D. 1274.

St. Thomas of Villanueva, surnamed the Almoner.   He was born in 1488.   His parents were of moderate fortune, but distinguished for their charities.   They supplied seeds for the fields of the poor, and lent their money without interest.   The son inherited their charity to an intense degree.   As a child he would take off his own clothes to give away to children in the street.   He showed from his infancy a singular fitness for the ministry of the Church.   He studied fourteen years at Alcala and Salamanca, and entered the Augustinian Order at thirty years of age.   In his life it is related that he pronounced his vows in the self-same hour in which Luther publicly renounced his.   He passed two years in penance and prayer, and then became an eloquent and distinguished preacher.   Charles V., the Emperor of Spain, held St. Thomas in great veneration ; and when he would not listen to the entreaties of friends or the requests of his son Don Philip, he yielded to St. Thomas, saying that he considered his request as a divine command.   In 1544 Charles named Thomas Archbishop of Valencia.   He reluctantly accepted the office, and arrived in Valencia so poorly clad and provided for, that his canons sent him four thousand crowns to buy him an outfit ; he thanked them, and sent it to the hospital for the sick ; and this, when his only hat had been worn twenty-six years !   His whole life was but a grand series of beneficent deeds.   He divided the poor into six classes : (1) The bashful poor, who had been independent, and were ashamed to beg ; (2) The poor girls, whose poverty exposed them to temptation, to sin and shame ; (3) The poor debtors ; (4)

---

[1] Later times have not produced his equal, much less his superior ; and his Holiness Pope Leo XIII. urges on all ecclesiastics the study of the works of the Angelic Doctor St. Thomas Aquinas.

Orphans and foundlings; (5) The lame, sick, and infirm; (6) Strangers and travellers who came to the city without the means to pay for food and lodging. For these he had a large kitchen, always open, where they could have food; rooms where they could sleep; and in addition a small sum of money when they went on their way. Amid all these cares, he did not forget his duties as a spiritual teacher. When the hour of his death came, he had given away everything except the pallet on which he lay, and this was to be given to a jailer who assisted him in executing his benevolent designs. So strange was it, that, in spite of all he had given away, he still left no debts, that it was believed that his money had been miraculously increased according to his wants. Thousands of poor people followed him to his grave. When he was beatified it was also decreed that he should be represented with an open purse, in place of the crosier; but the latter is not always omitted. He is usually surrounded by poor people, kneeling. The finest pictures of this saint are Spanish. One of Murillo's, of great beauty, represents him as a child dividing his clothing among four ragged little ones. The one called the "Charity of San Tomas de Villa Nueva," Murillo called "his own picture," and preferred it to all his other works. In this the saint stands at the door of his cathedral, relieving a lame beggar kneeling before him. September 17, A. D. 1555.

St. Tibertius. April 14. See St. Cecilia.

Tobias, the Son of Tobit. The pictures of the Archangel Raphael are so often illustrative of his journey with the young Tobias, that the story of their companionship rightly belongs here. Now Tobit was a rich man and just; and he and his wife Anna were carried away into captivity by the Assyrians. He then gave alms to all his brethren that he could help, and lived a just life, not eating the bread of the Gentiles. But in one way and another his misfortunes were increased, and he became blind; and nothing was left to him but his wife and his son Tobias. And he was so afflicted that he prayed for death. At this same time there dwelt in the city of Ecbatane a man called Raguel, and he had an only daughter, Sara, who had had seven husbands, and they were all killed by the evil spirit Asmodeus, as soon as they were married to her. Her maid reproached her, and said she had strangled her husbands. Sara was so wretched at this that she too prayed for death, that she might be at peace. So God sent his angel Raphael, that he might take away the blindness of Tobit and the reproach of this unhappy woman. Then Tobit remembered that he had given to Gabael, in Media, ten talents in trust, and he determined to send Tobias to ask for this money. So he called him, and gave him directions concerning it. Then Tobias said, "But how can I receive the money, seeing I know him not?" Then Tobit gave him the handwriting, and commanded him to seek for a guide who would show him the way. So Tobias sought a guide, and Raphael offered to go with him; and it happened that Tobias knew not that his guide was an angel. So he took him to his father, and they agreed upon the wages of the guide; and Tobit gave directions for their journey, and they departed. Anna was much grieved to part from her son Tobias. At evening the angel and Tobias came to the river Tigris, and lodged thereabout; and when the latter went to wash himself, a fish leaped out at him. And the angel told him to take the fish, and take out the heart and the liver and the gall and preserve them carefully. This Tobias did, and they roasted the fish and ate it. Then Tobias asked the use of the parts they had kept; and the angel said the heart and the liver would cure any one vexed with an evil spirit, if a smoke were made of them before the person, and the gall would take away blindness from one who had whiteness in the eyes. Now, when they were come near to Rages, the angel said, "Brother, to-day we shall lodge with Raguel, who is thy cousin; he also hath one only daughter named Sara; I will speak for her that she may be given thee for a wife." And he added that according to the laws she belonged to Tobias, and as she was fair and wise, he could marry her on their return. Then Tobias said he had "heard that she had been married to seven husbands, who all died in the bridal chamber; and he feared that he too should die and thus bring his parents to their grave in sorrow, since he was their only son." But Raphael assured him that she was the wife intended for him by the Lord, and he should be preserved if when he came into the marriage chamber he should make a smoke with the heart and liver of the fish, for at the smell of it the devil would flee away forever. "Now, when Tobias had heard these things, he loved her, and his heart was effectually joined to her." So when they were come to Ecbatane they met Sara, and she took them to the house of Raguel her father; and when they made themselves known unto him, he rejoiced to see them, and wept to hear of the blindness of his cousin Tobit; and Edna his wife and Sara wept also. And they killed a ram of the flock, and prepared a supper; but Tobias said unto Raphael, "Speak of those things of which thou didst talk in the way, and let this business be despatched." So they asked Raguel for Sara, that he should give her to Tobias as his wife. Then Raguel answered and told of the fate of the seven husbands she had had already; but he could not deny the request of Tobias, for by the law of Moses, Sara belonged to him. And so it was settled before they did eat together, and Raguel joined their hands and blessed them. Then Edna prepared the marriage chamber and brought her daughter in thither, and Sara wept; but her mother comforted her and blessed her. Then when Tobias went in, he took heed to make the smoke with the heart and liver of the fish, as Raphael had directed; and when the evil spirit perceived the odor thereof, he fled away to return no more. Then Tobias and Sara knelt down, and Tobias prayed as Raphael had commanded him, and Sara said Amen. And in the morning Raguel went out and dug a grave; for he counted Tobias as one dead, and he desired to bury him quietly, that none should know what had taken place. And he sent a servant to see if he were dead; and the servant found him and Sara quietly sleeping. Then did Raguel and Edna rejoice, and they prepared to keep the marriage feast of their daughter. And this feast lasted fourteen days. Meanwhile the angel went to Gabael, and received from him the money that Tobit had left with him. And when the feast was ended, Tobias with Sara and the angel departed to go to his father. And Raguel and Edna blessed them, and gave them half of their goods, servants, cattle, and money. Now, as they approached to the city of Nineveh, the angel said to Tobias, "Let us haste before thy wife and prepare the house, and take in thine hand the gall of the fish." So they went, and the little dog which they took away went with them. Now Anna was watching for them; and when she saw them she told Tobit that they were coming, and they were exceeding glad; for they had both been troubled at their long absence, and feared lest some evil had overtaken them. Then said Raphael to Tobias, "I know that thy father will open his eyes; therefore anoint thou his eyes with the gall, and being pricked therewith, he shall rub and the whiteness shall fall away and he shall see thee." Then Tobias did so, and it was as the angel said, and the sight of Tobit was restored to him. Then they all rejoiced and blessed God, and Tobias recounted what had happened to him. And they went out to meet Sara and the servants and all that he had brought with him. And the people wondered when they saw that Tobit was no longer blind. And they brought in Sara, and made a feast which they kept for seven days. Then Tobit said to his son, "See that the man have his wages that went forth with thee, and thou must give him more." And Tobias answered, "O father! it is no harm to me to give him half of those things which I have brought; for he hath brought me again to thee in safety, and made whole my wife, and brought me the money, and likewise healed thee." And Tobit said, "It is due unto him." So they called Raphael, and made known unto him their intentions. Then told he them to praise God, and glorify him for all this good. And he told Tobit that all his acts and his goodness had been known in heaven, and his weariness of life and his desire for death; and also those of Sara, who had so great troubles. Then he said, "And now God hath sent me to heal thee, and Sara thy daughter-in-law. I am Raphael, one of the seven holy angels, who present the prayers of the saints, and who go in and out before the glory of the Holy One." Then were they both troubled and fell upon their faces; for they feared. But he said unto them, "Fear not, for it shall go well with you; praise God therefore." After a few more words he vanished, and when they arose they could see no one. From this time forth all did go well with Tobit and Anna his wife, with Raguel and Edna his wife, and with their children. And while they lived they never ceased to praise God for all the wonderful things he had showed them. And when Tobit and Anna were dead, Tobias took his wife and children and went to Ecbatane to Raguel, his father-in-law. When Raguel died, Tobias inherited his riches and abode in honor; and lived to hear of the destruction of Nineveh, and died at Ecbatane, being an hundred and seven and twenty years old.

St. Torpè, or **Torpet**, is a Pisan saint. According to the legend he was a Roman, and served in the guards of Nero. He was converted by St. Paul. He was beheaded. When there was no water in the Arno and all were suffering for want of rain, the head of the saint was carried in procession; and so effectual was his intercession that the rain fell in floods and swept away a portion of the procession, and, *mirabile dictu*, the head of the saint also ! The people know not what to do, when two angels appeared, dived beneath the water, and brought again the head of the saint and gave it to the archbishop. St. Torpè was the patron of Pisa before St. Ranieri. For a time the latter saint was the more popular, but St. Torpè's fame revived in the seventeenth century. He is represented as a Roman soldier, and bears a white banner with a red cross.

True Cross, History of the. A long time after Adam was driven out of Paradise, he grew so weary of his life of toil and hardship that he longed for death, and he sent his son Seth to the angel who guarded the Tree of Life to ask him to send him the oil of mercy which God had promised him when he was driven out of Paradise. After his father had pointed out the way, Seth went ; and when he asked the angel for the oil, the latter replied, " The oil of mercy which God promised to Adam can only be given after five thousand five hundred years shall have elapsed ; but take these three seeds, they will bear fruit for the good of mankind." Then he gave him three seeds, believed to have been from the same tree of which Adam had eaten. And the angel told Seth that his father should die after three days, and commanded that after his death these seeds should be put under his tongue. Then Adam was joyous, for he much desired to die. And on the third day he died, and Seth buried him in the Valley of Hebron, and the three seeds were under his tongue. These seeds soon sprung up ; and the three saplings thus formed united into one, thus becoming a symbol of the Trinity. It was with a part of this tree that Moses sweetened the waters of Marah ; and with it also he struck the rock without calling on God ; for which fault he was forbidden to enter the Promised Land. David also did miracles with this tree, and at last brought it to Jerusalem, and placed it in his garden, and built a wall about it. When Solomon was building the Temple, he saw that this tree was good and strong, and it was cut down for a beam ; but the workmen could never make it fit in any place : sometimes it was too long, and again too short, so at last it was given up and thrown aside. After some years a woman, Sibylla, sat down upon it, and immediately her clothes took fire ; and she prophesied concerning it, that it would be for the destruction of the Jews. Some men who were near by cast it into a pond, and it rose to the surface of the water, and formed a bridge upon which many passed. But when the Queen of Sheba came to visit Solomon, as she neared this bridge she had a vision of its future, and she would not step upon it, but knelt down and venerated it; and she took off her sandals and walked through the stream, and she told Solomon that One should hang on that tree who would redeem the human race. Then Solomon took it, and cased it in silver and gold, and put it above the door of the Temple, that all who came in might bless it. But when Abijah, the son of Rehoboam, reigned, he desired the gold and silver, and he took them away and buried the wood deep in the earth. Now after a time a well was dug over the spot where the Tree of Mercy was buried, and its waters were powerful to heal the sick, and it was called the Pool of Bethesda. As the time for the death of Jesus drew near, this beam was cast up to the surface of the waters, and the Jews took it and made from it *The Cross ;* and so the tree which had grown from the seeds from Paradise, and which had been nourished by the decaying body of Adam, became at length the tree of the death of the second Adam. Another legend relates that the Jews believed that the body of Jesus would hang as long as the cross would last, and that it was made of four different kinds of wood, but the stem was of cypress wood, because this would not decay in earth or water. After the crucifixion the cross was buried deep in the earth and there remained for more than three centuries, until Constantine and his mother, the Empress Helena, were converted to Christianity; and the latter made a pilgrimage to Jerusalem, where she was seized with an uncontrollable desire to discover the Cross of Christ. Helena therefore commanded that all the wise men of the Jews should come to her palace. They were alarmed, and questioned one with another why this should be. But there was one named Judas, who said, "Know, my brethren, that the empress hath come hither to discover the cross on which Jesus Christ suffered. Take heed that it be not revealed; for in the hour that the cross comes to light, our ancient law is no more, and the traditions of our people are destroyed. My grandfather Zaccheus taught this to my father Simon, and my father Simon hath taught it to me. Moreover, he told me that his brother Stephen had been stoned for believing in him who was crucified, and he bade me beware of blaspheming Christ or any of his disciples." The Jews obeyed the injunction of Judas; and when the empress questioned them they all declared that they knew not where the cross was hidden. So Helena commanded that they should all be buried alive. Then were they alarmed, and they said, " Here is a just man, and the son of a prophet, who knoweth all things pertaining to our law, and who will answer all questions." Then she released the others, but Judas she retained. And when she questioned him he exclaimed, " Alas! how should I know of these things which happened so long before I was born?" Then the empress was so filled with wrath that she declared he should be starved to death, and for that purpose he was cast into a dry well. Here he endured hunger and thirst for six days; but on the seventh day he yielded, and led the empress to the temple of Venus, which Hadrian had built above the place where the cross was buried. Then Helena commanded that the temple should be destroyed. After that, Judas began to dig, and when he had dug twenty feet, he found three crosses; but they were all alike, and no one knew which was that of Jesus. As Helena and Macarius, the Bishop of Jerusalem, were consulting as to what should now be done, behold, a dead man was carried past to his burial. Macarius desired that the corpse should be laid on the crosses, and it was done. Now, when he was put upon the first and the second he stirred not, but when he was put upon the third he was restored to life; and the demons were heard to lament in the air above because Satan was overpowered and Christ reigned, while the man raised from the dead went on his way rejoicing. Then was Judas baptized, with the name Syriacus, or Quiriacus. But the nails of the cross were still wanting; and when Helena prayed for them, they appeared on the surface of the earth shining like gold. Then Helena divided the cross, and left a part at Jerusalem, and a part she carried to Constantinople. Constantine kept a portion of it, which was inserted into a statue of himself; and the rest was carried to Rome, where the church of Santa Croce in Gerusalemme was built to receive and preserve it. One of the nails the empress placed in the crown of Constantine; another she made into a bit for his horse; and a third she threw into a whirlpool in the Adriatic, and immediately the sea was calm. In the year 615, Chosroes, King of Persia, came to Jerusalem, and carried away the portion that had been left there. Then the Emperor Heraclius gathered his army together and defied Chosroes to battle. When they met, the king and the emperor decided to settle their difficulties by single combat.

Heraclius overcame Chosroes, and when the latter refused to be baptized, cut off his head. Then the emperor returned to Jerusalem in great triumph, bearing the cross with him; but when he would, he could not enter, for the walls were all closed up by a miracle. He was astonished at this, and an angel came to him and said, "When the King of Heaven and Earth entered through this gate to suffer for the sins of the world, he entered not with regal pomp, but barefoot and mounted on an ass." Then Heraclius wept that pride should have so blinded him; and he descended to the earth, took off his crown, and also his shoes, and took the royal robes off even to his shirt. Then he put the cross on his shoulder, and the wall opened that he might pass in. Then was the cross exalted on an altar and displayed to the people. There is scarcely a point in this legend which has not been the subject of art. It is also related in the legends that *The Title* of accusation was found and sent to Rome by St. Helena; that it was placed on an arch in the church of Santa Croce, and was there found in a leaden box, in 1492. The inscriptions in the Hebrew, Greek, and Latin were in red letters, while the wood on which they were painted was white. Since then it has faded, and the words "Jesus" and "Judæorum" are eaten away. The board is now only nine inches long, but was originally about twelve. *The Sponge* which was used for the vinegar, to wash the wounds of Christ,[1] as was the custom in crucifixions, is preserved with great veneration at the church of St. John Lateran at Rome. *The Lance* which pierced his side is also at Rome, but the point is at Sainte Chapelle in Paris. According to various authorities, the lance was buried with the cross. St. Gregory of Tours and Venerable Bede agree that in their day this lance was at Jerusalem. In order to guard it from the Saracens, it was buried at Antioch; and there it was found in 1098, when by use of it were wrought many wonderful miracles. It was then carried to Jerusalem, and thence to Constantinople. Baldwin II. sent the point of it to Venice in order to raise money for his necessities. St. Louis of France obtained it by paying the sum Baldwin had received. The rest of the lance remained at

---

[1] "Afterwards, Jesus . . . said, I thirst. Now there was a vessel set there full of vinegar; and they put *a sponge* full of vinegar about hyssop, and put it to his mouth. When Jesus therefore had taken the vinegar, he said, It is consummated." — *St. John* xix. 28–30.

Constantinople after it was taken by the Turks until 1492, when the Sultan Bajazet enclosed it in a beautiful case, and sent an ambassador with it to Rome to present it to Pope Innocent VIII.

The Crown of Thorns was given to St. Louis by Baldwin, for motives of gratitude and friendship, and also because Constantinople was no longer a safe place for it. St. Louis, with his mother-in-law, his brother, and many priests and members of his court, met the ambassadors who carried it to him five leagues from Sens. St. Louis and his brother Robert of Artois were barefoot and in their shirts; thus they bore the crown of thorns to Sens and to the cathedral of St. Stephen, where it was received with great ceremony. It was taken to Paris with equal honor, and St. Louis built for its reception the Sainte Chapelle, to which was attached a rich foundation for a chapter of canons. St. Louis also received the portion of the cross which was at Constantinople, and other relics which St. Helena had given her son. Some of the thorns from this crown have been given to other churches, and they have been imitated many times. They are very long.

The Nails of the cross have already been spoken of. These have been multiplied by imitation, and many made in this way and touched to the true nails, are considered holy.

The Pillar to which Christ was bound to be scourged, or a portion of it, is preserved at Jerusalem. The inscription above it says that it was placed there in 1223 by Cardinal Columna.

The Blood of Christ. The Rev. Alban Butler says that this relic, " which is kept in some places, of which the most famous is that of Mantua, seems to be what has sometimes issued from the miraculous bleeding of some crucifix when pierced in derision by Jews or Pagans, instances of which are recorded in authentic histories." Representations of all these different relics, of circumstances connected with their discovery, of the ceremonies which have taken place on their account, and of the miracles performed through them, are very numerous in works of art.

St. Umilita, or **Humility**, was the wife of Ugolotto Caccianemici of Faenza. She was the foundress of the Vallombrosan nuns. She had desired to remain a virgin, but was compelled to marry on account of the avaricious interests of her family. Her husband was also virtuous and pious. Not long after their marriage, Rosane (for this was her name) thus addressed her husband : "Dost thou not feel that we can find no real permanent happiness here on earth, and should we not aspire to that peace and bliss which we can attain in heaven ? Let us therefore separate for a while, and in the silence of some cloister make a sacrifice of ourselves to God, for our country, our kindred, and for all those whom we love. Time fleets by with lightning speed, and we shall soon be reunited in the kingdom of heaven, where we shall enjoy all that felicity which has been denied us here below." Ugolotto consented, and they both lived strict lives according to the Vallombrosan rule. This legend has been illustrated in a series of eleven pictures by Bufalmacco. One of them represents Rosano persuading her husband to the separation. Her face is alight with the inspiration of the project of self-sacrifice she has conceived, while that of Ugolotto is sad at the thought of parting with her.

St. Ursula, and her Virgin Companions (*Lat.* Sancta Ursula ; *Fr.* Ste. Ursule ; *Ital.* Santa Irsola). This legend, which from its very improbability and surpassing strangeness is so fascinating, can be traced to the year 600. All the discussions as to its signification have not (happily) changed the legend, and the Cologne version is the one followed by most painters who have attempted to depict its wonderful incidents. The manner in which this legend is told is so charming in its quaintness of thought and expression that even when I consider the brevity that is here desirable, I cannot find it in my heart to do otherwise than give it *verbatim et literatim.* "Once on a time there reigned in Brittany a certain king whose name was Theonotus, and he was married to a Sicilian princess whose name was Daria. Both were Christians, and they were blessed with one daughter, whom they called Ursula, and whom they educated with exceeding care. When Ursula was about fifteen, her mother, Queen Daria, died, leaving the king almost inconsolable ; but Ursula, though so young, supplied the place of her mother in the court. She was not only wonderfully beautiful, and gifted with all the external graces of her sex, but accomplished in all the learning of the time. Her mind was a perfect storehouse of wisdom and knowledge : she had read about the stars, and the courses of the winds ; all that had ever happened in the world from the days of Adam she had by heart ; the poets and the philosophers were to her what childish recreations are to others; but above all, she was profoundly versed in theology and school divinity, so that the doctors were astonished and confounded by her argumentative powers. To these accomplishments were added the more excellent gifts of humility, piety, and charity, so that she was esteemed the most accomplished princess of the time. Her father, who loved her as the light of his eyes, desired nothing better than to keep her always at his side. But the fame of her beauty, her virtue, and her wondrous learning was spread through all the neighboring lands, so that many of the neighboring princes desired her in marriage; but Ursula refused every offer. Not far from Brittany, on the other side of the great ocean, was a country called England, vast and powerful, but the people were still in the darkness of paganism; and the king of this country had an only son, whose name was Conon, as celebrated for his beauty of person, his warlike prowess, and physical strength, as Ursula for her piety, her graces, and her learning. He was now old enough to seek a wife; and his father, King Agrippinus, hearing of the great beauty and virtue of Ursula, sent ambassadors to demand her in marriage for his son. When the ambassadors arrived at the palace of the King of Brittany, they were very courteously received, but the king was secretly much embarrassed, for he knew that his daughter had made a vow of perpetual chastity, having dedicated herself to Christ; at the same time he feared to offend the powerful monarch of England by refusing his request; therefore he delayed to give an answer, and having commanded the ambassadors to be sumptuously lodged and entertained, he retired to his chamber, and leaning his head on his hand, he meditated what was best to be done; but he could think of no help to deliver him from this strait. While thus he sat apart in doubt and sadness, the princess entered, and learning the cause of his melancholy, she said with a smile, ' Is this all? Be of good cheer, my king and father! for if it please you, I will myself answer these ambassadors.' And her father replied, ' As thou wilt, my daughter.' So the next day, when the ambassadors were again introduced, St. Ursula was seated on a throne by her father's side, and having received and returned their salutations with unspeakable grace and dignity, she thus addressed them: ' I thank my Lord the King of England, and Conon, his princely son, and his noble barons, and you, sirs, his honorable

ambassadors, for the honor ye have done me, so much greater than
my deserving. I hold myself bound to your king as to a second
father, and to the prince his son as to my brother and bridegroom,
for to no other will I ever listen. But I have to ask **three things.**
First, he shall give for me as my ladies and companions ten virgins
of the noblest blood in his kingdom, and to each of these a thousand attendants, and to me also a thousand maidens to wait on me.
Secondly, he shall permit me for the space of three years to honor
my virginity, and with my companions to visit the holy shrines
where repose the bodies of the saints. And my third demand is
that the prince and his court shall receive baptism ; for other than a
perfect Christian I cannot wed.' Now you shall understand that
this wise princess, Ursula, made these conditions, thinking in her
heart, 'either the King of England will refuse these demands, or, if
he grant them, then eleven thousand virgins are redeemed and dedicated to the service of God.' The ambassadors, being dismissed
with honor, returned to their own country, where they made such a
report of the unequalled beauty and wisdom of the princess that
the king thought no conditions too hard, and the prince his son was
inflamed by desire to obtain her; so he commanded himself to be
forthwith baptized ; and the king wrote letters to all his vassals in
his kingdom of France, in Scotland, and in the province of Cornwall, to all his princes, dukes, counts, barons, and noble knights,
desiring that they should send him the required number of maidens,
spotless and beautiful, and of noble birth, to wait on the Princess
Ursula, who was to wed his heir the Prince Conon ; and from all
parts these noble virgins came trooping, fair and accomplished in all
female learning, and attired in rich garments, wearing jewels of gold
and silver. Being assembled in Brittany, in the capital of King
Theonotus, Ursula received them not only with great gladness and
courtesy, but with a sisterly tenderness and with thanksgiving,
praising God that so many of her own sex had been redeemed from
the world's vanities ; and the fame of this noble assembly of virgins
having gone forth to all the countries round about, the barons and
knights were gathered together from east and west to view this
spectacle, and you may think how much they were amazed and edi-
fied by the sight of so much beauty and so much devotion. Now,
when Ursula had collected all her virgins together, **on a fresh and**

fair morning in the spring-time, she desired them to meet in a meadow near the city, which meadow was of freshest green, all over enamelled with the brightest flowers; and she ascended a throne which was raised in the midst, and spake to all the assembled virgins of things concerning the glory of God, and of his Son, our Lord and Saviour, with wonderful eloquence; and of Christian charity, and of a pure and holy life dedicated to heaven. And all these virgins, being moved with a holy zeal, wept, and, lifting up their hands and their voices, promised to follow her whithersoever she should lead. And she blessed them and comforted them; and as there were many among them who had never received baptism, she ordered that they should be baptized in the clear stream which flowed through that flowery meadow. Then Ursula called for a pen, and wrote a letter to her bridegroom, the son of the King of England, saying, that as he had complied with all her wishes and fulfilled all her demands, he had good leave to wait upon her forthwith. So he, as became a true knight, came immediately; and she received him with great honor; and in presence of her father, she said to him, 'Sir, my gracious prince and consort, it has been revealed to me in a vision that I must depart hence on my pilgrimage to visit the shrines in the holy city of Rome, with these my companions; thou meanwhile shalt remain here to comfort my father and assist him in his government till my return; or, if God should dispose of me otherwise, this kingdom shall be yours by right.' Some say that the prince remained, but others relate that he accompanied her on her voyage; however this may be, the glorious virgin embarked with all her maidens on board a fleet of ships prepared for them, and many holy prelates accompanied them. There were no sailors on board, and it was a wonder to see with what skill these wise virgins steered the vessels and managed the sails, being miraculously taught; we must therefore suppose that it was by no mistake of theirs, but by the providence of God, that they sailed to the north instead of the south, and were driven by the winds into the mouth of the Rhine as far as the port of Cologne. Here they reposed for a brief time, during which it was revealed to St. Ursula that on her return she and her companions should on that spot suffer martyrdom for the cause of God; all which she made known to her companions; and they all together lifted up their voices in hymns of thanksgiving

that they should be found worthy so to die.   So they proceeded on
their voyage up the river till they came to the city of Basil; there
they disembarked, and crossed over the high mountains into the
plains of Liguria.   Over the rocks and snows of the Alps they were
miraculously conducted; for six angels went before them perpetually,
clearing the road from all impediments, throwing bridges over the
mountain torrents, and every night pitching tents for their shelter
and refreshment.   So they came at length to the river Tiber, and
descending the river they reached Rome, that famous city wherein is
the holy shrine of St. Peter and St. Paul.   In those days was Cyriacus Bishop of Rome ; he was famous for his sanctity ; and hearing of
the arrival of St. Ursula and all her fair and glorious company of
maidens, he was, as you may suppose, greatly amazed and troubled
in mind, not knowing what it might portend.   So he went out to
meet them, with all his clergy in procession.   When St. Ursula,
kneeling down before him, explained to him the cause of her coming,
and implored his blessing for herself and her companions, who can
express his admiration and contentment !   He not only gave them
his blessing, but commanded that they should be honorably lodged
and entertained ; and to preserve their maidenly honor and decorum,
tents were pitched for them outside the walls of the city, on the
plain towards Tivoli.   Now it happened that the valiant son of King
Agrippinus, who had been left in Brittany, became every day more
and more impatient to learn some tidings of his princess-bride; and
at length he resolved to set out in search of her, and by a miracle, he arrived in the city of Rome on the self-same day, but by a
different route.   Being happily reunited, he knelt with Ursula at the
feet of Cyriacus, and received baptism at his hands, changing his
name from Conon to that of Ethereus, to express the purity and
regeneration of his soul.   He no longer aspired to the possession of
Ursula, but fixed his hope on sharing with her the crown of martyrdom on earth, looking to a perpetual reunion in heaven, where neither
sorrow nor separation should touch them more.   After this blessed
company had duly performed their devotions at the shrine of St.
Peter and St. Paul, the good Cyriacus would fain have detained
them longer ; but Ursula showed him that it was necessary they
should depart, in order to receive the crown 'already laid up for them
in heaven.'   When the bishop heard this, he resolved to accompany

her. In vain his clergy represented that it did not become the pope of Rome, and a man of venerable years, to follow a company of maidens, however immaculate they might be. Cyriacus had been counselled by an angel of God, and he made ready to set forth and embark with them on the river Rhine. Now it happened that there were at Rome in those days two great Roman captains, cruel heathens, who commanded all the imperial troops in Germania. They, being astonished at the sight of this multitude of virgins, said one to the other, 'Shall we suffer this? If we allow these Christian maidens to return to Germania, they will convert the whole nation; or if they marry husbands, then they will have so many children, — no doubt, all Christians, — that our empire will cease; therefore let us take counsel what is best to be done.' So these wicked pagans consulted together, and wrote letters to a certain barbarian king of the Huns, who was then besieging Cologne, and instructed him what he should do. Meantime St. Ursula and her virgins, with her husband and his faithful knights, prepared to embark; with them went Pope Cyriacus, and in his train Vincenzio and Giacomo, cardinals; and Solfino, Archbishop of Ravenna; and Folatino, Bishop of Lucca; and the Bishop of Faenza, and the patriarch of Grado, and many other prelates; and after a long and perilous journey they arrived in the port of Cologne. They found the city besieged by a great army of barbarians encamped on a plain outside the gates. These pagans, seeing a number of vessels filled, not with fierce warriors, but beautiful virgins, unarmed youths, and venerable bearded men, stood still at first, staring with amazement; but after a short pause, remembering their instructions, they rushed upon the unresisting victims. One of the first who perished was Prince Ethereus, who fell, pierced through by an arrow, at the feet of his beloved princess. Then Cyriacus, the cardinals, and several barons sank to the earth or perished in the stream. When the men were despatched, the fierce barbarians rushed upon the virgins just as a pack of gaunt hungry wolves might fall on a flock of milk-white lambs. Finding that the noble virgins resisted their brutality, their rage was excited, and they drew their swords and massacred them all. Then was it worthy of all admiration to behold these illustrious virgins, who had struggled to defend their virtue, now meekly resigned, and ready as sheep for the slaughter, embracing and encouraging each other! Oh, then, had you seen the glorious St. Ursula, worthy to be the captain and leader of this army of virgin martyrs, how she flew from one to the other, heartening them with brave words to die for their faith and honor! Inspired by her voice, her aspect, they did not quail, but offered themselves to death; and thus by hundreds and by thousands they perished, and the plain was strewed with their limbs and ran in rivers with their blood. But the barbarians, awed by the majestic beauty of St. Ursula, had no power to strike her, but carried her before their prince, who, looking on her with admiration, said to her, 'Weep not; for though thou hast lost thy companions, I will be thy husband, and thou shalt be the greatest queen in all Germany.' To which St. Ursula, all glowing with indignation and a holy scorn, replied, 'O thou cruel man! blind and senseless as thou art cruel! thinkest thou I can weep? Or dost thou hold me so base, so cowardly, that I would consent to survive my dear companions and sisters? Thou art deceived, O son of Satan! for I defy thee, and him whom thou servest!' When the proud pagan heard these words, he was seized with fury, and bending his bow which he held in his hand, he with three arrows transfixed her pure breast so that she fell dead, and her spirit ascended into heaven, with all the glorious sisterhood of martyrs whom she had led to death, and with her betrothed husband and his companions; and there, with palms in their hands and crowns upon their heads, they stand around the throne of Christ, and live in his light and in his approving smile, blessing him and praising him forever, Amen!" It has been very troublesome for the artists who have represented this legend to devise any means by which they could represent the idea of the eleven thousand virgins; and in spite of all their ingenuity, several thousands still remain to whom justice has never been done. The attributes of St. Ursula are the crown of the princess; the staff of the pilgrim; the arrow, as a martyr; the white banner with the red cross, as the victorious Christian; and the dove, because a dove disclosed her burial-place to St. Cunibert. She is frequently represented as spreading out her broad mantle, underneath which many virgins cluster. There are many series of paintings giving the scenes of her life. Patroness of all young maidens; especially of school-girls and of such women as instruct the young of their own sex.[1]   October 21.

---

[1] Of the Ursuline nuns, especially.

St. Valerian. See St. Cecilia.

St. Valerie. See St. Martial.

Vera Icon, The. See St. Veronica.

St. Verdiana is seen in Florentine pictures. She is in the habit of a Vallombrosan nun, and bears a basket from which serpents feed. A. D. 1222.

St. Veronica (*Ital.* Santa Veronica; *Fr.* Ste. Véronique). There are two quite different legends concerning this saint. The most ancient relates that she was the woman who was healed by touching Christ's garment, and that she greatly desired a picture of his face. She first took a cloth to St. Luke, and he painted a picture that both he and Veronica thought to be like Christ; but when next she saw him, she found his face quite different. Then the Saviour said to her, "Unless I come to your help, all Luke's art is in vain, for my face is known only to Him who sent me." Then he told her to go to her house and prepare him a meal, and before the day ended he would come to her. Veronica did this joyfully, and when Christ came he first desired water to wash. Veronica gave him this, with a cloth whereon to wipe. He pressed the cloth to his face, and his image remained on it. He then gave it to Veronica, saying, "This is like me, and will do great things." About this time the Emperor of Rome was ill of a dreadful disease. Some say the emperor was Vespasian, and others Tiberius; that he had worms in his head, or a wasp's nest in his nose. It was a fearful sight. Now he hears that a great physician performs wonderful cures in Judæa. So he sends his messengers to Jerusalem, and finds that Jesus, the physician, had been slain three years before. Then Pilate is filled with alarm, and accuses the Jews of the deed, while they, in turn, make him responsible for it. Then the messenger inquires for the followers of Jesus, and at last Veronica is brought to him. He then desires to see the portrait. At first she denies having it, but at length acknowledges that she treasures it with great care, and brings it to him. The messenger desires to take it to Rome, but she will not consent unless she goes also. They therefore depart, and arrive after a very short and prosperous voyage. When all is explained to him of the death of Jesus, the miracle of the picture, and its inherent virtue, the emperor regards it, believing, and is healed. Pilate, who has been brought to Rome, is then cast into prison; he kills himself and his body is thrown into

the Tiber, where demons attack it. Then the emperor determines
to avenge the death of Christ upon Jerusalem. He besieges the city,
and so many Jews are slain that they cannot be buried. Captives
are crucified ; the thieves who divided the garments of Jesus are cut
in quarters, and many are sold for thirty pence each. Now this
cloth, which is the subject of this legend, is the " Volto Santo," or
" God's image," and these words were used as an imprecation in the
Middle Ages. Vera Icon, another name for it, signifies " The Sacred
Picture," and is the same as the name of the saint ; and in fact, the
picture is sometimes called " a Veronica." It is well to compare this
legend with that of King Abgarus, as they probably came from the
same source, and are very likely different versions of one legend.
The later legend of St. Veronica does not make her the healed
woman, but merely a woman of Jerusalem whose house Christ passed
when bearing his cross. Seeing his sufferings, she pitied him, and gave
him her veil to wipe his brow. When he returned it to her, it was
impressed with the sacred image. This legend is recognized by the
Catholic Church. The house of St. Veronica is shown at Jerusalem on
the Via Dolorosa. This latter legend also takes Veronica to Rome,
but the emperor has died before her arrival, and she remains with St.
Peter and St. Paul, and at last suffers martyrdom under Nero. Still
another version makes her go to Europe with Lazarus and his sisters,
and suffer death in Provence or Aquitaine. The image is the Vera
Icon, or the true image, and the cloth is the Sudarium (*Ital.* Il
Sudario ; *Fr.* Le Saint Suaire). A chapel in St. Peter's at Rome is
dedicated to this saint ; and therein is the face of Christ impressed on
a linen cloth, the veritable Vera Icon. St. Veronica is unmistakable in
art, as she is represented holding the napkin. The festival of St. Veronica (*Fr.* La Sainte Face de Jesus Christ) is held on Shrove Tuesday.

St. Victor of Marseilles (*Ital.* San Vittore) was a soldier
under Diocletian, and suffered martyrdom in the tenth persecution.
He endured terrible tortures with wonderful strength and devotion. In the midst of them a miniature altar was brought him on
which to sacrifice to Jupiter and thus save himself, but he dashed
down the image and destroyed it. He was then crushed with a
millstone, and afterwards beheaded. When he died, angels were
heard to sing, " Vicisti, Victor beate, vicisti ! " He is represented
as a Roman soldier with a millstone near him. July 21, A. D. 303.

St. Victor of Milan (*Ital.* San Vittore) was another Roman soldier who suffered also in the tenth persecution. He was a native of Mauritania, but suffered at Milan, where there is a church dedicated to him. He is the favorite military saint of northern Italy. It is said that he was thrown into a heated oven, and an oven with flames bursting out is sometimes near him in pictures; but he is more frequently represented as the Victorious, sometimes on horseback, and always in the dress of a soldier. May 8, A. D. 303.

St. Vincent, Deacon and Martyr (*Lat.* S. Vincentius Levita; *Ital.* San Vincenzio Diacono, San Vincenzino; *Fr.* St. Vincent). The principal facts concerning this saint are so established by good authorities that they cannot be denied; but imagination has had great license in the legend, as it is illustrated by those who paint; whether it be with brush or pen, artist or poet. It is as follows: Vincent was born in Saragossa. At the time of the terrible persecution under Diocletian he was about twenty years old, and already a deacon. The proconsul Dacian caused all the Christians of Saragossa to be brought together, with a promise of immunity, and then ordered them all to be massacred. St. Vincent did all in his power to encourage and sustain the people of God, and at length was himself arrested and brought before the tribunal. With him was his bishop, Valerius. When they were accused, Valerius answered first; but he had an impediment in his speech, and was moreover old and feeble, so that his answers were almost unintelligible; then Vincent exclaimed, " How is this, my father? canst thou not speak aloud, and defy this pagan dog? Speak, that all the world may hear; or suffer me, who am only thy servant, to speak in thy stead!" When the bishop therefore gave him leave, he proclaimed his faith aloud, and defied all tortures and sufferings. Then was Dacian very wroth, and he commanded that the young man should be reserved to the tortures, but the old man sentenced only to banishment from the city. The most fearful tortures were invented for Vincent, to which he submitted with miraculous strength. Prudentius says, in his celebrated hymn to St. Lawrence, " When his body was lacerated by iron forks, he only smiled on his tormentors; the pangs they inflicted were to him delights; thorns were his roses, the flames a refreshing bath; death itself was but the entrance to life." After his terrible sufferings they laid him on the floor of his dungeon strewed with potsherds; but angels came and ministered to him, and when his jailers looked in they beheld the place filled with celestial light, and a sweet perfume came out from it; they heard the songs of angels, in which Vincent joined with thanksgiving; and he called to the jailers to come in and partake of his bliss. Then these fell on their knees and were converted. After this, Dacian, being convinced that tortures could not conquer his spirit, resolved to try the seductions of luxury. He had the saint placed on a bed strewn with roses; his friends were admitted, and everything was done to ease his pain. But no sooner came these seductions than he died, and angels bore his soul to glory. Then the furious Dacian ordered his body to be thrown to the wild beasts; but God sent a raven to guard it, and it remained untouched for many days. Then the consul commanded that it should be sewed up in an ox-hide, as was done to the bodies of parricides, and thrown into the sea. So it was thus prepared, and carried out in a boat, and thrown over with a millstone attached to it; but lo, when the boatmen reached the shore, it was returned before them, and lay upon the sands! Then they ran away terrified; and the waves hollowed out a grave and buried it. Here it remained for many years, until at last it was miraculously revealed to certain Christians of Valencia, and they removed these holy remains to their own city. When the Christians of Valencia fled from the Moors, they bore with them these blessed relics. The vessel in which they were was driven upon a promontory on the coast of Portugal, where they stopped, and interred the body; and that point has been called Cape St. Vincent from that day. Here, too, the ravens guarded the remains; and a portion of the cape is called in remembrance of them, "el Monte de las Cuervas." When in the year 1147 Alonzo I. removed the remains to Lisbon, two crows accompanied the vessel, one at the prow and one at the stern; these crows multiplied greatly in Lisbon, until rents were assigned to the chapter for their support. Vincent has been surnamed *the Invincible*, both on account of his character and the signification of his name. St. Vincent is represented as young and beautiful, in a deacon's dress, and his proper attribute is a crow or raven. Patron of Lisbon, Valencia, and Saragossa; of Milan; of Chalons, and many other places in France. January 22, A. D. 304.

St. Vincent Ferraris was born at Valencia in 1357. His parents denied themselves greatly in order to educate him and his brother Boniface. He was a Dominican, and took the habit when only eighteen. He became one of the most celebrated preachers and missionaries. He went all through Spain, Italy, and France, and by invitation of Henry IV. to England. He so moved the hearts of his hearers that he was often obliged to pause that the sobbing and weeping might subside. He did many miracles; and it is related that when he preached in Latin he was understood by all who heard him, of whatever nation, learned or unlearned. He spent the last two years of his life in Brittany and Normandy, and died at Vannes. Jeanne de France, Duchess of Brittany, washed his body and prepared it for the grave with her own hands. His proper attribute is the crucifix, which he holds aloft in reference to his labors as missionary. He sometimes has wings as symbols of his fervor, but with the Dominican habit they have a strange effect. April 5, A. D. 1419.

St. Vincent de Paul is loved and venerated not only in his native France and by Catholics everywhere, but also by the majority of non-Catholics. He was born in 1576, at Puy, in Gascony. His father was a farmer, and Vincent tended the flocks. But his temper was so sweet, and his mind so active, that his father desired an education for him; so he was sent to a convent of Cordeliers, Franciscan Fathers, at Acqs. After he was well advanced in his studies, he accepted the place of a tutor, that he might continue his studies without being burdensome to his poor parents. He finally attained to the priesthood in 1600. He went to Marseilles, on business, and when returning by sea, was seized by African pirates and carried into slavery. He remained thus two years, and had several masters. The wife of the last one pitied him, and when she spoke to him was charmed by his conversation. One day she asked him to sing, and he, bursting into tears, sang, "By the waters of Babylon we sat down and wept," and then the glorious "Salve Regina." This woman was converted, and in her turn instructed her husband, who also received the truth. Then they all escaped, and came to Aiguesmortes. Vincent placed his companions in a religious house, and went himself to Rome, whence he was sent by the pope to Paris. This was in 1609. He had been greatly moved at the sight of the sufferings of the galley slaves. He had been in captivity. He was not able to do much for them, but he preached to them and comforted them as much as possible. He then turned his attention to the Magdalenes of Paris, and founded the hospital of "La Madaleine." He also founded the Congregation of the Sisters of Charity, and established a foundling hospital. This is no place wherein to speak of all the good he thus did ; and indeed, who can tell it? He was a friend of Richelieu until his death. He was called to the side of Louis XIII. in his last moments. During the wars of the Fronde he ministered to the sufferers, and greatly desired to do something for the Catholics of Ireland, who were suffering cruel oppression. In short, he has been named by general consent, " L'Intendant de la Providence et Père des Pauvres." He died at St. Lazare. He is represented in the clerical cassock, with a new-born infant in his arms, and a Sister of Charity kneeling before him. July 19, A. D. 1660.

St. Vitalis of Ravenna was the father of St. Gervasius and St. Protasius. He was condemned to be buried alive for having taken up and cared for the body of a Christian martyr. He was a soldier in the army of Nero, and had been converted by the preaching of St. Peter. His wife, Valeria, fled with her two sons to Milan. The church dedicated to him, and erected over the spot where he was buried, is a remarkable monument of Byzantine architecture. The fame of this saint extended all over Europe. He is represented as a soldier with the martyr's crown, and sometimes on a white charger, with the standard of victory. April 28, about 62.

St. Vitus (*Ital.* San Vito ; *Fr.* St. Vite or St. Guy ; *Ger.* Der Heilige Veit, Vit, or Vitus) was the son of a noble Sicilian, who was a pagan ; but the nurse and foster-father of Vitus were secretly Christians, and they brought him up in the faith, and had him baptized. When only twelve years old, he declared himself a Christian, which so enraged his father and the governor that they attempted to compel him to retract. They shut him in a dungeon after beating him ; but when his father looked through the key-hole, he saw him dancing with seven beautiful angels, and so dazzling was the sight that the father was made blind, and was restored to sight only through the intercession of his son. After this, he once more persecuted Vitus, who fled with his nurse and her husband in a boat, which was steered by an angel, to Italy. But here they were again accused as Christians, and were thrown into a caldron of boiling oil. He is represented as a beautiful boy. He has many attributes: the palm; the caldron of oil; a lion, because he was once exposed to lions; a wolf, because his remains were guarded by one; and a cock, the reason of which is not known, but on account of which he is invoked against drowsiness. He is one of the fourteen Noth-helfers, or patron saints of Germany. He is patron saint of dancers and actors; and is invoked against the nervous disease, St. Vitus' dance. Patron of Saxony, Bohemia, and Sicily. June 15, A. D. 303.

St. Walburga, whose Anglo-Saxon name is the same as the Greek Eucharis, and signifies "gracious," is also called Walpurgis, Walbourg, Valpurge, Gualbourg, and Avangour. When her uncle, St. Boniface, and her brother, St. Willibald, determined to take a company of religious women from England to the continent to assist in teaching the pagans, Walburga left the convent of Winburn, where she had lived twenty-seven years, and went with ten other nuns to Mayence. She was afterwards made first abbess of the convent of Heidenheim. After the death of Willibald, on account of her learning and talents she was called to Eichstadt, and governed the two communities there, — the monks as well as the nuns. She wrote a history of her brother in Latin. She had studied medicine, and did some wonderful cures. After her death she was entombed in a rock near Eichstadt, from which exuded a wonderful oil. This was thought to proceed from the remains of the saint; and it was called Walpurgis oil, and many remarkable cures were effected through its use. The cave became a place of pilgrimage, and a church was built on the spot. On the night of her festival, Walpurgis' night, the witches were said to hold their orgies at Blocksberg. The saint's chief festival is on the 1st of May. She is represented in the Benedictine habit with a crosier, and a flask; the latter a symbol of the Walpurgis oil. May 1, about 778.

Wandering Jew, The. This legend is given in several different ways. According to Matthew Paris, an Armenian archbishop came to England to visit its shrines, and was entertained at the monastery of St. Albans. He was questioned in regard to his own country and his travels, and was asked if he had ever known anything of a miraculous person who was present at the crucifixion of

Christ, and who still lived. The archbishop testified that it was true that such a man lived, and that he knew him well. He said he had been the porter of Pontius Pilate, and was named Cartaphilus. When the Jews were dragging Jesus from the judgment hall, Cartaphilus struck him with his fist, saying, "Go faster, Jesus, go faster! why dost thou linger?" Then Jesus turned and said, "I indeed am going, but thou shalt tarry till I come." Afterwards the porter was converted, and baptized by the name of Joseph. At the end of every century he falls ill, and is incurable; at length he goes into an ecstasy, and when he comes out of it, he is the same age that he was when Christ died, which was about thirty years. He is a grave and holy man. He remembers all the circumstances of the crucifixion, the resurrection, and ascension; of the composing of the Apostles' Creed, and the separation of the Apostles when they went forth to preach.

Another legend gives his name as Ahasuerus, and relates that as Jesus was bearing his cross, he stopped before his door to rest, and Ahasuerus drove him away with curses. Then Jesus told him that he should wander until he came to judgment; and ever since he wanders, bowed down with grief and remorse, and unable to find a grave.

St. Wenceslaus of Bohemia. See St. Ludmilla.

St. Werburga figures among the early Benedictine saints in England. She was abbess of Repandum, and had jurisdiction over monks as well as nuns. She was the niece of St. Ethelreda, and was brought up with her at Ely. She founded several monasteries, and had the care of them, besides that of Repton, — Weedon, Trentham, and Hanbury. The cathedral of Chester was dedicated to her in 800, and a part of her shrine now supports a pew erected for the Anglican bishop of the diocese. About 708.

St. William of Aquitaine. See St. Benedict of Anian.

St. Zeno of Verona was bishop of that city in the fourth century, and was remarkable for the wisdom with which he governed his diocese during those troublous times. He is represented in one picture holding a long fishing-rod, and the legend of Verona says he was fond of fishing in the Adige; but it is quite probable that the fish which hangs from the line is symbolical of baptism. It is doubtful whether he was martyred, although he is said to have been, by Julian the Apostate. It is related that King Pepin desired to be buried in the same grave with St. Zeno, so great was his esteem for him.   April 12, A. D. 380.

St. Zenobio of Florence was the son of noble parents, Lucian and Sophia, but they were pagans.   He was born in the last year of the reign of Constantine.   He was converted while at school, and succeeded in converting his parents.   He lived in Rome, and was a deacon, and the secretary of Pope Damasus I.   He was sent to Florence in a time of great distraction, but both Catholics and Arians desired to have him for their bishop.   He restored to life a man who had fallen down a mountain precipice, when on the way to bring some sacred relics to him, sent by St. Ambrose.   A lady on her way to Rome stopped at Florence, to see this good man of whom she had heard much, and she left her son in his care until she should return. The day before her return the child died ; but when she took it and laid it at the feet of St. Zenobio, he restored it to life.   He led a most holy life, and died in the reign of Honorius.   When he was being borne to his grave, the people so pressed about his bier that in the Piazza del Duomo his body was thrown against the trunk of an elm that was withered.   It immediately put forth buds and leaves. He is represented in his episcopal robes ; his attribute is frequently a tree which is putting forth leaves.   May 25, A. D. 417.

INDEX.

AARON, 19.
Abbondio, St., 37.
Abdelraman, 152.
Abelard, 66.
Abgarus, King, 11, 37, 39, 316.
Abiathar, Priest, 167.
Abijah, 304.
Abishag, 19.
Abraham, 15, 16, 227, 232.
Academy of Painters, 223.
Achaia, 50.
Achilleus, St., 39.
Achmet, 241.
Acquapendente, 269, 297.
Acqs, 319.
Acre, 46.
"Acts of Paul and Thecla," 291.
Adam, 266.
Adam and Eve, 16.
Adam and the Tree of Mercy, 303.
Adam, Symbol of, 12.
Adelaide, St., 39, 40.
Adelbert, St., 189, 287.
Adoration of the Magi, 169, 196, 279.
Adoration of the Shepherds, 196.
Adrian, Castle of, 190.
Adrian, Emperor, 111.
Adrian, St., 7, 40, 41, 141.
Adriatic, the, 305.
Ægæ in Cilicia, 90.
Ægean Sea, 240.
Ægeus, 50.
Æmilia, 49.
Æsculapius, 90.
Ætna, Mt. 43.
Afra, St., of Augsburg, 41, 95, 110, 111.
Afra, St., of Brescia, 42.
Agabus, 168.
Aganum, 129, 230.
Agar, 15.

Agatha, St., 7, 42, 43, 44, 187.
Agen, in Aquitaine, 111.
Aglæ, Roman lady, 47.
Aglaë, St., 44.
Aglaides, 92.
Agnes of Austria, 183.
Agnes of Montepulciano, St., 45.
Agnes, St., 4, 44.
Agnus Dei, 21.
Agostino, Sant', Church of, 30, 31.
Agricolaus of Sebaste, 69.
Agrippa, 151, 281.
Agrippinus, 309.
Ahasuerus, 322.
Aidan, St., 91, 247.
Aiguesmortes, 319.
Aix, 219.
Aix-la-Chapelle, 65.
Aix-la-Chapelle, Council of, 61.
Albano, Cardinal of, 70.
Albano, Painter, 96.
Albanopolis, 60.
Alban, St., 46.
Alban's, St., in Hertfordshire, 46.
Albert, St., 28, 46.
Albertus Magnus, 47.
Albigenses, the, 96, 257.
Albizeschi. Family of, 67.
Alcala, 95, 298.
Aldrovanski, 145.
Alexander Severus, 222.
Alexander, Son of Felicitas, 112.
Alexander the Martyr, St., 40, 47.
Alexander VIII., 185.
Alexandria, Bishop of, 56.
Alexandria, City of, 51, 56, 58, 85, 93, 190, 217, 223, 238.
Alexandria, Clement of, 159.
Alexandria, St. Catherine of, 76.
Alexis, St., 47, 48.

Alfonso, St., 147.
Alfred the Great, 101, 132, 236, 248, 290.
Alice, mother of St. Benno, 66.
Alice of Germany, St., 39.
Allston, Washington, 284.
Almachius, Prefect, 78.
Alonzo I., 318.
Aloysius, St., 34, 185.
Alpaïde, 179.
Alphege, St., 48, 107.
Alphonso, Don, 151.
Alphonso, King of Leon, 113.
Alsace, Duke of, 248.
Alva, Duchess of, 290.
Alvare, 243.
Alveida, Plain of, 152.
Alverna, Mount, 120.
Alviano in Tuscany, 215.
Amalaberga, St., 137.
Amand of Belgium, St., 61.
Amboise, Castle of, 121.
Ambrogio Maggiore, Sant', Milan, 131.
Ambrose, St., 48, 49, 57, 71, 130, 236, 254, 323.
Amethyst, Symbolism of, 9.
Amiens, 179, 264.
Anachronisms, 34.
Anacletus, 66.
Ananias, Servant to King Abgarus, 37.
Anargyres, 90.
Anastasia, St., 49.
Anchor, Symbolism of, 8.
Andernach, 89.
Andrea del Sarto, 30, 164, 260.
Andrea of Corsini, 50.
Andrea Orcagna, 33.
Andrea Riccio, 32.
Andrew, St., 25, 50, 133.
Andrew, St , Cross of, 3, 50.
Angel of Judgment, 182.
Angelico da Fiesole, 33.
Angelico, Fra, 33, 55.
Angelo, Michael, 30.
Angelo, St., 242.
Angelo, St., Castle of, 243.
Angels, Symbols of, 14.
Angelus, St., 28, 51.
Anghiari, Battle of, 50.
Angiolo, Sant', Church of, 115.
Angles, the West, 109.
Anian, the, 65.
Anianus, or Annianus, St., 51, 217.
Anna, St., 51, 156, 191, 199.
Anne of Austria, 145.

Annunciation, the, 5, 6, 12, 124, 192, 274, 279, 283.
Annunziata, the, 260.
Ansano of Siena, St., 51.
Ansric, England, 58.
Antemius, 50.
Anthony of Padua, St., 27, 28, 32, 54.
Anthony, St., 30, 51.
Anthony, St., Cross of, 3.
Anthony, St., Order of, 60.
Antioch, 55, 59, 92, 146, 162, 205, 214, 292, 306.
Antonio-di-Padova, Church, 32.
Antonio, St., 54.
Antony, St., 133, 137.
Antwerp, 34, 245.
Anvil, Symbolism of, 7.
Aoust, Archdeacon of, 67.
Apocalypse, Woman of the, 210.
Apocalyptic Lamb, 4, 322.
Apollina, 49.
Apollinare in Classe, Sant', 271.
Apollinaris-in-Classe, Basilica of, 55.
Apollinaris of Ravenna, St., 55.
Apollo, 120.
Apollo, Temple of, 64.
Apollonia of Alexandria, St., 7, 55.
Apollonius, 138.
Apollonius, St., 111.
Apostles' Creed, the, 24.
Apostles, the Twelve, 4, 24, 31, 204.
Apparition of Christ to the Virgin, 208.
Appian Way, 255.
Apple, 19.
Apples, Symbols, 98.
Apulia, 141.
Aqua Salvias, 251.
Aquila, House of, 263.
Aquila in Abruzzi, 68.
Aquitaine, 111.
Aquitaine, Duke of, 65.
Ara Cœli, 190, 195, 222, 282.
Aragon, 180, 187.
Aragon, King of, 106, 226.
Arba, the River, 51.
Archangels, 15, 124.
Archangel Gabriel, 5.
Archangel Raphael, 299.
Archilochus, 49.
Ardennes, Forest of, 143.
Ardents, St. Geneviève des, 126.
Area di San Domenico, Bologna, 33.
Arezzo, 97, 142, 272.
Arezzo, Cathedral of, 98.

Argyropolis, 41.
Arians, the, 60, 125, 258, 268.
Aristodemus, 159.
Arius, 56.
Armenia, 60.
Armor, 16.
Arno, 302.
Arnold de Brescia, 66.
Aroas, 123.
Arphaxad, King, 173.
Arrow, Symbolism of, 7.
Arrows, 82.
Artemius, 256.
Artesius, Count, 130.
Arthur, King, 132.
Arthusia, 162.
Artists of Spain (Stirling), 273.
Artois, Robert of, 307.
Arviragus, King, 132.
Ascension, the, 22, 203, 274, 279.
Ash Color, 20.
Asmodeus, 299.
Asperges, or Rod, 54.
Ass, Symbol, 195.
Assisi, 54, 121.
Assisi, Church at, 32.
Assisi, Clara of, 85.
Assumption, the, 2, 8, 29, 204, 207, 274, 279.
Assyrians, 173.
Asterius, 110.
Asti, 279.
Athanasius, St. (Bishop), 53, 56.
Athens, 60, 85, 95, 136, 177.
Attila, King of the Huns, 125, 126.
Aubert, St., 233.
Audrey, St., 109.
Augsburg, City of, 41.
Augustine of Canterbury, St., 57.
Augustine Order, 87, 298.
Augustine, St., 1, 27, 30, 56, 63, 72, 96, 166, 235, 245, 250, 252, 254, 281, 290.
Augustines, the, 30, 33.
Augustus, Emperor, 281.
Aurelian, 39, 46, 264.
Aureole, Symbolism of the, 2.
Austria, 166, 264.
Autun, 89.
Avalon, Island of, 132.
Ave Maria, Gratia Plena, 125.
Ave Marias, 96, 193, 274.
Aventine, the (Rome), 44, 243, 263.
Avignon, St. Catherine at, 76.
Avila, 289.
Avila, St. John of, 171.

Avranches, 233.
Awl and Shoemaker's Knife, 91.
Axe, Symbolism of, 7.
Aza du Plessis, 149.

BABYLON, 288,
    Babylonians, the, 61.
Baccio della Porta, 33.
Bagnarea, Tuscany, 69.
Bajazet, Sultan, 307.
Balaam, 196, 232.
Balbina, St., 58.
Baldwin II., 186, 306, 307.
Bamberg in Germany, Monastery of, 29, 142.
Bamborough Castle, 247.
Bangor, 58.
Banner, Symbolism of, 7.
Barachiel the Helper, 15.
Barbara, St., 7, 36, 58.
Barbarossa, Emperor. 197.
Barberini, Cardinal, 222.
Barcelona, 110, 267.
Bardney, 248.
"Barefoot Carmelites," "Scalzi," and "Padri Teresiani," 290.
Bari, 241.
Barking, in Essex, 108.
Barmherzigen Brüder, 170.
Barnabas, St., 59.
Bartholomew, St., 25, 60, 137.
Bartolomeo, 244.
Bartolommeo, Fra, 33.
Basileo, San, Church of, 244.
Basilians, Order of, 60.
Basilica of San Paolo-fuori-le-mura, 29.
Basilica of Sant' Ambrogio Maggiore, 49.
Basilissa, 177.
Basil, St., Order of, 93.
Basil the Great, St., 60, 136, 231, 243.
Basket with Roses, 98.
Basle, 132.
Bassi, Paolo di, 116.
Bathsheba, 19.
Baths of Caracalla, 79.
Bavaria, 70, 248.
Bavon of Ghent, St., 29, 61, 184.
Beasts, the Four, 21.
Beato, Il, 55.
Beatrix de Cepeda, 289.
Bede, 143.
Bede the Venerable, St., 61, 306.
Beehive, Symbol, 67.

Bees, St., 143.
Bega, 143.
Beggars, 28.
Bel and the Dragon, 61.
Belcastro, 297.
Belem, Monastery of, 34, 155.
Belgium, 264.
Belgrade, Siege of, 162.
Bell, 54.
Bellerophon, 129.
Bell, Symbolism of, 7.
Bembo, Cardinal, 33.
Benedetto da Maiano, 32.
Benedict, Bennet Biscop, or St. Bennet of Wearmouth, 65.
Benedictine Habit, 58.
Benedictine Order, 57, 63, 64, 88, 231.
Benedictines, the, 28, 274.
Benedict of Anian, St., 29, 65.
Benedict, St., 28, 29, 63, 67, 94, 109, 115, 154, 164, 230, 261, 275.
Benevento, 153.
Benizi, St. Philip, 30.
Bennet Biscop, St., 65.
Bennett, St., 29.
Benno, St., 65.
Berengaria of Castile, 113.
Berengarius III., 39.
Berenger, Count, 51.
Berg, Duchy of, 289.
Bergamo, City of, 40.
Bernardino da Feltri, St., 68.
Bernardino of Siena, St., 32, 67.
Bernard of Clairvaux, St., 28, 66.
Bernard of Menthon, St., 67.
Bernardone, Pietro, 117.
Bernardo Ptolomei, St., 29, 67.
Bernard, St., 192.
Bernard, St., Monasteries of, 67.
Bertha of Beindeleben, 103.
Bertha, Queen of England, 57.
Berthaire, King, 264.
Berytus or Beyrout, 127.
Bethany, Mary of, 224.
Bethesda, the Pool of, 304.
Bethlehem, 24, 138, 155, 156, 168, 196, 251.
Bethsaida, 258.
Bethulia, 173.
Betrayal of Christ, 279.
Bibiana, St., 68.
Birds, 19.
Bithynia, 40, 50.
Black Sea, 281.
Black, Symbolism of, 9, 29, 30.

Blaise of Sebaste, St., 68.
Blanche of Castile, 148, 186.
Blocksberg, 321.
Blood of Christ, the, 307.
Blue Mantle, 9.
Blue, Symbolism of, 9.
Blue Tunic, 9.
Boatmen, Patron of, 178.
Bodleian Library, Oxford, 73.
Bogaris, King of Bulgaria, 93.
Bohemia, 116, 166, 189, 263.
Boleslaus, 189.
Bologna, 33, 51, 54, 76, 97, 107, 115, 145, 258, 263.
Bolsena, Cathedral of, 81.
Bolsena, Lake, 81.
Bonaventura, St., 28, 32, 69.
Boniface, St., 27, 29, 70, 71, 111, 184, 276, 319, 321.
Boniface (St. Aglaë), 44.
Bons-hommes, Les, 122.
Book, 59, 67, 75, 94, 97.
Book of Decrees, the, 55.
Book, Symbolism of, 7, 16, 20, 27.
Book, the Sealed, 21.
Borghese, Scipio, Cardinal, 50.
Borgia, Francis, 286.
Borgognone, 30.
Brabant, 127, 259.
Brabant, Duke of, 61.
Brancacci Chapel, 33.
Brandeum, Miracle of, 134.
Brera, Milan, 93.
Brescia, City of, 42, 111, 176.
Brice, St., 71, 184.
Bride of Christ, the, 6, 209.
Bridget of Ireland, St., 71.
Bridget of Sweden, St., 27, 30, 71.
Brigittines, or Brigitta, Order of, 30, 71.
Brignolles, 187.
Britain, 57.
Brown, Dark, 31.
Brun, Le, 187.
Bruno, St., 29, 30, 72, **144.**
Brussels, 137.
Bufalmacco, 308.
Builder's Rule, 25.
Bull, Symbol, 90.
Burgos, Cathedral of, 113.
Bury St. Edmunds, 101.
Butler, Rev. Allan, 243, 307.
Butler's, Allan, "Lives of the Saints," 93.
Byzantium, 41.

CADWALLADER, 247.
Cædmon the Poet, 72.
Caernarvonshire, 220.
Cæsar Augustus, 194.
Cæsarea in Cappadocia, 60, 98, 184, 294.
Cain, 179.
Cairo, 200.
Caius, Pope, 287.
Calabria, 72, 105, 121.
Caldron, Symbolism of, 7.
Calista, 98.
Calocerus the Martyr, 42.
Calvary, Procession to, 274.
Calvinists, the, 70.
Camaldolesi, the, 28-30, 272.
Campo-Maldoli, 272.
Campo Santa, Pisa, 108, 179, 190, 266.
Cana of Galilee, 227.
Candace, Queen, 259.
Candelabrum, Symbolism of, 8.
Candlestick of Moses, the, 13.
Canterbury, 57.
Canterbury, Archbishop of, 48, 99.
Canterbury Cathedral, 48.
Capistrano, St. John, 162.
Capitoline Hill, 222.
Cappadocia, 50, 127, 133, 268.
Capua, 243.
Capuccini, the, 113.
Capuchins, the, 31, 113.
Caracalla, Baths of, in Rome, 39, 79.
Caracci, Annibale, 96.
Cardinal's Hat, 28.
Carducho, 30.
Caritad, Church of, Seville, 106.
Caritad, the, 170, 172.
Carlos, Don, 95.
Carlstein, 160.
Carmelite, Barefooted, 172.
Carmelite (St. Angelus), the, 51.
Carmelites, the, 33, 46, 204.
Carmel, Mt., 33, 168, 204.
Carmel, Mt., Order of, 290.
Carmine, Church of, 33.
Carpophorus, St., 264.
Carsagamala, 286.
Cartaphilus, 322.
Carthage, 92, 235, 252.
Carthage, Bishop of, 57.
Carthusians, the, 29, 30, 72.
Casimir, St., 28, 73.
Caspar, 197.
Cassian, St., 73.
Cassino, Monte, 244.

Castello, 185.
Castiglione, Marchese di, 185.
Castile, 148, 170.
Castile and Leon, 113.
Castle of St. Angelo, 232.
Catalonia, 267.
Catalonia, Governor of, 123.
Catania, 42, 187.
Caterina de Vigri, St., 76.
Cathari, the, 256.
Catherine, St., 6, 7, 35, 36, 97.
Catherine of Alexandria, St., 73, 76.
Catherine of Bologna, St., 76.
Catherine of Siena, St., 27, 28, 32, 46, 76.
Catherine of Sweden, St., 77.
Cato, 89.
Cecilia, St., 6, 7, 9, 36, 77.
Cecilia-in-Trastevere, Church of, 78.
Cedar of Lebanon, 21.
Cedd (St. Chad), 79.
Cedon, 225.
Celestine, Pope, 250.
Celsus, St., 78, 130.
Cemetery of Calixtus, Rome, 78.
Centa, 171.
Cerfroy, 165.
Certosa at Rome, 30.
Certosa di Pavia, 30.
Cesarea, 268.
Cesarea, St., 136.
Cesareo, or Cæsarius, St., 79.
Cesena, 269.
Ceslas, 145.
Chad of Lichfield, St., 79.
Chains, 58.
Chalcedon, 163.
Chalcedonia, 110.
Chalcis, 154.
Chalice, Symbolism of, 7.
Chalice, with the Serpent, 25.
Chalons, 318.
Chamuel, the Archangel, 15, 16.
Chant, the Gregorian, 133.
Chantal, la Mère, 79.
Charity, Brothers of, 170.
Charlemagne, 65, 80, 179, 184.
Charles Borromeo, St., 80, 260.
Charles of Provence, 226.
Charles V., 155, 298.
Charles VIII., 121.
Chartres, 81.
Chartres, Cathedral of, 13.
Chartreuse, 144.
Chartreuse, La Grande, 72.

Chartreux, Monastery at, 72.
Cheron, St., 81.
Cherub, the, 22.
Cherubim, the, 14, 16.
Chester, 58, 322.
Childeric, 126.
Childibert II., 233.
Children, 28.
China, 123.
Chlodomir, King, 283.
Chosroes, 3, 305.
Christ and Abgarus, 37.
Christ crowned with Thorns, 274.
Christ in the Temple, 274.
Christ lost by his Mother, 279.
Christ, the Infant, 27.
Christ with the Doctors, 279.
Christeta, 98.
Christina, St., 7, 81.
Christopher, St., 36, 82.
Chrysanthus, St., 85.
Chrysogonus, St., 49, 50, 85.
Chrysostom, St. John, 162, 178.
Church of Santa Croce, Florence, 68.
Church, Symbolism of, 7, 11.
Cilicia, 60, 178.
Cimabue, 33, 164.
Cinque Martiri, 264.
Circus Maximus, 49.
Circus of Caligula, 255.
Cistercians, the, 29, 30.
Citeaux, Monastery of, 66.
Citta Ducale, Umbria, 113.
City of David, the, 20.
Clairvaux, Abbey of, 66.
Clara of Monte Falco, St., 87.
Clara, St., 28, 32, 85, 118, 120.
Claudius, 254.
Clavijo, 152.
Clement of Alexandria, 159.
Clement, Pope, 95.
Clement IV., Pope. 297.
Clement X., Pope, 273.
Clement, St., 8, 87, 146.
Clemente, San, Church of, 87, 146.
Clemente, San, Convent of, Seville, 114.
Cleodolinda, 127, 128.
Cleophas, 153.
Cloaca Maxima, 278.
Closed Gate, the, 20.
Clotaire II., King, 107.
Clothaire V., of France, 264.
Clotilda, St., 81, 88, 126, 283.
Cloud, St., 88.

Clovis, King of France, 88, 271, 283.
Club, 25.
Club. Symbolism of, 7.
Cluniacs, the, 29.
Coals in Hand, Symbol, 71.
Cock, Symbolism of, 8.
Cœlian Hill (Rome), 47, 133, 166, 180, 264, 279.
Cœli-Syria, 138.
Coifi, 252.
Coliseum, 264.
Colle d'Inferno, 120.
Coln, the River, 46.
Cologne, 72, 91, 99, 111, 129, 142, 230, 244, 311.
Cologne, Cathedral of, 31.
Cologne, Kings of, 197.
Colors, Symbolism of, 8.
Columelle, 283.
Columna, Cardinal, 307.
Commodus, 109.
Communion of Mary, 204.
Como, Cathedral of, 37.
Company of Jesus, the, 147.
Compostella, 72, 151, 153, 170.
Comtes-de-Saint-Gilles, 131.
Concordia, 143.
Congregation of Sisters of Charity, 320.
Connaught, 250.
Conon, Prince, or Ethereus, 309, 312.
Conrad, Confessor of St. Elizabeth, 106.
Constance, 132, 270.
Constantia, 45, 134, 166.
Constantine, Cross of, 4.
Constantine, Emperor, 45, 73, 88, 138, 176, 220, 239, 279, 304, 306, 323.
Constantine Porphyrogenitus, Emperor, 38.
Constantinople, 38, 41, 51, 59, 60, 93, 103, 125, 136, 162, 163, 176, 186, 197, 237, 238, 249, 287, 305.
Constantius, 176.
Constantius Chlorus, 138.
Conti, Sigismund, 212.
Conventuals, the, 31.
Cope, the, 58.
Copenhagen, 153.
Cord, Knotted, Symbol, 31.
Cordeliers, the, 118.
Cordova, 113, 242.
Corfe Castle, 101.
Corn, Ears of, Symbolism of, 8.
Cornelius, St., 35.
Cornwall, 236.
Coronati, the, 264.

Coronation of the Virgin, 13, 207, 208, 209.
Coronation, the, 274, 279.
Correggio, 35.
Corsica, 176.
Cortes, the, 291.
Cortona, 55, 215.
Cosmo, St., 36, 90.
Costanzo, St., 91.
Costis, 73.
Coucy, 245.
Councillors of God, 14.
Coventry, 132.
Craco, 145.
Crediton, Devonshire, 70.
Creed of St. Athanasius, 56.
Creed, the Apostles', 24.
Creed, the Nicene, 14.
Cremona, 30, 34, 215, 245, 283.
Cremona, Cathedral of, 46.
Crescentius, 243, 244.
Crescent, Symbolism of, 11.
Crispianus, St., 91.
Crispin, St., 91.
Croatia, 264.
Croce, Santa, Church of, 68.
Cromwell, 250.
Crosier, 25, 67.
Cross, St. Andrew's, 25, 50.
Cross, Symbolism of the, 3, 8.
Cross, the Greek, 21.
Cross, the True, 3, 138.
Crown, 75, 82.
Crown of Roses, Symbol, 78.
Crown, Symbolism of, 6, 27.
Crown of Thorns, Symbolism of, 8, 27.
Crown of Thorns, the, 307.
Croyland Abbey, 137.
Crucifix, the, 27.
Crucifixion, the, 202, 274, 279, 283.
Crucifixion, Symbols of the, 8, 10, 12.
Crutch, 54.
Ctesiphon, 176.
Cuevas, Santa Maria de las, 72.
Cumæ, 281.
Cunegunda, St., 91, 141.
Cunibert, St., 91, 314.
Cup, the, 16.
Cuthbert of Durham, St., 91, 111, 247.
Cybele, 293.
Cypress, the, 20.
Cyprian, St., 35, 92.
Cyprus, 59.
Cyriaca, 180.

Cyriacus, 312.
Cyril, St., 93, 254.
Cyrus, King of Babylon, 61.

DACIAN, 111, 128.
Dagnus, King of Lycia, 84.
Dagobert, King, 91, 95, 107.
Dale Abbey, 94.
Dalmatia, 275.
Damascus, 176.
Damasus I., Pope, 323.
Damian, St., 36, 90, 94.
Damiano, San, Convent of, 86.
Damiano, San Perugia, 117.
Damietta, 119.
Danegelt, 102.
Daniel, 19, 21, 61, 124, 232.
Daniel, the Book of, 288.
Daria, 308.
Daria, St., 85, 94.
David, 13, 19, 303.
David, Race of, 156, 167.
Dead Nuns, Legend of, 94.
Dead Sea, 158, 254.
Death of Joseph, the, 201.
Death of the Virgin, 204.
"De Bono Mortis," the, 71.
Decius, Emperor, 42, 234, 268, 279, 280.
Decius, Persecution of, 111, 279.
Delphi, 281.
Delphine, St., 94, 102.
Demon, the, 67.
Denis, St., 36, 81, 91, 94, 100, 132, 143, 136, 229.
Deposition, the, 202, 279.
Descent from the Cross, the, 202.
Descent of the Holy Ghost, 203, 274.
Diana, 292.
Diana at Ephesus, 159.
Diana, Temple of, 263.
Dice, Symbolism of, 8.
Didron, 2, 3.
Didymus, 293.
Diego d' Alcala, St., 95.
Dies Iræ, 280.
Digna, 41.
Digna, St., 95.
Dijon, 66.
Diocletian, 90, 92, 108, 109, 114, 127, 128, 145, 182, 187, 236, 248, 256, 264, 276, 287, 317.
Diocletian, Persecution of, 46, 49, 51.
Dion Chrysostomus, 254.

Dionysius, 279.
Dionysius, King of Portugal, 106.
Dionysius the Areopagite, 14, 94, 207.
Dioscorus, 58.
Dispute in the Temple, the, 201.
Dniester, the, 145.
Dog, Symbol, 97, 216.
Dolphin, Symbolism of, 2.
Domatilla, Flavia, 39.
Domenichino, 29, 156, 244.
Domenico, San, 190.
Dominations, the, 15.
Domine quo vadis? 255.
Dominican Nuns, Order of, 97.
Dominican Order, 45, 77, 267.
Dominicans, the, 31-33, 55, 145.
Dominick, St., 32, 96, 145, 256, 274.
Dominick, St., Convent, Siena, 76.
Dominick, St., Order of, 273.
Domitian, Emperor, 39, 87, 159, 162, 229.
Domitilla, 87.
Donatello, 32, 227.
Donato of Arezzo, St., 97.
Donato, St., 36, 142.
Dorat, Cross of, 4.
Dorothea, St., 5, 28, 98.
Dottore Serafico, Il, 32, 69.
Dove, 61, 91, 107, 109, 134, 167.
Dove, Symbolism of, 5, 12, 24, 28.
Down, 250.
Dragon, Symbolism of, 4, 13, 28.
Drahomira, 189.
Drusiana, 160.
Dublin, 250.
Duns Scotus, 90.
Dunstan, St., 29, 98, 100, 101.
Durandus, 33.
Durer, Albert, 127.
Durham, Bishop of, 20.
Durham, Cathedral of, 92.
Dusseldorf, 290.

EAGLE, the, 22, 25, 161.
Ear of Malchus, Symbolism of, 8.
Earth, Symbolism of, 11.
Ebba of Coldingham, St., 99.
Ebb's Head, St., 109.
Ebro, the, 150.
Ecbatane, 173, 299.
Ecce Agnus Dei, 4, 158.
Ecclesiastical History, St. Bede, 61.
Edessa, 37, 38, 47.
Edgar, King, 99-101.

Edinburgh, 131.
Edith of Polesworth, 100, 235.
Edith of Wilton, St., 100.
Edmund, King, 99, 100.
Edna of Ecbatane, 301.
Edward, King and Confessor, St., 101, 114, 160.
Edwin, King, 99, 142, 252.
Egbert, King, 235.
Egfrid, King, 109.
Egidio, St., 246.
Egregius Doctor Hispaniæ, 149.
Egypt, 168, 186, 190, 217, 229.
Egyptian Cross, 3.
Eichstadt, 29, 321.
Eisenach, 103.
Eleazar de Sabran, St., 94, 102.
Elenora of Spain, 114.
Eleutherius, 95.
Elfleda, 248.
Elfrida, 101.
Elgiva, 99.
Elijah, the Prophet, 33, 204.
Elisabeth, St, 102.
Elizabeth, 158, 194, 201, 250.
Elizabeth of Austria, 73.
Elizabeth of Hungary, St., 6, 28, 32, 103.
Elizabeth of Portugal, St., 106.
Elizabeth, Queen, 106.
Elmo, St., 108.
Eloy of Noyon, St., 107, 127.
Elphege, St., 107.
Ely, 322.
Ely, Cathedral of, 109.
Emeric, St., 287.
Enclosed Garden, the, 20.
England, 181, 182.
Enns, the River, 116.
Entombment, the, 202.
Enurchus, or Evurtius, St., 107.
Ephesus, 159, 204, 205, 279.
Ephesus, St., 108.
Ephrem of Edessa, St., 108.
Epiphany, the, 196.
Erasmus of Formia, St., 108.
Ercolano, St., 108.
Eremitani, the, Padua, 31.
Erhard, 248.
Erythræa, 281.
Escurial, the, 34, 155, 181.
Esdras, 15.
Espinosa, 185.
Esquiline, the, 217, 262.
Esther, 19.

Ethelberga, St., 108.
Ethelbert, King of England, 57.
Ethelfrid, 58.
Ethelred, 101.
Ethelreda, St., 109, 322.
Ethelwald, St., 100.
Ethiopia, 229.
Eucharist, the Holy, 8, 161, 180.
Eudoxia, Empress, 163, 255.
Eugenia, St., 109.
Eulalia, St., 109, 182.
Eunomia, 41, 110.
Euphemia, St., 110.
Euphemian, 47, 48.
Euphrosina, 97.
Eusebius, 37, 111, 154.
Eustace, St., 5, 110.
Eustochium, St., 252.
Eutropia, St. 41, 111.
Eutychia, 187.
Evangelists, the, 16, 23, 31, 157.
Evangelists, Symbols of, 12.
Eve, 16, 19.
Eve, Second, 210.
Ewald the Black, and Ewald the Fair, Sts., 111.
Ezekiel, 14, 19, 21.

FABER, Frederic Wilfrid, 260.
    Fabian, St., 111.
Fabricius, 98.
Face in the Clouds, Symbolism of, 10.
Faith, St., 111.
Falcon, 61.
Farnese, Cardinal, 244.
Father of Orthodoxy, 56.
Fathers of the Church, the Latin, 48, 66, 281.
Faucon, 165.
Faustinus, St., 42, 111.
Felice, San, 218.
Felicitas, St., 112.
Felix de Cantalicio, St., 32, 113.
Felix de Valois, St., 112, 165.
Felix, or Felice, St., 113.
Felix, Son of Felicitas, 112.
Felix, St., 230, 236.
Ferdinand of Castile, St., 113, 149.
Ferdinand, Prince, 96.
Ferdinand, St., 149.
Ferdinand the Catholic, 146.
Fermo, 242.
Ferrara, 59, 96, 229.

Ferrymen, Patron of, 178.
Fescennius, 95.
Festival of St. Blaise in Yorkshire, 69.
Festival of the Rosary, 275.
Fidanga, Giovanni, 69.
Fiesole, 50, 55, 272.
Fiesole, Angelico da, 33.
Filippino Lippi, 33.
Filomena, St., 114.
Fina of Gemignano, St., 115.
Fire, Protector against, 54.
Fire, Symbolism of, 6.
Fish, Symbolism of the, 2, 14, 25, 28.
Fish with Key in its Mouth, 66.
Fitzurze, Reginald, 296.
Five Wounds, Symbolism of, 8.
Flagellation, the, 274.
Flames of Fire, 54.
Flames, Symbolism of, 6.
Flaming Heart, Symbolism of, 6, 27.
Flaming Sword, 16.
Flanders, 131.
Flavia Domitella, 39.
Flavia, St., 29, 115, 261.
Flavian, 162.
Flavius Claudius, 176.
Fleur-de-Lys, 187.
Fleur-de-Lys, Symbol, 88.
Fleur de Marie, 193.
Flight into Egypt, 168, 199, 279.
Florence, 31, 33, 50, 55, 68, 70, 91, 107, 158, 163, 164, 208, 227, 234, 235, 259, 261, 268.
Florence, Archbishop of, 55.
Florentius, 64, 231.
Florian, St., 115.
Flowers, Symbolism of, 6, 20.
Foligno, 91.
Fontaine, 66.
Fonte-Branda, Siena, 76.
Fontevrauld, France, 29.
Forli, 231.
Formia, 108.
Forum, the, 222.
Fossa-Nova, 298.
Fossa-Nova, Cardinal di, 97.
Fountain, the, 20.
Fountain of Mary, 200.
Fra Angelico, 33.
Fra Bartolommeo, 33, 257.
Fra Farina, 80.
Francesca Romana, St., 116, 255.
Francis I., 122.
Francis, St., 27, 28, 31, 32, 54, 55, 68, 69, 86, 97, 216.

Francis, St., Order of, 102, 187, 273.
Francis Borgia, St , 123.
Francis de Paula, St., 121.
Francis de Sales, St., 27, 79, 122.
Francis of Assisi, St., 117, 121.
Francis Xavier, St., 34, 122.
Franciscans, Founder of, 117.
Franciscans, Order of, 31, 32, 54, 186.
Francisco da Lucia, 115.
Francisco, San, Church of, at Aquila, 68.
Francisco, San, Church of, at Pisa, 115.
Frascati, 244.
Frati Minori, 119.
Frederick II., Emperor, 105.
Frediano of Lucca, St., 124.
"Fridolin," Schiller's, 107.
Freiberg, 242.
Frères de l'Observance, 68.
Friesland, 70, 111, 289.
Frondisia, 42, 43.
Fruit of the Spirit, 6.
Fruit, Symbolism of, 6, 20.
Fulda, 71, 184.

GABAEL, 300.
    Gabriel, St., the Archangel, 5, 15, 16, 124, 169, 193, 236.
Gaddi, Taddeo, 29, 32, 33.
Gaeta, 244.
Gaius, 42.
Galerius Maximian, Emperor, 40, 115, 249.
Galgano, Monte, 232, 244.
Galilee, 150.
Galilee, Cana in, 201.
Galla Placida, Empress, 161.
Gamaliel, 286.
Garcilasso de la Vega, 123.
Garden of Eden, 16.
Garter, Order of the, 129.
Gaudentius of Novara, St., 125.
Gaudenzio, St., 125.
Gaul, 154, 230.
Gemignano, San, 115.
Geminianus, St., 125.
Geneva, 67.
Geneva, Bishop of, 122.
Geneva, Lake, 230.
Geneviève, St., 95, 125.
Geneviève of Brabant, 127.
Genoa, City of, 38, 40, 78, 181, 182.
George of Cappadocia, St., 127.
George, St., 4, 35, 36, 40, 141, 218, 293.
Gereon, St., 129.

Germain, St., 125, 131.
Gertrude of Nivelle, St., 137.
Gervais, St., Church of, 115.
Gervasius, St., 78, 130, 236, 320.
Gervii, Prince of the, 109.
Gesu, Church of, Rome, 124.
Gethsemane, Garden of, 274.
Geysa, Duke, 287.
Ghent, 61, 184.
Ghirlandajo, 30.
Ghost, the Holy, 5, 12.
Gibbon, 279.
Gibraltar, 171.
Gideon, 10, 232.
Gilbert à Becket, 295.
Giles, St., 5, 29, 131, 263.
Giorgio-in-Alga, San, 185.
Giorgio Maggiore, San, 218.
Giorgio, San, Convent of, 86.
Giottino, 32.
Giotto, 32, 119.
Giovanni, Fra, 55.
Giovanni in Olio, San, 159.
Giovanni Patricio, 216.
Giovita, St., 42.
Giralda, the, 178.
Giulia, St., 143.
Giulio Campi, 284.
Giustina, San, Church at Padua, 29.
Glanfeuil, 231.
Glastonbury, 98, 99, 236.
Glastonbury, Abbey of, 131.
Globe, the, 10.
Gloria in Excelsis, 195, 246, 266.
Gloria Patri, 274.
Glory, Symbolism of the, 2.
Gloucestershire, 248.
Goa, 123, 294.
Godfrey of Bouillon, 132.
Godfrey of Boulogne, 129.
God the Father, Symbols of, 9.
God the Son, Symbols of, 11.
Gold Color, Symbolism of, 9.
Golden Fleece, Order of, 50.
Golden Gate, the, 157.
Gondoforus, 294.
Gondobald, 283.
Goose, Symbol, 222.
Gordian, 133.
Gorgonia, St , 136.
Gospel, the, 58.
Goths, the, 140.
Gourd, the, 16.
Governors, the, 15.

Gracchi, the, 155, 251.
Grado, 185.
Grammont in Flanders, 41.
Granada, 171.
Grapes, Bunches of, Symbolism of, 8.
Grata, St., 40, 133.
Gray, 29, 31.
Gray, Symbolism of, 9.
Great Litanies, 232.
Great Martyr, 129.
Greece, 50.
Greek Cross, 3, 4, 21.
·Green, Symbolism of, 9.
Greenwich, 43.
Gregorian Chant, 133.
Gregorio, San, Church of, 133.
Gregory IX., Pope, 267.
Gregory XI., Pope, 77.
Gregory XIII., Pope, 274.
Gregory, St., 57, 61, 115, 133, 190, 232, 278.
Gregory of Nazianzen, St., 60, 136.
Gregory of Tours, St., 306.
Grenoble, 72.
Grève, Place de, 127.
Grisogono, St., 49.
Grotta Ferrata, 244.
Grotta Ferrata, Convent, 29.
Gualberto, St. John, 163.
Guastala, 50.
Gudula, St., 137.
Guelphs and Ghibellines, 68.
Guido, 261.
Guido da Siena, 33.
Guthlac of Croyland, St., 137.
Guyenne, Duke of, 220.
Guzman, House of, 96.

HABAKKUK, Prophet, 63, 205, 232.
     Habits of various Orders, 32.
Hades, 158.
Hadrian, 232, 275, 305.
Haerlem, 61.
Hagar, 232.
Halberd, the, 25.
Hammer, Symbolism of, 8.
Hanbury, 322.
Hand, Symbolism of, 9.
Hanover, 40.
Haroun al Raschid, 241.
Hart, Symbolism of, 5.
Heart, Flaming, 27.
Heart, Symbolism of, 6, 8.

Hebron, Valley of, 303.
Heidenheim, 321.
Heifer, Sacrifice of, Symbolism of, 12.
Helena, 254.
Helena, Empress St., 89, 137, 197, 220, 304.
Helen of Troy, 255.
Heliodorus, 138.
Heliogabalus, 251.
Heliopolis, 58, 94, 199.
Hellespont, the, 281.
Henry II. of England, 295.
Henry II., St., of Bavaria, 41, 141, 181, 287.
Henry IV., Emperor, 65.
Henry IV., of England, 244, 319.
Henry VIII., 250.
Heraclius, Emperor, 305.
Herefordshire, 58.
Herman-Joseph, St., 142.
Herman of Thuringia, 103.
Hermengildus, St., 142, 149.
Hermione, St., 258.
Hermits of St. Francis, 121.
Hermogenes, 150.
Hermolaus, 249.
Herod, 150, 158, 196, 199.
Herrera, 142.
"Hidden Gem, The," by Cardinal Wiseman, 48.
Hierapolis, City of, 38, 258.
Hierotheus, 207.
Hilaria, St., 41.
Hilarion, St., 97, 142.
Hilary, St., 142.
Hilda of Whitby, St., 72, 142.
Hildegarde, Empress, 184.
Hind, Symbolism of, 5, 28.
Hippo, Bishop of, 57.
Hippo, St. Augustine of, 30.
Hippolytus, St., 143, 181.
Hircanus, 139.
Hog, Symbolism of, 54.
Hohenburg, 248.
Holofernes, 143, 173.
Holy Cave, 226.
Holy Family, 200.
Holy Ghost, Symbols of, 12, 13.
Holy Island, 92.
Honoria, Princess, 125.
Honorius, Emperor, 47, 48.
Honorius, Pope, 120.
Honorius III., Pope, 256.
Hospitallers, Order of, 170.
Howard, Cardinal, 33.
Hubert, St., 5, 143, 178.

Huesca, 180.
Hugh Capet, 243.
Hugh, Bishop of Lincoln, St., 144.
Hugh of Grenoble, St., 144.
Hugh, St. Martyr, 144.
Hugo, 163.
Hugo, Bishop of Grenoble, 72.
Humbert, Bishop, 101.
Hungarians, the, 162.
Hyacinth, St., 145.
Hydrophobia, 144.
Hypatia, 93.

IAGO, St.. or St. James, 113.
Iconium, 201.
Ignatius Loyola, St., 34, 122, 124, 146.
Ignatius of Antioch, St., 87, 146.
I. H. S., 27.
Ildefonso, St., 29, 147, 182.
Illyria, 49.
Immaculate Conception, Doctrine of, 99.
Immaculate Conception, Our Lady of, 209.
Imola, Patron of, 73, 229.
Ina, King, 109.
Incarnation, the, 19, 22, 283.
Incoronata, the, 208, 209.
Infant Christ, the, 27.
Innocent I., Pope, 47, 48.
Innocent II., Pope, 66.
Innocent III., Pope, 119, 280.
Innocent IV., Pope, 86.
Innocent VIII., Pope, 307.
Innocents, Massacre of the, 148.
Intarsiatura, 30.
Invention of the True Cross, 138.
Iphigenia, 229.
Irenæus, 254.
Irene, 277.
Iria Flavia, 151.
Isaac, 16, 232.
Isabel de Paz, 106.
Isabella, Empress, 123.
Isabella of France, St., 148.
Isaiah, 19, 21, 192, 198, 283.
Isaiah, Raphael's Picture of, 31.
Isidore, St., Bishop of Seville, 142, 149, 159.
Isidore of Pelusium, 254.
Isidore the Ploughman, St., 148.
Islam, 124.
Italian Trinity, the, 14.
Ives of Bretagne, St., 149.
Ivo, 145.

JACOB, 16, 196.
Jacobins, the, 97.
Jacques, Rue St., Paris, 97.
Jago, St., Order of, 151.
James Major, St., 24.
James Minor, St., 25, 153.
James of Aragon, King, 257, 267.
James the Great, St., 149, 159.
Jameson, Mrs., 23, 204.
Januarius, St., 36, 153.
Januarius, Son of Felicitas, 112.
Japan, 122.
Jarrow, 61, 65.
Jean de France, 319.
Jehudiel, the Angel, 15.
Jehoshaphat, Valley of, 206.
Jeremiah, 21.
Jericho, 232.
Jerome, St., 4, 7, 13, 21, 28, 34, 35, 50, 63,
    154, 168, 219, 223, 251, 281, 290.
Jeronymites, the, 34, 155.
Jerusalem, 50, 138, 147, 153, 196, 204, 206,
    208, 223, 226, 254, 265, 287, 303, 306, 316.
Jerusalem, Symbol of, 12, 24.
Jesuit Order, 123, 146.
Jesuits, the, 34.
Jew, the Wandering, 156.
Jews, 124.
Joachim, St., 156, 191.
Joacim, 288.
Joan, Countess of Ponthieu, 113.
Joan of Bavaria, 166.
Joanna II. of Sicily, 77.
John, 279.
John XVI., 243.
John, Abbot of San Martino, 65.
John, St., 25, 201, 205, 209, 291.
John, St., and St. Paul, 166.
John, St., Gospel of, 61.
John conducting the Virgin to his Home,
    202.
John de Matha, St., 112, 165, 257.
John of Avila, 171.
John the Baptist, St., 4, 16, 22, 64, 102,
    157.
John the Evangelist, St.. 7, 9, 12, 13, 22,
    25, 135, 146, 158, 201, 202, 204, 227.
John Capistrano, St., 162.
John Chrysostom, St., 162.
John Gualberto, St., 28, 163.
John Nepomuck, St., 165.
Jophiel, the Angel, 16.
Joppa, 151.
Jordan, the, 158, 223.

Joseph, St., 6, 9, 12, 30, 36, 167, 192, 194, 196, 201, 290.
Joseph of Arimathea, 132, 202.
Joshua, 232.
Jovita, St., 111, 170.
Joys, Seven, of the Virgin, 13.
Juan de Dios, St., 170.
Juan de la Cruz, St., 172.
Juan de Vargas, 148.
Judæa, 159, 169.
Judah, Tribe of, 167.
Judas, 180, 229.
Judas, Dress of, 9.
Judas Iscariot, 172.
Judas Syriacus, or Omriacus and the True Cross, 304.
Jude, St., 173, 196, 284.
Judith, 19, 156.
Judith and Holofernes, 173.
Julia, St., 176.
Julian, 81, 178.
Julian the Apostate, 60, 68, 97, 136, 166, 176, 221, 231, 322.
Julian Hospitator, St., 177.
Julian of Rimini, St., 178.
Juliers in Flanders, 131.
Julius II., 244.
Juno, 5.
Just, St., 34, 155.
Justa, or Justina, St., 178.
Justin, St., 254, 255.
Justina, St., 5, 178.
Justina of Antioch, St., 5, 92, 178.
Justinian I., 51, 249.

KAISERWERDT, 290.
Kent, England, 57.
Keys, the, 25.
Kildare (St. Bridget), 71.
Kiov, in Russia, 145.
Kloster Neuberg, 183.
Knife, the, 25, 60.
Knife, the Sacrificial, 16.
Koran, the, 13, 279.
Kostka, St. Stanislaus, 34.

LABARUM, the, 4.
Lactia, wife of Lubrius, 95.
Ladder, Symbolism of, 8.
La Madaleine, the, 320.
"La Madonna della Cintola," Legend of, 293.

Lamb of God, 24.
Lamb, Symbolism of, 4, 24, 28.
Lambert, St., 144.
Lambert of Maestricht, St., 179.
Lamech, 179.
Lamp, Symbolism of, 6.
Lance, the, 25, 306.
Lance, Symbolism of, 7.
Landolfo, 297.
Languedoc, 29, 257, 268.
Lantern, Symbolism of, 6, 8.
Laodicea, 47.
Lastingham, Priory of, 79.
Last Supper, 33, 153, 159, 180.
Lateran, St. John, Church of, 306.
Lateran, the, 77, 89, 114, 119, 135, 264.
Latin Cross, 3, 4.
Latin Fathers of the Church, 48.
Latin Gate, 159.
Laurati, Pietro, 190.
Laurence, St., 35, 141, 143, 180, 287, 317.
Lazare, St., 320.
Lazarus, 214, 225, 316.
Lazarus, St., 182.
Leander, 149.
Leander, St., 142, 182.
Lebanon, 205.
Lebbeus, St., 284.
Legend of the Holy Girdle, 207.
"Legends of the Monastic Orders," by Mrs. Jameson, 295.
Lemnos, 110.
Leo I., Pope, 37.
Leo X., Pope, 33, 260.
Leo XIII., Pope, 298, *note.*
Leo the Iconoclast, 110.
Leocadia, St., 147, 182.
Leofric, Earl of Murcia, 132.
Leon and Castile, 113.
Leonard, St., 36, 183.
Leonardo da Vinci, 33.
Leontine, St., 56.
Leopold of Austria, St., 183.
Leopoldsberg, 183.
Leovigild, King, 142.
Lepanto, Battle of, 274.
Lepers, 28.
Lerina, Duke of, 124.
Le Sueur, 30.
Leuchtenberg Gallery, 267.
Levi, 228.
Liberius, Pope, 217.
Libya, 127, 217, 281.
Lichfield, 79.

Licinius, 293.
Liege, 144.
Lievin, or Livin, St., 184.
Liguria, 49.
Lily, 97, 125.
Lily, Symbolism of, 6, 16, 20, 28.
Lima, 272.
Limoges, 107, 183, 220.
Lincoln, 144.
Lincolnshire, 248.
Lindisfarne, 92, 247.
Lioba, St., 184.
Lion of Judah, 4.
Lion, Symbolism of, 4, 22.
Lippi, Filippino, 33.
Lisbon, 318.
Lodbrog, Ragnar, 100.
Lombardi, 32.
Lombardy, 115.
London, 111, 131.
Longchamps, 148.
Longinus, St., 184.
Lorenzo Giustiniani, St., 185.
Lorenzo, San, in Cremona, 30.
Lorenzo, San, in Florence, 31.
Loretto, 275.
Lothaire, King of Italy, 39.
Louis VIII., 186.
Louis XI. of France, 121.
Louis XII., 122.
Louis XIII., 320.
Louis Beltran, or Bertrand, 185.
Louis Gonzaga, St., 185.
Louis, King, 148.
Louis, King of Bavaria, 71.
Louis-le-Debonnaire, 65.
Louis, Prince of Thuringia, 103.
Louis, St., 32, 70, 186, 226, 233, 306, 307.
Louis, St., of Toulouse, 32, 187.
Louise d'Angoulême, 122.
Louise de la Miséricorde, Sœur, 187.
Loyola, Ignatius, 34, 122, 133, 146.
Luca della Robbia, 32.
Lucas van Leyden, 179, 215.
Lucca, 124.
Lucia, St., 6, 7, 187.
Ludmilla, St., 189.
Luini, 30, 192.
Luke, St., 22, 25, 124, 189, 223, 290, 315.
Lupa, 151.
Lupo, St., 40, 190.
Luther, 106, 238.
Luxembourg, 259.
Luxembourg, Count of, 141.

Lycia, King of, 84.
Lycias, Proconsul, 90.
Lyons, 70.
Lystra, 59.

MACARIUS, St., 190, 305.
Maccabees, Book of, 138.
Maccabees, the Seven, 112.
Macheronta, 158.
Macrina, St., 60.
Madonna, the, 6, 9, 191, 209.
Madonna della Sedia, 213.
Madonna di Foligno, 212.
Madonna di San Sisto, 29.
Madonna Purissima, 210.
Madre Pia, 195.
Madre Serafica, 32, 86.
Madrid, 124.
Maestricht, 179.
Maestricht, Bishop of, 61.
Magdala, or Magdalon, 225.
Magdalen, the, 9.
Magdalen, Pictures of the, 187.
Magdeburg, 245.
Magi, Adoration of the, 169.
Maguelonne, Languedoc, 65.
Mahometans, 267, 274.
Maiano, Benedetto da, 32.
Maisons de Charité, 170.
Majorca, 267.
Malacca, 123.
Malchus, 279.
Malmedun, Forest of, 61.
Mal ardent, 126.
Malta, 42, 43.
Maltese Cross, 4.
Mamertine Prison, 255.
Manasses, 174.
Mandorla, the, 2.
Manresa, 147.
Mantle, Blue, 9.
Mantua, 59, 185, 307.
Marah, 303.
Marbourg, City of, 106.
Marcella, St., 155, 214, 225.
Marcellinus, St., 214, 256, 277.
Marcian, 279.
Marco, San, 217.
Marcus, 277.
Marcus Aurelius, 91, 112.
Margaret, St., 4, 36, 214, 220.
Margaret of Cortona, St., 32, 215.
Maria-del-Fiore, Santa, 268.

Maria della Navicella, Santa, 165.
Maria della Vallicella, Santa, 261.
Maria in Capitolio, St., 281.
Maria in Organo, Santa, Church of, 30.
Maria Maddalena de' Pazzi, 27, 216.
Maria Maggiore, Santa, 216.
Mariamne, St., 258.
Maria-Sopra-Minerva, Church, 33.
Maria Theresa, 287.
Marina, St., 216.
Marinus, 263.
Marius and Sylla, Wars of, 281.
Mark, St., 22. 35, 51, 59, 217, 293.
Mark, St., Convent of, 33.
Marmoutier, France, 29.
Marmoutier, Monastery of, 221.
Marriage at Cana, 201.
Marriage of St. Catherine, Legend of, 74.
Marriage of the Virgin, 192.
Mars, 258.
Marseilles, 182, 187, 219, 225, 227.
Martel, Charles, 70.
Martha, St., 4, 36, 155, 214, 219, 225.
Martial, Son of Felicitas, 112.
Martial, St., 220.
Martina, St., 222.
Martinian, 255.
Martinmas-Tide, 222.
Martin of Tours, St., 57, 64, 71, 220, 293.
Mary, 158.
Mary and Martha, 182.
Mary Cleophas, 207.
Mary Magdalene, 35, 36, 97, 201, 203, 207, 219, 223.
Mary, Mother of St. James, 153.
Mary of Egypt, St., 223.
Mary Salome, 207.
Mary the Penitent, St., 227.
Masaccio, 33.
Masolino, 33.
Massacre of the Innocents, 148, 283.
Massa, Town of, 67.
Massimi Family, 260.
Massimi, Palazzo, 260.
Mass of St. Gregory, 134.
Matarea, 200.
Mater Amabilis, 212.
Mater Apostolorum, 203.
Mater Dolorosa, 210.
Mater Sapientiæ, 19.
Matha, St. John de, 165.
Mathurins, 165.
Matilda, Queen, 131.

Matthew, St., 22, 228, 284.
Matthew, St., Gospel of, 59, 60.
Matthias, St., 25, 229.
Maurelio, or Maurelius, St., 229.
Maure-sur-Loire, St., 231.
Maurice, Order of St., 230.
Maurice, St., 129, 229.
Maurisa, 147.
Maur, St., France, 29.
Maurus, St., 29, 64, 230.
Maxentius, 89.
Maxima, 51.
Maximian, Emperor, 113, 129, 179, 230, 279.
Maximilla, 50.
Maximin, 225, 226.
Maximin, Tyrant, 75.
Maximus, 78, 288.
Mayence, 321.
Mayence, Cathedral of, 31.
Mayence, First Bishop of, 70.
Medici Family, 91.
Meissen, Bishop of, 66.
Meliapore, 294.
Melrose, 247.
Memmi, Simone, 33.
Mendicant Orders, 117.
Mercuriale, St., 231.
Mercurius, St., 177, 231.
Mercy, the Oil of, 303.
Mercy, the Order of, 30, 267.
Mercy, the Tree of, 303.
Merida, 109.
Merry, St., Church of, 115, 224.
Merseberg, Church of, 141.
Mesopotamia, 47, 284.
Messengers of God, 15.
Messina, 115, 261.
Methodius, St., 93, 232.
Michael Angelo, 30, 33, 282.
Michael of Prato, 207.
Michael, St., 4, 8, 182.
Michael, the Archangel, 15, 16, 206, 232.
Milan, 49, 57, 66, 67, 76, 78-80, 93, 130, 197, 235, 236, 318, 320.
Milan, Bishop of, 59.
Milan, Duke of, 68.
Millstone, Symbol, 82.
Miniato-del-Monte, San, 163.
Miniato, or Minias, St., 234.
Minimes, the, 31, 121.
Minstrels, Patron of, 178.
Miriam, 157.
Miserere, 290.

Misericordia, the, 170.
Missal, the, 280.
"Missus Est," 66.
Mitre, 28, 58, 67.
Modena, 125, 179.
Modwena, St., 100, 234.
Mohammed, 13, 102.
Mohammedans, 124, 173.
Mola di Gaeta, 108.
Moldau, the, 166.
Monachism, Founder of, 54.
Monasteries of St. Bernard, 67.
Monastery of Novara, 67.
Monastic Orders, 26.
Mongibello, the Volcano, 43.
Monica, St., 30, 56, 235.
Monreale, Church of, 186.
Mons Janicula, 255.
Monte Calvo, 88.
Monte Cassino, 64, 275, 297.
Monte Cassino, Monastery of, 29.
Monte Celio, 165.
Monte-Joye, Monastery of, 67.
Monte-Mayor, 170.
Monte Pellegrino, 273.
Mont Martre, 95.
Montpelier, 268.
Mont-Saint-Michel, 233.
Monts-de-Piété, 68.
Montserrat, 147.
Montserrat, Lady of, 147.
Moon, Symbolism of, 11, 20.
Moors, the, 113, 267.
Morocco, 54, 119.
Morselle, 137.
Moscetta, 164.
Moses, 19, 232, 235, 282, 289.
Moses, the Candlestick of, 13.
Mother of Humanity, 209.
Mother of Wisdom, 19, 203.
Mount of Olives, near Siena, 67.
Mount Sinai, 75.
Mourning Mother, 210.
Mugnano, 115.
Munich Gallery, 256.
Munster, 250.
Murcia, Leofric, Earl of, 132.
Murillo, 32, 96, 106, 116, 172, 267, 273, 299.
Musciatino, 208.
Muscovites, the, 50.
Myra, 238, 292.
Mysteries of the Rosary, 274.
Mystic Thorn, 132.

NABOR and Felix, St., Church of, 130.
    Nabor, St., 113, 236.
Nabuchodonosor, King, 173.
Nails of the Cross, 307.
Nails, Symbolism of, 8.
Naked Bodies, Little, Symbolism of, 8.
Nanterre, 125.
Naples, 29, 76, 115, 153.
Naples and Sicily, 187.
Napoleon, Lord, 97.
Narbonne, 276.
Narcissus, St., 41, 236.
Natalia, Wife of St. Adrian, 40, 41, 236.
Nativity, the, 12, 169, 194, 274, 283.
Nativity, Church of, 138.
Nativity of the Blessed Virgin, 191.
Nativity of John the Baptist, 158.
Navona, Piazza (Rome), 45.
Nazareth, 156, 167, 169, 200.
Nazarius, St., 78, 130, 236.
Nazaro-e-Celso, SS., Church of, 79.
Nazaro, San, Church of, Milan, 79.
Nazianzum, 136.
Neot, St., 236, 290.
Nepomuck, St. John, 165.
Nereus, St., 39, 237.
Nero, 130, 254, 272, 302, 316, 320.
Nero de' Neri, 261.
Neuberg, Kloster, 183.
Newman, Cardinal, 260.
Nicaise, St., 237.
Niccolo di Lido, San, 218.
Niccolo Pisano, 83.
Nice, Council of, 56.
Nicene Council, 90.
Nicene Creed, 14.
Nicholas V, Pope, 33.
Nicholas of Myra, St., 237.
Nicholas of Tolentino, St., 28, 30, 242.
Nicholas, St., 36, 218.
Nicodemus, 202, 287.
Nicomedia, City of, 40, 92.
Nile, the, 235.
Nilus of Grotta Ferrata, 243, 244.
Nilus, St., Life of, 29.
Nimbus, Symbolism of, 2, 26.
Nineveh, 173, 301.
Nineveh, Winged Bulls, 23.
Nismes, 137.
Noah, Sons of, 16.
Nocera, Fortress of, 86.
Nolasco, St. Peter, 30.
Nomentana, Via (Rome), 45.
Nonna, St., 136.

Nonnatus, 267.
Norbert, St., 244.
Norcia, 63.
Norfolk, 100.
Norica, Prince of, 72.
Normandy, 233.
Northumberland, 61.
Northumbria, 100.
Norwich, 145.
Novara, 67, 125.
Novatus, 262.
Noyon, 107.
Numerian, 85.
Numidia, 56.
Nunc Dimittis, 199.
Nuremberg, 182, 276.
Nutsall, or Nuscella, Abbey of, 70.

OAK, Augustine's, 58.
    Obsequies of St. Ephrem, Picture of, 108.
Observants, the, 31.
Ocean, Symbolism of, 11.
Offa, King, 46.
Offero, St. Christopher, 82.
Olive Branch, 125.
Olive, Symbolism of, 5, 20.
Olivetani, the Order of, 29, 30, 67.
Olybrius, 214.
Olympias, Baths of, 181.
Omobuono, St., 245.
Onesiphorus, 291.
Onias, the High Priest, 138.
Onuphrius, St., 246.
Oratorians, Order of, 260.
Oratory of St. Catherine, Siena, 76.
Orcagna, Andrea, 33.
Ordeal, Trial by, 246.
Order of Mercy, 30.
Order of Our Saviour, 72.
Order of St. Anthony, 60.
Order of St. Basil, 93.
Order of St. Francis, 102.
Order of the Basilians, 60.
Order of the Benedictines, 63.
Order of the Carthusians, 72.
Order of the Holy Trinity for the Redemption of Captives, 165.
Order of the Hospitallers, 170.
Order of the Olivetani, 67.
Order of the Poor Clares, 86, 118.
Order of the Visitation, 79.
Orestes, 93.

Organ, Symbol, 78.
Orientius, St., 180.
Origen, 58.
Orleans, 126, 149, 283.
Oropesa, 170.
Or-San-Michele, Church of, 107.
Ortolana, St. Clara, 85.
Osca, or Huesca, 180.
Osma, Bishop of, 96.
Osservanti, Order of, 68.
Osthrida, 248.
Ostia, 47, 165.
Ostian Gate, 251.
Oswald, St., 92, 247.
Otho I., Emperor, 39.
Otho III., 243, 244.
Otter, the Symbol, 92.
Ottilia, St., 248.
Our Lady of Mercy, Order of, 257.
Ox, the, 22.
Ox, Symbol, 195.
Oxford Library, 73.
Ozias, 174.

PADLOCK, Symbol, 166.
    Padre Serafico, 32.
Padron, 151.
Padua, 29, 31, 54, 179, 259.
Palatine Hill (Rome), 49.
Palermo, 186, 273.
Palestine, 186, 223.
Pallium, the, 55, 58.
Palm, 56, 59, 75, 82.
Palm, Symbolism of, 5, 20, 27.
Palm Tree and Palm Leaves, 54.
Palm Tree, Legend of, 109.
Pamoisin, Du. 202.
Pampeluna, 147.
Pancras, St., 248.
Pannonia, 220.
Pantaleon of Nicomedia, St., 249.
Panthera, in Lycia, 237.
Paola, 121.
Paola delle Tre Fontane, San, 251.
Paolo-fuori-le-mura, San. 29, 251.
Paolo, St., Convent of, 86.
Paphnutius, 246.
Paradise, Rivers of, 21, 24.
Paris, 30, 54, 66, 69, 72, 81, 95, 97, 99, 107, 115, 128, 131, 145, 147, 149, 165, 186, 224, 259.
Paris, Matthew, 321.
Parma, 35, 142.

Pascasius, 187.
Paschal, 78.
Passion, Symbols of the, 8.
Passion, the, 22.
Passion Week, 202.
Pastoral Staff, 28.
Pastorus, 262.
Paternosters, 96, 274.
Patienza, St., 180.
Patmos, 159, 161.
Patras, 50, 189.
Patriarchal Cross, 4.
Patrick, St., 71, 249.
Pau'a, St., 155, 251.
Paular, near Seville, 72.
Paulina, 256.
Paulinus of York, St., 252.
Paul, St., 25, 30, 47, 59, 87, 88, 90, 95, 130, 134, 162, 189, 250, 253, 262, 286, 290, 291, 302.
Paul, St., and St. John, 166, 251.
Paul's, Old St., London, 111.
Paul's, St., Cathedral of, 48.
Paul's, St., Monastery at Jarrow, 65
Paul the Hermit, 53, 54, 251.
Paul V., 209.
Paul Veronese, 93.
Pavia, 30, 39, 57, 284.
Pax Vobis, 151.
Peacock, Symbolism of, 5.
Peeping Tom of Coventry, 132.
Pega, St., 137.
Pelagius, Pope, 133, 287.
Pelican, Symbolism of, 4, 12.
Pembroke, Earls of, 100.
Pentecost, the, 5.
Penziano, Lorenzo, 116.
Pepin d'Heristal, 91, 143, 179.
Pepin, King, 322.
Pepin-le-Bref, King, 65, 70.
Père des Pauvres, 171.
Perfetto Legendario, Il, 219, 229.
Perpetua, St., 252.
Perseus, 129.
Persia, 281.
Peru, 185, 272.
Perugia, 91, 117, 192.
Perugia, Bishop of, 108.
Perugino, 29.
Peter Exorcista, St., 256.
Peter Igneus, 164.
Peter Martyr, St., 28, 32, 256.
Peter Nolasco, St., 30, 257.
Peter of Alcantara, St., 255.

Peter of Clugny, St., 29.
Peter Regolato, St., 257.
Peter, St., 7, 9, 24, 25, 36, 42, 55, 58, 88, 90, 130, 134, 144, 159, 180, 205, 217, 226, 250, 253, 262, 263, 272, 286, 290, 320.
Peter, St., Sword of, 8.
Petersburg, St., 116.
Peter's, St., 108, 185.
Peter's, St., Monastery at Wearmouth, 65.
Petronilla, St., 257.
Petronius, St., 258.
Philagatus, 243.
Philastrius, 254.
Philetus, 150.
Philip Benozzi, St., 259.
Philip, Deacon, St., 236, 259.
Philip, Emperor, 42.
Philip II., King of Spain, 95.
Philip III., 291.
Philip Neri, St., 260.
Philip, Proconsul of Egypt, 109.
Philip, Son of Felicitas, 112.
Philip, St., 25, 229, 258.
Philip the Apostle, 132.
Philistines, the, 129.
Phocas of Sinope, St., 261.
Phrygia, 239, 258, 281.
Piacenza, 29, 269.
Pianta Leone, War-cry, 249.
Piazza del Duomo at Florence, 323.
Piazza Navona (Rome), 45.
Piedmont, 49, 230.
Pietà, La, 210.
Pietro da Cortona, 222.
Pietro di Pavia, 164.
Pietro in Montorio, San, 255.
Pietro in Vincoli, San, 255, 278.
Pietro Martire, San, 33.
Pillar, the, 307.
Pillar and Cord, Symbolism of, 8.
Pillars of Hercules, 151.
Pincers, 56.
Pincers, Symbolism of, 7, 8.
Pinturicchio, 32.
Pisa, 108, 115, 132, 179, 190, 208, 265, 303.
Pisano, Niccolo, 33.
Pius I., Pope, 263.
Pius IV., Pope, 80.
Pius VII., Pope, 114.
Pius IX., 210.
Placentia, 243.
Placidus, St., 27, 29, 64, 110, 115, 261.
Plato, 49, 73.
Plautilla, 262.

Plessis-le-Tours, 121.
Poissy, 186.
Poitiers, 142, 265.
Poland, 141, 286.
Poland, Patron of, 73.
Polesmartu, 234.
Polycarp, 146.
Pomegranate, 19, 171.
Poniard, Symbolism of, 7.
Ponthieu, Joan of, 113.
Pontius Pilate, 172, 315, 322.
Pontoise, 145.
Pontus, 261.
Poor Clares, 32, 76, 117.
Porphyry, 75.
Porta Clausa, 20.
Porta Pia, Rome, 45.
Porta St. Sebastiano, Rome, 79.
Porte Maggiore, Rome, 68.
Portugal, 34, 155.
Porzioncula, the, 86.
Potitus, St., 108, 262.
Poussin, 108.
Povere Donne, 32.
Powers, the, 15.
Prætorian Guards, 276.
Prague, 166.
Prassede, Santa, Church of, 263.
Prato, Cathedral of, 207.
Prato, Michael of, 207.
Pratum Monstratum, 245.
Praxides, St., 262.
Preaching Friars, 32.
Pré-Montré, 245.
Presburg, 287.
Presentation in the Temple, 279.
Presentation of the Virgin, 191.
Princedoms, the, 15.
Principalities, the, 15.
Prisca, St., 263.
Priscilla, 263.
Priscilla, Catacomb of, Rome, 11
Priscilla, Cemetery of, 90, 262.
Priscus, 110.
Probus, 40.
Procession of the Spirit, 14.
Procession to Calvary, 202.
Processus, 255.
Procino, 45.
Procopius, St., 5, 263.
Proculus, St., 263.
Prophecy of Simeon, 279.
Protasius, St., 78, 130, 236, 263, 320.
Protevangelion, the, 167.

Protus, St., 145.
Provence, 165, 187, 227.
Prudentius, 109, 317.
Psalm, the 114th, 206.
Ptolomeus, Prince, 60.
Ptolemy Philadelphus, 198.
Publius, Prefect, 112.
Pudens, 262.
Pudentiana, St., 262, 264.
Puerta del Cambron, Toledo, 183.
Pulciano, Monte, 46.
Purification of the Virgin, 198.
Purification, the, 274.
Purse, Symbolism of, 8.
Purse, the, 25.
Puy, 319.
Pyx, the, 86, 145.

QUATTRO Coronati, 264.
Queen of Angels, 209.
Queen of Heaven, 6, 209.
Quintianus, King of Sicily, 42, 43.
Quintin, St., 264.
Quirina, 185.
Quirinus, St., 264.
Quirinus, the Prefect, 58.

RADCLIFFE, Mrs., 284.
Radegunda, St., 264.
Ragnar Lodbrog, 100, 265.
Raguel of Ecbatane, 299.
Ragusa, Patron of, 69.
Ralph II. of Burgundy, 39.
Ramirez, King, 152.
Ranieri, St., 265, 303.
Raphael, 31, 32, 202, 214.
Raphael, the Archangel, 15, 16, 266.
Ravenna, 55, 79, 161, 271.
Raymond of Peñaforte, St., 267.
Raymond, St., 72, 267.
Razzi, 33.
Red and Black, Symbolism of, 9.
Red, Symbolism of, 8.
Reggio, 121.
Regina Angelorum, 6, 125, 193, 209.
Regina Cœli, 200.
Regina Cœli lætare, Alleluia, 263.
Regulus, St., 268.
Rehoboam, 304.
Remi, St., 88.
Repandum, 322.

Reparata, St., 7, **268.**
Repose in Egypt, 168.
Repose of the Holy Family, **199.**
Repton, 322.
Repton, Monastery of, 137.
Resurrection, the, 22, 274, **283.**
Reuben, Tribe of, 172.
Rheims, 237.
Rheims, Cathedral of, 13.
Rheims, School of, 72.
Rhine, the, 290.
Rhone, the, 131.
Riccio, Andrea, 32.
Richard I., 129.
Richard of Normandy, **233.**
Richard, St., 145.
Richelieu, 320.
Rictius Varus, 264.
Rimini, 125, 269.
Rinaldo, 297.
Riposo, a, 200.
Riva di San Marco, 217.
Rivers of Paradise, 21.
Robbia, Luca della, 32.
Rocca-Secca, 297.
Rocco, San, 270.
Roch, St., 35, 36, 268, 278.
Roll of Music, Symbol, 78.
Roll, the, 16.
Romain, St., 271.
Roman Cross, 3.
Romano the Hermit, 64.
Rome, 29, 30, 31, 33, 38, 39, 45–47, 49, 55,
  57, 58, 63, 66, 68, 72, 77–79, 85, 87, 88,
  90, 91, 95, 97, 99, 111–114, 116, 119, 121,
  124, 133, 145–147, 154, 159, 161, 165, 166,
  180, 181, 185, 186, 190, 216, 217, **222, 232,**
  236, 243, 312.
Romualdo, St., 28, 271.
Romulo, St., 36, 272.
Rosa di Lima, Santa, 272.
Rosa di Viterbo, St., 32, 273.
Rosalia of Palermo, St., 273.
Rosary, the, 96, 202, 274.
Rosary, Mysteries of the, **21.**
Rose of Sharon, 6.
Roses, 20, 28.
Roses, Miracle of the, **105.**
Roses, Symbols, 98.
Rouen, 271.
Rubens, 34, 184.
Rufina, St., 178, **275.**
Rusticus, 95.
Ruth, 19.

SABERIA, 220.
  Sabina, St., 145, 275.
Sabinc, St., Convent of, 97.
Sabinella, 262.
Sabinella, Queen of Egypt, 73.
Sabran, Count of, 102.
Sacro Speco, Subiaco, 29.
Sainte Beaume, La, 226.
Sainte Chopelle, La, 186, 306, 307.
Salamanca, 208.
Sales, St. Francis de, 79.
Sallust, 181.
Salutation of Elizabeth, 194.
Salutation, the, 102.
Salvi, Monastery of, 164.
Samia, 281.
Sammichele, 32.
Samos, 84.
Samson, 124, 129.
Sancha, Queen of Naples, 102.
Sanchez de Cepeda, Don Alphonso, **289.**
Sancian, Island of, 123.
San Domingo, 185.
San José, 290.
Sansovino, 32.
Santa Casa, 275.
Santa Croce, Rome, 68, 161, 305.
Santa Maria Novella, Florence, 83.
Santiago, 150, 152, **291.**
Saône, the, 70.
Sapor, King, 176.
Sapritius, 98.
Sara, 15.
Saracens, the, 65, 141, 241, **275.**
Sara of Ecbatanc, 299.
Sardinia, 108.
Sardinian Order, 230.
Sargossa, 317, 318.
Sarmatia, 50.
Sarto, Andrea del, 30.
Satan, Black, Symbol of, 9.
Savia, 207.
Savonarola, **257.**
Savoy, 230.
Saw, the, 25.
Saxony, 70.
Scaccieri, 265.
Scales, 16.
Sceptre, 125.
Schiller's "Fridolin," 107.
Scholastica, St., 29, 64, 94, **275.**
Sciffo Favorino, 85.
Scipios, the, 155, **251.**
Sclavonia, 141, 214.

Scotists, 99.
Scotland, 50.
Scourge, Symbolism of, 7, 8, 28.
Scroll, 125.
Scrolls, Symbolism of, 24.
Scythia, 50, 258.
Sealed Book, the, 21.
Sealtiel, the Praying Spirit, 15.
Seamless Garment, Symbolism of, 8.
Sebald, St., 276.
Sebaste in Cappadocia, 69.
Sebaster, 158.
Sebastian, St., 7, 35, 36, 171, 249, 276.
Secundus, St., 279.
Seine, St., Abbey of, 65.
Selene in Libya, 127.
Seleucia, 292.
Sempronius, the Prefect, 44, 45.
Senario, Monte, 259.
Sens, 186, 252.
Seraph, the, 27.
Seraphia, 275.
Seraphic Order, 69.
Seraphic, the, 116.
Seraphim, the, 14, 16.
Serapion, 279.
Serapis, 217.
Serena, Empress, 288.
Sergius, 271.
Serpent, the, 25.
Serpent, Symbolism of, 5, 12, 19.
Serracina, 133.
Servi, or Serviti, Order of, 259.
Servi, the. 30.
Servius Tullius, 263.
Seth and the Tree of Mercy, 303.
Seven, the Mystic Number, 13.
Seven Churches, 159.
Seven Joys and Sorrows of the Virgin, 13, 21.
Seven Joys of the Blessed Virgin, 279.
Seven Maccabees, 112.
Seven Sleepers of Ephesus, 279.
Seven Sons of St. Felicitas, 112.
Seven Sorrows of the Blessed Virgin, 279.
Severianus, 264.
Severino, San, Church of, 29.
Severus, Emperor, 109, 130, 252, 264.
Sevigné, Madame de, 79.
Seville, 72, 106, 149, 170, 172, 178.
Seville, Cathedral of, 114.
Seville, Isidore of, 149.
Seward, Siward, or Sigward, 276.
Sforza, Francesco, 283,

Shaftesbury, 101.
Shears, Symbolism of, 7.
Sheba, Queen of, 281, 304.
Sheep, 24.
Shell, Symbolism of, 7.
Shepherd, the Good, 24.
Ship, Symbolism of, 7.
Shtaneshalck, 142.
Sibylla, 303.
Sibylla Cimmeria, 281–283.
Sibylla Cumana, 281–283.
Sibylla Delphica, 281–283.
Sibylla Erythræa, 281–283.
Sibylla Europa, 281–283.
Sibylla Hebraica, 281–283.
Sibylla Hellespontina, 281–283.
Sibylla Libyca, 281–283.
Sibylla Persica, 281–283.
Sibylla Phrygia, 281–283.
Sibylla Samia, 281–283.
Sibylla Tiburtina, 281–283.
Sibylline Leaves, 281.
Sibyls, 35, 280.
Sicily, 77, 187, 261.
Siegfried, Count, 127, 141.
Siena, 33, 67, 118, 132.
Siena, Duomo of, 51.
Sigismond, St., 34, 80, 283.
Silesia, 145.
Silvestro, St., Church of, at Rome, 38.
Simeon, 196, 198, 284.
Simone Memmi, 33, 266.
Simon Magus, 254.
Simon Peter, 50.
Simon, St., 25, 145.
Simon the Pharisee, 225.
Simon Zelotes, or the Zealot, St., 284.
Sinai, Mount, 75.
Sion, 67.
Sion, Mount, 204.
Siponte, 232.
Sisiberto, Archbishop, 148.
Sissek, 264.
Sisto, San, 190.
Sisto, San, Madonna di, 29.
Sixtus II., 180.
Sixtus IV., Pope, 121.
Skull, Symbolism of, 7, 12.
Slaves with Broken Chains, 28.
Smyrna, 146.
Society of Jesus, 185, 286.
Socrates, 93.
Soissons, 91.
Solomon, 303.

Solomon's Temple, 303.
Sophia of Thuringia, 103.
Sorbonne, the, 210.
Sorrows, Seven, of the Virgin, 13.
Spagnuoli, Chapel of the, 33.
Spagnuoli, San Giacomo degli, Church of, 96.
Spalatro, the, 284.
Spasimo di Sicilia, Lo, 202.
Spear, the, 25.
Spear, Symbolism of, 8.
Spice, Boxes of, Symbolism of, 8.
Spoleto, 63.
Sponge, the, 306, *and note.*
Sponge, Symbolism of, 8.
Stabat Mater, 210.
Staff, 16, 58.
Staff, Pastoral, 28.
Staff, the Pilgrim's, 25.
Stag, the, 28.
Standard, Symbolism of, 7.
Standard, the, 27.
Stanislaus Kotzka, St., 34, 286.
Star. Symbol, 97.
Star, Symbolism of, 20, 28.
Stem of Jesse, 20.
Stephanie, 244.
Stephen II., Pope, 95.
Stephen of Hungary, St., 287.
Stephen, St., 7, 35, 180, 286, 304, 307.
Stigmata, the, 27, 77.
Stirling, Mr., 172.
Stirling's "Artists of Spain," 273.
Strada di Costanza, 91.
Strasburg, 248.
Strasburg, Cathedral of, 31.
Stridonium, 154.
Strozzi, Chapel, 33.
Suabia. 183.
Subiaco, 64, 115, 230, 261.
Subiaco, Cave of, 20.
Sudarium, 287, 316.
Suetonius, 281.
Sueur, Le, 30.
Sun, Symbolism of, 11, 20, 28.
Susanna, 288.
Susanna, St., 287.
Sweden, 71.
Sweden, St. Catharine of, 77.
Swidbert, St., 289.
Swithin, St., 290.
Sword, 59.
Swords of the Apostles, 8.
Sword, Symbolism of, 7, 16.

Sylvanus, Son of Felicitas, 112.
Sylvester, Bishop of Rome, 88, 89, 290.
Sylvester, St., 4.
Sylvia, 133, 134.
Symbolism of Colors, 8.
Symbolism of the Monastic Orders, 25.
Symbols of Angels, 14.
Symbols of God the Father, 9.
Symbols of God the Holy Ghost, 12.
Symbols of God the Son, 11.
Symbols of the Apostles, 24.
Symbols of the Evangelists, 21.
Symbols of the Trinity, 14.
Symbols of the Virgin, 17.
Synagogue, Symbolism of, 11.
Syracuse, 187, 189.
Syria, 119, 227.
Syro, or Syrus, St., 284.
Syrus, 225.
Syrus, St., 284.

TABLET, Symbol, 94.
Tacitus, 281.
Taddeo Gaddi, 29, 33.
Tagaste, 56.
Tankelin, 245.
Taper, Symbolism of, 6.
Tarantaise, 67.
Tarascon, 219.
Tarentum, 243.
Tarquin, 281.
Tarragona, 293.
Tarsia, 30.
Tarsus, 47.
Tarsus, Ships of, 197.
Tasso, 246.
Tau Cross, 3.
Te Deum, 57.
Templars, the Laws of, 66.
Temple of Solomon, 20.
Temptation, the, 9.
Teresa, St., 13, 27, 185, 273, 289.
Terracina, 39, 79.
Tertullus, 261.
Tetramorph, the, 20, 23.
Thaddeus, St., 25, 38, 284.
Thamyris, 291.
Thebais, the, 217, 230.
Theban Legion, 40, 129, 229, 279, 293.
Thebes, 246.
Thecla, St., 291.
Theoclea, 291.
Theodobert, King, 183.

Theodora, 90.
Theodore, St., of Heraclea, 293.
Theodore, St., of Venice, 293.
Theodoret, 254.
Theodosius, Emperor, 49, 136, 162, 163, 279, 287.
Theonestus, St., 293.
Theonotus, 308.
Theophania, 39.
Theophilus, St., 98, 293.
Theresa, St., 172.
Thermutis, 235.
Thessalonica, 49.
Thetford, 101.
Thirty Pieces of Silver, Symbolism of, 8.
Thomas à Becket, St., 27, 294.
Thomas Aquinas, St., 32, 47, 99, 297.
Thomas of Villanueva, St., the Almoner, 298.
Thomas, St., 25, 197, 206, 207, 293.
Thomas, the Disciple, 38.
Thomists, 99.
Θ, or Θεός, 54.
Thorwaldsen, 153.
Thrones, the, 15.
Thuringia, 70, 264.
Tiber, the, 47.
Tiberias, Sea of, 225.
Tiberius, Emperor, 315.
Tibertius, St., 299.
Tiburtina, the Sibyl, 195.
Tiburtius, 77.
Timotheus, 207.
Tiro, 81.
Titian, 33.
Title of Accusation, 306.
Titles of the Virgin, 17, 18.
Tivoli, 281.
Tobias, 139, 267, 299.
Toledo, 29, 113, 148, 182, 183.
Toledo, Castle of, 114.
Toothache, Patroness against, 56.
Torches, Symbolism of, 11.
Tortosa, 151.
Torpé, or Torper, St., 302.
Torre de' Spechi, 116.
Totila, King of the Goths, 65, 108, 268.
Toubert, or Touberch, 109.
Toulon, 226.
Toulouse, 54, 187.
Tours, 221.
Tours, Bishop of, 71.
Tower, 59.
Tower of David, 20.

Trajan, 87, 110, 135, 146.
Tranquillinus, Ausanus, 51.
Transfiguration, the, 159.
Trastevere, the (Rome), 50, 246.
Travellers, Patron of, 178.
Tree of Life, the, 303.
Trent, 145.
Trentham, 322.
Treves, 48.
Triangle, Symbolism of, 10, 14.
Trinità, Church of the, 164.
Trinità-di-Monti, 121.
Trinity, the, 16, 303.
Trinity, Symbols of the, 10, 14.
Trissina, 292.
Trojan War, 283.
Troyes, 126.
True Cross, the, 186, 303.
Trumpets, 16.
Tubal-Cain, 179.
Tunic, Blue, 9.
Tuscany, 260, 268.

UAVAS, Father G. de, 242.
Ubaldini, House of, 86.
Uberto, Bishop, 208.
Ugolotto Caccianemici, 307.
Ulpho, Prince of Norica, 72.
Ulrich, Prince, 263.
Ulster, 250.
Umbria, Citta Ducale, 112.
Umilita, St., 307.
Unicorn, the, 179, 193.
Unicorn, Symbolism of, 5.
Urban II., Pope, 72.
Urban VI., Pope, 77.
Uriel, the Archangel, 15, 16.
Ursula, St., 7, 36, 82, 91, 308.

VAGAO, the Eunuch, 175.
Valencia, 96, 185, 187, 298, 318, 319.
Valens, Emperor, 60.
Valentinian, Emperor, 222.
Valentinian III., 255.
Valeria, 320.
Valerian, St., 77, 85, 92.
Valérie, or Valère, St., 220.
Valerius, 317.
Valerius Flaccus, 258.
Valid, Daughter of Pharaoh, 235.
"Valley of Wormwood," 66.
Vallière, Louise de la, 187.

Vallombrosa, Order of, 164.
Vallombrosians, the, 28, 29.
Valois, Felix de, 165.
Vandals, the, 57, 237.
Van Dyck, 34.
Vannes, 319.
Varro, 281.
Vatican, the, 33, 156, 244, 251, 255, 264, 273.
Vaudois, the, 96.
Vega, Garcelasso de la, 123.
Veneziano, Antonio, 266.
Venice, 166, 173, 179, 185, 217, 242, 249, 270, 293, 306.
Venice, Patroness of, 75.
Venus, the Temple of, 305.
Venus, Worship of, 178.
"Verbum sum," 195.
Vercelli, Bishop of, 46.
Verdiana, St., 315.
Verdun, 141.
Verona, 30, 50, 89, 256, 322.
Veronese, Paul, 93.
Veronica, St., 11, 315.
Verulam, 46.
Verus, 129.
Vesica Piscis, the, 2.
Vespasian, Emperor, 315.
Vesuvius, Mount, 154.
Via Appia, Rome, 79.
Via Dolorosa, 202.
Via Nomentana (Rome), 45.
Via Tiburtina, Rome, 181.
Victor, St., of Marseilles, 316.
Victor, St., of Milan, 317.
Vienna, 183, 286.
Vienna, Cathedral of, 162.
Villani, Archbishop, 266.
Vincent de Paul, St., 319.
Vincent Ferraris, St., 319.
Vincent, St., 287, 317.
Vincent, St., Cape, 318.
Violet, Symbolism of, 9.
Virgil, 282.
Virgin Alone, the, 208.
Virgin and Child Enthroned, 211.
Virgin Mary, 2, 5, 6, 8, 12, 13, 16, 17, 156.
Virgin of Mercy, 211.
Virgin of Virgins, 209.
Virgin, Seven Joys and Sorrows of, 13.
Virgin, Titles of, 17, 18.
Virgo Sapientissima, 209.
Virtues, the, 15.
Vischer, Peter, 276.

Visconti, Bianca, 283.
Visitation, Order of, 79.
Visitation, the, 102, 194, 274, 279.
Vitalicino, King, 178.
Vitalis, Son of Felicitas, 112.
Vitalis, St., of Ravenna, 320.
Viterbo, 273.
Vitus, St., 320.
Voltaire, 186.
"Volto Santo," or Vera Icon, 316.
Votive Pictures, 34.
Vox clamantis in deserto, 158.
Vulgate, the, 154.

WALAIS, the, 67.
Walbeck Church, 141.
Walbeck in Saxony, 41.
Walburga, St., 184, 321.
Walking on the Sea, 28.
Walpurgis Night, 321.
Walpurgis Oil, 321.
Walpurgis, St., 20.
Wandering Jew, the, 321.
Wartburg, Castle of, 103, 105.
Warwickshire, 235.
Wastein, Monasteries, 72.
Wearmouth, Monastery of, 65.
Weedon, 322.
Well, the, 20.
Wenceslaus IV., 166.
Wenceslaus, St., 189.
Wenzel, St., 189.
Werburga, St., 322.
Westminster, 160.
Westminster Abbey, 102.
Westphalia, 111.
Wheels, Symbolism of, 7, 75.
Whitby, 142.
White Friars, 33.
White, Symbolism of, 8, 20, 32.
Wild Beasts, 28.
Wilfrida, 100.
William, Duke of Aquitaine, 65.
William, St., 145.
William the Conqueror, 233.
Willibald, St., 321.
Wilton, 100.
Winburn, Convent of, 321.
Winchester, 290.
Winchester, Abbey of Nutsall, 70.
Winfred, St. Boniface, 70.
Wings, 16, 23.
Wiseman's, Cardinal, "Hidden Gem," 48.

Woman of the Apocalypse, 2.
Wool-comb, Symbol, 69.
Worcester, Bishop of, 99.
Worcestershire, 58.
Work-basket, Symbol, 193.

XAVIER, St. Francis, 34.
   Xeres, Battle of, 113.

YELLOW, Symbolism of, 9.
   York, 252.
York, Archbishop of, 70.
Yorkshire, Festival, 69.

ZACHARIAS, 124, 167, 194, 201.
   Zadkiel, the Angel, 16.
Zambri, the Magician, 89.
Zebedee, 150, 159.
Zeno, 89, 264.
Zeno, Emperor, 59.
Zeno, St., of Verona, 322.
Zenobia, St., of Florence, 323.
Zingara, or Gypsy, the, 200.
Zingaro, Antonio lo, 29.
Zoccolanti, the, 31.
Zosimus, 223.
Zurbaran, 30.